SCOPES RETRIED

SCOPES RETRIED

A Novel About Creation and Evolution

Stephen Bartholomew Jr.

To my good friend Ed,
I hope you enjoy this book,
Ed. I sure enjoyed writing it!

Steve

2 Tim. 4:3,4
Rev. 4:11

Published by
Stephen Bartholomew Jr.
Virginia

Printed by Bethany Press

ISBN: 978-0-9857637-0-1

This book is dedicated to the memory of
Henry M. Morris (1918 – 2006) who is widely recognized
as the father of the modern creationist movement. Dr. Morris
was not only a brilliant scientist and theologian, but in his
tireless efforts to promote the truth about God's creation,
he was always humble and gracious, traits that are far
too often missing in the origins debate.

Contents

To accept as a truth that which is not a truth, or to fail in distinguishing the sense in which it is not true, is an evil having consequences which are indeed incalculable. There are some subjects in which one mistake of this kind will poison all the wells of truth and affect with fatal error the whole circle of our thoughts.

by the Duke of Argyle, a friend of Charles Darwin, from *The Road of Science and the Ways to God*, by Stanley Jaki

Foreword

As the author/publisher of the popular creationist book, *In the Minds of Men*, I have often been sought by would-be creationist authors for publishing advice. However, in most cases when the proffered manuscript arrives, a quick glance is sufficient to know that it would have little chance of success. Nevertheless, I always try to be encouraging. Then I received the manuscript for *Scopes Retried*; the author was not known to me, but the presentation looked professional. As I ran my eye across the pages for a first impression, I found the sentences were short and the grammar and spelling pretty well faultless! These were indeed encouraging signs. However, when I sat down to actually read it through, I couldn't put it down. Parts of it brought me to tears! I was stunned ... this was surely not your average creationist literature!

Perhaps the reader may wonder how a book about creationism could bring me to tears. In the first place, this book is completely unique in its field. It is a gripping story that rivets the reader's attention from the first page to the last ... and it's a *novel!* The idea is brilliant and the manuscript is a gem. Unlike the sea of nonfiction literature in this field, these pages have no technical terms, no equations, no figures, and no footnotes or references to divert the reader's attention. Nevertheless, through the mouths of an interesting cross-section of individuals, including Christians and atheists, high school students and university professors, a compelling and absorbing argument for creationism is presented. Using plain, easy-to-read language the author addresses most of the major issues in the creation/evolution debate. These include: global vs. local Flood, theistic evolution and Intelligent Design versus biblical creationism, science versus religion, the origin of life, the strict limit to mutations, transitional forms, fossils, and much more. Although the story is fictional, the scientific information sticks to the well-tested facts.

Held to the page by the story line, by the end of the book the reader will have received a powerful and compelling defense of creationism. While traveling the exciting journey through the book, all along the way the reader is being fed life-saving food – the truth about God's creation. It is a brilliant concept, and a truly remarkable achievement.

The issues addressed in this book, such as the Genesis Flood and the age of the earth, for example, are truly critical. Unfortunately, many churches have avoided these very issues, fearing that they are too controversial and may turn people away. Ironically, the truth is quite the opposite; ultimately, *not* facing these issues will slowly drain the power from these churches, for ultimately what is at stake here is the authority of God's Word, and when that is abandoned, the life of the church goes with it. *Scopes Retried* is a unique effort to ensure that this does not happen, and I strongly recommend it to anyone searching for the truth in this intense and critical debate.

Ian Taylor,
author of *In the Minds of Men*, now in its sixth revised edition.

1

Mr. Potter's Science Class

"To tell you the truth, Mike, nobody knows exactly how feathers evolved," Mr. Potter answered. "Various theories have been proposed over the years, but they're all speculative. As I told you yesterday, scientists are quite confident that birds evolved from reptiles in the Jurassic period, about 125-150 million years ago. Somehow, through many small mutational changes over millions of years, feathers probably evolved from reptilian scales."

Richard Potter had been teaching high school science, particularly biology, for almost twenty years in Madison, New Hampshire, a town of about fifteen thousand people near Durham, home of the University of New Hampshire. A good-sized man in his late forties, he was quite serious, a very good teacher who genuinely cared about his students. At the moment, he was in the midst of teaching evolution to the nineteen students in his advanced eleventh grade class. It was early April. For three days in a row the temperature had climbed into the mid-fifties, and the snow that had blanketed the ground over a foot deep only two weeks ago would soon be only a memory. Awakening from their long slumber in the frozen earth, here and there crocuses were breaking through the cold, dark soil with their eagerly anticipated message: spring was near.

"As I said, Mike, scientists aren't sure about the mechanics of the process. Perhaps in the early stages a mutation caused the edges of a reptile's scales to become ragged, or frayed. Somehow, this small change gave this animal a slight advantage over its peers, so this feature spread through the population. After many other such changes, over millions of years the scales became feathers."

"Why would ragged scales be an advantage to a reptile?" Mike Lawton asked. Mike was the resident bird expert in the school, and it was this interest that had attracted him to science. Fascinated by birds for as long as he could remember, Mike had several pet birds in his house, including an African Grey Parrot that his father had purchased over twenty years earlier. Named *Timmy*, after his technical classification, *Timneh African Grey*, this fascinating bird could not only speak over two hundred words but could also mimic many sounds he had heard in his living quarters, which was also the TV room. Occasionally, the Lawtons would be startled out of their sleep in the middle of the night by gunshots, or even exploding missiles … but it was just Timmy. As impressive as these imitations were, they fell short of Timmy's number one simulation: a dead-on rendition of the opening lines of Kate Smith's *God Bless America*.

"By increasing the surface area of the edges of their scales, it would make them more efficient at catching insects," Mr. Potter added.

Mike furrowed his brow. He wasn't quite sure why ragged scales would help reptiles in their insect hunting. Before asking about this matter, though, he had another question.

"Is there any evidence of these ragged scales, Mr. Potter? You know, like in the fossil record or something?"

"No, not really. As I said, at this point all the theories about the evolution of feathers are speculative."

"I'm not sure I get it, Mr. Potter," Mike continued. "What advantage would ragged scales give to a reptile? Feathers are so *awesome*. My dad has shown me some under a microscope and explained how they work. They're just so *different* from reptile's scales. I've looked at them under a microscope, too. The feathers are designed so perfectly for flight. I don't understand exactly how they work," he went on with growing enthusiasm, "but somehow when the bird pushes his wings downward, little tiny hooks hold the feathers tightly together so the feathers can push against the air and drive the bird forward, or upward, whatever. Then, when he lifts his wings back up, the hooks release and …"

"That's very interesting, Mike," Mr. Potter interrupted, ostensibly to keep the discussion from straying too far off course. In fact, Mike was pushing into territory where there was considerable uncertainty in the scientific community, and Mr. Potter didn't really want to go there. He knew very well that the subject he was currently teaching, the theory of evolution, could be very controversial, and he wanted to do everything he could to stick to the main points, because he deeply believed in the theory and thought it was very important for his students to get a good grasp of it. "And I see where you're coming from," he continued. "Remember, though, that I said that nobody is sure exactly how feathers evolved. The main point is that feathers *did* evolve. Think about it. It's really just simple logic. All birds have feathers. At some point in the distant past, they – or, more precisely, their precursors – did *not* have feathers. So, at some point between these two groups feathers *must* have evolved. Scientists may not have figured out the correct process yet, and maybe they never will. But they know that somehow this evolution occurred."

Jennifer Conley had been paying close attention to this discussion and had become increasingly agitated. She had been home-schooled through the eighth grade by her Christian parents who had taught her that the theory of evolution was not true. She was not entirely convinced that they were right, but nothing she had learned so far in Mr. Potter's class had given her any reason to doubt them. She knew that she would be in this class at some point and had discussed with her parents how she should react. They had told her to let the Spirit be her guide. By nature she did not like confrontation and had managed to remain quiet through the first couple of classes on this subject, but now she was getting a nudge from the Spirit and felt the need to speak up.

"Yes, Jennifer," Mr. Potter said.

"I don't see why you say that feathers *must* have evolved," Jennifer said, getting straight to the point. "Maybe birds were created with feathers from the very beginning."

"Hmmm," Mr. Potter said, nodding his head. "And how could this have happened, Jennifer? How could they have been created in this way?" He suspected what was coming next. It usually did when he was teaching this subject.

"Well ... by God," Jennifer answered, exactly as Mr. Potter had anticipated.

"And how long do you think it took him – or her – to do this?"

"Well ... not very long," Jennifer said, smiling gamely. "Not very long at all."

"How long is 'not very long,' Jennifer?"

"I – I don't know exactly," Jennifer responded, a bit surprised by Mr. Potter's persistence. "A few hours ... no, wait, maybe only a couple of min ... like I said, I don't know exactly. Just a real short time."

"You mean that one day – or one minute – there were no birds and then, poof! – suddenly, the whole earth was filled with birds? Sort of like a cosmic-scale magic trick?" Mr. Potter asked with a slight grin.

Jennifer fidgeted nervously, a bit embarrassed. Several of her classmates did too, sympathetic for Jennifer's plight, but thankful that they weren't in her shoes. Bravely, Jennifer continued.

"Well, uh, yes. I guess you could say that. Yes, that's what I believe."

"And why do you believe that? On what do you base that conclusion?"

Jennifer paused and took a deep breath. Her parents had warned her that being a Christian wasn't always going to be easy.

"Because that's what it says in the Bible. According to the Bible, birds were created on the fourth – no, wait, the fifth – day of creation. So, yes, one day there were no birds and the next they were everywhere, just like you said." This last comment elicited a few smiles among her classmates.

"Sooo, God filled the entire earth with birds in twenty-four hours?"

After a brief pause for reflection, Jennifer replied, "Not exactly. Actually, it didn't even take Him *that* long, because He filled the oceans with fish on the same day, so ..."

"So it must have taken him only about twelve hours, or even *less*, to create the birds, eh? Man, he sure was a fast worker, wasn't he, Jennifer?" Mr. Potter said with a big smile.

Jennifer didn't reply, and Mr. Potter decided that it was time for him to back off. He could see that Jennifer was a little embarrassed, and he felt a bit guilty, because he genuinely liked her, as he did almost all of his students. He did not, however, like the subject she had brought up, divine creation. In his mind, Mr. Potter didn't have anything against God. He just objected to a lot of the ideas espoused by creationists, like God creating the entire world in six 24-hour days, for example. As a teacher, he believed that education was the pathway to the Promised Land of success and happiness in life, and to him truth was the foundation of education. The ideas promoted by creationists, he believed, were stumbling blocks on this path and made the job of teaching the truths of science decidedly more difficult.

"Jennifer," he continued, "I know that you feel strongly about your beliefs, and what you're proposing is perhaps a theoretical possibility. However, it's not a possibility that we can consider here. This is a science class, and in this class we deal with the natural world, that is, nature. What you are talking about is the *supernatural*, the world that some believe exists outside of nature. Science cannot investigate this world, if indeed it exists. Therefore, we cannot consider it. Our answers *must* – let me repeat: *must* – come from *within* nature, Jennifer. There's a word for this approach; it's called *naturalism*. Do you see what I'm saying?"

"I think so. But I'm not sure I agree with you. I mean, I thought we were supposed to be searching for *truth* in this class. If scientists can't come up with a reasonable explanation for the evolution of feathers – which it doesn't seem to me they have – then why can't they consider that God created them? If they can't find an answer within nature, why can't they consider one outside of nature?"

Jennifer's persistence surprised everyone in the class, including Mr. Potter.

"Like I told Mike, Jennifer, just because scientists haven't come up with a completely satisfactory explanation for the evolution of feathers doesn't mean that it didn't take place. A good scientist ..."

"But, Mr. Potter, it doesn't sound to me like they've come up with *any* ..."

"Please, Jennifer," Mr. Potter said, holding up his hand, "let me finish. The theory of evolution, as I explained to you at the beginning of this section, is considered by many scientists to be the bedrock theory of science, the theory upon which all others rest. If you wish, you can believe that your God – or some god, at least – was somehow involved in the process. Like, maybe he or she designed it, or perhaps oversaw it in some way. Many church people choose such a belief. It's called theistic evolution. But, to repeat, discussion of such beliefs does not belong in a science class."

Jennifer was thinking about saying something, but the bell ending the period rang, and everyone began getting up to leave. She was just as glad it did.

2

Conversation in the Cafeteria

The day after Mr. Potter's science class David Newton and a few of his friends were having lunch in the Madison High cafeteria. Several of them, including David, had been in that class. The conversation turned to the exchange between Jennifer and Mr. Potter.

"Jennifer really surprised me," Eddie Romano said. "Mr. Potter was really challenging her. Actually, I thought he was getting a little rough. But she didn't back down. I didn't know she could be that way. She's always, like, so *nice*, you know what I mean?"

"Well, she was obviously a little embarrassed," Ray Corbett added. "I can't say that I blame her, though. Like you said, Eddie, Mr. P was getting a little nasty – you, know, sort of mocking Jennifer's belief about how long it took God to create the birds and stuff. *You mean that God filled the whole earth with birds in only ten minutes ... sort of like a cosmic magic trick? Man, he must be a real wizard, Jennifer!*" he said, nicely mimicking Mr. Potter and eliciting chuckles from his friends. "I was really surprised at his reaction. I don't ever remember seeing him that way. What about you guys?"

"Yeah, me neither, Ray," Nick Murray said. "To tell you the truth, I thought it was annoying. I didn't think it was fair. I don't see why he had to put Jennifer down the way he did. She was just trying to express her opinion."

"Which he obviously didn't agree with," Eddie quickly added.

"So what?" Nick shot back. "He's always encouraged us to speak our minds, right? How come he decided to make an exception in this case?"

"Even though he was pretty condescending to her – which ticked me off, too, Nick – he didn't *completely* reject what she was saying. At least he admitted that God *might* have had something to do with evolution," David said.

"Come on, Dave! Like he really meant it, right?" Eddie said. "He was just throwing Jennifer a bone, to make up for embarrassing her. It's obvious, man. He doesn't think that God has anything to do with evolution … and, I must say, I don't think I do, either."

"I guess that clinches it. Why not, genius?" Ray asked.

"Simple. In order for that idea to be true, there has to be a God, right?"

"And you don't think there is?"

"I don't know," Eddie replied. "Maybe I do, maybe I don't. I'm not sure. Anyway, like Mr. Potter, I believe that if there is a God I sure don't think that he could have created the world in such a short time, like Jennifer was talking about."

"Six days, Eddie. That's what the Bible says," David said.

"Yeah, that's just what I'm talking about. Ya see. *Six days!* And how long did it take according to our science textbook, and Mr. Potter? *Billions of years*, right?! I mean, even if the scientists aren't exactly right, even if their calculations are off by a few hundred million years, it's sure obvious that the creation took a heck of a lot longer than six days," Eddie said. "To me, what Jennifer was arguing makes no sense at all, Dave. None. Zero. It would be one thing if she suggested, like, a couple of hundred million years, or even a couple of million years. But *six days!* That's a *joke*, dude, a total joke. It's pathetic."

"Yeah, I know what you're saying," Dave replied. "Personally, I don't know what to think about all this. But let me ask you something. Just because you don't agree with what the Bible says about creation, does that mean you have to reject the whole book, and God, too? I mean the creation story is just a tiny part of the Bible, a few verses or chapters, maybe."

"It's a lot more than a few verses I have trouble with, Dave," Eddie replied. "I got issues with a lot of other things in that book, too. I mean, don't get me wrong. I haven't read much of it. But I used to go to Sunday school when I was younger, and I remember some of the stories. Like the one about Jonah in the belly of a sea monster for a few days and the Red Sea parting for some reason, and Jesus walking on water, and performing all those miracles – and, oh yes: rising from the dead. And then, of course, there's the famous Noah's Ark, which carried Noah's family and a few million animals safely through a flood that covered the whole world. Now, one thing's for sure: a worldwide flood would be a *major* news flash. If it really happened, don't you think that our science textbook, or our science teachers, would have to at least *mention* it? You know as well as I do that they haven't. Come on, Dave. You're a pretty smart guy. You can't believe all those stories are *literally true*.

This is the twenty-first century we're living in, man – the *scientific age* – not the Dark Ages."

"All right ... I admit it. You've got a pretty good point there, Eddie. I don't know what to tell you. But if those stories aren't true, what are they? Fairy tales?"

"No, I guess they're just made up to teach people things and help them get through their troubles in life. Sort of like Greek and Roman mythology, I guess. They can't be about real events, though. Like, people can't walk on water, or rise from the dead. Never have, never will. And I certainly don't think the Bible can teach us much about science. I mean, I don't know when it was written, but I know it was a long time ago. Hundreds of years ago, maybe even thousands. *Way* before the discoveries of modern science, anyway. Heck, people probably still thought the earth was *flat* when it was written."

"I totally agree with you, Eddie," Ray said. "I don't see how people living in today's world can still believe all that crap, either. What about you, Dave? What do you think about the stuff Jennifer was saying? Do you think she was making any sense?"

"Like I just said, I don't know *what* to believe about all this stuff. It's really confusing to me. I'll say one thing for Jennifer, though. She's got a lot of guts standing up for her beliefs the way she did."

"Yeah, you got that right, Dave," Eddie said. "I don't know if I could have done that."

"Yeah, and I know why," Ray pronounced.

"Oh? Why?" Eddie asked innocently.

"Because it doesn't sound like you have any beliefs to stand up for!" Ray said with a big grin.

"Hey, I'll say something else for Jennifer," John Mitchell said. "She made a pretty good point about the evolution of feathers, didn't she? When she pressed Mr. Potter for an explanation of how they evolved, he didn't have too much to offer, did he?"

"So what?" Eddie said. "So he couldn't tell us exactly how feathers evolved 500 million years ago, or whatever. What difference does it make? Does it prove that evolution didn't take place? Does it prove *anything*, for that matter? Other than that scientists haven't discovered this one little tiny piece of the puzzle? If you ask me, considering that all this stuff – you, know, all the changes that occurred during evolution – took place such a long time ago, I think it's amazing that scientists have figured out as much as they have."

"Hey, look," John Mitchell exclaimed. "There's Jennifer with Lisa in the lunch line. Let's ask them over. I'd like to hear what she thinks about all this."

"Good idea, Johnny. I would, too. Call her over," Dave quickly added.

In a couple of minutes, the girls were at their table. David quickly got to the point.

"Jennifer, we were talking about yesterday's science class and were wondering about some of the things you were saying."

"Yeah? Like what?"

As mentioned, Jennifer had been home-schooled through the eighth grade and therefore hadn't been a member of her class nearly as long as most of the others. Nevertheless, she had an inner strength and peace that other people naturally found appealing, and she made friends easily because she was kind and considerate and always found the good in other people. It didn't hurt that she was intelligent, attractive, and a good athlete ... She was a varsity gymnast. Lisa Knight was Jennifer's best friend. Her family, like Jennifer's, went to Grace Bible Church.

"Well," Dave continued, "it's just that you seemed *so* opposed to what Mr. Potter was teaching about evolution. It's almost like you don't believe *anything* about it."

"Yeah, right," John added. "That's the way it seemed to me, too. I mean, it's one thing to have some questions about it, but ..."

"I don't remember saying that I don't believe *any* of it," Jennifer corrected him.

"Maybe you didn't *say* it. But it sure seemed ..."

"Although if anything about it is true, I'm not sure what it is," Jennifer added.

"So, do you guys believe in evolution? I mean, *all* of it, like Mr. Potter's been teaching?" Lisa asked.

"Well, we were just discussing that," John replied. "I basically believe it, I guess. Not necessarily one hundred percent, though."

"I do," Ray offered. "Why shouldn't I? According to our textbook – and Mr. Potter – scientists have basically proven it's true. If you ask me, the only reason people wouldn't believe it is fear, or ignorance."

"Fear of what?" David asked.

"Fear that God may not be all He's cracked up to be. Fear that their faith may not have a solid foundation."

"What do you mean?" Jennifer asked.

"Well, as far as I can tell, the only people who question evolution are religious people. You know, Christians. People who read the Bible and go to church every week and all that … people like you, I guess, Jennifer. Like, you believe that God created everything, right? Not that things evolved, but that they were created by God. You know, like you were saying in science class."

"Yes, definitely," Jennifer replied.

"Well, you see, with the discoveries of science, it seems to me that you've got a problem, a *big* problem. Because as far as I can tell science has basically *proven* that everything came about through evolution. *Not* through creation, that is. Now, you gotta admit, Jennifer," Ray continued, "*both* of these explanations can't be true. I mean, according to the theory of evolution – at least as far as I can see – everything happened by accident, sort of. There wasn't any design or plan, or anything like that, which there would be if God created everything, of course. So, like I said, as far as I can tell, these two theories are … let's see … what's the word I'm looking for …"

"How about *mutually exclusive?*" Lisa suggested.

"Yeah, that's it," Ray exclaimed. "Mutually exclusive. Perfect, Lisa. Thanks. In other words, if one's true, the other's not. If you believe what the Bible says about creation, you can't believe what science says about evolution. And vice-versa. You gotta pick one or the other. You can't have both. That's the way I see it, anyway."

"Wait a second, Ray," David spoke up. "Aren't you forgetting something? What about the idea we were talking about a few minutes ago, that God thought up the plan of evolution and used it to create everything. If this was true, then the two ideas wouldn't be mutually exclusive. And people could believe in evolution and keep their faith in the Bible, and God, without having to change their beliefs in any way. As my mom likes to say, 'They could have their cake and eat it, too.'"

"You're talking about God being, like … let's see … like, the author of evolution, or, better yet, the one who wrote the program, then?" Jennifer asked.

"Yeah, that's a good way to put it."

"But this isn't what our teachers seem to believe, or the people who write our textbooks, is it?"

"How do you know, Jen?" John replied. "They basically don't mention God one way or the other. So how do you know what they're thinking about him?"

"That's exactly my point, Johnny," Jennifer said. "You just said it: *they never mention Him*. Don't you think that might just be a clue? Don't you think that suggests that they don't believe He had anything to do with the process? Come on, Johnny. Do you really think that Mr. Potter, for example, believes that God designed evolution?"

"Didn't he suggest that it…"

"No, he didn't suggest that it might be possible. He said that people can believe it if they want to, but it's perfectly obvious that he doesn't think it's possible himself."

"Yeah, I have to agree with you, Jen."

"Hey, I know why these guys don't mention God," Eddie said." Even if he's real, teaching about him belongs in the church, not in school – *especially* not in *science* class."

"I think that's stupid, Eddie," Jennifer replied. "If God really is the author of creation, even if He used evolution to make it happen, we certainly should be hearing *something* about Him. I mean, suppose that we were learning about a book in English class and were never told the name of the author – or, even crazier, that we were *legally forbidden* from learning anything about him, or her?!"

"So, Jen, are you admitting that evolution might be true?" David asked.

"Like I've said, Dave, I'm not sure. Maybe there's something to the idea of God designing evolution. At this point I can't say for sure. What I do know is that the more I hear about evolution, the more I don't like it. I can't put my finger on the exact reasons, but something about it just doesn't seem right. It's like I get the eerie feeling that someone's trying to put something over on me, trying to, like, deceive me almost. It's hard to explain … Hey, look at the clock. Lunch is almost over. But listen, before you go I want to tell you all something. Next Sunday our church youth group is going to be starting a study of creation and evolution, just what we've been talking about. What a coincidence, eh? Maybe you guys would like to come."

"Where is it going to be?" John asked.

"I'm not sure," Jennifer replied. "Maybe at my house," she added, knowing perfectly well that the study had been planned to take place at her church. "I'll let you know."

Shortly, they were all off to their next class.

3

Sunday Dinner at the Newtons

After a half hour or so of friendly dinner conversation, Gary Newton, David's father, said to his guest, Reverend John Strong, "I thought your sermon was very good, John. What you were saying seems so logical. If more people were exposed to your ideas, maybe this heated debate between creationists and evolutionists would simmer down. Some people get so worked up about this subject," he added, glancing at his wife. "Personally, I don't see why they make such a big deal of it. It doesn't really affect our daily lives in any way."

Gary was referring to the sermon that Reverend Strong had delivered that morning at St. Peter's Episcopal Church in Madison, which Gary attended fairly regularly. The topic of the sermon had been theistic evolution, which contends that the theory of evolution is entirely true, but that God, or at least some divine being, initiated and perhaps directs the process. Unlike most creationists, who utterly reject the theory of evolution, theistic evolutionists believe that the scientific evidence in support of evolution is overwhelming and, therefore, undeniable. In recent years theistic evolution has become the dominant belief about origins in most traditional Protestant denominational churches and Catholic churches, as well as an increasing number of nondenominational, evangelical and free churches.

"Thanks, Gary. I certainly do agree with you. You know, considering that it's been about 150 years since the publication of *The Origin of Species*, to me it's pretty unbelievable that this debate is still going on. I mean, I *know* that a lot of people are devoted to the Bible – heck, I certainly am – but that doesn't mean they have to turn their backs on scientific evidence. To the rest of the world such people appear to be – how should I put this – let's just say, to be polite, not very well educated. It's sad and, especially for someone in my position, frustrating. It's long past time that these people should stop fighting the great advances of science and accept that the Bible is a book about theology, not science," Reverend Strong replied, shaking his head slowly.

John Strong had been the Reverend at St. Peter's for almost ten years. He was in his late forties, and this was the fourth church that he had served, all of them Episcopal. He was married with three children, two of them still living at home, one at Princeton, where he himself had earned a doctorate in Religious Studies. Like many modern Episcopal ministers, his theology was decidedly liberal, and he believed that the burgeoning creationist movement in the conservative Christian community was hurting the church's efforts to spread the gospel.

Until the last couple of weeks, the subjects of creation and evolution had not been of particular interest to David. Suddenly, however, because of his recent classes with Mr. Potter and the discussion he had just had with his friends in the school cafeteria, things were different. His curiosity had been aroused, and he was paying close attention to the conversation. David thought back to what Ray had said about creation and evolution, that the two concepts were mutually exclusive. It seemed that the Reverend wouldn't have agreed with his friend.

"So, you're saying, then, that's there's no conflict between what the Bible says and the theory of evolution, that you can believe in both at the same time?" David asked.

"Exactly."

"And you believe in the theory of evolution one hundred percent, but you think that God was behind the whole thing ... like a computer programmer, or something?" David asked, remembering Jennifer's analogy.

"Yes, that's a good analogy."

"According to your idea, then, evolution couldn't have happened without God."

Hesitating for a moment, Reverend Strong replied, "That's right."

David nodded his head reflexively. He was definitely having difficulty trying to harmonize these two seemingly contradictory ideas.

Michelle, David's mother, had been paying close attention to the dialogue between her son and the Reverend. Taking advantage of the pause in the conversation, she spoke up. "Let me ask you, Reverend ... If evolution could not have taken place without God, I guess that means that we wouldn't be here – the whole world wouldn't be here, for that matter – apart from God, right?"

"Yes, of course."

"But if that's so, then how come teachers aren't allowed to mention God, or creation, in our public schools? According to what you're saying, on the one hand these teachers wouldn't even *be* here if it wasn't for God, but on the other they aren't allowed to *mention* Him!? It's sort of like teaching kids about a certain book but forbidding them to mention its author. I mean, think about it. Isn't it kind of crazy?"

David noted with interest that the analogy his mother used had been mentioned by Jennifer in the cafeteria. *They both go to the same church,* he thought to himself. *Maybe their pastor used it in a sermon, or something.* The church David was thinking about was Grace Bible Church, a nondenominational church in Madison. His mother went to it regularly. He would sometimes join her. Occasionally, he would also join the youth group, where he would see Jennifer and Lisa, who were regulars, and sometimes a couple of his other friends. If Jennifer didn't encourage him, though, he probably would never go.

Gary had observed his wife in conversations like this before, and he knew where she was headed. "Uh-oh," he said. "Here she goes. This is what I was talking about, John, when I said 'some people can't seem to let it go.'"

Ignoring her husband's remark, Strong replied to Michelle, "I understand your frustration, Michelle. I really do…"

"I'm not so sure," Michelle interrupted. By now it was reasonably clear to her that the Reverend's position in this debate was definitely not the same as hers. She didn't want to get into an argument, but, at the same time, she felt obligated to defend her beliefs, especially with her children at the table. She was a sixth grade teacher in the local school system and a faithful attendee at Grace Bible Church. The new pastor at this church, Peter Jenkins, was a passionate creationist and was trying to get his congregation excited about the subject. In fact, he was going to preach a sermon on it in a week or two. Michelle was just starting to learn about the subject and could already see why her pastor was enthusiastic. Also, unlike her husband, Michelle was a born-again Christian.

"No, really, I do," Reverend Strong said. "But, you see, any discussion of God as the Creator in the classroom would be obvious support for Christianity, and perhaps Judaism, and that would violate the First Amendment of the Constitution and the notion of the separation of church and state. The Supreme Court has made it perfectly clear that no religion can be endorsed in our public schools, and I totally agree with their decision. People are supposed to learn about science *in* the classroom, about religion *outside* the classroom. When Christians reject evolution they appear uneducated because virtually all scientists accept the theory. In the academic community, creationists are generally looked down upon. If we want to win souls for Christ, if we want people to listen to us, our beliefs must be reasonable and respectable, don't you think?"

"You say that all scientists accept the theory of evolution, but that's not true. There are quite a few that don't," Michelle replied, even more certain that she disagreed with the Reverend.

"Actually, I said 'virtually' all scientists. But, in any event, can you name some that don't?"

"Well, I can't name any off the top of my head" – Michelle wasn't very good at remembering names – "but there are a couple of great Web sites that are devoted to creation, and they have..."

As Michelle was speaking, Reverend Strong was thinking that she was exactly the type of person that gave Christians – or, to be more specific, creationists – a bad name, in the academic community especially. Her beliefs seemed to be based too much on faith, not enough on reason and knowledge. He imagined how her naive arguments would stand up against a real scientist.

"This is all very interesting, Reverend," David spoke up, "but what concerns me is, what's true? You know ... Is evolution true? Is the Bible true? The basic questions."

"As I've suggested, I believe they're both true. But what about you, David? What do you think about evolution? Do you believe it?"

"I don't know. Some of it just sounds kind of crazy to me."

"Like what?"

"Like the idea that birds evolved from reptiles. We were talking about this in one of our classes last week, and when I was thinking about it afterward, it just didn't seem to make much sense to me. Like, Mr. Potter – he's our teacher – was saying that birds' feathers probably evolved from reptiles' scales, but his explanation sure wasn't very convincing."

"Why not? What didn't make sense to you?"

"He said that somehow a mutation caused the edges of some reptile's scales to become ragged and that this somehow gave this creature an advantage over the other reptiles and that after a few million years these ragged scales became feathers. It sounds fishy to me. Mike Lawton, a friend of mine, asked Mr. Potter if there were any examples of these ragged scales, like in the fossil record, and Mr. Potter said that there wasn't. The two of them went back and forth for a few minutes, and Mr. Potter ended by saying that even though scientists don't really know *how* feathers evolved, they're positive that they *did* because …get this … because birds *have* them. I mean, what's up with that? Apparently there's no evidence to support the idea – none, zero – but we're supposed to believe it, anyway, just because our teacher says we should? I thought conclusions in science were supposed to be based on *evidence.*"

"I think you may be missing the forest for the trees here, David," Reverend Strong said gently. "Scientists freely admit that they don't have all the answers about evolution, and exactly how feathers evolved is one of the things that is still a mystery. But the overall evidence for the theory is overwhelming. You mustn't let one little obstacle prevent you from accepting the whole grand theory. The National Science Teachers Association has labeled evolution as one of the five unifying concepts of all science and, as such, is to be taught as fact and included on all state assessment tests that are required for school accreditation. If virtually the entire scientific community has accepted the theory of evolution as a fact, don't you think that we, being non-scientists, should accept it, too? I certainly do. Theistic evolution, you see, is an effort to harmonize evolution with the words of Scripture. It may not be perfect … but it's a lot easier to defend than the idea that the world was created 6,000 years ago, like some creationists believe!"

"Oh yeah, that's a good one!" Gary Newton quickly blurted out. "That one really kills me! I mean, give me a break! As far as I can recall, six thousand years ago the Egyptians were busy building their pyramids. How can anyone in his right mind believe that at that time the whole world was first *created*? I mean, what happened? One day God created the universe, a few days later he created man, and the next day the pyramids were under way? What a *joke*!"

David had to admit that it did seem pretty unbelievable.

Gary turned toward David. "You know, David, if creationists got their way, before long you won't just be learning about biology, geology, physics and astronomy in your science classroom. Pretty soon you'll be learning about Adam and Eve … and maybe even Noah's Flood, too!" he laughed, along with Reverend Strong.

Michelle flashed an icy glance at her husband and turned toward Reverend Strong. "I know you don't believe in these things, Gary, but I'm surprised at your reaction, Reverend. Apparently, you have doubts, too?"

"I'm sorry, Michelle. I just find your husband amusing and can't help laughing along with him sometimes. But, please, don't get me wrong. It's not that I don't believe these stories. It's just that I don't take them absolutely literally. They are allegories, intended to teach us powerful and important spiritual truths. They're obviously not literally true. I doubt if there's a geology textbook in the world, at least not a modern one, that mentions a word about Noah's Flood. If it were literally true, if it were really a worldwide flood, it would have been the greatest natural event in the history of the world, and according to the Bible it took place only about five or six thousand years ago. To geologists, events that occurred 6,000 years ago are recent history. Don't you think that an event of this magnitude, an event that would certainly have reshaped the entire surface of the earth, if it took place only 6,000 years ago, would have left an abundance of evidence in its wake, evidence that would have made its existence abundantly clear not just to scientists but to everyone? But based upon the teaching of our geology textbooks, not only is there not an abundance of evidence, there isn't *any*! Tell me, Michelle. Did any of the science textbooks you used when you were in school ever mention a single word about Noah's Flood?"

"I suppose not. I certainly can't remember one, at least," she answered, somewhat flustered.

"That's what I thought," Reverend Strong said. "By the way, I want to make it clear that although I certainly don't believe that Noah's Flood was worldwide, I'm not saying that it didn't happen. Perhaps it did, but if so, it must have been a local, not a worldwide, event."

For the first time, David's younger sister, fourteen-year-old Kristen, spoke up. "Um … I was wondering something, Reverend Strong," she hesitantly asked. "You said that the stories about Noah's Flood and Adam and Eve were not literally true, but that they taught us spiritual lessons, right?"

"Yes, that's right."

"What are the lessons?"

It was a good question, and Strong tried to explain what these lessons were, but David's thoughts were elsewhere. He was thinking about the exchange between his mother and the Reverend concerning the absence of any mention of a great flood in science textbooks. If it were true, he realized that it could be a significant argument against creation, at least the Bible's account of it. But he had trouble believing that it was. There must be at least a couple of books that discuss it, he figured. He determined that he would check this out for himself. And the next afternoon, he did. Somewhat to his surprise, he discovered that the Reverend was absolutely right. He scanned over a hundred books about science in his school's library and there was no mention of such an event, not a word. Naturally, this suggested that the Reverend had been right about this point.

After scanning the books, however, David turned his attention to the Internet. Here, what he discovered was quite different. Here he found a number of sites that claimed that this flood had been not only very real but worldwide, too. And their descriptions seemed very reasonable and solidly grounded in scientific evidence. Now, the fact that none of the science books in the school library had even mentioned this flood didn't make any sense to him. It almost seemed as if the books must have been very deliberately chosen to make sure that students were not exposed to any information about this subject. What else could explain such absolute silence about such an awesome event? But who would have done this, and why would it be done?

4

Moving Forward

Mr. Potter's class was almost over. The subject was the evolution of mammals. All that remained of this section on evolution was a look at primates, including man, and a summary of the material.

David Newton raised his hand. "In our last class, Sir, you were explaining the evolution of feathers. Jennifer was raising some pretty good questions – at least I thought they were good – and the class ended before you could completely answer them …"

"Yes, I remember," Mr. Potter responded. "She was getting into some areas that I didn't feel were appropriate for a science classroom."

"I understand – creation and God and things like that. But that's not what I was going to ask you about. I just don't see how feathers could have evolved from reptiles' scales. You were going over it with Mike, but I didn't get it. Could you go over it again?"

"Okay," Mr. Potter replied, relieved that David wasn't going to ask him about creation or God and things like that. "I had said that nobody knows exactly how this change took place." As he was speaking Mr. Potter noticed the clock on the back wall.

"We only have about a minute left, David, so I won't be able to answer your question very thoroughly. The key, though, is mutations. Whatever actually occurred, mutations played a vital role. The transformation was the result of a large number of very small changes over a very long period of time, and the changes were caused by natural selection acting upon these mutational changes. I suggest that you review your notes and textbook on mutations, which we covered in the first week of this section. That should help, I think."

Jennifer's hand went up, but she never got to ask her question, because the class ended just as it did. As she was leaving she stopped at Mr. Potter's desk. He was looking down at some papers and didn't notice her.

"Mr. Potter ..."

"Oh, Jennifer ... yes, yes, what can I do for you?" Mr. Potter stammered, surprised by Jennifer's presence.

"I've been meaning to ask you about something."

"Sure, sure ... Go ahead," he said, suspecting what the subject would be.

"That passage on the wall behind you. Why do you have it there? What does it mean to you?"

The passage was a verse from the eighteenth chapter of the Gospel of Matthew. It read:

Whoever causes one of these little ones who believe in Me to stumble, it is better for him that a heavy millstone be hung around his neck, and that he be drowned in the depth of the sea.

Relieved that Jennifer didn't want to discuss their recent confrontation, Mr. Potter replied, "That was given to me several years ago by the mother of one of my students. She was a Christian, I guess, and told me that it was from the Gospel according to Matthew. As I interpret it, the little ones are my students and I am the one they believe in. The way I see it, it lays a heavy responsibility on my shoulders to make sure that I teach my students the truth, for if I fail, and they stumble because of this failure, I will be held responsible and may one day be held accountable. I really like it."

Although Mr. Potter's interpretation was admirable, Jennifer knew that it was incorrect in one critical detail. She didn't feel that this was the right time to mention it, however.

"I do too," was the only response she could think of at the moment. "Well, I'll see you later," she added with a warm smile. "I gotta run."

There's something special about that young lady, Mr. Potter mused as he watched Jennifer head toward the door.

As she was hurrying down the hall towards her next class, English, David called to her. "Jennifer, wait a second. I saw your hand up at the end of class. What were you going to say?"

"I was going to ask something about mutations. I remember that Mr. Potter had taught us how important mutations are in the process of evolution ..."

"I think he called them 'the vehicle of change.'"

"Yeah, that's right. It seems to me that, according to Mr. Potter's definition, mutations have, like, an almost magical power. Through them, scales turn into feathers, wolves become whales, and monkeys become people. It just seems unbelievable to me, David. You know what I mean? Basically, I don't understand how mutations could possibly account for all the changes they're given credit for. As I was thinking about it – while you and Mr. Potter were talking – I realized that I really didn't understand mutations very well at all. I mean, I know we studied them a week or two ago, and I *thought* I understood them. But then I realized in class today that I really don't – not very well, at least. So I wanted to ask Mr. Potter a question about them ... Oops!" Jennifer exclaimed. "Here's my English classroom. I guess I didn't really answer your question, did I? I never told you what I was going to ask Mr. Potter!"

"That's okay," David said. "Maybe you can tell me some other time ... later, Jenn."

"All right. I'll see ya."

David had a free period ahead of him and decided to step outside for some fresh air. It was a beautiful, warm spring day. As he looked skyward, he noticed a hawk high above the western hills. Rhythmically flapping his powerful wings, he was flying upward into the wind. As he rose ever higher, his forward motion stopped, even though he was still flapping his wings; his speed and that of the wind had become equal. Suddenly, he stretched out his wings and, like a kite, sailed backward in the wind. After a few seconds, he tucked in his wings, banked to his left and plummeted downward in a headlong free fall. Soon, he spread his wings and turned in a broad sweeping arc until the wind was once again at his back, at which point he leveled off into a smooth, swift glide, like a sailboat running with the wind. David could tell by the speed at which he streaked across the sky that the wind was swift up there.

Shortly, the hawk circled back into the wind and began the same routine once again. After repeating this aerial show a couple of more times, with the wind once again at his back, he streaked off into the distance and disappeared.

David nodded his head in admiration. *That was awesome,* he thought. As the hawk disappeared from his sight, David pondered the purpose of the marvelous event he had just witnessed. *What was this hawk doing?* he wondered – *testing the wind? – or perhaps putting on a dazzling show for the unfortunate earth-bound creatures far below him?*

Quickly it dawned on David. The hawk had no ulterior purpose at all. He was soaring in the wind for the sheer joy of it. He was doing, and doing perfectly and beautifully, exactly what God had created him to do – soaring, flying, and gliding in the wind.

David recalled what Mr. Potter had been teaching about the evolution of birds, and he wondered how such a glorious and special creature as this hawk could ever have evolved by chance – and from an earth-hugging *reptile*, no less!

With a little smile, David gently shook his head in disbelief and headed to the library.

Shortly after his eleventh-grade advanced science class had ended, Richard Potter was in the teacher's room talking to Barbara Henrikson, a fellow science teacher. Prompted by the discussion in Mr. Potter's class, they were discussing creationist organizations, in particular one that had been mentioned by Jennifer, the Institute for Creation Research (ICR), which was one of the best known.

"So far as I can tell, Dick, they not only find fault with evolutionary theory, they utterly reject it," Barbara exclaimed.

"That's right, Barbara," Potter responded. "But that's hardly the end of it. They also believe in a worldwide flood that covered the entire earth only a few thousand years ago and – this is the one that really gets me – that the world is only about ten thousand years old!"

"I know! Isn't that absolutely *incredible!* My God, Dick, how can people that are apparently reasonably intelligent believe such utter nonsense? I mean, come *on* ... *ten thousand years!* ... and some of them think it's only *six thousand!* In terms of earth history, anyone who knows the slightest thing about science is aware that the earth is about 4.5 *billion* years old and that ten thousand years is only a blink of an eye. Heck, once the conditions were right, it probably took about a thousand times longer than that for the first amino acids to form from inorganic chemicals."

Mr. Potter shook his head in amazement. "The thing that really bothers me about these people is the way they promote these myths so aggressively. If they want to believe this foolishness themselves, it's one thing. But, trying to make everyone else believe it, that's quite another."

"I know, Dick. I know. We see it in our classrooms all the time, don't we? Every time the subject arises, there's almost always one or two students, sometimes more, who actually seem to believe this baloney. And it's usually tough to change their minds, to get them to see the truth."

"Yeah, it's like they've been brainwashed or something. I hate it when they bring it up, because I can see how confusing it is for the rest of the students. I've even seen some of these others actually start to believe this stuff! Did you ever notice how often these doubters are kids who have been home-schooled?"

"I certainly have. Jennifer was home-schooled, wasn't she?"

"Oh, yeah. She sure was."

After a brief pause, Mr. Potter continued. "Have you noticed that if you ask one of these kids to point out a specific problem with evolutionary theory, they almost always have trouble? Like today, I asked Jennifer to name one."

"Did she come up with anything?"

"She tried – first, with the evolution of birds, but we had already covered that, so I asked her to try something else. And you know what she brought up? Seriously, see if you can guess, Barbara."

"Hmmm," she pondered. "The evolution of 'organs of extreme perfection,' as they're sometimes called, like the eye? You know what Darwin said about this: *The eye to this day gives me a cold shudder.*"

"That would have been a good one, Barb, but it's not the one she brought up … thankfully, I might add. That's not an easy one to defend, is it? Try again."

"How about the statistical odds against life arising completely by chance?"

"Nope. Wrong again – Hey, I'm glad you weren't in my class, by the way!" Mr. Potter chuckled. "I'll tell you what it was: radiometric dating."

"No! Come on, Dick! You're kidding, right?"

"No, really. I swear. That's what she said."

"Amazing. It's practically the Holy Grail of evolutionary theory. What did she say about it?"

"That the dates determined by the method sometimes vary."

"That's it? That's all she said?" Barbara inquired, somewhat incredulously. "And just where did she say she discovered this little pearl of wisdom?"

"From one of these creationist organizations. In fact, I think she said it was the one we were just referring to, the Institute for Creation Research."

Barbara shook her head in disbelief. "What about the other kids. Were any of them raising questions about the theory?"

"Yeah, there were a couple of others – Mike Lawton, for one."

After a pause, Barbara asked, "Hey, what about Josh Siegel? Has he had anything to say in your evolution classes?"

Josh was Mr. Potter's top student, actually the best student he had ever had, and Barbara knew that her friend had a special place in his heart for this brilliant young man.

"Josh? Oh, well, Josh missed a couple of these classes … some sort of illness, I've heard. Anyway, when he has been in class he hasn't seemed particularly interested in what's been going on. Maybe he's just been bored. You know Josh, Barbara. You've had him in class. No matter what subject we're on, he's usually so far ahead of everyone else."

"Yes, I know exactly what you mean, Dick. He is quite an amazing young man." Pausing for reflection, Barbara then continued. "Speaking of Josh, I was wondering something about him the other day. He's seventeen, isn't he?"

"Yes."

"Well, as bright as he is, how come he hasn't skipped a grade or two?"

"Good question," Mr. Potter nodded. "A number of years ago, when he was about eight or nine years old, Josh had a prolonged battle with Hodgkin's disease, a battle, which, thankfully, he eventually won. But it kept him out of school for the better part of two years."

"Very interesting. I never knew anything about that."

"It was quite a few years ago. I don't imagine a lot of people in the high school do."

The period was almost over, and Mr. Potter got up to leave. "It looks like we'll have to keep fighting these brushfires in our classrooms for a little while longer, doesn't it, Barb?"

Suddenly spreading his arms, Mr. Potter began speaking in a voice that resembled Martin Luther King's. "But don't worry, my dear sister, our battle won't last forever. One day, I'm sure that the blazing light of truth will shine over *all* the land! And then, yes, and then the reigns of ignorance that are holding us back from progress will finally be severed, and we'll all be free, free at last!"

Amused, Barbara exclaimed, "Right on, Brother Richard, right on … And what a grand and glorious day that will be!"

Laughing, they exchanged a high-five.

As Mr. Potter turned to leave, Barbara left him with a question. "That day of truth, Dick … I wonder if we'll be around to see it shining."

It was a damp, dreary Saturday morning, and Tom Lawton was driving home from soccer practice with his son, Mike. Mike was one of the best players on his team, but his team was only the junior varsity. He was small and not particularly strong, but he was blessed with one invaluable weapon: speed. He loved the sport with a passion. Tom went to all of his games. While they were driving, Mike told his dad about the recent dialogue he had had with Mr. Potter about the evolution of birds. He had just told him what Mr. Potter had said about the evolution of feathers from reptiles' scales.

"When I asked Mr. Potter what advantage these ragged scales would give to a reptile, he said that they would help when they were trying to catch insects. I couldn't understand why that would be. What do you think, Dad? Does that make any sense to you? Do you think that Mr. Potter was right?"

Tom Lawton looked over at his son and gently shook his head. He had majored in biology at the University of New Hampshire and had planned to go into teaching. But those plans hadn't worked out, and at present he worked in a small start-up software company north of Boston. He had a keen interest in birds, an interest that had been kindled many years ago, when he was a teenager. The story behind this attraction is intriguing. Genealogical research his mother had done had revealed that he was a distant relative of the famous naturalist, John James Audubon. Inspired by this discovery, Tom's family decided to take a weekend trip to the New York Historical Society in New York City to view Audubon's original paintings of American birds, the collection that had made the great naturalist famous throughout the world. There are over four hundred of these paintings, and each one measures 26 ½ by 39 ½ inches. Dazzled by these spectacular paintings, Tom fell in love with their subject. A couple of years ago, he had taken his own family to New York so they could see the paintings. The glory of these magnificent works of art had the same effect upon them that they had had upon Tom: they, too – all six of them – fell in love with birds.

During his high school and college days Tom had been thoroughly subjected to the theory of evolution, of course, but something had always prevented him from fully accepting it. He wasn't aware of it, but that something was his love for birds that had been inspired in him by his distant relative, John James Audubon. Tom had read a couple of biographies of Audubon and knew that he believed deeply in the Creator and considered birds, which he referred to as "his little sisters," to be wonderful exhibitions of the Master's handiwork. Audubon's faith had reached down

Great Blue Heron

through the years and touched Tom's heart. Tom's faith wasn't as strong as his distant cousin's, but he had enough to know that birds probably didn't evolve from lizards.

He owned a small camp in North Conway, New Hampshire, where he grew up, and his family would go camping there as often as possible. They all loved hiking in the White Mountains and fishing in the mountain streams and lakes. He was also a member of the Madison School Board.

"No, Mike, I don't believe that Mr. Potter was right. If you ask me, the whole idea that birds evolved from reptiles is an evolutionary myth. I've showed you feathers under a microscope. It seems simply impossible to me that these magnificently designed objects could have evolved from reptile scales by random mutations, which is what evolution claims."

"So what should I do, Dad?"

"What do you mean?"

"Well, should I object when my teachers bring up these ideas? If you were in my place, would you?"

Tom Lawton paused before he answered his son's question.

"I think you should do what you think is right. Stand up for what you believe in, Mike."

"Would you?"

Looking at his son with a warm smile, Tom replied, "I hope so!"

After a few minutes of silence, Mike said, "Hey, can we go up to the camp next weekend? I want to go to Mt. Washington and see how much snow there still is."

"That's a great idea. This time of the year the trout fishing should be great!"

"Could I bring a friend?"

"Yeah, sure. Who do you have in mind?"

"I was thinking about Scott Martin."

"The hockey player? I didn't know you were friends with him."

"He's co-captain of the varsity soccer team, too. And guess what ... After a scrimmage against the varsity a few days ago, Scott came up to me and said that his team could really use someone with my speed. He said he was going to talk to Coach Stone and see if he could bring me up for a game. Can you believe it, Dad? I might get a chance to play on the varsity soccer team! Scott loves to fish, just like me. I was telling him about our camp in North Conway, and he said it sounded really cool and that he'd love to go up with us sometime. He's a great guy, Dad. I'm sure you'd really like him."

"That would be great, Mike. I look forward to meeting him."

5

An Interlude

It was Friday night, and as they often were on Friday nights, David Newton and a few friends were gathered at Dino's pizza parlor on Main Street in Madison. Adorning the walls were large prints of Italian scenes so common in such restaurants – harbors, small villages, and colorful street scenes. They were hardly great works of art, but there was something very appealing about them; the more you saw them, the more you liked them. Most of Dino's patrons had never been to Italy, but because of these scenes some of the regulars almost felt that they had been. A large jukebox kept up an endless stream of music, from different eras, and in one corner was a large screen TV that faithfully transmitted every Red Sox game. Like most people in Madison, David and his friends – or, most of them, at least – were Red Sox fans.

"So, here we go, guys," Josh Siegel, a passionate Sox fan, pronounced, as he observed the Red Sox take the field against the hated Yankees for the first time that year, "spring time in New England, and The Great Rivalry begins again."

"Did you see who the Yankees picked up over the winter?" John Mitchell asked. "Once again, it looks like they think they can buy a pennant by adding a few aging superstars."

"If the past few years are any indication, it looks like it might be time to scrap that plan and think of something new, eh?" David grinned.

"Hey Ray," Josh said to Ray Corbett, a Yankee fan, "when are you going to give up on those losers you support and join Red Sox Nation? You know that we'd welcome you with open arms, right? We especially like pinstripe converts."

"I believe that you guys have a little more practice at losing than us, man. Does the number twenty-six ring a bell?"

"That's ancient history, dude. We prefer focusing our attention on more recent events, like last year's World Series. Sweep, Ray – four games straight.

Does that ring a bell? Oh, yeah – and if I'm not mistaken, I believe that the loser in game four was an ex-*Yankee*," Josh smiled.

"Yeah – Shultz. He should have retired years ago."

After several minutes of eating pizza, watching the game and friendly chatter, John asked David a question. "Hey Dave, I've been meaning to ask you …Are you going to that youth group meeting Sunday night at Jennifer's church?" John was in Mr. Potter's advanced eleventh grade science class and had been very intrigued by the questions stirred up during the recent study of evolution. It was the first time he had become aware that anyone even had doubts about the theory.

"I don't know, Johnny. Were you thinking about it?"

"What meeting are you guys talking about?" Josh interrupted.

Mitchell proceeded to tell Josh about the discussion that took place in the high school cafeteria after Mr. Potter's class on evolution a few days ago – Josh had been absent – and Jennifer's invitation to the upcoming youth group in which they would be discussing creation and evolution.

"Wait a second," Josh responded somewhat incredulously. "You guys are thinking about going to a *church* to talk about *creation?!* You gotta be *kiddin'* me, man."

"Uh, it's not actually going to be at a church, Josh. It's going to be at Jennifer's house, I think," David responded.

David and Josh were life-long friends. They grew up on the same street, only a few houses apart. Although Josh was unusually bright, David wasn't too far behind him. During Josh's two-year battle with Hodgkin's disease, David proved to be Josh's most loyal friend, checking in on him almost daily. Josh's family was Jewish, of the Reformed – that is, liberal – variety.

"I don't care if it's right here at Dino's, Dave. I still don't see why any of you would want to go to such a stupid meeting. I mean, what is there to *discuss* – how God carved Eve from Adam's rib?" Josh said, laughing.

"Hey, you weren't in class the day that Mike got into a discussion with Mr. Potter about the evolution of feathers," Dave replied. "Let me tell you, Mike was making some really good points – he's quite the bird freak, as you know – and I, for one, wasn't very satisfied with Mr. Potter's answers to his questions. To tell you the truth, their discussion left me with more questions than answers."

"Me, too," Mitchell chimed in.

"Ditto," added Ray Corbett.

Josh looked around the table and shook his head. "So, what – are *all* of you going to this little revival meeting?" He paused for a moment. "Wait a minute ... Wait just a minute," he picked up. "You said the meeting's going to be at Jennifer's house, right, Dave?"

"Yeah, that's right."

"I think maybe I'm starting to get the picture here. Dave, don't you go to Jennifer's church?"

"Yeah, sometimes, like once every month, or two, when my mom drags me there."

"Have you ever been to their youth group?"

"Occasionally."

"So, you know who goes to the group, right?"

"Yeah, I guess – generally, at least."

"Who else is going to be there, besides Jennifer?"

"I don't know. Lisa, probably, and Ginny ... maybe Cindy and ..."

"Just like I thought!" Josh interrupted, with a big smile. "I know why you're going – there'll be a bunch of chicks there!"

Everyone had a good laugh. They knew Josh was right – partially, at least.

"You know, I hadn't even thought about that, Josh ..." John said.

"Yeah, sure you hadn't!" Nick Murray said, pointing his finger at John with a big grin. "Like, it never even crossed your mind that Lisa might be there!"

Smiling, John nodded his head. "To tell you the truth, Nick, I really hadn't thought of that ... But, now that you mention it, that clinches it for me: I'm *going!*"

"All right," Josh said. "Johnny's got an excuse ... maybe Dave, too. But the rest of you sure don't!" Turning to Dave, Josh added, "Who's going to be leading this thing, Dave – Jennifer?"

"No. Actually, I think it's going to be the new youth pastor at the church."

"Yeah? What's his background? What does he know about science? And what's he like?"

"Regarding his background, I have absolutely no idea. I've only been to one youth group that he was leading. But I have to say, he seemed like a pretty decent dude."

"How old is he?" John asked.

"I don't know – maybe about 30, or 35, I'd say. His wife was there, too. She seemed cool. Hey, by the way, I just remembered a couple of other guys that go to the youth group: Peter Bernardo, and Scott Martin." The mention of these two caught the attention of the group, for they were both well-liked and respected seniors, Scott in particular. He was a star defenseman on the hockey team, co-captain of the soccer team, and vice-president of their class.

Shortly, the conversation about the upcoming youth group ended, and the boys' attention turned back to the baseball game, which the Red Sox won with a two-out walk-off home run by David "Big Papi" Ortiz in the bottom of the tenth inning. For everyone except Ray Corbett, the only Yankee fan in the group, it was a sweet beginning to the Great Rivalry.

6

The First Meeting of the Youth Group

A few days after her conversation with David and his friends in the high school cafeteria, Jennifer ran into her youth pastor, Paul Hopkins, one evening at Grace Bible Church. She told Paul about the conversation, adding that some of the kids had expressed curiosity about the youth group and might even decide to visit one. She then raised the suggestion that, since some of these kids did not attend church, it might be more inviting to them if the group was held in her home rather than the church. Paul didn't need any convincing. He thought it was a great idea.

So, the following Sunday the Grace Bible Church youth group met at the Conley's home at 27 Lake Hill Road in Madison. By 7 p.m. everyone had arrived. As Jennifer had explained to the group in the cafeteria a few days earlier, the topic they would be focusing upon would be creation and evolution. There were fifteen people altogether: Lisa Knight, Kristen Macdonald, Peter Bernardo, Mike Lawton, Scott Martin, Sue Peterson, Ginny Corbin, David Newton, John Mitchell, Nick Murray, Ray Corbett, Jennifer, Paul Hopkins, and his wife, Sarah – and Jennifer's thirteen year old sister, Kelly. Mike, Ray, Nick, Kristen and John were at the group for the first time. It wasn't David's first time, but he was hardly a regular.

The Conley's home was a century old center-hall Colonial, pale yellow with off-white trim and black shutters, that they had purchased eighteen years earlier, shortly before Jennifer was born. It needed a considerable amount of work when they bought it, but Jennifer's father, Jason, was in the construction business and over the next several years he had done a marvelous job of renovating the home. Set well back from the road, the house featured a lovely wraparound front porch with solid mahogany decking that Jason had built himself. Upon entering through the front door, the den was to the right and the hall to the spacious country kitchen directly ahead. A moderate-sized dining room was between the den and the kitchen, and to the left of the main hall was the large family/living room. This was where the youth group would meet. Two large couches, two easy chairs, and a few dining chairs in the living room provided seating for most of the kids. The others sat on the floor.

After the initial introductions and a couple of games, Jennifer's mother, Laura, brought out some homemade pizzas and soda. Besides home-schooling her two younger children, Laura did medical bookkeeping out of her home. In addition to Jennifer, they had three other children: Elizabeth, nine, Kelly, and James, nineteen and a sophomore at UNH. They were all devout Christians … all, that is, except for James, who, like so many other college students from a similar background, was reevaluating his faith at this point. About 7:30 Paul decided that it was time to get the discussion started.

"I want to welcome you all here," he began, "especially those of you that are here for the first time. Jennifer told me that we might have some extra people here tonight, and she gave me some idea why. She said that you were studying evolution in school and that some issues came up that you wanted to check out. As you will soon find out, I'm not a big fan of evolution, but since it got you to come here tonight, I guess it can't be all bad! God does work in mysterious ways. Now, before we get started, let's give Mrs. Conley a hand for that fabulous pizza!

"Great. Thanks a lot … Okay, first of all, I want to let you all know that we're not having this meeting just because some of you were studying evolution in school and had some questions about it. I actually planned this study a while ago. I deeply believe that the topic that we're going to be talking about is incredibly important. I've had a passionate interest in it for many years. Perhaps I'll get a chance to tell you why sometime. I don't know how long we'll spend on this topic – perhaps three or four weeks, maybe more, maybe less. We'll just see where God leads us. Sometimes, you know, we just can't figure Him out … just like a *lot* of times, I'm sure He must have trouble figuring *us* out!

"So, then, our topic is creation and evolution. We'll look at it from both a biblical perspective and a scientific perspective. Our goal is to discover the truth. It's not only an extremely important subject, but it's also very fascinating. I think we're in for an exciting journey, and I hope that you'll all be with us until it's over. Now, to get started, how about if you guys ask me some questions."

Since nobody volunteered to respond, Paul turned to David.

"I hope you don't mind me picking on you, Dave, but Jennifer said that you and she had had some good discussions about this topic recently, and I thought maybe you could share with us some of the things you talked about."

"Yeah, sure," David replied. "I don't mind. Basically, I'm confused about this subject. I've got a lot of questions, and I'd really like to find out the truth about it. Let me give you an example. It's not something that I was talking to Jennifer about, but … never mind. I think you'll get the point. The other day, we had the Reverend from my dad's church over for Sunday dinner. His name is John Strong. His sermon that morning had been about something he called *theistic evolution*. At dinner we were talking about his sermon, and somehow the subject of Noah's Flood came up. I think my dad mentioned it. He doesn't believe in it himself. In fact, he thinks it's a joke. Well, apparently, the Reverend doesn't believe in it, either … at least not as a real event, as something, you know, that really happened."

"What does he think it was?" Paul asked.

"I'm not really sure," David replied. "Some kind of spiritual allegory or something, I guess. He did say that it might have happened, but that if it did, it must have been only a local, not a worldwide, flood. Anyway, to prove his point, he asked my mom – she had asked him whether he believed it was real or not – whether she had ever seen this flood mentioned in a single book when she was in school. She had to admit that she hadn't. It seemed like he believed that this proved his point that it couldn't have been real – because, you know, if it had been real, at least *some* school book would have mentioned it. Well, I thought he had a pretty good point, but I wasn't *absolutely* convinced. I just couldn't quite believe that this flood wasn't mentioned in *any* science book – I mean, like *everybody's* heard of it, right? – so I decided to check it out for myself. And guess what? When I checked the science books in the high school library, it seemed that the Reverend *had* been right. I checked over one hundred books, and not a single one mentioned one word about any worldwide flood …"

"That doesn't really surprise me, David, because …" Paul interrupted.

"No, wait, I'm not finished yet. Later that night, at home, I checked out the subject on the Internet, and I found out that there are actually quite a few people that *do* believe that this worldwide flood actually happened. But – and here's where I got a problem – Reverend Strong *never mentioned them*. He never let us know that there were other opinions about the subject, opinions that didn't agree with his. The way I see it, he *must* have known about these other opinions. I mean, like, he *preaches* about this stuff. Certainly he must know a lot more about it than the people in my family do. He must know that there are plenty of intelligent people who believe that this flood was worldwide."

David paused for a moment.

"I don't know," he continued. "It just seems to me that Reverend Strong was kind of deceiving us, if you know what I mean. I know that sounds kind of rough – my dad thinks he's a great preacher – but I don't really know what else to think. I mean, maybe the guy *is* a great preacher and all that, but still, I got a problem with the way he presented his case about the flood. It didn't seem fair, if you know what I mean. Maybe I'm missing something, though. What do you think?"

"You are definitely *not* missing something, Dave. Actually, you are *getting* something, something very important, in fact. Thanks a lot. That was *really* interesting, a very sharp insight, and we will *definitely* come back to it. But before we do, I want to hear from some of the others, to hear what they hope to get out of this group. Is that okay with you, Dave?"

"Yeah, sure. No problem."

"How about someone else?" Paul asked.

"Okay. I'll give it a shot," Scott Martin spoke up. Scott was a senior at Madison High, and his family had been going to Grace for several years. He was a regular at the youth group. Along with David, Nick Murray, and John Mitchell, he was on the varsity hockey team and was generally admired by everyone who knew him. Unlike several of the other kids who were there that night, he was not in Mr. Potter's advanced eleventh grade science class. "I came tonight because, well, because I almost always come to youth group," he smiled at Paul. "I really like it. I think it's interesting. But, aside from that, I'm really looking forward to this study, because, like Dave, I'm confused about this whole creation/evolution topic. Like everyone else here, I've been taught since the seventh grade that the theory of evolution is basically a proven fact. I mean, that's the way it's presented to us in school, right guys?" he asked, scanning the room and nodding his head. "But as I've been coming to this youth group the last couple of years and learning more about God, I'm having more and more trouble putting these two things together – God and evolution, I mean. The more I learn about God, and the Bible, the more trouble I have believing in evolution. So, I'm hoping these meetings will help me get some of this stuff straightened out."

"Why are you having trouble putting these things together, Scott?" Paul Hopkins asked. "What doesn't seem to fit?"

"Well, let me see if I can come up with something … All right, here ya go. We've been talking here about the Fall – you know, where Adam and Eve ate the fruit in the Garden of Eden and how that brought sin into the world, and then, because of that, how we all need a Savior, right?" Scott said, glancing at Paul for approval, which was granted. "Okay, then, if we all evolved from monkeys or whatever a few million years ago, this story just wouldn't make any sense."

"Why not?" Kristen Macdonald, a friend of Lisa and Jennifer, immediately asked. "What's the problem?"

"The problem is," Scott responded, "how the heck do Adam and Eve fit into the theory of evolution? The Bible doesn't say anything about them evolving from monkeys, or from anything else. Furthermore, if we all evolved, how can God blame us for any of our sins? If evolution is true, we're just glorified monkeys, as far as I can tell. Also, according to the Bible, man was created on the exact same day as the monkeys, so how the heck could we have *evolved* from them?!"

"What do you mean that man was created on the exact same day as monkeys?" John Mitchell asked. John's family didn't go to any church, and John was, basically, completely unfamiliar with the Bible. Thus, he had never read, or heard, the creation account found in the first chapter of Genesis.

"According to the Bible, Johnny, the whole world was created in six days, and all the land animals, including monkeys and people, were created on the sixth day," Scott answered.

"Oh, man, that's just what Jennifer said the other day in science class. According to Mr. Potter, though, the world is, like, fifteen billion years old, and people started to evolve about two or three million years ago, maybe even earlier. This idea that the world was created in six days sounds *crazy* to me, man."

Knowing that John was probably not the only one in this group who had little or no exposure to the Bible, Paul knew that he had his work cut out for him with this group. But he had been a youth pastor for over six years, and this certainly was not unfamiliar territory to him. He had come across quite a few young people just like John – more and more all the time, in fact.

"Hey, I'm just telling you what it says in the Bible, man," Scott responded.

"And you *believe* it?!"

"That's right, Johnny. I do." Raising his eyebrows, John nodded, surprised at Scott's firm convictions. He knew Scott quite well but was unfamiliar with this side of him. It definitely piqued his interest.

"That was great, Scott. Thanks a lot," Paul said. "I want to hear from all of you at some point, but before we do, let me provide some background to this subject, some information that can begin to provide you with some perspective.

"To begin, it's critical for you to understand that evolution is based *entirely* – absolutely, completely, *entirely* – upon chance ... upon, in other words, the completely *random* interaction of *natural* events. When all the fluff and all the rhetoric are eliminated, we are left with this stark truth: there are *only two* possible ways that life, or more broadly speaking, the world, could have come into existence: by chance or by design. There is no room for a compromise between these two possibilities. If one is true, then the other isn't. Evolution is based entirely upon chance; there is absolutely no room for a Creator or God in the process."

"Wait a minute, Pastor Paul – Hey, is that what we're supposed to call you: Pastor Paul?" Mike Lawton spoke up for the first time.

"You can if you want to," Paul replied, "but just plain old 'Paul' is fine with me."

"Okay, good. Thanks – Paul. Like I started to say, why can't there be a compromise? Why can't evolution have been designed by God? That would make everyone happy! I don't see any problem with that." Others in the room nodded their heads. Obviously, they thought that Mike had a good point. David thought back to the recent discussion at his house with Reverend Strong when they had been discussing this very point.

"That's a very good question, Mike," one that Paul Hopkins had heard many times before. Although he wasn't aware of it, Mike, like Reverend Strong, was referring to theistic evolution. "Let me try to answer it for you. Suppose, for the sake of argument, that life did evolve in some warm little pond a few billion years ago by completely random interactions of, first, atoms and then molecules – just like you've been taught in school – but that God was actually behind these events, directing them to make sure that everything was running smoothly, that exactly the right interactions were always occurring at exactly the right time. This is about what you mean by God designing evolution, right?"

"Yeah, that's pretty good. That's about right, I'd say."

"Okay. Now – and this is the critical point – if God, or some Creator, was actually doing this, *the process would no longer be evolution*, because, like I just said, evolution rests entirely upon random, *not* planned or designed events. If God were *directing* everything, the events would no longer be *random*. And if they weren't random, it wouldn't be evolution. Also, let's keep in mind that the people who wrote your science textbooks sure don't think God had anything to do with evolution. It's perfectly obvious; they never mention Him!"

Paul looked around the room. Everyone was paying attention. He went on.

"Another problem with the idea of God being behind evolution is the incredible amount of *time* it requires. It just doesn't make sense. I mean, think about it. Supposedly there is this awesome, all powerful being – God – behind the scene of nature causing one form of life to change into something entirely new, like causing a reptile to change into a bird." As Paul said this, Mike, and everyone else in the room who had been in the class, instantly thought about the recent advanced science class in which Mike had discussed this very subject with Mr. Potter. "But He can't do it *quickly*. He needs countless millions of years. Don't you think something's wrong with this picture, Mike?"

"Hey, maybe you're missing something," Sue Peterson spoke up. "Maybe God isn't quite as powerful as you believe. Maybe he can make these things happen, but he needs time for trials and errors. Like, he can do them, but he just can't do them instantly."

Paul was aware that the concept he was trying to convey was rather sophisticated, but at the same time fundamental to understanding the whole debate, so he was more than willing to spend whatever time was required to make sure the kids understood it.

"So, although God might somehow be involved in evolution, He might not be great or powerful enough to make stuff happen *quickly*, or instantly. Like, although He might have *designed* monkeys, for example, and planned a place for them in the natural world, He needed a few million years and lots of trials and errors in between to produce a monkey from something that lived earlier. Is this kind of what you mean?"

"Yeah, that sounds about right," Sue replied.

"Okay, good. Now here's the problem with God planning, or being in any way involved with, evolution. Think about the origin of light. In the beginning God created the whole universe, the whole *world,* out of *nothing,* and the universe was absolutely dark, inky black. Then, all of a sudden, God said 'Let there be light!' and the whole world was filled with light! Now, here's the point, Sue: if God is so powerful that He can instantly fill the *entire universe* with light just by ordering it with His spoken word, why in heaven's name would he need a few million years to turn some little creature into a monkey?"

"How can you be so sure that God filled the universe with light by His spoken word?" Mike asked.

"That's a very good question, Mike – and the answer is very simple. I believe it because that's the explanation that the Bible offers."

"But just because the Bible says it doesn't necessarily make it true."

"You've raised a very important issue, Mike: the authority of the Scriptures. It's fundamental to the subject we're talking about here tonight, but we don't have time to get into it right now. I'm sure we'll address it in the future, though ... so I guess you'll just have to come back, eh?" Paul added, with a warm smile.

Smiling back, Mike said, "We'll see."

"There's another problem with trying to combine the biblical account of creation with the theory of evolution," Paul said. "In evolution the only way new creatures can arise is for old ones to die. Evolution, in other words, demands death and suffering, millions and millions of years of it. If God was able to create the entire world out of nothing simply through His spoken word – creation ex nihilo it's called – why would He need countless numbers of His creatures to suffer and die over countless millions of years in order for new ones to arise? Surely, such an all-powerful Creator could have figured out a better way, don't you think?"

"Also, after God had finished creating everything, in the first chapter of Genesis, didn't He say that He was very pleased, or that it was very good, or something like that?" Lisa, a regular at this youth group, observed.

"He sure did, Lisa," Paul replied. "Genesis 1:31: *And God saw all that He had made, and behold, it was very good.*"

"Right, that's it. I don't think God would have said that if there had already been millions of years of suffering and death. I mean, why *would* He?"

"You're exactly right, Lisa. That's an excellent point."

After a few minutes of lively discussion, Peter Bernardo brought something to Paul's attention.

"We were talking about this meeting at dinner tonight, and my dad told me about a story that his teacher had told him when he was in high school to prove that evolution could take place. His teacher asked his students to imagine a million monkeys at a million keyboards that were typing like mad, like nonstop. The teacher said that if they typed for a long enough time, they might type almost anything – like even a Shakespeare play, or even *all* of Shakespeare's plays. The idea was supposed to be that if monkeys typing randomly at a keyboard could eventually produce a Shakespeare play, then random events in nature could also produce anything – including monkeys, and even us! I thought it was a pretty cool idea, and my dad wanted to know what you thought about it."

"The story – actually, it's an analogy – is an interesting one, Peter, and it used to be used by evolutionists regularly to support their theory. You don't hear it too often anymore – most likely because there's no truth to it at all. The fact is that a million monkeys at a million keyboards would be extraordinarily lucky to produce a single short line of Shakespeare, or any other writer, in a *billion* years. And I'll tell you why …

"The idea of using monkeys here, of course, as opposed to humans, is that they would have absolutely no idea what they were typing … sort of like the way I type sometimes when I'm *really* tired! The letters they typed, in other words, would be completely *random*. Now, suppose that there were fifty keys on each keyboard … Hey, does anyone know how many keys there *really* are on a standard keyboard?"

Everyone looked around. No one knew the answer.

"A hundred and four!" Sarah shouted from the back.

"Okay, okay. You've heard this before. That's not *fair*," Paul said with a grin.

"I sure have," Sarah replied with a smile. "More than once, too."

"Anyway, on our monkeys' keyboards there are fifty keys," Paul went on. "Now, imagine that the monkeys were typing at a good clip, say ninety words a minute, and that each word averaged four letters, not including spaces. They would be typing, then, about three hundred sixty letters a minute, or about six letters a second. Let's say the line we were waiting for them to type was … hmmm, let's see … Anyone have an idea?"

"Romeo, Romeo, wherefore art thou, Romeo?" Lisa called out.

"Okay, fine … 'Romeo, Romeo, wherefore art thou, Romeo?' Now, let's see – that's … thirty-one letters, plus nine spaces and punctuation marks. Is everyone following me?"

Paul looked around the room. Everyone seemed to be paying attention, so he went on.

"Now, the monkeys start typing – one million monkeys, one million keyboards, six letters per second per monkey. And we're looking for, 'Romeo, Romeo, wherefore art thou, Romeo?' After hitting the first key, how many 'R's' would there probably be?"

After a brief pause, Mike provided the answer: twenty thousand.

"Perfect," Paul replied.

"Hey, Mike, how did you figure twenty thousand?" Scott asked.

"Easy. If there are one million monkeys and fifty keys on the keyboard, only one monkey out of fifty would be likely to hit 'R.' So, the answer is one million divided by fifty."

"How many of the 'R's' are *capitals*, Mike?" Jennifer's younger sister, Kelly, inquired, eliciting a few chuckles from the group.

"Hey, that might appear to be a funny question," Paul replied, "but actually it's a very good one, because writing obviously does include capital letters, as well as spaces, punctuation, paragraphs, chapters, etc. And don't forget – we're not requiring our monkeys to include any of these. We're really letting them off easy. Think of how unlikely it would be for a monkey sitting at a keyboard to *ever* type a capital letter, let alone get it in the right place.

"So now, after the first key has been struck, there are twenty thousand 'R's'. Now the monkeys hit the second keys. How many 'Ro's' will there be?"

Hardly pausing, Mike answered, "four hundred."

"That was pretty quick, Mike. You must have seen where I was headed, eh?" Mike nodded his head, and Paul continued. "All right, after two keys have been hit, there are four hundred 'Ro's'. Now the monkeys hit the third key. How many 'Rom's' will there be?"

By now, several of the kids had gotten the picture, and the answer "eight" was quickly provided.

"Right. And, obviously, after one more key has been struck, the chances are pretty slim – less than one out of six, to be exact – that there will be any 'Rome's.' So, the bottom line is that in less than one second any possibility of any monkey typing 'Romeo, Romeo, wherefore art thou, Romeo' has been completely eliminated. The truth is that a million monkeys typing at a million keyboards for one second are going to produce almost entirely gibberish – and the same monkeys typing for a million seconds, or a million years, are going to produce millions of times *more* gibberish. The chances of them ever producing one *line* of Shakespeare, let alone an *entire play*, are about a zillion to one."

"But wait," Mike said. "I'm not sure I agree with you. Maybe you've set up an unfair goal for these poor monkeys. You have demanded that they type, 'Romeo, Romeo, wherefore art thou, Romeo.' So, maybe they didn't type what you wanted them to. But there are an awful lot of other lines from Shakespeare's works. Don't you think they might eventually type some other one?"

Judging from the reaction, it appeared that some of the others might have agreed with Mike.

"First of all, Mike, let's keep in mind that what we were looking for from these monkeys was an entire play of Shakespeare's, not just a single line. But, anyway, it doesn't matter what line we have in mind. The result will always be the same. In every case, the first letter must be followed by exactly the right second letter, the second letter must be followed by a specific third letter, and so on. So, in every case the odds against any of the monkeys getting the first letter right are fifty to one, the first two letters right fifty times fifty to one, or 2500 to one, etc. By the fourth letter, the odds against a million monkeys having four letters correct are six to one – exactly the same as the example we just looked at. The end result is that no matter what line you have in mind for the monkeys to type, the odds against them doing it are going to be the same: a zillion to one. Are you all getting this?"

Paul could see that not everyone had.

"Listen, think of it this way," he said. "Suppose that you're one of the people who has been chosen to scan the monkeys' typing, to see if they're making any progress ... What a great job *that* would be, eh? Watching a monkey type a bunch of gibberish at a computer twenty-four hours a day! Imagine this little critter sitting at his keyboard banging away for hours and hours on end, at the rate of five or six keys a second. The letters flow endlessly onto the monitor screen with absolutely no order or thought ... CNHUGHNFX, on and on. Every now and then, you see a three-letter word – CAT, DOG, HOT, THE, etc. Much less frequently you would see a *four-letter* word. Spaces would be scattered about here and there, with a small chance of ever being next to a word.

"Now, here's the question: given this scenario, how long do you think you'd have to wait to see 'Romeo, Romeo, wherefore art thou, Romeo'? – including, if we really want to make it tough on your furry little friend, all the spaces, capitals, and punctuation marks in the correct places?"

"Oh ... about a zillion years?" Mike offered with a big grin.

"I think you've got it, Mike!" Paul said, laughing. "At first glance, the analogy seems to make sense, but further analysis, like we just did, makes it clear that it really doesn't. Ironically, unlike its original intention, which was to demonstrate that given enough time a large number of random events could produce virtually anything, what it actually demonstrates is how *unlikely* it is that random events can ever produce a complex finished product. Instead of confirming that evolution *could* happen, in other words, it demonstrates that it could *not!*"

"I'm a little confused," Peter Bernardo said. "From this discussion, it seems so obvious that a bunch of monkeys jabbing away at a keyboard could never produce a single line of Shakespeare's plays, no matter how many of them there were. How come my dad's teacher, not to mention my dad, never figured that out? Are they just stupid?"

"No, Peter, they aren't stupid, not at all. It's just that the theory of evolution has incredible power to deceive people, to lead intelligent people to believe in illusions. As we proceed with this study we'll see this again – over and over, in fact."

For the first time that evening, Jennifer decided to join the discussion.

"This discussion of the monkeys at the keyboards made me think of something we've been studying in Mr. Potter's class – mutations. As you were talking, I got this feeling that there's something similar between the keys on the keyboard and the nucleotides in DNA, but I can't figure out what it is. Does this make any sense to you, or am I nuts? Do you know much about mutations?"

"No, you're definitely not nuts, Jennifer. It's actually a very perceptive observation … and, yes, I do know something about mutations, and I'd love to talk about them with you all. But before we leave here tonight, I want to get back to what Dave was saying earlier regarding his discussion with Reverend Strong about Noah's Flood, and it's getting pretty late." Paul paused in reflection for a moment. "I have an idea, though. Why don't you, Jennifer – and anyone else who's interested – investigate this topic on your own and see what you can find out, and then we can talk about it next week? It really is a fascinating and very important subject, and I definitely think we should discuss it. What do you say?"

"Yeah, that sounds good. I like the idea," Jennifer replied. Turning to the group, she added, "If anyone wants to do this with me, let me know before you leave."

"That's great, Jennifer. I'll be looking forward to a very interesting discussion next week … Now, back to David and Reverend Strong's discussion about Noah's Flood. If you will recall, Reverend Strong claimed that this Flood was not a real, historical event … or, if it was, it certainly wasn't worldwide, like the Bible claims. To support his claim, he pointed out that not a word about this flood was ever mentioned in your school's science textbooks. When David checked the Internet, however, he discovered that there actually are many people, including many scientists, who believe that this flood actually was an historical event, and that it was worldwide. Assuming that the Reverend did know about these contrary opinions, it seemed to David that the Reverend was being *deceptive,* that he was purposefully hiding information from them in order to support his point. What else could he conclude? The information he had discovered on the Internet certainly hadn't been difficult to locate. He couldn't imagine that the Reverend was completely unaware of it.

"When you step back and take an objective look at the situation, it almost seems like there was a conspiracy, doesn't it? Not only was there no mention of the Flood in any of the science textbooks that anyone there had read or any of the books about science in the school library – by the way, that's pretty unbelievable, isn't it? ... not a single word about any worldwide flood in over one hundred library books about science! – but Reverend Strong gave no indication that there are actually many people in today's world, including thousands of scientists, who definitely believe that this worldwide flood was an historical event. As David pointed out, it's pretty hard to believe that the Reverend is not aware of these contrary opinions. He's been a leader in the Episcopal Church for many years and must surely be familiar with the different opinions about the scope of Noah's Flood – including, of course, that it was worldwide. After all, for most of Christian history that was by far the most common belief, and there are still many ..."

Before he could finish his point, Ray Corbett spoke up.

"Uhh ... I got a little problem with what you're saying," he said. "Our family doesn't go to church very often, but when we do, we go to Reverend Strong's church, St. Peter's Episcopal. I'm not sure how my parents would take it if I told them that you believed that the Reverend was deceptive, like you were saying."

Suddenly, Paul was faced with a dilemma. If Ray went ahead and told his parents that he had learned at this youth group that Reverend Strong might be guilty of deception, it obviously could create a problem. On the other hand, Paul believed, sadly, that his assessment of the exchange between David and the Reverend about the Genesis Flood was probably accurate.

"Reverend Strong was withholding information to strengthen his argument, Ray. People do it all the time – especially lawyers," he added with a forced smile. "Whether it's deception or not is a judgment call."

"So how do you call it?" Ray asked. "Do you think he was being deceptive?"

"I'll leave it up to you, Ray. What do you think?"

"To tell you the truth, it sounds to me like he was."

"Hey, Ray," John Mitchell called out with a big smile on his face. "Are you going to tell your parents that their Reverend is a deceiver?"

"I don't know, Johnny. I'll have to think about it," he added with a shrug of his shoulders.

Paul started to say that it was time to end the group, but Mike interrupted him. "Earlier you said that you were going to tell us why you were so interested in this topic. Could you tell us now?"

"It's kind of late, Mike," Paul smiled. "The group lasted a little longer than I planned, and there's not time to tell you tonight. But I promise, I'll tell you in the next week or two, okay?" Mike agreed, and shortly the meeting came to a close.

Paul and Sarah were the last to leave. As they were walking to the door, Paul stopped to say something to Jennifer. "Good luck with your investigation into mutations, Jennifer. You probably won't find what you're looking for right away, but keep searching, and I think you will. I'm really looking forward to hearing your report. By the way, did anyone offer to help you?"

"Yes," Jennifer responded enthusiastically, "Dave and Mike."

"Oh, that's terrific. You all should have a good time together. Well, good night – and thanks again for letting us use your home. It was a great idea to meet here instead of at the church!"

As Paul and Sarah headed toward their car, Paul looked upward to the stars twinkling in the clear night sky. The balmy air was filled with the smells of spring. He put his arm around his wife.

"That was a great meeting, wasn't it, honey?"

"Yeah, it sure was," Sarah smiled. "What a *wonderful* group of kids!" Pausing, she added, "I hope Ray doesn't decide to inform his parents that he learned here that their Reverend is a deceiver. That wouldn't be the greatest PR for this group, you know what I mean?"

"No, I suppose it wouldn't ... But, hey, sometimes the truth hurts, eh, honey?" he added with a big smile. "Also, when you think about it, it could open up a worthwhile conversation at Ray's home. Perhaps it would cause the Corbett family to rethink their choice of a church. From what I've heard about Reverend Strong's theology, that might not be a bad idea."

The next afternoon David was driving home from track practice with Josh Siegel, and he mentioned the previous night's meeting at Jennifer's house.

"Oh, yeah," Josh declared. "I meant to ask you about that. For one thing, I can't believe that you went to it."

"Whadduya mean? It was really interesting. Maybe you should ..."

"*Interesting?*" Josh interrupted. "A church youth group in which you talked about *creation,* and you say it was *interesting?* What's come over you, man?" Josh paused for a moment. "Wait a second. Where did you say the meeting was?"

"At the Conley's."

"Oh yeah. I forgot. That's why you went ... to see Jennifer. You dig her, don't you?" Josh said with a big grin.

"No, no ... That's not it," Dave replied with a sheepish smile. "That's not it at all ... well, maybe a tiny bit, I guess. But seriously, I find this stuff really interesting. Like I was starting to say, maybe you should come with me next week to check it out."

"Listen, Dave, let me lay it on the line for you. I think creationists are basically morons. You know as well as I do that *no* legitimate scientist believes in creationism, so why do you want to waste your time hearing about it." Josh paused for a moment. "Was that youth pastor you mentioned Friday night leading the discussion?"

"Yeah."

"So you were being taught about origins by a *church youth pastor?* That's crazy, man." Josh paused for a moment for reflection. "You know, maybe I will join you next week. It might be fun," he added with a mischievous grin.

Dave looked over at his friend. "Are you serious? You really want to come?"

"Yeah, maybe so."

Dave furrowed his brow. He was a little concerned about what kind of fun Josh had in mind.

"On second thought, maybe you shouldn't come," he said. "Knowing how you feel about creation, you'd probably be bored."

"Maybe not. Maybe I'd find it *interesting*. After all, *you* do."

Dave looked over at Josh and shook his head in concern. He was fairly sure that Josh wouldn't follow through on his threat to attend the youth group – but he was a little concerned that he might. He sensed that Josh might have an ulterior motive in mind. He tried to discuss it, but Josh wasn't interested.

7

Mutations

After dinner Monday night, Jennifer checked her email. There was a message from David.

```
     hey Jen
     good meeting last night, eh - I've talked to a
few of the guys that were there and they all had a
good time - they thought Paul was cool ... Sarah,
too ... about that mutation study - have you done
anything yet? I talked to Mike. he's already start-
ed to check it out. let me know.
     Dave
```

Jennifer replied,

```
     glad you liked the group. i thought it was
great - Lisa and Kristen did too. about mutations -
haven't done anything yet, but might a little later
tonight - talk to you tomorrow.
     Jen
```

Shortly after this exchange, Jennifer decided to give David a call to see what he wanted to do about their mutation investigation. After getting over his initial surprise, and joy, from the call, David asked Jennifer what she found interesting about this subject.

"Okay, let me see if I can explain it to you," Jennifer replied. "You know what Mr. Potter told us about mutations, that they're supposed to be the 'primary vehicle of evolutionary change' – that evolution couldn't take place without them, right? Well, from what we learned about them, I just *can't* understand how they can possibly do everything he claims they can. It doesn't make sense to me. I figure that I must be missing something, and I want to try to find out what it is."

"Hey, I don't know, Jen. From what we've been taught, it seems like every scientist agrees with what Mr. Potter said about them. Who the heck are *we* to prove these guys wrong? I mean, I think it would be interesting to take a look at them, but it's pretty hard to believe that ..."

"No, wait, Dave. I understand what you're saying – that if there's a major problem with mutations, plenty of people would have already discovered it and it would be mentioned in our textbooks, or something like that, right? But, hey, remember what Reverend Strong said about Noah's Flood and what you found out when you looked it up on the Internet for yourself. Well, just like you checked out Noah's Flood, I want to check out mutations."

"But I just don't see what the problem could be with mutations."

For a moment, Jennifer wondered why David wanted to investigate mutations with her if he didn't see any problem with them, but she let it go.

"All right. I'll ask you a question. Maybe that will help you see where I'm coming from. Exactly what is a mutation?"

"Well," David replied hesitantly, trying to recall his notes on the topic, "the way I remember it, a mutation is a change in an organism's genetic code, in the DNA, right?"

"Yeah, that's what we were told. But be more specific. *Exactly* what is the change? How does it occur? And what are the actual *observed* results of these changes?"

"Whadduya mean? I just told you *exactly* what changes: the genetic code, the DNA. What have I left out?"

"I know what you said, Dave. But what I'm asking you is, What *really* happens? What *happens* to the DNA?"

"You're tough, Jen."

"Hey, I'm not trying to give you a hard time. I'm just trying to point out that spouting back the words we were taught in school is one thing, but understanding them is another. You see what I'm saying?"

"Hmmm ... Yeah, I think I'm starting to. I have to admit that when I think about it, like you're saying, I'm not *really* clear about what a mutation is."

"Exactly. That's exactly my point. Before we can understand the role mutations play in evolution – if there is one – we have to first understand exactly what a mutation *is*, and I don't think we *really* do. At least I know *I* don't."

"I guess I have to agree with you, Jen. Now that I think about it, I guess I don't either."

By the time they finished their phone call a few minutes later, Jennifer and David were eager to get started on their research project, and the next afternoon they did, along with Mike. Over the next few days, they spent several hours on it, both together and alone. Some of their time was spent in the school library, some at home on the Internet, and a couple of times they met together in the University of New Hampshire library in Durham. They were all very good students, and they enjoyed going to the University library. It was much larger and more extensive than the one at their school. In particular, their computers were more sophisticated than the ones in their school library. The University administration encouraged local high school students to use their facilities. It was good PR, plus they wanted to do whatever they could to promote education – after all, that *is* their *raison d'etre*. Another thing they enjoyed at this library was their occasional conversation with the college students, who usually seemed to be impressed when they discovered why they were there. David couldn't help noticing that most of these conversations were initiated by male college students – with Jennifer.

They had a good time not only sharing their discoveries, but also just hanging out together, and they learned some very interesting things about mutations. In Mr. Potter's class they had learned that mutations took place in the nucleus of the cell, in DNA molecules, chains made up of tiny components called *nucleotides*, that in turn are made up of four kinds of nucleic acid molecules (<u>c</u>ytosine, <u>a</u>denine, <u>t</u>hymine, and guanine – *c a t* ... plus "g"). A single DNA molecule may have well over a million nucleotide links. In fact, human DNA has over three *billion* such links. In order to envision a DNA molecule, Mr. Potter told them to imagine a ladder. The rungs on the ladder, he said, are analogous to the nucleotide links. Imagine the ladder being twisted, sort of like a spiral staircase, he said, and you would have an idea of the actual shape of the molecule, the famous Double Helix first discovered by James Watson and Francis Crick in 1953.

In one of their group discussions, it became apparent to Jennifer, David, and Mike that where Mr. Potter's teaching had fallen short was in regards to the question of *exactly* what happens in the DNA during a mutation. They knew that *something* happened, and that it was in the DNA, but they just didn't know exactly what it was. As they probed into this question, they learned that a mutation occurs when one or more of the nucleotide links of the DNA is in some way altered, or damaged. Such mutations are called *point mutations*. The cause of this damage can be either natural, for example cosmic rays or ultraviolet light, or man-made, through chemicals or x-rays, for example. Whatever its origin, however, every author they came across agreed that, according to the theory of evolution, *this cause is completely random*. In regards to what happens to the affected nucleotide links, they discovered that they can be transformed into a different nucleotide, either one of the four base kinds, or perhaps a completely different one, or they can be knocked right out of the chain.

Mike came across an intriguing analogy in which DNA, which provides the *perfect* instructions for every physical detail of our bodies, was compared to the head office of a factory which contained the master blueprints, or instructions, for every operation in the entire factory. Another author he came across compared the instructions contained in DNA to a printed instructional manual, or a computer program. The information, or instructions, encoded in the nucleotide links is, in a very real sense, like the letters in printed instructions, with each nucleotide corresponding to an individual letter, or the bits in a computer program, with each nucleotide corresponding to an individual bit. In the analogy to printed instructions or a computer program, he learned that these alterations would be comparable to the changing or elimination of a letter, in the former, or a 'bit' in the latter. He thought that these analogies were very helpful, and when he shared them with Jennifer and David, they heartily agreed.

In addition to point mutations, they discovered that DNA can also be altered by a process called *recombination,* which occurs when a *group* of nucleotides, perhaps an entire gene, which typically consists of a thousand or more nucleotide links, shifts its location or is otherwise altered. These are referred to as chromosomal mutations. Just like point mutations, these, too, can cause an alteration in the physical characteristic of an organism. In the analogy to the printed instructions, this transposition would be like the shifting, or altering, of an entire word, perhaps even a sentence or a paragraph, as opposed to a single letter.

One evening Jennifer came across these words: "When the nucleotide becomes altered, or damaged, in one of these ways, one of three things can happen. First ..."

Suddenly, one of the words in this description struck her like a bolt of lightning: *damaged.*

Damaged! She thought. *...How can something be improved if it is struck by a foreign object and **damaged**?! ...especially if it was supposedly perfect in the first place?*

Jennifer leaned back in her chair, and her mind drifted to the wondrous creatures in the natural world: colorful winged birds, beautiful flowers, the incredible variety of creatures that filled the seas, the fascinating insects, the mighty lion, the enormous elephant, the swift gazelle, and all the other animals that roam the forests and plains of the world. She reflected upon these creatures' meticulously designed organs, their eyes, hearts, nervous systems, etc., and she pondered the mind-boggling fact that according to the theory of evolution all of these wondrous creatures, and everything about them, are the result of *damaged* nucleotides in some ancestor's DNA. As far as she was concerned, this was not only absurd, it was the fatal flaw she had suspected. Paul Hopkins, she recognized, had been right.

Jennifer's suspicion regarding a possible flaw in evolutionary notions regarding mutations may seem rather extraordinary for a seventeen year old high school student. There is, however, a very good explanation for this unusual circumstance. Because of her years of being home-schooled by her devout fundamentalist Christian mother, Jennifer deeply distrusted the theory of evolution, and was unusually resistant to accepting it. Her mother and father had instilled in her a burning faith in the truths expressed in the Bible, and she *believed* what her parents had taught her with all of her heart. She was, in other words, *programmed* to be on the lookout for fatal flaws in the theory. From her perspective, the idea that mutations were, essentially, the foundation of evolution, should be viewed very skeptically, because she viewed the entire theory of evolution very skeptically. From her perspective, in other words, *anything* that supported the theory of evolution was, at the very least, highly suspicious. Very few of her peers were similarly programmed.

Something else was motivating her research into mutations, also: her embarrassment in Mr. Potter's class a short while earlier. Despite her friendly and congenial outward nature, Jennifer had a competitive streak, too, and she felt that Mr. Potter's condescending attitude toward her was not only unjust and unfair, but, more seriously, an attack against her God. She wasn't going to take it sitting down. Mr. Potter didn't know it yet, but he had grabbed a tiger by the tail.

Immediately after these thoughts crossed her mind, Jennifer hurried over to the table where David and Mike were taking a break.

"I've come to a conclusion, guys," she announced triumphantly. "Mutations can't possibly be the vehicle of evolutionary change, because the only thing they cause is *damage*! How can *damaged* molecules *possibly* create new forms of life?"

Mike had come across the same information as Jennifer, but it didn't impress him in the same way. Unlike Jennifer, he wasn't looking for the fox in the hen house. He wasn't programmed to. "That's very interesting," he replied. "And your proof of this startling conclusion is …?"

"I haven't found that out, yet. I figured that should be *your* job!" Jennifer replied with a big smile, stretching out her uplifted palms towards her two companions.

"Oh, great!" David responded. "And just what do you expect us to come up with?"

"Well, here's what I figure," Jennifer proceeded. "I was just blown away by the fact that mutations are basically the result of random *damage* to nucleotides, and I find it impossible to believe that damaged nucleotides could be the catalyst for everything that has ever lived, like the theory of evolution claims. So, I figure what we need to look at is the results of research that has been done on mutations, to see what they've *really* caused, to see if we can find any good ones … you know, ones that show some new feature evolving on some animal. Surely, if evolution is true, there must be *some* examples of this, right?"

"But what if we do find such things, Jen? What then?" Mike asked.

"I don't know, Mike. Let's cross that bridge when, and if, we come to it, okay?"

A few minutes later, the three teens set off on their search. Before long, David began to get a little discouraged. All he found were statements that essentially agreed with what Mr. Potter had taught about mutations. Some writers emphasized the role of recombinant DNA more than others, but none of them seemed to find any fatal flaw with mutations, like Jennifer apparently did. Whether neo-Darwinist (the current designation for believers in evolution) or saltationist (one who believes in Punctuated Equilibrium), they all apparently believed in the theory of evolution and conferred upon mutations a primary, actually critical, role in the evolutionary process. David was beginning to think that maybe Jennifer was on a wild goose chase. And he wasn't so sure he wanted to go along with her.

Who the heck are we to be questioning the wisdom of all these brilliant scientists? he thought. *I mean, hey, let's face it, we're just high school students. These scientists have devoted their lives to this stuff, and most of them have an advanced degree, or two, to back up their words.*

Suddenly, it was as if these thoughts were the voice of another person whispering in David's ear. *That's right - get realistic!* the voice continued. *Before you or Jennifer or Mike can possibly take issue with these learned scientists, you've got a LOT more to learn. Come on, David, who are YOU to be questioning these people? They know A LOT more than you do! Do you REALLY think you can see something about mutations that all of these others have missed? Don't you think you're being just a wee bit PRESUMPTUOUS?*

A flush of embarrassment momentarily reddened David's cheeks. The thoughts that had run through his mind seemed to make a lot of sense. It *did* seem that he and Jennifer and Mike were being awfully presumptuous. After all, mutations do cause real changes in the physical structure of organisms. And if this is so, he thought, then, given enough time, like the hundreds of millions of years proposed by the theory of evolution, why couldn't they cause all of the changes required by evolution?

Yeah ... Yeah, he thought, *that's right. Given enough time, and enough mutations, just about anything could probably happen. Given enough time, why* **couldn't** *a reptile evolve into a bird, a scale into a feather, or a wolf into a whale?*

The voice hissed again, *"Now you're getting it, David. Time. Time, David. That's the hero of the plot!"*

David decided that he needed to back off and reconsider this project. He went to look for Jennifer and found her at a computer.

"Hey, Jen."

"Hey ... What's up, Dave. How is it going?"

"Uh, well, I think I'm going to pack it in for the night. I'll just go read a magazine or something 'till you and Mike are ready to go."

"Oh, man, Dave. What happened? I thought you were really into this."

"Yeah, I was ... but all of the stuff that I've looked at so far seems to agree with what Mr. Potter taught us about mutations. Plus, Jen ... I'm also wondering, like, who the heck are we to be questioning what all these brilliant scientists believe about mutations. I mean, we're only high school students …" David proceeded to repeat to Jennifer the thoughts that had occurred to him a few minutes earlier.

Jennifer paused for a moment to consider what David had said.

"Let me ask you something, Dave. Did you find any examples, even one, of a mutation causing an animal to evolve into a *different* animal, or some brand new feature evolving in an animal? After all, that's what mutations are supposed to cause, right? That's what we're *looking* for."

"No. No, I didn't. But still, Jen, like I said, aren't we being awfully *presumptuous* to think we can see something about mutations that all of these scientists can't? I mean, look …"

"Hey, I know what you're thinking, Dave," Jennifer interrupted, "but maybe you just haven't found the right stuff yet. Here, look at this," she added, pointing at her computer monitor. "Here's something I was just looking at. It's from a book named *The Neck of the Giraffe*, by some guy named Francis Hitching. It's only a quote, but look at what he says: *it is highly doubtful that scientists can point to a single mutation that was unqualifiedly beneficial to the organism in which it appeared.*[1] You see, Dave. That's *exactly* what I'm talking about!" Jennifer exclaimed excitedly. "Mr. Potter's been teaching us that mutations are the foundation of *every living creature* – all the dead ones, too! – and here's a real scientist who says that it's hard to find even *one, single beneficial mutation*. So, you see, I'm not crazy, no matter what you might think!" she added, spinning around and looking David in the eye with a big smile.

David smiled back and gently nodded his head. Until now, he wasn't really fully committed to this project, not like Jennifer was, at least. As far as he was concerned, it wasn't *that* big of a deal. After all, it was only going to be a presentation to a church youth group. Truth to be told, David had somewhat of an ulterior motive in participating in this project. As Josh had suspected, he was attracted to Jennifer and thought that this project would be a good excuse to spend some time with her. This is not to say that he wasn't interested in the subject they were investigating, for he really was. It just wasn't his *only* reason for getting involved. At this moment, however, it became clear to him that Jennifer was not only committed to the project, she was *passionate* about it. It crossed his mind that there might be more to this little research project than he had imagined, that there might be something going on that he wasn't aware of, not at the moment, at least. Jennifer certainly acted like there was.

Jennifer had returned her attention to the monitor screen.

"Hey, Jen," David said.

"Yeah, what?" Jennifer responded casually, not turning away from the monitor.

"You're pretty psyched about this study, aren't you?"

Jennifer turned to look at David. "Yeah, I guess I am."

"Why?"

"I'm not really sure. I just think it's interesting, I guess," she smiled. After a pause, she added, "Also, I want to make sure we have a good report ready for the group this Sunday. After all, that's what Paul asked from us." Here was reflected another attractive aspect of Jennifer's nature: she was eager to please others. In this case, it was Paul.

David nodded his head and smiled back. He thought *she* was interesting, too.

"Hey," he pronounced. "I've got an idea. What's the name of that author you just mentioned?"

"Hitching – Francis Hitching."

"Yeah, that's it. I'll check him out in the reference file. Maybe that book you were quoting, *The Neck of the Giraffe*, is in the library.

"That's an *awesome* idea, Dave. Go for it!"

"By the way ... Where did you find that quote from Mr. Hitching?"

"On the Internet – *Answers in Genesis*. Just go to Google and enter AIG. It's a really great Web site. And you know what? They don't believe in the theory of evolution at all. They think it's a big *lie!*"

"Wow! That's pretty radical. I knew you had a lot of doubts about the theory, but I didn't know you thought that the whole thing was a complete *lie.*"

Jennifer tilted her head and raised her eyebrows, with a little smile.

"On the other hand, based upon what you said the other day in Mr. Potter's class, maybe I should have known, I guess," David smiled back. "All right, I'm off. Catch you later."

Within a few minutes David had found the book he was looking for, *The Neck of the Giraffe... Glad we came to the UNH library tonight,* he thought. Scanning the index, he quickly found a description of artificially induced mutations in the fruit fly, drosophila. According to Mr. Hitching, there have been more mutations induced in this insect, through radiation, than in any other organism. These radiation bombardments have, indeed, induced a large number of mutations, which have resulted in many mutant individuals, some of them quite bizarre:

The geneticist's favorite laboratory animal is the common fruit fly, Drosophila melanogaster. Since the early 1900's, starting with the work of the biologist T.H. Morgan, tens of millions of flies have been involved in experiments. They have been selectively crossed with each other, and bombarded with various strengths and frequencies of x-rays so that the mutation rate has sometimes been 150 times faster than normal. Passing under the microscope have been flies with elongated or shortened bodies and limbs, monstrously wrinkled wings, a leg instead of an eye, and so on ... in spite of the enormously increased mutation rates, all the fruit flies have remained fruit flies. Indeed, out of the millions of mutations, only two are arguably 'fitter' than the parent stock of flies, and even this is strongly debated ...

Ernst Mayr, who remains convinced that small-scale gene substitution is the answer to evolution, conducted one striking piece of research on Drosophila which, ironically, seemed to demonstrate the opposite.

He selectively bred successive generations of flies to try to increase or decrease the number of bristles they grew, normally averaging 36. He reached a lower limit, after 30 generations, of 25 bristles; and an upper limit after 20 generations, of 56 bristles. After that the flies rapidly began to die out. Then, Mayr brought back non-selective breeding, letting nature take its course. Within five years, the bristle count was almost back to average. This resistance to change has been given the label genetic homeostasis and elsewhere in the literature there is an even more mysterious example. In a remarkable series of experiments, mutant genes were paired to create an eyeless fly. When these flies in turn were interbred, the predictable result was offspring that were also eyeless. And so it continued for a few generations.

But then, contrary to all expectations, a few flies began to hatch out with eyes. Somehow, the genetic code had a built-in repair mechanism that re-established the missing genes. The natural order reasserted itself.[2]

Hmmm, David mused. *This sure does seem to support Jennifer's belief that mutations can't change some creature into another one. I mean, no matter what* *these scientists did to these fruit flies, they never changed into anything else – and this includes <u>millions</u> of mutations!*

David thought over all the information he had seen on mutations in the past few days, trying to recall any examples of mutations changing one creature into another, or creating a brand new physical feature in one, and he really couldn't remember a single one. Even in these experiments with fruit flies, he realized, even though bodies and features were altered, distorted, moved, perhaps even eliminated, no *new* features ever emerged.

Just as he was thinking that Jennifer might be right, something occurred to him... The voice whispered in his ear again: *This is interesting,* he thought, *and it certainly seems to cast doubt on the idea that mutations could be the "primary vehicle of evolutionary change." But Mr. Hitching is only one man. He seems to be a lonely voice in a big crowd of people that don't share his opinion. I'm not sure this is the greatest evidence ..."* His thoughts trailed off. He decided to find Mike and Jennifer and talk things over.

Mike, David discovered, had found plenty examples of harmful mutations, including diseases such as sickle cell anemia, Down's syndrome,

albinism (the condition that causes albinos), animals and people with extra or distorted members, and many others. He found that examples of beneficial mutations, however, were much rarer. One that was occasionally mentioned was the resistance developed by mosquitoes, and other insects, to certain deadly chemical sprays, or pesticides. Many examples of new and improved species of crops or livestock were given: seedless, larger, or sweeter fruits and vegetables, cattle with increased muscles, altered flowers, etc.

"So, it seems like we've all found pretty much the same pattern in what we've been reading, then, doesn't it?" David said. "Practically everyone that we've read seems to agree with the standard evolutionary mantra about mutations, the one Mr. Potter taught us, that mutations, in conjunction with Natural Selection, are the main vehicle of evolutionary change. But they don't back up their position with many good, clear examples of *positive* – you know, *beneficial* – mutations. Maybe an example here or there, like Mike mentioned, but not that many."

"Yeah, that's about right, I'd say," Jennifer spoke up. "But, you know, I thought of something that didn't seem to occur to these people, at least not the ones I came across. If evolution is true, and mutations are all they're cracked up to be, there should be a *huge* number of examples of beneficial mutations, not only from the past but in the present, too. The world should be *teeming* with them. There shouldn't be just a few examples here and there."

"Nice, Jen. I like it," David agreed.

"Yeah, me too – totally," Mike added.

There was a pause.

"Hey, it's after eleven o'clock, and we've been here for almost four hours. Whadduya say we go to Dino's for a pizza?" David suggested.

"What about the presentation we're supposed to make at the youth group Sunday night?" Jennifer asked. "When are we going to put that together?"

"Hey, we'll be fine, Jen," David replied. "I'm sure Paul doesn't expect, like, a formal presentation or anything. We'll just discuss the stuff we've discovered over the past few days with the group. We've found out some great stuff. It'll be cool. Don't worry."

The next morning, Saturday, Mike wanted to talk to his father about his recent investigation into mutations. His father was in his office, preparing some things for an upcoming School Board meeting. Mike loved this room, primarily because of the many objects that exhibited Tom Lawton's love of birds. It was like a mini museum of ornithology. There were half a dozen stuffed birds, including a magnificent snowy owl and a blue heron, and four beautiful full-sized prints of John James Audubon's famous bird paintings. On the wall behind his desk was a quotation from Audubon:

Ah! How often, when I have been abroad on the mountains, has my heart risen in grateful praise to God that it was not my destiny to waste and pine among those noisome congregations of the city.

His father had told him how often he thought of these words when he was hiking and fishing in his beloved White Mountains. This love had certainly been passed on to Mike. Scattered about the room were photographs of the White Mountains. One that Mike particularly liked was an autumn scene of the famous Mt. Washington Hotel. The bright red and yellow foliage around the hotel and in the surrounding foothills glistened vividly in the clear afternoon sunlight. Towering majestically in the background stood Mt. Washington, its snow-covered peak shimmering brilliantly against the deep azure sky. It was a breathtaking scene that never failed to capture the attention of visitors to this room. Mike had an additional reason for liking this photo, though: he had been with his father when he had taken it a few years earlier.

After telling his father about the exciting information that he and his friends had discovered about mutations, Mike asked his dad a question.

"You know, Dad, the more I learn about these things, the more trouble I have believing in the theory of evolution. But according to our biology textbook, evolution is a proven fact. What do you think about this?"

"I have a lot of trouble believing in the theory, too, Mike. I think that when your teacher is going over the chapter in your textbook on evolution he should make it clear that not everyone accepts evolution as a proven fact, that there are alternatives that should be considered."

"I hate to break the news to you, Dad, but there's not just one chapter that covers evolution in our textbook. The theory is referred to throughout the whole book. In fact, there's hardly a chapter that *doesn't* mention it."

"Come on, Mike. I think you're exaggerating."

"Not really. You want to see my textbook for yourself?"

"Yeah, sure. Go get it."

A couple of minutes later Mike returned with his textbook. A quick glance at the Table of Contents quickly confirmed what Mike had said. It was obvious that at least four chapters were devoted primarily to the theory of evolution: chapter 11, *The Origin of Life*; chapter 12, *The Theory of Evolution*; chapter 13, *History of Life on Earth*; and chapter 14, *Human Evolution*. As Mike was quick to point out, this was hardly all, however. A lengthy quotation from Charles Darwin, accompanied by a picture of the scientist, was featured at the very beginning of the book, on page two. This quotation was followed by a comment from the authors: *Today we know more about the structure and function of living things than scientists in Darwin's day could have ever imagined. The findings of modern scientists reveal how species change over time, supporting Darwin's observations in a multitude of ways.* Lawton also noticed that an ancient age for the earth was promoted on the first two pages, a notion that was repeated throughout the book, including a colorful chart on the inside of the back cover teaching that the earliest life on earth, ancient bacteria, first appeared about three and a half billion years ago.

Picking up on his father's love of birds, Mike turned to chapter thirty-three and showed his father that the book explicitly taught that birds evolved from reptiles and that feathers were "derived from reptilian scales." Lest there be any doubt about the certainty of the authors' position regarding evolution, Mike showed his father a box at the beginning of chapter twelve titled *Authors' Rationale,* which began with the sentence, *Evolution is the central unifying concept of biology – almost everything biological can be explained in terms of evolution.*[3] Tom Lawton found this statement to be particularly disconcerting. Years earlier, when he was majoring in biology at college, he would have known that this statement was speculation, at best. Today his evaluation of it would not be so generous.

Mike and his father spent about forty-five minutes going through the textbook, and by the time they had finished it was perfectly obvious that Mike's accusation about the book, that the theory of evolution was woven throughout its pages, was exactly right.

"So, what do you think now, Dad? I guess I was right, eh?" Mike asked with a mischievous grin, knowing that his father's doubts about his claim had been thoroughly shattered.

Tom Lawton smiled. "Yeah, I guess you were – for once! Seriously, though, Mike, this investigation really surprises me. I knew that you were being taught the theory of evolution in school, but I had no idea that it was being taught this aggressively. There's something wrong here, something *seriously* wrong."

"You're on the School Board, Dad. Why don't you do something about it?"

"Like what, Mike?"

"I don't know. You're the one on the Board, not me. Maybe you can come up with something."

"I'll think about it, Mike. Who knows … Maybe I can."

Lying in bed that night Tom Lawton was having trouble getting to sleep. He kept thinking about his conversation with his son Mike earlier in the day. He knew that he was being taught the theory of evolution, of course, but he had no idea how insistently it was being taught. Because of his own doubts about the theory, doubts that were only increasing with time, the matter deeply disturbed him.

There was one thing, however, about which he had no doubts at all. He knew that feathers never evolved from reptiles' scales!

8

The Second Meeting of the Youth Group

The second meeting regarding creation and evolution of the Grace Bible Church youth group gathered at the Conley's on Sunday evening at 7 p.m.. Everyone that had been at the first meeting was present. There was also one newcomer: Josh Siegel. He had come with David. After some of Mrs. Conley's pizza, Paul Hopkins opened the meeting with a brief prayer. He then turned to Jennifer.

"Jennifer, were you able to come up with anything on mutations for us?"

"Yes, I was. Actually, David and Mike and I were, that is. We spent several hours investigating them and found out some pretty interesting stuff."

"That's great," Paul replied. "Let's hear what you learned." For the next half hour or so, the three youths related to the group what they had discovered about mutations. Everyone seemed very interested in what they said. They were particularly intrigued by the analogy Mike had read in which the nucleotide links in the DNA molecules were compared to the letters in an instructional manual, or the bits in a computer program. It was a very effective illustration.

Upon finishing, Paul praised the trio for their effort and asked if there were any questions or comments.

"I have one," Kristen Macdonald spoke up. "I'm not sure I quite get this. Jennifer was suggesting that since mutations are basically damage to nucleotides, they can't do anything positive. That is, they can't create anything new, right?"

Paul turned to Jennifer and asked for her response.

"Yeah, that's basically what I think," she said.

"But if you think about it, damaged DNA *is* different. So, in a sense, isn't it new?"

"If you think of 'new' and 'different' as being equal, you're right, Kristen," Paul responded. "But using this definition of new, you could create a 'new' marble statue by hitting an existing one with a sledge hammer. But this certainly isn't the 'newness' that evolution requires. In my analogy of the statue, in order to get the type of change required by evolution, a blow from a sledgehammer would have to cause something new to be added to the statue. Like, if the statue that was hit was Michelangelo's famous statue of David, a spear would suddenly appear in his hand, for example. Needless to say, this is completely impossible. Damaging things does make them different, but it doesn't make them better, or new, in any realistic sense."

As he glanced around the room, Paul was not confident that everyone was getting the picture about mutations. Believing that it was very important that they did, he pressed on.

"Let me give you a specific example of what I'm talking about," he continued. "Jennifer was telling me the other day about a science class in which she was being taught that birds evolved from reptiles – a belief, incidentally, that is now widely accepted in the scientific community. According to this theory, some place during this evolution, reptiles' scales evolved into birds' feathers. Now, can you tell me how this could have happened as a result of mutations?"

After a pause, John Mitchell spoke up. "Hey, I'll give it a try," he said. "What have I got to lose? Okay, we start off with these reptile scales, right? Then, some mutations start happening, and little by little the scales start to change. First, they get longer. Then they start to slowly change their shape. Instead of one flat disc, like a little pancake, they slowly break up into a bunch of little, you know, hair-like shapes," he said. Looking around the room, he added, "You know what I mean. You've all seen feathers. After awhile – a *long* while, I guess," he noted with a grin – " and a few more changes, you've got feathers. There you go. How's that?"

"That was a great try, John, and I appreciate it," Paul replied. "However, it doesn't really work. I'll explain why in a second. First, however, let me ask Jennifer something: When your teacher was going over the evolution of birds, did he spend any time describing feathers to you?"

"He didn't – but Mike did," Jennifer replied, pointing at Mike Lawton.

"Mike, I'm sure that not everyone here tonight was in that science class. Could you go over your description of feathers for the rest of us?"

Mike didn't need any encouragement. He enthusiastically granted Paul's request.

"That was very good, Mike" Paul said. Turning to the group, he continued. "As you can see, feathers are perfectly and wonderfully designed for a very specific purpose: flight. As Mike's description made very clear, they are far more than just reshaped scales. Not only do they consist of a very intricate, wonderfully designed network of hooks and barbules, without which flight would be utterly impossible, but they allow birds to vary the shape and aerodynamic properties of their wings at take-off and landing, and for various sorts of flight: flapping, gliding, and soaring, for example. One skill that feathers provide which I only recently became aware of is the ability to instantaneously stop upon landing. Next time you get a chance, check it out for yourselves; watch a bird streak toward a branch and instantly come to a complete stop the moment his feet touch the branch. It's not the grasping of the branch that causes him to stop; it is something that he does with his wings. It's quite incredible. It is comparable to an airplane coming to a complete stop the second its wheels touch the runway.

"Now, here's the critical point: like I just said, feathers are far more than just reshaped scales. It would be one thing if feathers were something like a petal on a flower, or a leaf – you know, a larger but thinner and lighter version of a scale. But they aren't. They are *completely different* than scales. They are as different from scales as your eye is from your ear. The evolution from a scale into a feather requires far more than the *alteration* of existing information in the DNA, which is all that mutations are capable of; it requires *completely new and different information*. Remember how Jennifer and David and Mike just explained that DNA is analogous to an instructional manual, or a computer program, and that the nucleotides are analogous to the letters in the manual or the bits in the computer program. Well, the information, or instructions, for feathers simply does not exist in the DNA of a reptile, and mutations cannot create it. No matter what was done to a reptile's DNA, the instruction for a feather would never arise.

"Think of it like this. Imagine that the instructions for the reptile's design, or physical appearance, which is encoded in the DNA, is comparable to a complete set of instructions to build a brand new Ford pick-up truck – 1,000 pages in total, let's say, all in English. Now, imagine that someone invents a brand new fuel system for the car, one which operates on *water*, rather than gasoline. Obviously, in order for this system to be included in new models, new information must be added to the instructions. But suppose that this designer is told that he cannot personally add the necessary new information to the manual. He can only *randomly* change the letters, one at a time, and hope that the new information will eventually appear. How successful do you think he would be? Oh, one other requirement … The new information must be in *Chinese*."

Judging from the expressions on the kids' faces, Paul felt satisfied that they understood what he was trying to explain. He was relieved, because he believed very strongly that the subject being discussed, mutations, was critical to this debate and that an informed opinion required a good grasp of it.

Mike raised his hand.

"Mr. Hopkins – er, Paul –I've got a question for you. You don't believe in evolution at all, do you?"

Paul was not surprised by Mike's question. He had anticipated it would come up at some point. He glanced at his wife Sarah in the back of the room. She knew, too. She smiled, raised her eyebrows, and gave him a thumbs up.

"To tell you the truth, Mike, no, I don't."

"Not at all?" Mike responded. "Not even a tiny bit?"

"No, Mike, I have to admit, not even a tiny bit."

"But you must have been taught in school that it's true, just like we are. What caused you …"

Mike was interrupted by a question from the rear of the room. "You say that evolution isn't true, eh?"

It was from Josh Siegel.

Paul replied, "Actually, what I said is that I don't *believe* it's true. I'm aware, of course, that not everyone agrees with me and that …"

"That's for sure!" Josh interrupted again. "Like no legitimate scientist, for example."

The combative tone of Josh's remark took everyone by surprise. The truth was that, except for David, the kids were surprised that Josh was even there. No one was aware that he had any interest in religion. One thing they *were* aware of, however, was Josh's reputation as a brain. Just like some kids in high school are known for unusual ability in athletics or art or music, Josh was known for his intelligence. Furthermore, Josh was well aware of this, and he liked it very much. For his entire life, he had *always* been the brightest among his peers, and in his mind it was the one thing that made him special and unique.

Like everyone else, Paul was also surprised by the somewhat hostile tone of Josh's remark. It certainly wasn't the first time he had seen such an attitude in a youth group, but it nevertheless caught him off guard. As opposed to almost everyone else in the room, Paul knew nothing about Josh's reputation. In fact, he knew nothing at all about Josh.

"Well, I don't know that *no* legitimate scientist shares my opinion, Josh, but I'd certainly have to agree that the majority don't!" he said with a big smile, hoping to defuse the tension.

Josh wasn't going to let Paul off the hook, however. He didn't inform anyone, but the truth was that his only purpose in coming to this meeting was to show everyone how foolish creationism is. As generally intelligent as he was, science was his real forte, the discipline that he loved and excelled in more than any other. He had been taught that evolution was the grand unifying theory of all science, and he believed this with all his heart. From David he had learned what had been discussed in the previous meeting, and he looked upon creationism as an attack upon science. He came to defend it – and he figured it should be easy, like taking candy from a baby. After all, his only opponents would be a bunch of high school students and a youth pastor. He knew that the students wouldn't be able to counter his arguments, and he didn't imagine that some Christian youth pastor could, either.

"Here's the problem I have with all this," Josh replied. "You are claiming that mutations couldn't possibly be the driving force behind evolution, because they cannot produce the new information which evolution requires, right?"

"Yes, that's right," Paul responded somewhat tentatively.

"But it's pretty obvious that what you are *really* claiming is that *evolution* can't be true. I mean, let's be honest – your opposition to mutations is actually opposition to evolution. The problem is that your whole argument is made irrelevant by one simple fact: laboratory experiments have already proven that evolution *can* happen, that life *can* evolve from non-living chemicals through completely random, natural events. And if such events can bridge *this* great gap and create the first forms of life, they can surely cause the evolution of the succeeding forms of life, where the gaps are much less formidable. The only thing that is required is time – and considering that the earth is over four billion years old, there's plenty of that!"

David quickly recognized what was happening, and tried to think of a way to head off trouble. He knew now that the uneasiness he felt a few days earlier regarding Josh's attendance at the meeting was justified. Also, he felt somewhat responsible for what was happening. After all, he had invited Josh to the meeting.

"Josh," he said. "Maybe it would be a good idea if you discussed any disagreements you have with Paul after the meeting, eh? I'm sure that he wouldn't mind. There's other things we need to go over tonight, and ..."

"Look, Dave," Josh snapped. "I appreciate your concern, but I came here tonight to discuss the truth about these matters, and that's exactly what I intend to do. I mean, that's supposedly what you guys are here for, to learn the truth, right?" he added, staring straight at Paul.

"Yeah, Josh, that's right. That's what we're here to discover – the Truth," Paul said. Paul knew exactly what experiment Josh had been referring to, and during the exchange between Josh and David, he had quickly weighed the pros and cons of allowing this discussion with Josh to continue. It was clear to him that, first, Josh was looking for an argument and, second, that Josh was undoubtedly very bright. Of course, he also knew that Josh wasn't aware that he knew a little about science, too. As always in such situations, his primary concern was for the kids and how they would be affected. Would it be better for them if the discussion proceeded or if he avoided it? It was a difficult decision, but he felt the issues at stake were very important. Also, if he backed down from an exchange at this point, he was concerned that it might give the kids the impression that Josh's analysis was right, and he certainly didn't want to risk that, because he knew that it wasn't.

"So, let's talk about this experiment you mentioned, Josh. Which one was it?"

"It was by Stanley Miller, in 1953. He created an atmosphere similar to that which would have existed in the early earth several billion years ago. Then he introduced an electric charge into the atmosphere, simulating lightning, and – bingo! – several amino acids, the building blocks of life, were formed."

"That's the experiment I thought you were referring to," Paul responded. "But you said this experiment produced life from non-living chemicals. But it didn't. Amino acids aren't life."

"Of course they aren't. And I didn't say they were. They are small organic compounds consisting of about ten to twenty atoms. But here's the point ... Your argument about mutations is basically that random natural events cannot be the cause of evolution, because random natural events cannot cause something of a lower order to evolve into a higher order. But in Stanley Miller's experiment this is exactly what happened. Entirely as a result of random natural events, non-living chemicals evolved into amino acids. As you said, they're not life. But they're a critical building block of life."

"Josh," Paul said, "I doubt that everyone here is familiar with this experiment. Perhaps it would be a good idea if you explained its basic details."

Josh looked at Paul and slowly nodded his head, wondering if Paul was perhaps testing him with this request.

"Sure, no problem. Like I said before, Mr. Miller created an atmosphere consisting of methane, ammonia, water vapor, and hydrogen, gases that scientists suspected were likely present in the atmosphere of the early earth. Circulation in the chamber was maintained by boiling the water in one limb of the apparatus and condensing it in the other. At the end of the week some particles were caught in a trap and analyzed by a process called paper chromatography. To Mr. Miller's great delight, it was found to have a mixture of amino acids! Glycine and alanine, the simplest amino acids and the most prevalent in proteins, were definitely identified in the solution, and there were indications it contained aspartic acid and two others. The yield was surprisingly high. This amazing result changed in a single stroke the thoughts concerning the probability of the spontaneous formation of amino acids, and, by extension, living cells."

Josh scanned the room to see if everyone was impressed. They were, as he expected. He proceeded to explain exactly what amino acids were, and their importance in the structure of living organisms.

"This experiment forever dashed the belief, which up until then had been quite widespread in the scientific community, that, because of the laws of probability, amino acids could never have formed by purely random events in nature. It is not difficult to see that this same reasoning extends to all other forms of life. That is, if amino acids can form by completely random events, then there is no reason why they, in turn, should not eventually combine to form proteins. And so on, right up the chain of life."

Josh looked at Paul with a proud smile, confident that his defense of evolution was successful and would undermine whatever might be said in this group from now on about creation. Along with everyone else in the room, Paul was impressed with Josh's grasp of the subject.

"Does anyone have any questions?" Josh asked.

Lisa spoke up. "Yes, I've got one. Have any forms of life higher than amino acids ever been created in a laboratory by random processes?"

"Good question, Lisa," Paul quickly interjected. "I just wanted to remind everyone that, as Josh pointed out, amino acids are not life. They are small organic compounds, the building blocks from which living organisms are eventually formed. It's very important that you keep this fact straight."

Paul turned to Josh and added, "Sorry, Josh. Go ahead"

Josh nodded back brusquely. In fact, he was glad to have a few extra seconds to formulate an answer to Lisa's question. He knew the answer was not going to do anything to strengthen his case.

"Quite surprisingly, Lisa, the answer to your question is 'no.' Structures more complicated than amino acids, like proteins, have not yet been created in a laboratory through strictly random processes in conditions like those of the ancient earth. They have been produced, but only when the experiments have been carefully controlled and directed.

"Anyway, scientists all over the world are working on this problem, and I'm sure that it won't be long before they're successful."

Lisa nodded, not entirely satisfied with Josh's answer.

For the next few minutes, Josh answered a few more questions about the experiment. Believing that his work was finished, he turned to Paul.

"Anything you'd like to add … or ask," he said with a slight smirk.

"Yes, there is," Paul responded. "I'd like to start with a question, about the gases that Stanley Miller chose for his experiment. You said that they were selected because scientists think that they were the gases in the atmosphere of the early earth. How come they didn't include oxygen? After all, oxygen is the second most common gas in the earth's atmosphere."

"That's an easy one," Josh replied. "There are two things that destroy organic compounds, such as amino acids. One is the decay of living organisms; the other is the attack of oxygen. Decay, of course, is a process that requires living organisms, and we are talking of a time before life existed. The thinking about oxygen is that since organic compounds *must* have formed – if they hadn't, life couldn't have evolved – and since they could not have formed if oxygen had been present in the atmosphere, then obviously oxygen must *not* have been present. Pretty basic."

Ignoring Josh's swagger, Paul responded, "I have another question, but before I ask it could you tell us how oxygen destroys organic compounds?"

"Sure, no problem. It just eats them up – just like we gobbled up Mrs. Conley's delicious pizza a little while ago!"

"Interesting," Paul said. "My question is, What *evidence* is there that this reducing – that is, oxygen-free – atmosphere ever existed?"

"Basically, I just told you," Josh replied, under the impression that Paul hadn't understood what he had just said. "Oxygen *couldn't* have ..."

"I understand exactly what you said," Paul interrupted. "That oxygen couldn't have been present because if it had been, then the molecules couldn't have possibly formed, because oxygen consumes such molecules as soon as they form. But I asked you for *empirical evidence* that such an atmosphere ever existed. What you gave us isn't evidence, Josh. It's a *requirement* based upon Miller's presuppositions."

"What do you mean, Mr. Hopkins? I'm not following you," Scott Martin spoke up.

Paul nodded, aware that his statement needed some explanation. Josh was very glad for this interlude, because Paul's request had caught him completely off guard. At the moment, he couldn't think of *any* empirical evidence that supported Miller's decision to omit oxygen from the atmosphere of his experiment. It simply never occurred to him to question this feature of the experiment. His textbook certainly didn't question it. Why should he?

Thus, while Paul was answering Scott's question, Josh was racking his brain for the evidence Paul had requested.

"Okay, Scott, let me see if I can make myself clear," Paul replied. "I asked Josh a question: Why didn't Miller include free oxygen in his experiment? What was his answer?"

"He said that oxygen couldn't have been present at the time amino acids formed because oxygen would have immediately eaten them," Scott answered.

"Right. And what was the purpose of Miller's experiment? What was he trying to do?"

"Hmmm, let's see," Scott replied, his brow furrowed in thought. "I guess you'd say he was trying – uh, hoping – to produce amino acids."

"Right again. So then, one could certainly suspect that the main reason, perhaps the *only* reason, he omitted oxygen from his experiment was that the presence of oxygen would have totally prevented the achievement of his goal, the creation of amino acids. Do you see anything wrong with this picture, Scott?"

"Not really," Scott replied. "If he was hoping to produce amino acids, and oxygen would have made this impossible, why shouldn't he have eliminated it?"

"But Scott, look what he did in order to accomplish this," Paul said with growing passion in his voice. *"He completely changed the atmosphere of the earth!* He didn't just adjust it a little – you know, fine-tune it. He eliminated the two gases, free nitrogen and oxygen, which make up over 99% of our current atmosphere. Practically speaking, Scott, the atmosphere of Miller's experiment bore absolutely no relationship to our current one, which is, of course, the only one that has ever been observed. To assume that such an atmosphere ever existed is a HUGE assumption ... Absolutely *HUGE*.

"The point I'm trying to make, the reason for my question to Josh, is that if you're going to make such an assumption, you'd better have some darned good evidence to back up your claim. You see, Scott, I don't believe that there's a single shred of real evidence that this atmosphere in Miller's experiment *ever* existed in the earth's history. I believe that Miller selected the gases of his experiment for only one reason: to make his goal, the production of amino acids, possible. The notion that this atmosphere had some basis in reality is, in my opinion, simply an evolutionary myth.

"The only thing that will prove this speculation wrong is some real evidence, chemical traces in ancient rocks, perhaps, or something like that, of this utterly bizarre atmosphere. And this is what I've asked Josh for ...

"Does that help, Scott?"

"Yeah, it does. I think I get it now."

After a brief pause, Paul turned his attention back to Josh.

"So, Josh, how about it? Can you provide us with some evidence that the atmosphere in Miller's experiment ever existed?"

Josh was taken aback by Paul's penetrating analysis of Miller's experiment. His logic appeared very sound, although Josh was sure that it must somehow be flawed. As far as Josh knew, the conditions and results of this experiment, including the composition of its atmosphere, were just about universally accepted in the scientific community. At least, that's the impression he had gained from the description of the experiment in his textbook. Josh just couldn't believe that Paul could possibly locate a critical flaw in the experiment that all of these scientists had overlooked. After all, he was only a *youth pastor.*

At the moment, however, these reflections didn't make much difference. Josh needed to come up with an answer to Paul's question.

"Well, uh, I'm not sure you'd exactly call it evidence," Josh began hesitantly, "but this notion that the atmosphere of the early earth was oxygen-free is just about universally accepted in the scientific community. And since this is the case …"

"Come on, Josh! Mr. Hopkins asked you for *evidence*, dude. That's not evidence. Those are just *opinions*. How about some cold, hard *facts*?!"

The speaker was Jennifer's younger sister, Kelly.

For the moment, at least, Josh was speechless. He couldn't answer Kelly's question for the simple reason that he couldn't think of any cold, hard facts to support his position. To the utter surprise of almost everyone in the room, Paul had forced Josh –Josh, the walking brain – onto the defensive. Those that knew Josh well, David in particular, had never seen him in such a position. That Paul was several years older didn't matter. As far as they knew, on the intellectual battlefield, Josh *never* lost. Of course, the battle was not yet finished.

As everyone stared at him, waiting for an answer, Josh became tense. He felt a little flushed. He wasn't used to being in such a situation, to say the least. He felt like just getting up and leaving, but he couldn't, of course. It would be embarrassing. His intellect, the thing that he prized above all, the only thing that gave him any confidence, was being challenged, so he had to fight with all his strength to avoid defeat. *Paul is only a youth pastor,* he thought. *What am I worried about? I can pull this out.* Thinking quickly, he came up with something that he hoped would turn things around for him.

"Some scientists base their notion of a reducing atmosphere around the primitive earth upon the atmosphere of other planets in our solar system. The atmosphere Miller chose mirrors some of these."

"I don't get it," Sue Peterson spoke up. "What are you talking about?"

"Well," Josh replied, "if the earth formed around the same time as the other planets, it would be logical that the ingredients of its original atmosphere would be the same, or at least similar, to theirs. And since there is hardly any oxygen in the atmospheres of the other planets, it is logical to suppose that there probably wasn't any in the early earth's atmosphere, either."

On the surface, this response seemed to make sense, but the logic was only superficial, and Paul saw right through it.

"So, then, you're saying that Stanley Miller's atmosphere makes sense because of its similarity to the atmosphere of some of the planets?"

"That's right," Josh responded.

"Which one?"

"What do you mean?" Josh replied.

"Which planet do you have in mind?"

"I ... I don't know," Josh stumbled. "Probably Mars ... Yeah, Mars. That's the planet that most closely resembles the earth."

"But think about it, Josh. What were the four gases in Miller's atmosphere?"

"Methane, ammonia, water vapor, and, uh ... let's see ... hydrogen."

"And what are the gases in Mars' atmosphere?"

"Uh ... I think it's mostly carbon dioxide. Beyond that, I ... I'm not really sure."

"Well, here's what's interesting. Out of the four gases in Miller's experiment, only one, water vapor, appears in measurable amounts on Mars. Therefore, the notion that Miller selected the gases for his experiment's atmosphere because of their similarity to those found on Mars just doesn't make sense – because there really isn't any similarity."

"It looks like you better try another planet, Josh!" Mike challenged. Over the years, Josh had occasionally picked on Mike when a disagreement arose – intimidating him with his superior intellect – and Mike was taking advantage of this opportunity for a little payback.

Josh was silent.

With barely a pause, Paul picked up the conversation. "Before we leave this topic, I want to point out that in addition to the fact that there's no real evidence to support it, there's something else wrong with the idea that the atmosphere of the early earth was oxygen-free."

There were two reasons Paul spoke up at this point. First of all, he could see that Josh was becoming increasingly uncomfortable, and he wanted to deflect attention away from him as quickly as possible. Second, knowing that this outdated and largely rejected experiment was still common in high school textbooks – as Josh had just proven – he wanted to make absolutely sure that the kids in that room clearly understood that scientists most definitely have *not* proven that life has evolved from non-living chemicals, as Miller's experiment implied. Back in Darwin's day, it was not particularly unreasonable to speculate that under certain conditions, and with enough time, non-living chemicals could perhaps become organized through random natural events into living cells. After all, viewed down a microscope at a magnification of some several hundred times, such as would have been possible in Darwin's time, a living cell is a relatively disappointing spectacle. It appears as an ever-changing and apparently disordered pattern of blobs and particles which, under the influence of unseen turbulent forces, are continually tossed haphazardly in all directions.[4] Paul was well aware, however, that scientific discoveries over the past century, especially in more recent years, have completely discredited this quaint notion of the cell and that the gap between lifeless chemicals and any living cell, rather than decreasing – as many scientists expected – has become a yawning chasm that appears increasingly *unbridgeable* as time passes.

"If there was no oxygen, there would be no ozone," Paul continued. "Ozone is an isotope of oxygen consisting of three atoms of oxygen, rather than two, and is formed naturally in the upper atmosphere by a photochemical reaction between oxygen and solar ultraviolet radiation. Ozone forms a canopy nine to eighteen miles above the earth's surface, protecting life on the planet from the deadly effects of these ultraviolet rays. As I just said, without oxygen ozone could not exist. And without the protection of this ozone canopy, amino acids could not exist."

"So, let me see if I've got this straight," Mike offered. "*With* oxygen in the atmosphere amino acids could never have gotten started because oxygen would have eaten them up. And *without* oxygen they wouldn't have been able to get going either, because without oxygen there wouldn't have been any ozone, and without ozone, they would have been destroyed by cosmic rays … right?"

Mike paused and looked around the room. With a big grin, he concluded, "It sounds to me like those poor little critters just had no chance of getting any place – just like the Yankees against the Red Sox!"

Everyone laughed. Everyone, that is, except Josh. Josh was completely distraught. As far as he was concerned, he had been completely humiliated in front of his peers by a church youth pastor. His fragile ego was shattered, and he desperately needed to escape so he could grapple with his turbulent emotions alone. But, still, he couldn't. To leave now would only worsen his humiliation.

Laura Conley, Jennifer's mother, had been observing the meeting from the back of the room; she was actually very interested in the topic being discussed. She had been watching Josh closely, and it was clear to her that something was wrong. She didn't know exactly what it was, but she knew that he needed an escape, right away.

"Hey, listen everybody," she spoke up. "It's getting pretty late, and some people may have to leave. Kelly and I baked a big batch of chocolate chip cookies. We'll bring them in. Anybody that needs to leave, feel free. Come on, Kelly. Give me a hand."

"You're right, Laura," Paul quickly responded, glancing at his watch. "It is about time to end. We were having such an interesting discussion, I hadn't even noticed the time!" he added, looking at Josh with a friendly smile. Paul had recognized that something was wrong with Josh, also, and if Laura had not brought the discussion to an end, he would have himself.

Josh didn't notice Paul's smile. As soon as he heard Laura Conley's words, his only thought was to get out of that house as quickly as possible. Immediately, he headed for the door. Just before he got there, Jennifer caught up to him in the hallway. It was an awkward moment, but Jennifer also knew that something was wrong with Josh. Furthermore, as opposed to her mother and Paul, who really didn't know Josh at all, she had a sense of what the problem might be.

"Josh," she said, "thanks for coming. You did a great job of explaining the Miller experiment. Your discussion with Mr. Hopkins was really interesting. I was really surprised at how much he knew about this stuff, weren't you? I sure learned some things that we never were taught in Mr. Potter's class, you know what I mean. I hope that you…"

"That's okay, Jennifer," Josh interrupted. "Don't worry, I'll get over it." He appreciated what Jennifer was trying to do, but at the moment he had no desire to talk to Jennifer or anyone else. He wanted only one thing – to be alone.

He turned away from Jennifer to leave.

"Wait, Josh. I have a couple of things for you. Here." Some cookies wrapped up in a napkin was the first thing she handed him. "Fresh from the oven – food for your body. Take this, too … This one's food for your soul."

She handed him a pamphlet, which Josh stuffed in his pocket.

"Thanks, Jennifer."

In a moment, Josh was out the door. Before he took a step, he felt a grasp on his arm. It was David.

"Hey, man, wait for me! I'm ready to split, too," he proclaimed. Josh had come to the meeting in David's car.

Josh wrenched himself out of David's grasp.

"Let me *go*, man! I gotta get out of here!"

"Whadduya mean? It's almost two miles, and I'm going right by your house. Don't be an idiot!"

"*Back off, Dave!* You heard that discussion tonight. Couldn't you see? I already *am* an idiot!"

With that, Josh spun around and headed toward the street. Well aware of Josh's fragile psyche, David anxiously watched him.

"Hey ... be careful! I'll see you tomorrow," he called out.

Without turning around, Josh held up his arm and raised his thumb, suggesting that he'd be all right.

Not convinced, David shook his head and headed back into the house.

In the kitchen he found Jennifer, her mother, and Paul and his wife, Sarah. Jennifer had told them about Josh's reputation regarding his intelligence and had speculated about the bearing this reputation may have had on his feelings at the end of the meeting.

"I think his pride may have been shattered," Jennifer suggested.

"Well, whatever it was," Laura Conley said, "by the end of the meeting Josh was in pretty tough shape. I think ..."

"Yeah, you're right, Laura," Paul interjected. "I feel kind of bad about it. I got so wrapped up in the discussion we were having that I failed to notice what was going on with him. But, hey, it wasn't all that bad, I don't think. You know, *sticks and stones can...*"

"I don't know, Paul. I hope you're right. But I was watching him very closely, and I think he was *really* hurting," Laura said.

After a moment of silence, she turned to Jennifer.

"I saw you speaking with Josh at the door, Jennifer. What did he say?"

Jennifer explained what she had given to Josh.

"That's great!" her mother exclaimed. "Gosh, could he ever use it," she added, referring to the pamphlet.

"Hey, we have to get going," Paul said. "Could we pray for a minute? I think that God is really at work in these meetings, and we need to continually seek His blessings and guidance. Also, I think you're absolutely right about Josh, Laura. He really needs our prayers."

After praying for a few minutes, Paul and Sarah were ready to leave. Before they did, Laura asked Paul a question.

"You certainly seemed to know a lot about that Stanley Miller experiment, Paul. How come?"

"Well, actually, I majored in biology in college."

"*That's* news. Where did you go?"

"Yale."

"If you majored in biology at Yale, how did you end up being a youth pastor?"

"I'd love to tell you, Laura, but I don't have time right now. Sarah and I promised a friend we'd visit her in the hospital tonight, so we really have to run. But I promise I'll tell you the story before long, okay?"

"Sure, that's fine. I'll be looking forward to it."

"So will I!" Jennifer said, with a big smile.

"Me, too," David added.

After Paul and Sarah left, Laura went into the living room to clean up, leaving David and Jennifer in the kitchen.

"I saw you and Josh outside," Jennifer said to David. "What happened?"

David answered Jennifer's question and then added, "Your mom is definitely right about Josh being hurting, Jen. You probably know as well as I do what the problem is. This is not going to be an easy thing for him to get over."

"Well, you're a good friend of his, Dave. You'll be there for him, right?"

"Yeah, sure. Of course I will. But Josh can get into these funks sometimes that last for weeks. I've seen it happen quite a few times. When he does, he gets really down and goes into, like, you know, a shell. I'll do what I can, but … I don't know.

"Hey, by the way … I've gotta give your mom credit for recognizing that Josh was hurting and needed to get out of here. She definitely came through in the clutch."

"Thanks, Dave. I have to agree – She is pretty special."

9

A Step Out in Faith – The Science Exam

David and Jennifer pulled up their chairs before Mr. Potter's large old oak desk. It was Friday afternoon, after school. Outside, it was a warm, beautiful spring day. A few kids were playing Frisbee on the nearby soccer field and a robin was feeding her hungry chicks in her nest in the great old maple tree on the edge of the field near Mr. Potter's room. In this room, however, the atmosphere wasn't quite as pleasant. The windows were closed and the air was cool, almost dank. Jennifer, in fact, felt chilly and wished she had brought a sweater.

As the two teens settled nervously into their chairs, Mr. Potter watched them carefully. After an uncomfortable pause, he took a deep breath, and then spoke.

"Do you know why you're here?"

They did – but neither was inclined to admit it.

"Okay, then, I'll tell you – even though I'm quite sure you already know. I've brought you here this afternoon to discuss your science exams. Several of your answers, most of the ones having to do with evolution, in fact, were remarkably consistent – and almost all wrong. The remarkable similarity would normally suggest cheating, except when people cheat they generally try to get the *right* answers, not the *wrong* ones. Furthermore, I've never had even the slightest suspicion that either of you were ever cheating in my class. Could you please tell me what in the world you were up to."

The truth was that Mr. Potter had a very good idea of what David and Jennifer were up to, but he wanted to hear it from them; he wanted to force them to admit it. It wasn't the first time one of his students had pulled a stunt like this on his final exam, but it irritated him whenever it happened. He strongly objected to it, because he so strongly believed in evolution. In his opinion, these two naïve youngsters, like their misguided predecessors, had mistakenly chosen the wrong side in the raging battle between evolutionists and creationists, and he passionately believed that it was his duty to rescue them from intellectual suicide. To him, the battle was over truth, in particular the great truths of science, and in his mind the theory of evolution was perhaps the greatest truth of all. Mr. Potter saw himself as a general in this battle – and the creationists were his primary enemy.

He believed with all his heart in the verse hanging on the wall behind him:

Whoever causes one of these little ones who believe in Me to stumble, it is better for him that a heavy millstone be hung around his neck, and that he be drowned in the depth of the sea.

The way he saw it, if a student of his fell for the irrational propaganda of the creationists, his teaching would have to be at least partially to blame, and he, therefore, would be at least partially guilty. Thus, he believed that he was in some way responsible for David and Jennifer's stumble and that it was his solemn duty to pick them up and protect them from future falls. The way he saw it, he was looking out for their best interests.

After another awkward pause, David spoke up. "Well, Sir, in the last few weeks, we've developed some doubts about the theory of evolution. We've done some research outside of class, and we believe …"

"You've done some research outside of class, eh? And just what have you been researching?"

"Well, uh, one thing we've looked into is mutations."

"Mutations, eh? That's interesting. And what have you discovered about them that you didn't learn in my class?" Mr. Potter added, a bit annoyed that they didn't find his teaching on the subject to be adequate.

Under pressure, David struggled to explain to Mr. Potter some of the things that they had found out about mutations, but before getting very far Mr. Potter inexplicably turned his attention to Jennifer.

"Excuse me, David … What about you, Jennifer? What do you think about these things?"

"But, Mr. Potter," David spoke up, "I hadn't even …"

"Don't worry, David," Mr. Potter interrupted. "You'll get your chance to finish your explanation. Of course, I've heard all this before. Now, I want to hear from Jennifer." The truth was that Mr. Potter *had* heard the things that David was saying before. He knew very well that in order to defeat your enemies, you had to know them, and he was very familiar with creationist arguments. It exasperated him that these arguments were so readily available to impressionable young people, however, and he knew where the blame lay: the Internet. At the touch of a key, these arguments were instantly available to anyone with access to a computer. The battle was no longer limited to the classroom, the library, and the traditional media, as it always had been until recently. Now it was being waged in cyberspace. And now young people didn't need adults to guide them to information, like they did in years gone by. Now they found it on their own – often quicker and more efficiently than adults. In the battle for people's minds, the rules of engagement had certainly changed, and Mr. Potter was well aware that this was making his mission a lot more difficult. Under the old rules, he felt that he had a reasonable amount of control over the information his students were exposed to. With the Internet this control had virtually vanished. Now, anyone could click onto Google and instantly find *seven million* entries about mutations – and a lot of them would be from creationists. He knew, of course, that David and Jennifer had utilized the Internet in their search and, based upon twisted logic, David symbolized these changes that were making his teaching more difficult, and for this reason he resented him.

Mr. Potter's brusque attitude toward David upset Jennifer, and she didn't understand it. It was making her very uncomfortable. Before it started, Jennifer had had a strong intuition that this meeting probably wasn't going to be a pleasant one. Her fears were proving to be well-founded.

"Miss Conley?" Mr. Potter said, shifting his attention back to Jennifer.

"Basically, Sir," Jennifer began haltingly, "I think you probably know from some of the things I have said in your class that I … I just, uh, have a lot of doubts about evolution. And since this is the case, I just couldn't answer the questions on your exam the way I know you wanted me to. I mean, I knew what answers you *wanted* me to give, but I just couldn't …"

"Jennifer, you say that you have a lot of doubts about evolution. Why don't you simply admit it – You just don't believe in the theory of evolution at all, do you?"

"Well, Sir," Jennifer sheepishly replied, "that's right."

"And exactly why is this? It's because of things you've been told in your church, isn't it?"

"Well, yes, that's part of it. But that certainly isn't the *only* reason."

"It's not? What else could possibly lead you to this utterly senseless – I mean, *surprising* – conclusion?"

"Hey, wait a minute," David spoke up. "I don't think you should call our position 'senseless.' We've found out that there are a lot of other people that feel the same way that we do about this subject, and some of them are ..."

"Maybe there are, David, but there's a lot *more* that don't, and I'm certainly one of them – and I'm your teacher, and I wrote the exam that you two just ... Never mind, we'll talk about that in a minute."

"No, wait," David quickly said. "What were you going to say? What happened to Jennifer and me on the exam?"

"Don't worry, David, we'll get to that in a minute," Mr. Potter brusquely replied. "Would you like to continue, Jennifer?"

"Well, um ... Like David was just saying, over the last few weeks, some of us have become really interested in this whole creation/evolution controversy, and we've been doing some research ..."

"I know. I've already been informed of this little detail. And where did you do this research? In your church library?" Mr. Potter said with a disdainful chuckle.

As she looked at Mr. Potter, Jennifer was suddenly jolted by the thought that there was something more going on in that room than an academic discussion about evolution and their final exam. A Bible verse flashed into her mind:

> *For our struggle is not against flesh and blood, but against the rulers, against the powers, against the world forces of this darkness, against the spiritual forces of wickedness in the heavenly places.*

She recognized that the struggle in that room was not really about creation and evolution but about souls – Mr. Potter's, specifically, but also, she dimly sensed, perhaps others.

"No," Jennifer responded, "We did our research in the school library, and at the UNH library ... and, of course, on the Internet. And as we studied, we began to see some serious problems with the theory of evolution."

"Perhaps there are some problems. *Every* scientific theory has its weaknesses. But that certainly doesn't mean that the entire theory is *wrong*, Jennifer."

Kicking Jennifer under the table, David quickly responded. "Mr. Potter, we were simply trying to do what was right, to answer the questions honestly, based upon what we believed. You have always encouraged us to think for ourselves and not just to echo what our teachers tell us. This is what we've tried to do here. With all of our doubts, we decided that we couldn't just spit back the answers we knew that you were looking for if we didn't believe them ourselves."

Mr. Potter was faced with a dilemma. He certainly had encouraged his students to think for themselves. But this free-thinking was supposed to have a limit. It certainly wasn't supposed to include rejection of Darwin's mighty theory, the bedrock of modern science, as far as he was concerned. Nevertheless, he couldn't help feeling a little pleased about David's principled adherence to his teaching philosophy.

Momentarily stumped, Mr. Potter turned to a different subject. "You two are regular church-goers, aren't you?"

"Not exactly," David answered. "Jennifer is, but I sure am not. I mean, I go sometimes, but I'm hardly a regular."

"I don't really care about your attendance record. You both go to church, so let me ask you. Be honest with me. Isn't your resistance to evolution really based upon your religious beliefs rather than upon empirical evidence? Aren't you rejecting Darwin's theory, in other words, primarily because it contradicts what you learned in church?"

Raising his eyebrows, David looked at Jennifer and pointed his finger at her.

"Well, you're right," Jennifer said. "Evolution *does* contradict the Bible. And that's definitely a big problem for me – for us, I guess. But it's not the *only* problem, Mr. Potter. Our study – you know, the research we've done on our own – has shown us that there are serious problems with the theory besides."

"Yeah," David blurted out, "you might say that in order to fail, the theory doesn't really need any help; it fails completely on its own!" Needless to say, Mr. Potter didn't see the humor in David's remark. Jennifer couldn't resist a little chuckle, however.

"I'm glad you're able to find a little humor in this situation, David. I don't think you'll find your grades too funny, however," Mr. Potter snapped.

"Whadduya mean?" David asked concernedly. "What are they?"

"Like I told you earlier, we'll discuss them in a few minutes. First of all, I'd like to find out what these 'serious problems' in Darwin's theory are."

For the next few minutes, David and Jennifer presented a few of what they believed were fatal weaknesses in the theory of evolution, including the statistical improbability of life evolving by chance from non-living chemicals, the impossibility of mutations introducing new information into living creatures, and the questionable evidence regarding the age of the earth. Mr. Potter listened patiently, but agreed with nothing they said, of course.

"You realize, I suppose, that this isn't the first time I've heard these arguments. They are common among creationists. I've had other students who have raised them. *Every* scientist has heard them – over and over again, in fact. And just about all of these people completely reject them." Mr. Potter paused for a moment. "You mentioned awhile back my encouragement to think for yourselves. You must realize, however, that this independent thinking has its limits – and you've crossed over them here. The theory of evolution is the foundation of modern science, and Charles Darwin was unquestionably one of the greatest scientists in history – some would argue *the* greatest. Don't get me wrong; I *do* want you to think for yourselves. However, like I said, this notion has its limits. For example, if I was your math teacher, I wouldn't want you to question that two plus two equals four, would I? Do you see what I'm talking about?"

David glanced at Jennifer and rolled his eyes. Mr. Potter saw it.

"I can see you don't agree with what I'm saying, eh, David? Perhaps you'd rather talk about your grades?"

A little embarrassed, David was silent.

"I'll get right to the point," Mr. Potter continued. "Your grades on the final exam dropped more than two full letters, from an A to a C minus. And your semester grades dropped from an A to a C plus."

"What?!" David exclaimed, almost jumping out of his chair. "How could our semester grades have dropped all the way to a C plus?! I thought you said that our final exams only counted 25% of our final grade. If we went in with an A average, how could a C minus on the exam bring us all the way down to a C plus for our semester grade?"

"Well, you see, my rules for grading are not entirely rigid. If a student does particularly poorly – or well – on their final exam, I will sometimes weigh this grade more heavily in determining their final grade."

"But you never told us that before the exam!" David exclaimed.

Mr. Potter leaned toward David. "Suppose you had known about this policy, David. Would it have affected your answers to the questions concerning evolution on the exam?" Now it was David who was caught on the horns of a dilemma.

Glancing at Jennifer, David dropped his eyes. "No … No, I suppose it wouldn't have."

Again, there was a tense pause.

Finally, Jennifer spoke up. "Are we finished, Mr. Potter? I'd really like to leave. I have a bunch of homework to do." The meeting had been more unpleasant than Jennifer had anticipated, and she didn't feel any good could come from extending it.

Mr. Potter genuinely liked these two youngsters, and he suddenly sensed that he might have been too rough on them, especially concerning their grades. He *had* taught them to think for themselves, and, after all, that is exactly what they had done. At the moment, however, he was reluctant to admit that he may have been wrong. His pride was in the way.

Turning away from them and looking out the window, he responded to Jennifer's question. "You have been two of my best students this year. I had great hopes for you. It's too bad the year had to end like this." He kept looking out the window. For the moment, he couldn't face them.

As he spoke, Jennifer thought that Mr. Potter looked very worn out, as if he was going through a great struggle. Her heart went out to him.

"Aw, don't worry, Mr. Potter. Everything will work out somehow. We'll be all right. One C on our report card isn't going to kill us, I suppose." Jennifer looked over at David and with a look of intensity nodded toward Mr. Potter, inviting David to back up her attempt at reconciliation. David shook his head and remained silent.

"Well, I guess we'll be going, Mr. Potter," Jennifer said.

Mr. Potter turned towards Jennifer. "Okay. Thanks for coming," he responded. He started to say something else but checked himself.

Jennifer and David got up from their chairs and headed toward the door. As Mr. Potter watched them, he couldn't help feeling begrudging admiration for their principled stand.

"Hey!" he called out to them as they were about to exit his room.

David and Jennifer turned around, surprised at his call.

"Maybe I was a little too harsh about your final grades," he said. "I'm going to think them over."

Smiling for the first time since they entered the room, Jennifer quickly responded. "Gee, thanks a lot, Mr. Potter. That would be great!"

"Don't thank me yet. I didn't say I'd *change* them!"

Glancing back as she headed out the door, Jennifer saw a little smile on Mr. Potter's face.

"That sure was a blast, wasn't it?" David said as they walked down the hall. "Mr. Potter got a little rude, cutting me off and stuff, you know what I mean? He's just so in love with the theory of evolution, thinking, like, it's the foundation of modern science and all that. Doesn't he know that not everyone agrees with him? Gimme a break. What about his big idea of *thinking for ourselves?* I don't remember him telling us that this applied to everything *except* evolution, do you?"

"I know what you mean, Dave. But, you know what – Mr. Potter's just got one main problem … He needs to find Christ, just like everyone else in the world. And you know what else? I think we might just be able to help him. What do you think? You think there's any hope?"

Although David was familiar with the phrase "finding Christ" – his mother had used it occasionally since she had been going to Grace Bible Church and Paul Hopkins had mentioned it a few times in youth group – he wasn't sure exactly what it meant.

"You mean hope of Mr. Potter becoming a Christian?"

"Yeah, that's right," Jennifer replied.

"Whew … I don't know, Jen. As far as I can see, Mr. Potter's certainly not the most likely candidate for sainthood. But who knows, with God anything's possible, I guess."

"That's right, Dave. It is … It certainly is," Jennifer said with a big smile.

After a pause, David said, "Listen, Jen, I gotta ask you something. What exactly do you mean when you talk about 'finding Christ?' I've heard my mom say that a few times, and Paul Hopkins, too. But I'm not real sure what it means."

Jennifer was excited that David had asked her this question. Despite David's recent involvement with the youth group and apparent interest in Christian things, she was not really sure whether he had committed his heart to Christ. His question made it pretty clear to her that he hadn't. The truth was that Jennifer had deliberately tossed out this phrase – *find Christ* – to see what David's response to it would be. She was fishing for David's soul, and this phrase was the bait.

"That's a good question, Dave. I'm glad you asked. I'll try to answer it for you … First of all, it doesn't mean that you've just *heard* of Christ, because millions of people have heard of Him but haven't *found* Him.

Finding Him, I guess you could say, means finding the message He came to give the world and then – and this is really important – accepting the message for *yourself*."

"But exactly what message are you talking about? Didn't He bring a *lot* of messages?"

"Yeah, sure He did. You're absolutely right. But there was one *main* message:

God so loved the world that He gave His only begotten Son, that whoever believes in Him should not perish but have eternal life. John 3:16."

"Oh yeah – the verse you always see these yahoos holding up on signs at football games, right?"

"Yup – That's the one."

"Huh – that's funny … I never knew what those signs meant. What exactly is it again?"

For God so loved the world that He gave His only begotten Son, that whoever believes in Him should not perish but have eternal life.

"Okay – So what do you mean that you have to *accept* it for yourself, Jen – just that you have to believe in Jesus, like the verse says?"

"Well, not exactly. I mean you do have to believe in Him, of course. But there's a little more you need to do, too. You have to confess Jesus as your own Lord, your own Savior. A lot of people *believe* in Jesus that haven't accepted Him as their own, personal Lord."

"Where does it say you have to do that?"

"In Romans … *If you confess with your mouth Jesus as Lord and believe in your heart that God raised Him from the dead, you shall be saved*."

"But I don't see why you have to confess it if you believe it in your heart."

"Do you believe it?"

"Well, uh … Yeah, I think so."

"Have you actually opened your mouth and asked Jesus to be your Lord, like the verse says?"

"I don't know. Probably not, I guess"

"Well, that's what you need to do, Dave, to be sure of your salvation … Open your mouth and ask Him to be your Savior. You see, God knows that our hearts are wicked and *deceitful*, and that we can fool ourselves into thinking that we have accepted Jesus as our Lord when we really haven't. There's a verse in the Bible that says, *The heart is desperately sick*. That's why we need to openly confess Jesus as our Lord – to make sure that we're not fooling ourselves into thinking that He *is* when in fact He *isn't*. It's kind of like the feelings a husband has toward his wife. If he believes that he loves her, but never opens his mouth and tells her, don't you think his wife would have reason to wonder whether he actually does? In order for her to really believe that her husband loves her, he needs to *tell* her. Same with God. In order for Him to really believe that we have accepted Him as our Lord, we need to *tell* Him. Then, when we do, He'll be sure – and so will we. You get it?"

"Yeah, I think so – or, maybe I should say, I'm *getting* it! But I have another question. You said that we need to confess Jesus as our Lord and *Savior*. What's He saving us from?"

"From our sins, Dave – and beyond that, from hell, which is where you'll end up if you *aren't* saved," Jennifer added with raised eyebrows.

David nodded his head. For the first time, it was perfectly clear to him what he needed to do to be "saved." It was equally clear to him that he hadn't done it yet.

As they stepped outside the building, Jennifer and David looked at each other and smiled. They were happy … And why wouldn't they be? The meeting with Mr. Potter was behind them, it was a beautiful spring afternoon, and – best of all, in their minds – they were together.

"Look out!" someone yelled.

Looking up, David saw a stray Frisbee headed in his direction. Instinctively, he took a few quick steps to his right, reached up and snatched it. With a snap of his wrist he whipped it back to its sender, about forty yards away – a perfect strike.

"Nice toss!" came a call from the building behind him.

Spinning around, David replied, "Hey, thanks, Mr. Potter!" With a big grin, he added, "Thanks a *lot*!"

That night, while alone in his bed, David thought about his conversation with Jennifer earlier in the day and began to reflect upon the sins in his life. The more he thought about them, the more he discovered: selfishness, pride, lust, anger, jealousy, and greed, to name a few. It wasn't a real pretty picture, but, thanks to Jennifer, he knew what he needed to do now. He opened his mouth and confessed his sins – and asked Jesus Christ to be his Lord and Savior.

He was born again.

10

A Downward Spiral

As Josh walked home from the Youth Group meeting at the Conley's, he desperately tried to rationalize the aching humiliation he was feeling, but no matter how hard he tried he couldn't escape what seemed to him to be the awful truth – that he had been totally humiliated in front of his friends and peers by a church youth pastor in a debate about *science*. For most other people, this experience would have been unpleasant, but hardly traumatic. They would soon have gotten over it. For Josh, however, the event was devastating, because his self-esteem rested almost entirely upon his extraordinary intelligence. To be so thoroughly outdone in a debate about *anything*, by *anybody*, was an utterly unique experience for Josh. But for the subject of the debate to be the one in which he most prided himself, science, and for his opponent to be a church youth pastor was just more than he could stand. Josh kept hoping the whole experience was a bad dream. He knew, however, that it wasn't.

For the next few days, Josh remained in his room as much as possible, leaving only for school and an occasional trip into town for a bite to eat. Although he had been warned not to, he doubled up on his prescription antidepressant pills, Prozac, which he had been taking for the past three years, but it didn't seem to help. His parents knew that something was wrong with their son, but he did tumble into these valleys periodically – that's why he took Prozac – and they figured he'd climb out of it before long, like he always had before. "It's his demons – They come with his brains," his father, Benjamin, would say. Benjamin was the editor of the *Manchester Daily Messenger*, a good-sized daily newspaper. His wife, Rachel, was a guidance counselor at Hebrew Academy of Durham. Josh was their only child.

Almost two weeks had passed since the youth group meeting. It was Friday afternoon, and Josh was sitting at a booth in the Main Street Diner having a cheeseburger when he felt a hand on his shoulder. Turning around, he saw Paul Hopkins.

"Hey, Josh ... I was sitting down on the other side and noticed you over here. Mind if I join you for a minute?" Paul said with a friendly smile.

"Uh ... yeah, sure. Why not?" Josh stammered, completely caught off guard.

Even though Paul had heard about Josh's condition from some of the kids in the youth group, particularly his close friend, David, he was alarmed by Josh's careworn appearance. He had actually tried to contact Josh a couple of times but had not been successful. Josh was not responding to any attempts at communication, aside from an occasional email from David. The situation was awkward.

"I've been trying to get in touch with you. Did you get my emails?" Paul asked.

"Yeah, I did ... Sorry I didn't get back to you. I haven't been feeling too well."

"That's all right." After an uncomfortable pause, Paul continued. "I wanted to talk to you about our discussion the other night at Jennifer's house. I got kind of carried away and I felt bad about it afterward. If I embarrassed you in any way, please forgive me. I certainly didn't mean to show you up or anything. It's just that I believe that the experiment we were discussing is so important, and I wanted to make sure ..."

"Don't worry, Mr. Hopkins. I'm okay about it," Josh lied.

"You know, Josh, the truth is that that experiment by Stanley Miller has been essentially disregarded by scientists for many years. Scientists who tried to repeat it had difficulty. The only place people still read about it is in school textbooks."

Josh was surprised at this information. He was completely unaware of it.

"That's kind of weird. If it's been disregarded in the scientific community, how come it's still in our textbooks?"

"Because when it comes to the issue of origins, your textbook is not exactly telling it like it is."

"By origins, do you mean the origin of life?"

"Not only life ... Actually, I mean the origin of *everything* in the natural world: the stars, the sun, the earth, *and* all living creatures."

Josh nodded his head. After a pause, he asked a question. "Say, I meant to ask you something. You seem to know a lot about science. Like, you knew the chemicals in Mars' atmosphere, for example – not exactly common knowledge. How come? What's your background?"

Paul proceeded to inform Josh of his undergraduate and post-graduate experience in biology at Yale.

"That's pretty radical," Josh responded. "If you got a Masters degree in biology at Yale, how the heck did you ever end up as a church youth pastor? That's *nuts!* I thought people that graduated from Yale ended up making the big bucks. I was even thinking of going there myself."

"You're certainly not the first person to ask me about this, but, if you really want to know, I'll tell you."

"Go right ahead."

"Okay … Here's what happened," Paul began. "The summer after my senior year at Yale, I got a job in a biological research lab in Cambridge, Massachusetts. At that time I was quite sure that I wanted to pursue a career in science, and this job presented me with a great opportunity for some serious hands-on training. One of the assistants who was working with me in the lab – he had graduated from Harvard – initiated some conversations with me about evolution and creation, and I started to have some questions about the subject. One day he invited me to a discussion group that he said might be able to provide answers to some of my questions. It turned out that the discussion group was a Bible study at this fellow's house. There was fresh-brewed coffee and homemade doughnuts, so I was hooked! After going to this study for a few weeks, I began to see things about evolution that really blew me away. In particular, I began to recognize that the notion that life evolved by random, natural events, as my biology professors were teaching, really didn't make sense … and for the first time, I started to see the logic of a supernatural Creator."

Josh was intrigued by what Paul was saying, but, at the same time, he still held him somewhat accountable for his current depression. After all, it was Paul who had made him appear so foolish at the youth group. For the moment, at least, he couldn't take any more of Paul. He had to get away.

"Listen, I think what you're saying is very interesting, and I'd like to hear more about it sometime, but I really have to hit the road right now. I gotta do some things at home." Sliding out of the booth, he added, "So, I'll catch you later, eh?"

With that, he picked up his bill and started to leave.

"Hey, wait," Paul said. "Leave your bill. I'll take care of it."

"Never mind. I got it … Thanks, anyway."

That night, exhausted after a long, fitful struggle to find some peace, Josh finally fell into a deep sleep. The next thing he knew he was in a large room, like an auditorium, filled with people. In the front of the room, on a long platform, was an extravagant, brightly lit apparatus consisting of a myriad of glass tubes and flasks of many different sizes and shapes, electric wires, and shiny silver containers. A man was moving back and forth behind the apparatus, talking excitedly as he pointed to different parts. The man looked strangely familiar to Josh. *Oh, my God!* he thought – *It's Mr. Potter!* Looking more closely, he wasn't sure. It appeared that the man was explaining the function of the various parts, but Josh couldn't hear what he was saying. The man flipped a switch and the apparatus suddenly lit up in different colors. He then began feeding things into an opening at one end of the contraption. Josh couldn't make out exactly what the things were – small stones, perhaps, mixed in with what looked like dirt, or sand. Next, he opened the valves on some cylinders that were connected to the glass tubing with rubber hoses, apparently releasing some gases into the mixture. The material was suspended throughout its journey in a clear liquid, which the man explained was water. As it flowed through the apparatus, the matter glowed and pulsated and began to conglomerate into little clumps. Apparently, a great deal of heat was being generated, for smoke, or perhaps steam, oozed from some of the connections. At the end of their long, twisting journey, the clumps dropped out onto the platform upon which the great contraption rested. To Josh's utter astonishment, as they landed, they slowly began to move about on the platform. They seemed to be *crawling!* Triumphantly, the man declared that they were *alive!*

The crowd sprang to their feet and broke into wild applause. Josh couldn't believe what he was seeing. He rushed to the platform to get a better view, but he was grabbed by two burly guards. Again, the man behind the platform looked like Mr. Potter to Josh.

"Stop! Let me go!" Josh cried out. "I know that man … Mr. Potter! Tell them to let me go! I have to get down to the platform to see what's going on!" The man at the platform stared coldly at Josh. It wasn't Mr. Potter.

The next thing Josh knew, he was lying face down on the ground outside in the cool night air, alone. His arms were sore, as if they had been twisted.

He had no idea where he was, and he had no desire to find out. He just wanted to get out of there, as quickly as possible.

Looking around to get his bearings, he discovered that he was in the middle of a completely unfamiliar wilderness. The breeze moaned eerily in the huge pine trees that towered all around him, and in the distance loomed some jagged mountain peaks. Aside from some scattered moonbeams filtering through the dense pine boughs, the only light was coming from the building he had just left. In the distance he could make out some cabins, but they were all pitch black. Across the parking lot, or field, he saw a narrow road that disappeared into the dark forest. An arrow with an Exit sign stood at the beginning of it. He was hesitant to take it – it looked ominous – but he couldn't see any alternative, so he headed toward it. Before disappearing into the forest, he turned to take one more look at the building he had left. It seemed much larger than he had pictured it, like a giant old castle. Suddenly, he felt a powerful grip on his shoulder. Spinning around, he was startled to see a large man staring him in the face. The man asked him where he was going.

Frightened, Josh replied, "I … I just wanted to step outside for a minute … to get a breath of fresh air. It was getting kind of stuffy in there."

"Who gave you permission to leave?" the man asked threateningly.

"Uh, no one. The door was open. I don't know …I …"

In a deep voice that seemed strangely distant, the man said something about Josh being carefully selected for the evening and how he should feel greatly honored to have been chosen. He added something about the importance of the experiment, like it was one of the most important in the history of science, or maybe of the world … Josh couldn't understand him very well; he had a weird accent. He just wanted to get away from this awful place, far away and as fast as he could. He tried to wrench free, but the powerful man just gripped his arm more tightly.

"I'm afraid you don't understand," his captor growled, his hideous face inches from Josh's. "You *cannot* leave. We've been watching you for many years now, and we have great plans for you. We've chosen you for our team, and once we have chosen someone, they cannot leave. Don't be a fool, Josh. Stick with us. One day you'll be rich and famous. *Fame and fortune*, Josh. Isn't that what humans dream of? Come on – Isn't that what you *live* for, Josh?" he added with a frightening laugh.

Terrified, Josh exclaimed, "Let me go, you monster! *Let me go!*"

The next thing Josh knew, he was racing through the forest of great pine trees. Aside from the bright shaft of an occasional moonbeam, the forest floor was dark and foreboding. He ran and ran, for a long time. Finally, on the side of a hill, he stopped to catch his breath. Illuminated by the full moon, some movement in the valley below caught his eye. To his dismay, it was the man that had stopped him on the exit road – along with two companions! He couldn't believe it. He was sure that he had left them far behind. They were headed right for him at a rapid, relentless pace. And, to Josh's horror, despite their distance from him, their glowing red eyes seemed to be looking right at him! He could tell that *they* wouldn't need to stop for breath.

Gripped by fear, Josh began running again, but with each step he knew that the three men were getting closer. Exhausted, he stumbled and fell. He heard a noise – footsteps! Overwhelmed with terror, he let out a primal scream. Suddenly, he felt a grasp on his shoulder.

"Josh! Josh, what's the matter?!" his father cried out anxiously, his hand on his son's shoulder.

Quickly, Josh awoke from his nightmare and saw his father and mother standing next to him.

"Oh, Dad … It's okay … Don't worry. I was just having a bad dream … I'll be all right," came the unconvincing reply.

"Whew!" his father responded. "It sure must have been awful. I was afraid you were going to wake up our neighbors! You want to tell us about it?"

"No, I don't, Dad. I just want to *forget* it! If I tell it to you, it will just make me remember it. Basically, it was one of those dreams where you're being chased by some terrifying people, and no matter how fast you run, they just keep getting closer and closer. Then, just before you get caught, you wake up, you know? Only this time I think I actually *did* get caught! It really scared the crap out of me, Dad. But you know what I mean, don't you?"

"Yeah, I sure do," his father replied. "I guess we've all had dreams like that."

"I've had them, too, Josh," his mother added. "They sure are frightening! Thank God, I always wake up just in the nick of time – just like you did."

Josh nodded. Although the terror of his dream was still fresh in his mind, his parents' compassion was at least somewhat comforting.

A couple of minutes later, as they were headed back to their bedroom, Rachel Siegel turned to her husband. "Ben, I'm really worried about Josh.

He just doesn't seem to be pulling out of his depression, like he always has in the past. It's been almost two weeks now and he hasn't shown any improvement at all. To tell you the truth, in my opinion he seems to be getting worse." After a pause, she added, "What do you think, honey?"

"I don't know. I think he'll be all right. It's not like he's never been like this before. He's always had his demons. You know that. He just has to learn to cope with them." Pausing, he added, "I hope he's taking his Prozac."

"Don't worry. I'm making sure that he does."

Josh spent the rest of the night trying to get back to sleep, but, haunted by the memory of his frightening dream, he never did. As he watched the soft light of the morning sun slowly creep into his room, he knew that his battle to get some sleep was lost – again.

11

A Chat with Mr. Potter

"Hey, Josh," Mr. Potter exclaimed cheerfully as he saw his prize pupil walk through the door into his office. "What's up?"

As the best student that he had ever had, Josh held a special place in Mr. Potter's heart. Not surprisingly, the two of them had grown very fond of each other over the past couple of years. Josh often stopped by after school to chat, sometimes about science, but about other things, also. Occasionally, they would go skiing together. Mr. Potter was aware of Josh's battle with depression – he had discussed it more than once with Josh's parents – and could usually tell when Josh had slipped into one. It pained him to see Josh in one of these gloomy spells, and he always tried to do whatever he could to help him get over it, usually without much success. Judging from the dark circles under his eyes and his unkempt appearance, Mr. Potter worried that the blues had once again overtaken his young friend.

"Uh, not too much," Josh replied.

Motioning to the old leather armchair in the corner of his office where Josh always sat, Mr. Potter said, "Have a seat. Is everything all right?"

"Yeah, I guess so" Josh lied. Then, without wasting any time, Josh got right to the point of his visit. "I want to ask you something, though: I know that you believe in the theory of evolution, of course. What I want to know is, how *certain* are you that the theory is true? I mean, do you have any doubts about it at all?"

"Hmmm … How certain am I that the theory of evolution is true, eh? Now there's an interesting question." Mr. Potter picked up a baseball from his desk and stood up. "Here, let me show you." Holding the ball out in front of him, he said, "How certain are you that this ball will fall to the floor if I drop it?"

"I don't know … maybe fifty-fifty," Josh chuckled.

"All right, wise guy – keep your eyes open," Mr. Potter said as he let the ball drop from his hand. "As far as I'm concerned, my faith in the theory of evolution is just as strong as my belief that that ball would fall to the floor when I dropped it. To me, in other words, the theory of evolution is just as valid as the theory of gravity. But why do you ask? Are you having doubts about it?"

"Maybe."

"Why? What caused them?"

Josh wasn't sure how to answer Mr. Potter's question. He definitely didn't feel like telling him about his experience at the youth group – it would be way too embarrassing – but since that was where his doubts originated, he was in a bit of a dilemma.

"*Something* must have caused them, Josh … something you read, or saw on TV, or the Internet, or maybe a conversation you had with someone. Come on, think about it."

"All right. I guess it was a conversation I had."

"That's a good start. Tell me something about it. Who was it with?"

"What difference does it make?" Josh replied evasively. "I don't think that's really important. It doesn't matter *who* I talked to. I just want to talk about the issue, all right?"

"Maybe you're right. But, on the other hand, it might be helpful if I knew who you were talking to. If I knew something about the person, it might give me some insight into the source of their skepticism … and it might help me answer your question."

"Could be, but, like I said, I don't want to get into that right now. I just want to talk about the scientific evidence for the theory. I want to find out why you're so convinced that it's true."

"Okay, I'll go along with you," Mr. Potter agreed. "Tell me, then: what parts of the theory are you doubting?"

"Like, maybe the whole thing," Josh replied.

Mr. Potter was surprised, almost shocked, at what Josh was telling him, because he considered the theory of evolution to be the bedrock theory of science, the theory that united all of the others, and he had assumed that his teaching on the subject would have caused Josh – especially Josh, in fact – to share this belief. Experience had taught him that there were always going to be some students who would have their doubts about the theory, especially Christians, and even more especially Christians with a home-school background, like Jennifer. But he never expected someone as bright as Josh to fall into this group.

Josh had arrived at the great fork in the evolution versus creation debate, and he had paused. To Mr. Potter's bewilderment, it appeared that Josh actually believed that the decision about which road to take was worthy of consideration. Mr. Potter was determined to straighten out his thinking as quickly as possible. He figured that a brilliant future in science awaited Josh, and he knew that doubts about, or even worse, rejection of, the theory of evolution, could be a major stumbling block in the career path of a scientist. He personally knew two scientists whose careers had been abruptly derailed by rejection of the theory, and he had read about a number of others. To prevent Josh from making a disastrous choice, Mr. Potter surmised that Josh needed a savior – and he knew exactly who it should be.

"Let me be honest with you, Josh. I don't know who you've been talking to, but I guarantee you that whoever it was, they're sadly misinformed. It's true that there are some elements of the theory of evolution that are uncertain, but taken as a whole no reputable scientist rejects it. Evolution is a *fact*, Josh. It is one of the most well-established and well-documented facts in the history of science, and to deny and attack evolution is to deny and attack one of the most fundamental facts of all nature and reality, one of the crucial foundation stones of modern science. I'm sure that this person you were talking with ..."

"The person I was talking to has an advanced degree in biology from Yale," Josh interrupted, "so I don't think you can say that he is 'sadly misinformed.'"

"That's interesting. And what does he do now?"

"Uh ... he, uh ... he works in a church, as a youth pastor," Josh replied hesitatingly, well aware that he had left himself wide open for judgment.

"A *youth pastor*, eh? That helps to explain things," Mr. Potter snickered. "And how did you meet him?"

"Like I said before, I really don't want to talk about it, Mr. Potter. Can't we just talk about the science behind the theory? Once again, what does it matter who I was talking to?"

"Well, what did he say that caused you to have doubts?"

Reluctantly, Josh proceeded to tell Mr. Potter about the debate that he had had with Paul Hopkins about the Stanley Miller experiment. "I'll tell you, he really seemed to know what he was talking about," he observed.

"Okay, Josh, I can see why you had a problem there. The fact is that that experiment by Stanley Miller has lost most of its luster over the past few decades, and very few scientists still acknowledge it as a milestone in the effort to produce life in the laboratory. The problem is that your textbook still portrays it as such a milestone."

That's just what Paul was saying, Josh thought.

"Then why is it still in the textbook?" Josh demanded, increasingly annoyed.

"That's a valid question, of course, and to be blunt it shouldn't be. But you must realize, Josh, that printing textbooks is a very expensive project and to reprint these books every time some bit of information in them was proven to be invalid would be prohibitively costly. If publishers had to do this, they wouldn't be in business very long."

"I get your point, but when these things happen – when something presented in a textbook as being true becomes invalid – it's up to the teacher to inform his students about it. Otherwise, the students are being deceived; they're being led to believe that something is true when it really isn't. And that's just wrong, Mr. Potter ... really, really wrong," Josh said, shaking his head in disappointment.

"You're right, Josh. It is, in a sense ... And I should have been more careful to explain the problems with Miller's experiment." Mr. Potter paused. "Actually, I thought I did. Perhaps you were out sick that day. You missed a couple of days about that time, remember? But listen; we're missing the forest for the trees here. Just because a textbook continues to include an outdated experiment about one small detail of a theory hardly seems to be a sufficient reason to reject the entire theory. The path to any scientific theory is always littered with trials and errors. That's exactly what the Miller experiment is: a trial whose conclusions eventually proved to be mistaken.

"But, Josh, please, *please* don't latch onto this little bump in the road as a reason to reject the mighty theory of evolution," Mr. Potter said with rising passion. "That would be a disastrous mistake! These fundamentalist Christians – and I strongly suspect that your youth pastor friend is one of them – are undermining the science curriculum in our entire nation, and if we back down and let them have their way, one day students across the land will once again be taught that the world was created in six twenty-four hour days about six thousand years ago by a superman with a long white beard that waved his magic wand from his magic kingdom high above the clouds, like they were in the distant past, when modern science was in its infancy. My God, Josh, do you want to see *that* come about? That would be *insane!*" he added, slamming his fist upon his desk.

Mr. Potter's eyes blazed with fury, and his crimson face evidenced the heightened pressure in his veins.

Taken aback by Mr. Potter's display of anger, Josh thought to himself, *Whew! This man's commitment to evolution is* **serious!**

"When you put it that way, it does sound pretty crazy, I guess," Josh replied. "But it's pretty hard to imagine anything like *that* ever taking place. That would be, like, a return to the Dark Ages."

"It sure would! But listen, that's exactly what these fundamentalist Christians are seeking. I know it's hard to believe, Josh, but I've been following their crusade for years, and, trust me, that's their goal. We're in a war, my friend, a battle for truth, and we've got to do everything in our power to make sure that the truth prevails. Make no mistake about it: our opponents are very dedicated and focused. They believe in their cause just as much as we believe in ours. They are not going to go away easily. Our side desperately needs capable warriors like you to defend our cause, the cause of truth. In my opinion, if we lose, our country is going to be in big trouble."

"Whew … thinking about the debate between creation and evolution as a *war*. I don't know – That's *radical*, man."

"It really isn't, Josh. Think about it. Prior to the Scopes trial in Dayton, Tennessee in 1925, the teaching of evolution was pretty much prohibited in public school classrooms. As a result of that trial a ray of light, of truth, finally filtered into these classrooms. It took awhile, but in time the ancient myth of a supernatural Creator creating the world in six days was completely, and mercifully, abolished from these rooms, and the students in them finally became enlightened with the *real* story of our origins. Well, these fundamentalists want us to return to the pre-Scopes days and reintroduce the biblical creation myth into the classroom. In the last one hundred and fifty years or so scientific discoveries have created an increasingly great gap between this ancient myth and reality, and to resurrect this myth as a real alternative to evolution as an explanation for the natural world would be an absolutely disastrous reversal of scientific progress. It would make us the laughingstock of the world and ensure that we lose our position as a world leader in the realm of science. It wouldn't necessarily return us to the Dark Ages, but it certainly would snuff out a lot of lights.

"Not a lot of people see this battle very clearly, Josh, especially younger people. But eventually everyone must choose which side he is on. As I'm sure you know, I care for you a great deal, and I want to make sure that you choose the right side. Use your wonderful mind to thoroughly research the issue, and I'm confident it will lead you in the right direction. One more thing ... You know that whenever you need help, with this question or with anything else, I'm *always* here for you, right?"

"Yeah, I know ... Thanks. Thanks a lot, Mr. Potter."

A few minutes later their conversation ended and Josh got up to leave. Mr. Potter gave him a hug and said, "Don't worry, Josh, everything will work out all right. I'm sure you'll figure things out."

As Josh was walking down the hall, he realized something: they never really did discuss any of the scientific evidence behind the theory of evolution, which really had been the purpose of his visit. Therefore, unfortunately, he left his meeting with Mr. Potter just as confused about the theory as he had been before he came. His troubled soul had desperately been seeking help. Unfortunately, it hadn't found any.

12

Breakthrough

"Hey, Dave, you heard anything from Josh recently?" Scott Martin asked David Newton. It was about 11 p.m. Saturday night and Scott, Dave, and John Mitchell were driving home after a post-movie pizza at Dino's.

"Not in the last couple of days. He's been really depressed recently – ever since that youth group meeting he was at a couple of weeks ago. You guys were both there. You saw what happened. I think he felt humiliated. You know Josh … Whenever he's involved in anything having to do with the intellect – whether it's a debate, a discussion, whatever – he *always* has to be on top, right?"

"Yeah, right," John said. "Especially if it's a debate with a church youth pastor, about his favorite subject, science. Oh, man, he *definitely* was not a happy dude that night."

David nodded his head in agreement. "We've exchanged some emails and I've been over to see him a couple of times, but he said he just needs to be alone for awhile." David paused for a moment, then added, "You know, my mom mentioned to me this afternoon that Josh's parents were going to be away tonight visiting some friends in Brattleboro or something. I wonder if it might be a good idea to stop over at his house to see how he's doing. Whadduya think? You want to go?"

"Yeah, why not?" John replied. "Let's go."

Fifteen minutes later the three boys were at the Siegel's house. David rang the doorbell. There was no response. He banged on the door. "Josh – Josh. Open up. It's Dave, and Scott and Johnny." Still, there was no response. The boys could see that Josh's Jeep Cherokee was in the driveway, so they figured he must be home. They also figured that it was much too early for Josh to be in bed, especially since it was a Saturday night and Josh was usually a night owl. David tried the door. It was open, so they entered the house.

"Josh," David called out. "Josh! *Where are you, man?* Speak up!" There was only silence. David looked at his companions with concern. "Let's see if he's in his room," he said, and they headed up the stairs, two at a time.

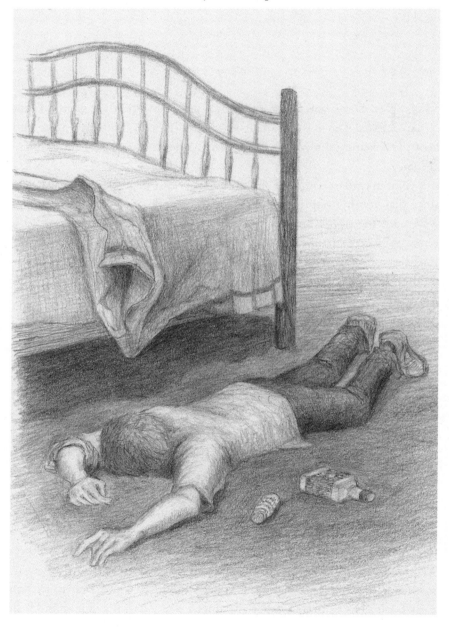

"Oh, my God!" David exclaimed as he entered Josh's bedroom. Josh was lying face down on the floor. Beside him were an open container of Prozac and an empty bottle of Jack Daniels. David rushed to his friend's side.

"Josh! Josh, are you all right?" he burst out, knowing in his heart that he wasn't.

Josh was completely limp. Frantically, David felt his pulse. It was there, but it was weak.

Scott grabbed his cell phone and dialed 911. Fifteen minutes later the police and an ambulance arrived. As soon as he entered the room, the leader of the ambulance squad quickly sized up the situation. "This is serious, boys – very serious. Prozac with alcohol is a dangerous combination."

"How dangerous?" David asked anxiously.

"Uh ... Let's just say we better not waste any time getting him to the hospital."

Opening her eyes from a good night's rest, Jennifer glanced at the computer on her desk and noticed that she had an email message.

"Oh, no! This is *terrible!*" she exclaimed as she opened it ...

```
    Jen
    josh is in the hospital. me and scott and johnny
found him in his room last night - it looks like
he od'd on his depression pills. i think it might
have been a suicide attempt!! i'll fill you in on
the details at church in the morning
    Dave
```

Jennifer and David arrived early at Grace Bible Church Sunday morning and as soon as they found one another they quickly hugged. David especially was pretty badly shaken by the events of the previous night.

"Have you heard anything this morning?" Jennifer asked.

"I called the hospital about an hour ago, and the woman I spoke to said that Josh was still in intensive care."

Jennifer paused before her next question. "You said in your email that you thought that what happened might not have been, uh ... an accident. Have you had any feedback about that?"

"Yeah, I have. I asked the leader of the ambulance squad, and he said that he couldn't say with any certainty, but that Prozac – the pills Josh was taking – was one of the drugs most commonly associated with suicide attempts, especially among teenagers. He added that it was especially dangerous when combined with alcohol."

"Was there any alcohol involved?"

"Yeah, there was an empty fifth of Jack Daniels lying next to him."

Suddenly, David saw Paul Hopkins walking into the sanctuary, and he called him over to tell him about Josh.

"That's really terrible," Paul declared, deeply concerned. "Listen, let's round up the youth group and go to our meeting room to pray about this."

"When do you want to meet?" David asked. "After church?"

"No – right now."

About ten minutes later, Paul, David, Jennifer, and eight other teens were gathered together in prayer for Josh. They were in their meeting room for about forty-five minutes, and for most of them it was the most intense prayer session they had ever participated in. One of the prayers was from Paul, asking God to forgive him for any role he may have played in Josh's crash. It wasn't the first time Paul had made this request.

As they were leaving, Paul stopped David to tell him something. "I'm going to go visit Josh as soon as I possibly can, Dave. If you see him before I do, tell him that we are all praying for him – and that we *really* care about him."

"Yeah, sure, Mr. Hopkins ... I sure will. I'll probably try to get over to the hospital this afternoon. Hey, by the way, I don't think you should feel guilty about this. What happened to Josh definitely wasn't your fault. He's been headed for some kind of a crash for a long time. In my opinion, it was sort of inevitable."

"Thanks, Dave. Thanks a lot. I needed that!" Paul replied with a warm smile, touched by David's insight and compassion.

Josh was in the hospital for three days. Due to the high level of fluoxetine in his system, his doctors determined that the event was very likely a suicide attempt. Based strictly on his physical condition, he could have gone home the next day. He was kept longer for observation.

Monday afternoon Paul stopped at the hospital to see Josh. It was obvious to Paul that Josh was still drained from the incident, so he made his visit brief.

"It looks like you could use a little rest, Josh, so I'll be taking off. How about if I stop in for a visit after you get home, towards the end of the week, perhaps?"

"Yeah, sure. That would be okay," Josh said, glad that Paul would be leaving. He was quite tired. Although Josh still harbored lingering resentment against Paul for the evening at the youth group, he had pretty much accepted that Paul's role in the incident was completely innocent. In fact, Josh was quite intrigued by Paul and, to his surprise, was looking forward to seeing him again.

Paul came to Josh's house the following Friday afternoon. Their conversation was a little awkward at first. It wasn't the first time that Paul had sat with a teenager who had attempted suicide, however, so he was able to relieve the tension quite quickly. After a few minutes, Josh steered the conversation to their recent meeting in town.

"Remember that conversation we had the other day in the Main Street Diner, when you told me that the Stanley Miller experiment was no longer relevant?"

"Yeah, sure I do," Paul replied.

"I gotta tell you, Mr. Hopkins, the more I thought about that, the more ticked off I got. How was I supposed to know that that experiment wasn't legitimate? There was a description of it, with a picture, right in our textbook, and our teacher never told us that there were any questions about it. I ended up looking like such a fool – and right in front of my *friends!* I can't get that awful evening out of my mind, man. It's like a *nightmare.*"

Paul could see that Josh's analysis of that fateful evening was exactly right. The memory of it was obviously plaguing his young friend. As it was with everyone, Paul's main goal in his relationship with Josh was to help break down the walls that separated him from God. Josh's comments had presented him with an opening.

"But you shouldn't blame yourself for what happened at that meeting, Josh. Think about it. You were presented incorrect information from sources that you had every reason to trust: your teacher, and more specifically, your textbook."

"*Incorrect information?* Our textbook claimed that that experiment essentially proved that amino acids could have formed in the early earth through purely random, natural events. Apparently that's not true. Let's call a spade a spade. It wasn't just incorrect information. It was a *lie,* Paul!"

Trying to be diplomatic, Paul replied, "I'm not sure 'lie' is exactly the right term here. Perhaps deception might be more accurate. I don't think ..."

"Deception, lie ... What's the difference? The point is that Miller rigged his experiment with a totally make-believe environment and conditions to achieve the end that he was looking for: amino acids. And then, ever since, innocent high school kids like me have been suckered into believing that this experiment proved that it was possible for life – or at least preorganic chemicals – to be created in a test tube. That's bullsh ... uh, just not right, man – not right *at all*."

"All right, Josh, I have to say that I agree with you. But you didn't know these things when we were discussing the experiment at the youth group. How could you? So, like I said, you shouldn't blame yourself for what happened. *It wasn't your fault.* You were working with bad information. You know the saying: garbage in, garbage out."

Josh took a long, hard look at Paul, and slowly nodded his head. He recognized that Paul was right – and he felt a weight lift from his shoulders.

"Thanks, Mr. Hopkins ... Thanks a lot," Josh said softly. "I really needed to hear that. I ..." Suddenly Josh became choked up and couldn't speak. Fighting to hold back tears, he turned away from Paul. Several seconds passed before he was able to continue.

"God, I was such an incredible jerk! Why did I ever do that – why, *why?*" he said, burying his head in his hands.

It was clear to Paul that his young friend was really hurting, and his heart went out to him. "*Please*, Josh – Don't feel guilty," he pleaded. "You were given bad information, so you mustn't ..."

"I'm not talking about what happened at that meeting. I'm talking about what I did *afterward* – last Saturday night!" As Josh blurted out these words, he burst into sobs. Paul rushed over and put his arms around him. He knew that what Josh needed right now wasn't words of wisdom. It was love, and Paul desperately wanted to provide it. Josh resisted for a moment, but soon gave in. Paul was offering him exactly what he needed.

"It's all right, Josh ... It's all right. Everything's going to be all right. I'm not leaving here until you're okay."

"But how ... how can I ever forgive myself, Mr. Hopkins? I tried to take my own *life!*" Josh cried out through his tears.

"I know you did, Josh, but it's over with now. It's in the past. Trust in God, my friend. He will forgive you, and then, through His strength and

His love, you will be able to forgive yourself. Trust me, Josh. You're going to be all right. Very often, people have to hit rock bottom before they finally want God in their lives. It's one of the ways God gets our attention … It's pretty effective, too!"

Wiping his tears with his shirt sleeve, Josh pulled away and gathered himself together. "But how can I ask God to forgive me? I don't even know Him. To be honest, I don't think I even *believe* in Him! How can I ask someone I don't even believe in to forgive me?"

"What's important, Josh, is not whether you *do* believe in God. What's important is whether or not you *want* to believe in Him."

Josh was confused. "But I can't *make* myself believe in God, no matter how much I *want* to. And even if I could, why would God want to have anything to do with someone who tried to *kill* himself?"

"That's a very good question," Paul replied, "and I'll try to answer it for you … but let's finish our discussion of belief first, because it's *really* important … You're all right now?"

"Yeah, I'm okay. Go ahead."

"Good. Now, like I was saying, the key question here is not whether or not you believe in God; it's whether or not you *want* to believe in Him. If you want to believe in Him, the Bible tells you exactly what you need to do to get this belief. If you follow these simple instructions, God will take care of the rest. He will create this belief in you. People don't have great faith in God *before* they reach out to Him, Josh. How can they have great faith in someone they are barely familiar with? They reach out to Him *first*, and then He provides them with faith … Does this make sense?"

"Actually, it does. Like you said, how can you possibly have faith in someone if you don't even know them … And, listen, I *do* want to believe in God. But exactly how do I reach out to Him? What are these instructions you were talking about?"

"The instructions are in the book of Romans: *If you confess with your mouth Jesus as Lord and believe in your heart that God raised Him from the dead, you shall be saved; for with the heart man believes, resulting in righteousness, and with the mouth he confesses, resulting in salvation.* According to this verse, in order to establish a permanent relationship with God, in order to reach out to Him, all you need to do is open your mouth and confess Jesus as your Lord. It doesn't say that you must gather as much information as you can about God and carefully weigh it to see whether you believe it or not, does it? It just says that you must open your mouth and confess Him as your Lord. Missionaries tell of people who make this confession the very first time they ever hear about God. The news they hear about Him rings true to them, and they immediately know that they need Him. So it's a simple choice. You can decide to either do this or not do it, at any moment. Believe me, Josh, you don't need any more information about God in order to make this decision. You have more than you need right now. To think that you need more information, or more time to think things over, or that you need to straighten your life up or start to read the Bible, etc.… All of these things are simply excuses, planted in your mind by the devil, to prevent you from making the simple confession presented in that verse in Romans. As the Bible says, *Today is the day of salvation.*"

"But wait a second," Josh protested. "According to that verse, there are *two* things you must do: confess with your mouth Jesus as Lord *and* believe in your heart that God raised Him from the dead. Even if I do the first thing, confess Jesus as my Lord, I'm not sure that I believe the second thing – that God raised Him from the dead. So where would that leave me? Would I be, like, *half* saved?"

"A very good question … and here's the answer. In response to this verse, the only thing that *you* can control is the confession of Jesus as your Lord. Anyone who *wants to* can make the decision to open their mouth and confess Jesus Christ as their Lord. Nothing can stop them, except their own will. As far as believing in the Resurrection is concerned, don't worry about it. God knows that from a human perspective that's a very difficult thing to accept. He will take care of that requirement *after* you ask Him to be your Lord. You do your part, and God will handle the rest. You make the confession, and He will give you belief in the Resurrection. Imagine that someone *really* wanted to have a relationship with God, and *really* wanted to accept Jesus Christ as their Lord and Savior, but was uncertain about the Resurrection. Do you think that an all-loving God would fold His arms and refuse this person's petition until he believed in the Resurrection with all of his heart? Doesn't that seem pretty ridiculous? … So, then, reaching out to God is really very simple, Josh."

Josh nodded. "Yeah, it sure is – almost too simple, I'd say. If it's that simple, why doesn't everyone just do it?"

"Because they *choose* not to. Take yourself, for example. You said a moment ago that you want to believe in God, right?"

"Yeah, I guess I did."

"Okay. Well, you just found out what you need to do: open your mouth and confess Jesus Christ as your Lord and Savior. Simple, right?"

"Right."

"Then why don't you do it – right now?"

Josh smiled. "Uh, right this minute? ... I don't think so. I need to think it over. Maybe later. I get your point, though: it's up to me – It's my choice. I promise, though: I'll give it some serious thought – really, I mean it. Now, what about my other question: why would God want to have anything to do with someone who attempted to take his own life? Isn't that breaking one of the Ten Commandments: *Thou shalt not murder*? How can God forgive something as awful as that?"

"What you did was wrong, Josh, no question about it. But *everyone* does things wrong. That's the main reason God provided the Ten Commandments: to prove to people that it's impossible to live a sinless life. The Bible says that we're all sinners and fall short of the glory of God. In God's eyes a sin is a sin. To Him there's no difference between lying, stealing, or murder. It's all sin, and He hates all of it. But the wonderful news of the gospel is that as much as God hates sin, He will forgive it – *all* of it."

"You mean he'll forgive *anything* – even ... even what I did?"

"That's right: *anything*. All you have to do is ask Him. Look, Moses, one of the greatest men in the Bible, committed murder. And I guarantee that he'll be spending eternity in heaven! Paul might have, too, and he wrote about half of the books in the New Testament. The apostle John writes, *If we confess our sins, He is faithful and righteous to forgive us our sins and to cleanse us from all unrighteous.* In fact, he takes this notion a step further. He says that if we say that we haven't sinned, we are deceiving ourselves and the truth is not in us. You know, Josh, from the world's perspective, attempting suicide is pretty horrifying. But, like I just told you, from God's perspective, it's no worse than any other sin. Maybe you needed to commit a really obvious sin in order for God to get your attention. Have you ever heard the saying, 'the strongest steel must go through the fire?' Well, my friend, I think you've just been through the fire – and now, just like a sword of tempered steel, you're ready for the battles that may be looming in your future ... or, I should say, *almost* ready."

"What do you mean *almost* ready?"

"The confession I just told you about. Remember?"

"Oh yeah. The one in the book of Romans … Okay, I think I'm getting the picture," Josh continued. "But what about those battles you mentioned. What did you have in mind?"

"Oh, nothing in particular. Everyone goes through battles in their lives. You've had yours, and you'll be having more."

"Yeah, I guess you're right … Say, I've been thinking about something and wanted to make sure that I asked you about it while you were here. I understand now that there are some serious problems with the Stanley Miller experiment, but you said that you didn't believe in *anything* about the theory of evolution. That seems pretty radical to me. I mean, I can see that it's not perfect. But to reject it *entirely* … I don't get it. Are you rejecting it primarily because of your faith – your belief in the Bible – or because of the evidence?"

"It's a little of both. First of all, the theory definitely does directly contradict the biblical account of creation. But, then, I don't believe that the scientific evidence supports it, either."

"How does it contradict the Bible?"

"In a number of ways. For example, the Bible states that God created the world in six days, and according to evolution the process took – shall we say – a little longer."

Josh chuckled. "Yeah, like about a few *billion* times longer! Hey, that reminds me of something else I've been wondering about. Does the theory of evolution refer just to the evolution of life, or to the evolution of the whole world from the very beginning – like, from the Big Bang? Mr. Potter said in one of our classes recently that technically the theory of evolution applies only to the development of life, but that sure doesn't seem to be what the authors of our textbook believe. The way it describes the Big Bang, and then the formation of the stars and the galaxies and the solar system and the earth, and then the evolution of life, it seems like it's all part of one seamless evolutionary process. What do you think?"

"That's an important question. Before I try to answer it, though, let's be clear that there's a difference between what people might *say* about this issue, on the one hand, and what they actually believe and what you learn in school, on the other. Just because a person *says* that the theory of evolution applies only to the development of life doesn't mean that it actually does, or even that they believe that it does … Let me try to show you what I mean. Ask yourself this question: if someone says that evolution applies only to the development of life, what does this imply about what happened in the world *prior* to this point?"

"Uhh … I guess it implies that prior to the origin of life, the world must *not* have developed by means of evolution," Josh replied with a shrug of his shoulders, uncertain about where Paul was headed here.

"Exactly. And if it did not *evolve*, then how did it develop?"

"I don't know. I never really thought about it. Like I just told you, the only thing I've ever heard is that it did evolve."

"All right. I think we need a little background here. Technically, evolution can be split into two major categories. The evolution of nonliving things is called inorganic evolution and the evolution of living things is called organic evolution. The first category covers the development of the world prior to the origin of life and according to evolutionary theory lasts about eleven or twelve billion years. The second covers the evolution of life, which supposedly lasted about two or three billion years, perhaps longer."

"You say 'supposedly' lasted two or three billion years. Apparently, you don't believe in this time scale, eh?"

"No, I don't. But let's save that discussion for later. For now, let's stick to our topic … So, what I was saying about organic and inorganic evolution – does it sound familiar? Did you hear this in your biology class?"

"Yeah, I guess so. I remember the terms *organic evolution* and *inorganic evolution*, but the distinction between them wasn't made as clear as you just did – or maybe I wasn't paying attention when Mr. Potter went over that stuff."

Paul smiled. "None of us are perfect, eh? Anyway, here are two important truths that you need to be aware of. First, the theory of evolution is based entirely upon the completely random interaction of *natural* events – upon chance, in other words. This belief is fundamental to the theory, its cornerstone, if you will. The word 'natural' is critical in this description. It limits the events to those that are *entirely within the natural world*. By definition, then, it completely excludes any intervention of a being that exists *outside* this world – of anything *supernatural*, in other words. The plain truth is that the main purpose of the theory of evolution, the main reason it exists, is to explain how the world evolved *naturally*."

"Without any help from God, in other words?"

"To be precise, from God or from any other supernatural Being. The second truth is that aside from chance there is *only one* other possible cause for the world, and for life: design. Because of this, the world must have come into being either by chance – which is equivalent to evolution – or by design. That's it. There are no other alternatives."

"Wait a second," Josh spoke up. "I'm not so sure I buy that. Are you *sure* there are no other possibilities? It seems like there must be."

"Well, go ahead. Give it your best shot. See if you can think of any."

After a couple of minutes of discussion, Josh saw that Paul was right, and Paul proceeded with his argument.

"Now, given this background, let me ask you the question I asked before: if prior to the origin of life, the world did not develop by means of evolution, how did it develop?"

"Based upon what you were just saying, it must have been created supernaturally. Apparently, it's the only other possibility."

"That's right. So then, let me ask you another question: do you think that this is what your teacher and the authors of your textbook believe?"

"You mean that prior to the origin of life the world was created supernaturally?"

"Right."

"I think I'd have to give that a negative."

"Why?"

"They never suggest it. If they never suggest it, they must not believe it."

"Of course. It's obvious, Josh. The authors of your textbook clearly believe that the world evolved, from the very beginning, entirely through random natural events. And I guarantee you that this belief is shared by the vast majority of people who believe in the theory, including your teacher – *no matter what they say.*

"So that's it, Josh. Your question has been answered. The *real* theory of evolution, the one promoted in your science class, applies to the entire development of the world, from the very beginning, and any true evolutionist who claims otherwise is either not being honest or he hasn't thoroughly thought through his position.

"Let me just say one more thing about this subject. There's one more reason for rejecting the idea that prior to the origin of life the world was created supernaturally and afterward it evolved by chance: common sense. Think about it. If you accept the evolutionary time scale – like anyone who believes in evolution would, of course – this would mean that God spent about eleven or twelve billion years creating the universe and then, two or three billion years ago, just before life began, He completely checked out of the scene and left everything up to chance. Seriously, does that make one bit of sense?"

"Maybe He never really left. Maybe before He checked out He designed the process of evolution to create life on earth and then, like, oversaw the process – you know, from a distance."

Paul was very familiar with this idea – theistic evolution – and it was very popular among Christians, certainly in liberal churches, but increasingly among evangelicals, also. He felt that it was a major cause of the erosion of faith in the Christian community.

"That idea is called theistic evolution. People who believe it don't understand what I just explained to you, that the very foundation of the theory of evolution is *naturalism* – random *natural* events, in other words – and that *by definition* this process absolutely and totally excludes anything supernatural. Like I said, *if anything supernatural is included in evolution, it's no longer evolution.* Sadly, people who believe in theistic evolution simply don't understand this very basic truth. They're living in a fantasy world."

Paul could see that Josh was getting tired and thought he'd better bring his visit to a close. "Listen, I'd love to discuss this with you more completely, but we've gone over a lot today, and I think maybe we should save that discussion for another day. Is that all right with you?"

"Yeah, sure. You're right. We have covered a lot of ground, and I'm pretty wiped out."

Josh paused for a moment.

"I'll tell you, Mr. Hopkins. What you're saying about these things definitely seems to make sense – a lot of it, in fact – but it's so contradictory to what I've been learning in school about evolution. Man, I don't know what to do! I gotta tell you, I'm really confused."

"I know it's confusing, Josh. Believe me; I was exactly in your place several years ago."

"Oh yeah? What did you do about it?"

"Well, for one thing, I investigated these things on my own."

"Yeah? What else?"

"Along the way, I got things straightened out with God."

"Like what you were telling me a few minutes ago, eh? Asking Jesus to be your Lord?"

"That's right. You see, in trying to wind your way through this minefield, ultimately what you are searching for is the Truth. And Jesus *is* the Truth. In

John 14:6, He says, *I am the way and the truth and the life*. So, if you have Him on your side, your search for the truth will be a whole lot easier."

"All right," Josh replied. "Suppose I did want to investigate these things on my own. You got any suggestions about where I should look?"

"Sure. Sure I do. There's an organization called Answers in Genesis that has a great Web site, www.answersingenesis.org. Go to Google and type in aig, or go to answersingenesis.org. Institute for Creation Research, ICR, is another great creationist organization. Creation Ministries International is also very good. I have a bunch of books about the subject. I'll pick a few out and bring them over. If you want any help, I'll be more than happy to help you in any way I can. And I'll guarantee you one thing, Josh. If you honestly seek the truth with all of your heart, you will find it."

Josh took a long hard look at Paul and slowly nodded his head. He sensed that Paul was indeed telling him the truth. "I might just take you up on your suggestion… Yeah, I might just do that."

"You should. I'm sure you would find the search to be most interesting and rewarding. Let me mention one more thing before I leave. If you decide to make the spiritual commitment we were talking about – you know, accepting Christ as your Lord – please make sure you let me know about it."

"I don't know, Paul. When it comes to things like that – you know, really personal things – I like to keep my feelings to myself. We'll just have to see what happens, okay?"

"Sure. That's fine. Anyway, if you have any questions about that matter, don't hesitate to get in touch with me, any time of the day or night."

Before he left, Paul thought about going over one more topic that had come up in their conversation, the Big Bang, but he decided that it would be better to save it for another day. It was a wise decision. Josh really needed some rest.

So, after a brief prayer, Paul departed.

13

Josh Searches for the Truth

The next day Paul stopped over to see Josh again.

"I brought you something," he said as he handed Josh a gift. It was a Bible.

Surprised, Josh fumbled for words. "Thanks. Uhh … thanks a lot. I have to tell you, though … I've never really read the Bible. In fact, I hardly know anything about it." Flipping through the pages of the massive book, he added, "I wouldn't even know where to begin."

"Why don't you come back to the youth group? We read something from the Bible there every week."

"Uhh … No, I don't think so. After what happened the last time I was there I don't know if I could ever show my face there again. That's just not gonna happen."

"All right. We'll see about that. In any event, I'd be happy to start a Bible study with just the two of us if you'd like. What do you say?"

"Yeah, maybe. I'll think about it. I'd kind of like to check it out on my own first, though. Do you read it like a novel – you know, starting at page one?"

Sensitive to Josh's Jewish heritage, Paul replied, "Some people do. Personally, I think that's an excellent place to start. The book of Genesis. It begins with the story of creation and then goes on to describe many other fascinating and well-known stories, like Noah's Ark, the Tower of Babel, and the amazing tale of Joseph and his family, a saga some scholars have called the greatest story in all literature. Alternate with readings from the New Testament … one book in the Old Testament, one in the New."

"What are the Testaments?"

Paul proceeded to provide Josh with a brief description of the Bible, including its chronology, authors, and purpose. A short while later, he left.

Shortly after Paul left, Josh opened the Bible on his own for the first time in his life. As Paul had suggested, he started at the beginning: *"In the beginning God created the heavens and the earth."* - Genesis 1:1, the most widely read ten words in the history of the world. The dramatic difference between the account of creation in Genesis and the one he had learned in school was quickly apparent to Josh. One was orchestrated by a Creator, the other by chance. One lasted six days, the other several billion years. In one account the earth came into existence after the sun and the stars; in the other, it preceded them. Josh wondered if there was any way these startling differences could be reconciled. Unless the biblical account was a myth – like the Greek myths he had studied in history class – he couldn't imagine how. That two such profoundly different theories could both be believed by intelligent people was a mystery to him. He was very intrigued.

The next morning Josh was sitting at the breakfast table having a bowl of cereal and rereading the first chapter of Genesis when his father walked into the room.

"Hey, Dad," Josh said in a surprised tone. "What are you doing home? I thought you got to your office about seven-thirty every morning. It's like after nine."

"I had some things I had to take care of at home this morning. I'm running a little late." After a pause, Benjamin asked his son a question: "What are you reading?"

"Oh, this?" Josh asked somewhat defensively. "Uh … it's just a, um, a Bible. I'm just checking a few things out. No big deal."

Benjamin was surprised at Josh's choice of reading material, for he had never seen Josh read the Bible, especially the one he was reading, which was obviously brand new.

"That's a little surprising. I didn't know you were interested in the Bible. Where did you get it?"

Josh was a little uneasy at his father's questioning. He knew that his father didn't read the Scriptures much himself, but that wasn't the problem. The problem was that the Bible Josh was reading was a Christian Bible, and his family was Jewish. If he was going to read a Bible, he knew that his father would want it to be a Hebrew Bible – the Old Testament in the Christian Bible. Josh knew that although his parents were liberal in regards to their religious beliefs, they nevertheless believed that there were boundaries that should not be crossed – and Josh knew that he had crossed one.

"A friend gave it to me," Josh said evasively.

"What friend?" his father probed.

"His name is Paul Hopkins. He stopped over yesterday to see how I was doing. He's a really nice guy, Dad. I'm sure you'd like him."

"What kind of a Bible is it? And who is this Paul fellow? "

"It's, uh, a ... a Christian Bible. There's some stuff that he thought I might be interested in ... and, you know, he was right. I am."

Now Benjamin was concerned. "Like what? What are you reading?"

"I followed Paul's suggestion. I started at the beginning, Genesis."

"Genesis, eh? That's good," Benjamin replied, slightly relieved. "Same book our Bible starts with. *In the beginning God created the heavens and the earth*, right?"

Josh smiled. "Hey, not bad, Dad. I didn't know you were a Bible scholar!"

"A Bible scholar I'm not, Josh," his father chuckled. "That's probably the only verse in the Bible I have memorized. But, listen, what do you find so interesting about Genesis? It's basically just a myth about how God created the world, along with some other stories, I guess."

"Well, to tell you the truth, I'm not sure about that, Dad. Some people think that it's the literal truth and that ..."

"Oh, come on, Josh! That's ridiculous! It says that the world was created in six days and that God made Eve from Adam's rib and other things like that. Those things *can't* be literally true. It's utterly impossible."

"Why, Dad? Why is it impossible?"

"Come on, Josh! Haven't you been paying attention in your science classes? The world is about fifteen billion years old and it took *billions of years,* not *six days,* for all of these things to happen. The only people who believe otherwise are these Christian fundamentalists who have buried their heads in the sand in their effort to maintain their hopelessly outdated faith. By the way ... your friend Paul ... He's not one of these fundamentalists, is he?"

"Uh, I don't know," Josh lied. "I don't really know him very well. All I know is that he sure has been supportive in the past few days. He's called me about three times and visited yesterday for about an hour. The only other person who has been over is Dave."

"Well, I'm glad for that. But you'd better be careful and check out his beliefs before you get any closer to him. These fundamentalists are nuts, if you ask me. I sure don't want you to get involved with any of them. You understand?"

"Yeah, sure, Dad. Don't worry. I can look out for myself."

Thinking about his son's recent suicide attempt, Benjamin was going to question Josh's last statement, but he thought better of it. "All right. Well, I have to get going now. Take it easy and have a good day, Josh. I'll see you tonight ... One more thing – don't spend too long on that Bible. If you're really interested in reading the Bible, read ours. Your mother can probably find it for you."

"Don't worry, Dad. I won't. I got other things I want to do. You have a good day, too."

As his father walked out the door, Josh's eyes followed him. He suspected that in regards to his opinions about the creation, his father was just parroting things he had been exposed to in the popular media, and in school – that he had not critically investigated the subject on his own, in other words. He certainly couldn't remember the two of them ever discussing the subject, or his father even mentioning it. As he was thinking these things, it struck him that he really wasn't much different from his father when it came to this topic. Until very recently, he, too, had accepted uncritically what he had learned about evolution. The only difference between him and his father in regards to this subject was that because of the things that he had recently been exposed to – in particular what he had learned about the Stanley Miller experiment – his belief in the theory of evolution was now tempered by doubt.

These doubts were nagging at him, calling for his attention. He recalled his recent conversation with Paul, in which Paul told him about his decision several years ago to investigate the subject of origins on his own and about the impact this investigation had had on his life. And he remembered Paul suggesting that such an investigation might benefit him, also. Paul's words flashed through his mind: *I'll guarantee you one thing, Josh. If you honestly seek the truth with all of your heart, you will find it.* Josh knew that Paul was right. Even though his exposure to creationism had been very brief, it was perfectly clear to him that the two accounts of origins were radically different and unless the biblical account was only a myth – not to be taken as literal truth, in other words, as his father believed – there was no way these competing theories could be harmonized; they were utterly contradictory. Only one of them could be true. Actually, as Paul had pointed out, since chance and design were the only two realistic explanations for the existence of the world, one of them *must* be true. Josh could not wait. He had to know which one it was. His investigation had to begin immediately.

While polishing off a second bowl of cereal, he thought over the first question he needed to address: Should his investigation start at the beginning of the universe or at the origin of life? He thought back to his recent conversation with Paul regarding inorganic versus organic evolution, and he recalled Paul arguing that the theory of evolution applies not only to the development of life but to the development of the whole natural world, beginning with the Big Bang. Paul had pointed out that evolutionists often dispute this notion, arguing that evolutionary theory addresses only the development of life, not the events prior to this point. Superficially, this claim appears to leave the door open for the possibility that prior to the origin of life the world was created. According to Paul, however, this is just a facade. He remembered Paul's words: *At least it's not supported by any evolutionary literature. Look at it. None of it supports such an idea. All of it is based upon the proposition that evolution began at the very beginning, at the Big Bang. Look at their textbooks. Do any of them say, "In the beginning God created the heavens and the earth, and once He created life, evolution took over?"* The answer was obvious. Of course they didn't. Josh found Paul's argument very convincing. His starting point, then, was clear: the Big Bang.

His plan of attack was simple. Beginning with the Big Bang he would carefully research the popular account of evolution, the one that he had learned in school and that was so widely championed in the media, to see if he could discover any serious flaws or problems. He had already been exposed to one: the Stanley Miller experiment. He wanted to find out if there were others. Of course, he had already studied much of this material in his science classes, but in those studies he hadn't approached the material critically. He had just been absorbing information, without ever questioning its truthfulness. This study was going to be a lot different. This time he would be examining every step along the way through the critical eye of a skeptical judge.

The theory of evolution was about to go on trial. The goal was to resolve a simple question: is it true?

Starting with Big Bang, Josh determined to search hard for flaws in the theory, for reasons to doubt it. If the theory withstood this examination, the credibility of creationism would be severely shaken. Among other things, since the Big Bang postulates that the world began about fourteen billion years ago, it would render absurd the idea that the world was created in six days a few thousand years ago, as Paul taught that the Bible claims. It would demonstrate that the biblical account of creation could not be literally true and would preclude the need for any further investigation. It occurred to Josh that if he had undertaken this study a short while ago, that is exactly the result he would have expected. Now, though, because of the things he had been exposed to in the past few weeks, he wasn't so sure. His faith in evolution had developed a few cracks. Creationism had slipped its foot into the door.

His study began that very morning. He had plenty of resources available, including his science textbook, a few books which he owned, some books Paul loaned him, and, of course, the Internet. Furthermore, he had access to a wealth of material at the UNH library in Durham, which has a particularly strong science section. He figured the study might last a few days, maybe even a week. Determined to discover the truth, he wasn't going to rush.

Concerning the Big Bang, it was clear to Josh that aside from some Christians, like Paul and some of the others in the youth group, most people believed that the theory is very securely established as a scientific fact. After all, that is the way it is presented in his science textbook and from just about every other source he had ever seen. Before long, though, he discovered that the theory did have a little competition, such as the steady state theory. Developed in 1948 by Fred Hoyle, Thomas Gold, and Hermann Bondi, this idea was once very popular. Its central premise is that the universe is eternal. Its creators accepted the firmly established notion that the universe is expanding, but this presented them with a difficult problem: if an eternal universe is expanding and the matter within it is finite, in time the matter would become so far apart that space would be virtually empty. In fact, it probably should have become empty already. They came up with a unique solution: in order to assure that the average density of matter remained equal over time, they speculated that new matter, mainly hydrogen atoms, was continuously being created – out of nothing.

That was all Josh needed to know about the steady state theory. *Hydrogen atoms created* <u>*out of nothing*</u>*! No way. Something can't be created out of nothing. No wonder this theory is no longer popular.*

Next, he came across the multiverse theory. The catalyst for this theory, Josh discovered, is the fact that our universe, particularly our solar system and the planet earth, appears to be designed, or fine-tuned, especially for life. One example of this is the earth's place in the solar system. If we were much further from the sun, our planet's water would freeze; if we were much closer, it would boil. It appears, in other words, that the earth is located in exactly the right place for life.

Josh found out that there are many other similar examples of apparent design in the universe, far too many, it seems, to be attributed entirely to coincidence. The conclusion from these things appears to be obvious: the universe is designed. To those whose world view is built upon the foundation of naturalism, however, this conclusion is unacceptable. Their world view has no room for a designer.

To overcome this roadblock, the multiverse theory was created. It offers believers in naturalism a solution to their dilemma: It eliminates the need for a designer. The idea is actually quite simple. If there are an infinite number of universes, then there would be an infinite number of possible options for these universes – including ours! Sort of like, if you could possess an infinite number of lottery tickets, you'd always win. Not exactly rocket science.

Josh quickly grasped the logic behind this theory, but he realized that there was a major problem with it: It is not supported by a scintilla of real evidence. The alternate universes are entirely imaginary. As far as he was concerned, it seemed obvious that the theory exists for one reason and one reason only: to avoid the conclusion that the world was designed. To him, the theory wasn't scientific. It wasn't even science fiction. At least science fiction has some basis in reality. It was more like magic, like pulling a rabbit out of a hat. He was amazed at the crazy ideas people could dream up to avoid something that seemed so obvious.

He slowly shook his head in dismay. *Hydrogen atoms created from nothing, an infinite number of imaginary universes. If these two theories are the best the competition has to offer, no wonder the Big Bang theory is so popular*, he mused.

As Josh turned his attention to the Big Bang, an immediate question arose: Supposedly, the Big Bang was a humungous explosion that launched the universe … What exploded? That is, what was there an instant before the Big Bang, and where did it come from? It didn't take him long to discover the answer that was proposed to these questions. But he could hardly believe it. Supposedly, an instant before the Big Bang all the matter in the entire universe was condensed into a space no larger than an apple, or perhaps an atom – or even a space that was *infinitely small*. As one writer suggested, "Our universe is thought to have begun as an infinitesimally small, infinitely hot, infinitely dense entity, called a singularity."

Wow, Josh thought. *All the matter in the entire universe squeezed into a space no larger than an atom – or something even smaller! In the natural world, that seems totally inconceivable. I wonder why I never heard about that in my science class. Maybe I was absent that day. Or maybe we never went over it … Or maybe my teacher didn't want to mention it … I can't say that I'd blame him. I wouldn't have wanted to, either.*

To Josh, aside from the intervention of a Being with supernatural powers, someone that had the power to do *anything* – like, the ultimate Superman, or God – this hypothesis made absolutely no sense. He remembered learning in biology class, for example, that a human body contains fifty to a hundred trillion cells, each of which contains ten trillion or more atoms. Thus, to squeeze all of the cells of a single human body – which would be approximately 1,000,000,000,000,000,000,000,000,000 atoms – into a single atom through natural forces alone seemed entirely inconceivable to him. *But if this seems impossible*, he thought, *what about the notion of squeezing all of the matter of the entire universe – a hundred billion galaxies each containing a hundred billion stars, or more – into such a space?*

Soon he learned that he wasn't the only one who thought this idea was impossible. Big Bang proponents recognized it, too. And they proposed a solution. Utilizing Einstein's famous equation, $E = MC^2$, which indicates that under certain conditions there is an equivalency between matter and energy, they propose that the original matter, the stuff in the singularity that existed prior to the explosion, rather than being *matter* was *energy* – "pure, pent-up, exquisitely hot energy," as one writer put it.

Josh quickly recognized the supposition that this notion required: energy doesn't occupy any space. If this is true, of course, then all the matter in the universe could indeed fit into a single atom. The question, of course, is, "Is it true?" Josh didn't think so. Here is what he reasoned: Even though energy, unlike matter – except for light – is intangible, it seemed to Josh that it must require space in order to exist. *Surely,* he reasoned, *energy can't exist in nothing, which is essentially what the singularity was – especially all of the energy in the entire universe!*

Naturally, Josh wondered what the evidence is for this astonishing idea. He found that it is supposedly supported by advanced mathematics, and after some digging, he located some of these formulas and equations. Unfortunately, as good as he was at math – and he was *very* good – much of what he located was over his head. Some of the calculations even utilized equations from Einstein's theory of relativity. Nevertheless, he was leery of their accuracy. To him, it strained credulity to the breaking point. He thought it would take a lot more than mathematical equations to squeeze all of the matter of the universe into an atom naturally – even if some of the equations were Einstein's!

Even though he wasn't able to grasp much of the mathematics, however, he certainly recognized at least one glaring flaw in the logic behind the theory. He knew that a scientific theory is "an explanation or model based on observation, experimentation, and reasoning, especially one that has been tested and confirmed as a general principle helping to explain and predict natural phenomena." He also knew that the tests that underpinned a theory must be repeatable. The problem this presented for the Big Bang theory was obvious: whatever it might have been, it certainly was not observed, and it surely can't be tested, because it can't be repeated!

Even if everything in the singularity was energy, Josh realized that there would still be a critical question that remained unanswered: What was the cause of the original energy?

This question brought to his mind the words he had read earlier that day in the Bible: "In the beginning God created the heavens and the earth" … *creation ex nihilo* – creation out of nothing. Of course, he realized that this verse wouldn't answer this question for Big Bang proponents, because their theory strictly excluded God. As Paul had made clear, according to them everything in nature must be explained by *natural* laws and processes.

Hardly surprisingly, the notion of God being the ultimate source of the creation raised another question in Josh's mind: *What, or who, created God?* For an answer he once again turned to the omniscient answering machine: Google. The best answer he found was from a creationist Web site. It was from the Bible, in Psalm 90. According to it, no one created God; He is eternal:

> *Lord, Thou hast been our dwelling place in all generations.*
> *Before the mountains were born,*
> *Or Thou didst give birth to the earth and the world,*
> *Even from everlasting to everlasting, Thou art God.*

Josh wasn't sure he accepted this answer, but he did think it was better than the explanation offered by the Big Bang theory for the origin of the world, which is that the matter, or energy, in the singularity that existed prior to the Big Bang evolved from nothing. He had no idea how God could have existed forever, but he did know that matter could not have evolved from nothing through natural processes because it would violate one of nature's fundamental laws, the first law of thermodynamics, which declares that according to natural processes neither matter nor energy can be either created or destroyed. Nothing comes from nothing.

In addition to the mathematics that supposedly justified all the matter of the universe being squeezed into an atom prior to the Big Bang, another evidence of the Big Bang that Josh came across was the so-called microwave background radiation, or MBR, that is coming in from all parts of the universe. Supposedly, this radiation is the left-over heat of the Big Bang. However, according to at least some scientists, Josh discovered, the notion has a critical flaw: wherever this radiation has been measured, it has been found to be extremely uniform, and this is not consistent with the fact that the matter and energy in the universe is *not* uniform. Rather, it is "clumpy," composed of endless intermittent galaxies and voids. If the Big Bang theory was true, there should be a correlation between the material composition of the universe and the corresponding radiation, because everything emits thermal heat. Although the criticism of the background radiation theory made sense to Josh, it was apparent that critics of the theory are definitely in the minority. He determined that he probably should spend more time investigating it. Maybe he was missing something.

Not now, though. He had spent almost two days, about twenty hours, investigating the Big Bang and the origin of the universe. Although he had uncovered some very problematic details connected to the theory, his study of inorganic evolution was hardly finished. In fact, it had just begun. He still had to investigate the evolution of the stars, the galaxies, the planets, and the solar system. This would have to wait, though. It was almost eleven p.m. He was tired and hungry. He was going to the Main Street Diner for a bite to eat and then to his home for a good night's rest.

Josh returned to the library at a little after nine o'clock the following morning. As he looked into the evolution of the stars and galaxies, he discovered that according to evolutionary theory, after the Big Bang the universe eventually began to be filled with the two simplest elements, first hydrogen and then helium. At various locations, for some inexplicable reason, these gases supposedly became particularly dense. As the density reached a critical point, so the story goes, gravity took over and contracted these huge masses of hydrogen and helium into stars.

Josh sensed a problem. From everything he had learned, under natural conditions gases always tend to expand or disperse, not contract. In nature, in other words, whether currently or fifteen billion years ago, apart from some external force or pressure, without being confined in some sort of enclosure, it doesn't seem possible that gases could ever contract and become a star. Just like the mathematical support for the compaction of matter into an atom prior to the Big Bang, Josh discovered that this contraction of gas into stars was also supported supposedly by very advanced mathematics. Not all authors accepted these formulas, however. Apparently acknowledging that gas in free space cannot come together unless it is confined, these people suggested that the gases may have been squeezed together by a mighty force, exploding stars called supernovas.

Josh tried to imagine this scenario. He envisioned the hugest explosion he could think of, like millions of hydrogen bombs, in outer space in the vicinity of a massive gas cloud. According to the theory, the force of this explosion would slam the atoms of the gas cloud together and create a new star.

No matter how hard he tried, Josh could not possibly imagine the proposed result. The way he saw it, an explosion near a gas cloud in free space could never *compact* the gas. It would blow it to smithereens!

*Who ever heard of an explosion blowing things **together**?* He wondered. *Explosions blow things **apart**!*

Quickly, Josh recognized another problem with this exploding-star theory. If star formation required the external pressure of a nearby exploding star, where did the *original* exploding star come from? In his research, the few authors who proposed this idea never addressed this problem.

Josh turned his attention to the origin of the solar system. He had learned at school that the most popular theory for this event is the nebula theory, which proposes that the solar system condensed from a large, lumpy cloud of gas and dust. Supposedly, for some reason this nebula began to condense, or pull together, under the force of its own gravity. After awhile, this mass began to spin, which in time made the material around the center flatten out into a disk-like shape. Over time the gas and dust particles in this disk supposedly came together to make tiny particles, which gradually joined with other particles, making larger and larger objects. Eventually these objects became the planets. One of them was the earth. The rest of the story, Josh knew, linked inorganic to organic evolution … A couple of billion years after the earth cooled the first cell evolved, and a few billion years after that McDonalds gave birth to the Big Mac.

This description was too much for Josh. It just seemed like an imaginative fairy tale to get from point A, in which the only thing that existed in the universe was stars, to point B, in which the solar system exists. As far as he was concerned, the idea didn't seem to have any basis in reality. Just because particles are in the vicinity of one another does not mean that they will begin to stick together. *If this was true*, he mused, *we wouldn't have any beaches to enjoy, because all the sand would have turned into concrete!*

As he was looking into the evolution of stars, he was reminded that, according to astronomers, the light from distant stars is supposedly millions, or even billions, of years old – which implies, of course, that the stars are that old, too. A thought flashed into his mind: *Doesn't that completely invalidate the creationists' claim that the world is only a few thousand years old?* Recognizing the dramatic potential impact that this notion could have upon the study he had embarked upon – bluntly put, it could end the study before it had barely begun – Josh immediately directed his attention to it. He became totally immersed in this investigation for the remainder of the day, and most of the next one.

By late afternoon the following day, Josh concluded that this question of starlight and time and the age of stars was far too complex for him to achieve anything more than a superficial understanding of it at this point. After all, PhD programs were devoted to this subject. Countless books were written about it. He had only spent less than two days looking into it. The literature about it was replete with complicated mathematical equations, including differential and integral calculus, advanced statistical analysis, etc., much of which was not familiar to him. It also included esoteric concepts such as black holes, white holes, dark matter and dark energy, time dilation, horizon events and many other unfamiliar terms. Although he was well aware that he had barely scratched the surface of this absorbing subject, he did come across a few scientists like Dr. Russell Humphreys and Dr. John Hartnett, who had developed fascinating theories that suggested how the great apparent age of stars and starlight could be harmonized with the young age of the world implied in the Bible. A key feature of these theories is the fact that time is affected by gravity and that this fact can have a dramatic effect upon calculations of the age of distant objects in the universe. This idea is called "time dilation," and it was originally proposed by Einstein in his theory of relativity.

Fundamental to the theories of Humphries and Hartnett, and which Josh found very interesting, is the hypothesis that the earth is at, or very close to, the center of the universe. Their notions regarding time dilation require this condition, in fact. According to the Big Bang theory, on the other hand, the universe is not expanding out from a center into space; rather, the whole universe is expanding and it is supposedly doing so equally at all places, as far as can be determined. To Josh, based upon Big Bang cosmology, in which the universe began at a particular point in space – the singularity that supposedly existed prior to the initial explosion – the notion that the universe had no center didn't seem to make sense. *If everything exploded uniformly from a particular point, the singularity*, he thought, *wouldn't that be the center of the universe?*

While reflecting upon the Big Bang, something curious occurred to Josh: among those who claim to believe in creation, some are very critical of the Big Bang theory, whereas others, including many followers of Intelligent Design and theistic evolution, appear to embrace it. Some in the latter group even take it a step further. They believe that the Big Bang is actually a boon to creationism, because it allegedly provides, for the first time, scientific evidence corroborating the creation account in the book of Genesis; to be specific, it proves that the universe had a beginning. The reason this is supposedly so special is that, again for the first time, it repudiates the ancient rival of creationism, the eternal universe theory, on the basis of scientific, rather than philosophical or theological, evidence. Finally, its supporters claim, at least in relation to creation, science and religion are no longer at odds.

Hmmm, Josh reflected – *I guess these folks must believe that the first verse of the Bible is somehow a reference to the Big Bang – pretty wild.*

Briefly, Josh thought this idea was kind of interesting. With a little more thought, however, his interest quickly waned. He decided that these people were making too much out of the notion that the universe had a beginning. *After all,* he mused, *everything in the world has to have a beginning … So what's the big deal about the universe having one?* He also began to recognize some problems with the idea – some big ones, in fact. First of all, recalling his recent conversation with Paul, it seems to overlook an essential feature of the Big Bang theory, which is that its foundation is naturalism, the notion that the universe came into being entirely through *natural* processes. By definition, then, the Big Bang theory seems to explicitly exclude intervention from God, or any other supernatural being. In support of this conclusion, none of the descriptions of the Big Bang that he had come across – most definitely including those in the textbooks he had used in school – attributed a supernatural cause to the event. It seemed to Josh, in fact, that it wouldn't be too much of a stretch to say that explaining how the world came into being without any supernatural intervention is the very reason for the Big Bang's existence.

How can people who supposedly believe in creation accept a theory that specifically denies a Creator? he wondered. Recalling Paul's words about evolution, *If anything supernatural is included in evolution, it's no longer evolution,* he thought the same thing might be said about the Big Bang theory: *If anything supernatural is included in the Big Bang theory, it's no longer the Big Bang theory.*

This wasn't the only issue that Josh had with these creationists who believe in the Big Bang theory, however. After his recent study, it was clear to him that the order and timing of the events that the Big Bang supposedly initiated was vastly different than that presented in the biblical creation account. Most obvious, of course is the staggering difference in the time required for the events to transpire – about fifteen billion years in the one and six days in the other. In addition, there is the order in which the components of the natural world appeared. According to the Big Bang theory, for example, the earth appeared billions of years after the evolution of the stars began and millions of years after the sun. In the biblical account, of course, the earth appeared on the first day of creation, before the sun and the stars, which came into being on the fourth day.

There were other differences, too, but Josh wasn't interested in studying them now. As far as he was concerned, it was pretty clear: the Big Bang theory and biblical creation simply weren't compatible. To him, the idea that they were was a big bust.

It was close to midnight, and the library was about to close. Josh had spent seven long days on his investigation of inorganic evolution, far longer than he had expected. Leaning back in his chair, he reflected upon what he had learned so far. To say the least, things had hardly proceeded as he had anticipated. The theory of evolution, at least the inorganic phase of it, seemed to be riddled with serious flaws. Not only was much of the evidence unconvincing, but in his opinion a lot of it was literally unbelievable.

But Josh knew that evolutionists would argue that all of the problems he had encountered with inorganic evolution were irrelevant, because their theory supposedly had nothing to do with this phase of the world's development. So now he would turn his attention to organic evolution, the evolution of life. After the things he had uncovered in his study of inorganic evolution, he couldn't imagine what lay ahead. One thing he was sure about, though: If there were anywhere near the number of problems with the theory of organic evolution as there was with inorganic evolution, he might have to conclude that Paul was right about these things. He might have to become a ... *creationist!*

His investigation into organic evolution began with amino acids, the building blocks of life. Without warning, these words unleashed a stream of memories in his mind: Stanley Miller, the youth group, his debate with Paul, the surge of depression that followed, the Saturday night when he couldn't handle the pain any longer and decided to end his life. The memories had blind-sided him, and he knew from past experience that he was suddenly at the edge of the viper's den. If he couldn't get away, in an instant the serpent could strike and plunge him into depression. This is the way it always happened; everything would be going along just fine, and then, completely by surprise, something happened that caused his thoughts to take a sudden turn into a labyrinth of dark and unhealthy thoughts. Before he could escape, he would be entangled in depression. He had never had any defense against these sudden twists in his thoughts. As usual, he felt helpless. Suddenly, an idea came to him, something he had never tried before: prayer.

Oh God, he quietly uttered, *you know how I've struggled with depressions … they're so awful, and I know I'm in danger right now of slipping into one …I can feel it. Oh! Please help me, God! Please! I've been there so many times before, and I hate it! I'm sorry I haven't asked you for help before, but …but, hey, you gotta start sometime, eh? Thank you and …well, I guess that's it."*

Josh had no idea whether God heard his prayer. He wasn't sure whether he even *believed* in Him. One thing he did know, however: he felt better. The fear that had gripped him only a moment ago had definitely subsided. He took a short break, had a cup of coffee and skimmed through a magazine. Twenty minutes later, he returned to his study with renewed determination. For the time being, at least, the enemy had retreated.

Returning to his study, right away he was faced with a problem. *Here we go again,* he thought. The issue was similar to the problem of how gases and rocks "stuck together" to eventually form planets. How did the building blocks of amino acids – oxygen, nitrogen, hydrogen, and carbon – acquire the ability to stick together in the beginning? Obviously, they have this ability now, but where did it come from? It's really quite extraordinary. Without it, in fact, the universe could not exist. Few authors, Josh discovered, even addressed this problem. Like so many other natural mysteries, it just seemed to be taken for granted.

Soon Josh came upon the notion of a reducing (oxygen-free) atmosphere which underpinned not only Stanley Miller's experiment but the entire theory of evolution, for without such an atmosphere life could never have gotten started on earth – not by purely *natural* events, at least. Josh flashed back to his debate with Paul at the youth group and the discussion they had about this very topic. He recalled Scott Martin's question regarding the logic behind Miller's decision to eliminate oxygen from the atmosphere of his experiment: "If he [Miller] was trying to produce amino acids, and oxygen would have made this impossible, why shouldn't he have eliminated it?" … and Paul's answer …

But Scott, look what he did in order to accomplish this. He completely changed the atmosphere of the earth! He didn't just adjust it a little – you know, fine-tune it. He eliminated the two gases, free nitrogen and oxygen, which make up over 99% of our current atmosphere. Practically speaking, Scott, the atmosphere of Miller's experiment bore absolutely no relationship to our current one, which is, of course, the only one that has ever been observed. To assume that such an atmosphere ever existed is a HUGE assumption … Absolutely HUGE.

He recalled Paul emphasizing that if one was going to make such a bold assumption – that the atmosphere of the early earth was completely without oxygen – he'd better have some darned good evidence to back up the claim … and Paul's assertion that there's not a single trace of real evidence that such an atmosphere ever existed in the earth's history.

Although he had been startled at the time by Paul's assertions, when he had thought it over later he had been forced to admit that his argument was quite convincing. In fact, he had investigated the matter on his own afterward and, as Paul's comments had implied, had been unable to find any convincing evidence for this oxygen-free atmosphere. Like so many other topics in the evolutionary tale, it seemed that its proponents *assumed* this condition with barely, if any, a shred of evidence.

Right away he came upon another problem that had surfaced in his debate with Paul at the youth group: the absence of oxygen would mean the absence of the ozone layer, since ozone is an isotope of oxygen; if there wasn't any oxygen, there couldn't have been any ozone. And the absence of the ozone layer would mean that there would be nothing to shield the earth from deadly ultraviolet light, which destroys organic chemicals like amino acids as effectively as oxygen.

With a little grin, Josh remembered Mike's succinct summation of this dilemma: *With oxygen in the atmosphere amino acids could never have gotten started because oxygen would have eaten them up … and without oxygen, there wouldn't have been any ozone, so they would have been wiped out by cosmic rays. It sounds to me like those little critters could never have evolved by chance!* He recalled the times he had been a little rough on Mike and vowed to never be again.

Committed to giving evolutionary theory every chance to prove itself, Josh searched for a resolution to this obvious conundrum. Eventually, he discovered one, although he wasn't too thrilled about it. It seemed too contrived.

The solution was that the amino acids were swept into a nearby – *very nearby!* – sea immediately after they formed, thus dodging the deadly ultraviolet light, because ultraviolet light doesn't penetrate very deeply into water. At this point, Josh discovered, the story becomes very confusing. Some authors point out that the watery environment of these floating amino acids present a huge hurdle to any further evolution, because the next phase in the evolutionary process, large chainlike molecules like DNA and protein, called polymers, *cannot* form in a dilute solution of water as would have existed in the ancient oceans, because water prevents the necessary bonding. These authors proposed various solutions to this problem, none of them particularly convincing to Josh.

Other authors seemed to completely ignore this problem, acting as if it didn't exist, and assumed – or, more accurately, *pretended* – that the amino acids and other organic compounds, nucleotides, for example, did form in the ancient seas.

Josh tried to figure out the logic of these people. *Even though this event is apparently physically impossible,* he mused, *of course it must have happened, because if it didn't, then evolution couldn't have happened – but evolution, of course, did happen. Therefore, this event must have happened … Not real convincing,* he reflected.

Despite its illogic, the majority view seemed to be that the polymers did, in fact, form in the sea. Josh noticed that the proponents of this position preferred terms other than "water" for the liquid home of these objects, terms like "primordial soup" or "ancient broth." Becoming increasingly jaded, he suspected the reason for these imaginative terms: knowing that it would have been impossible for the polymers to evolve in water, an alternative home for them had to be created. Of course, exactly how these objects could have evolved in "primordial soup" or an "ancient broth," as opposed to water, was never explained – perhaps, Josh thought, because such liquids only existed in the imaginations of those who wrote about them. To Josh, it seemed that these people were attempting to solve the problem with *semantics*, not *science!* As far as he was concerned, water by any other name was still water.

Logic aside, the evolutionary story rolled on, claiming that over vast periods of time some amino acids eventually conglomerated into proteins, while other nucleotides joined together to form DNA – deoxyribonucleic acid, the famous double helix molecules found within the nucleus of every cell which are the "blueprints" for the construction of cells. Josh came across a few authors who pointed out that the statistical odds against such highly complex organic molecules evolving purely by chance were astronomically high. The typical human DNA molecule, for example, consisted of over three *billion* base pairs, or nucleotides, all arranged in a very precise order. According to these authors, statistically speaking the odds against such an object evolving entirely by chance is essentially zero.

One of these authors offered a colorful analogy to illustrate the irrationality of such an event: Imagine a million tennis balls, numbered one through one million, scattered about on a sandy beach. Based upon the logic behind the theory of organic evolution, over time it would be possible for random natural events – wind, rain, surf, etc. –to cause these balls to be lined up in perfect order, one through one million. Upon reflection, it crossed Josh's mind that the analogy didn't require a million balls to make its point – ten would have been sufficient.

As he dug deeper into this particular area of study, Josh encountered what appeared to be an insurmountable obstacle: proteins depend upon DNA for their formation, but DNA cannot form without preexisting proteins. A cannot exist without B, but B cannot exist without A. *Which came first?*

He discovered that a similar problem exists with DNA and RNA, both vital ingredients of every living cell. These two molecules exist in a symbiotic relationship. Whereas the DNA originates the "blueprint" or design for the cell, the RNA transfers this information from within the nucleus to various parts of the cell. Without the RNA, in other words, the blueprint for the cell's organization, in particular the creation of proteins, never leaves the office, and the cell cannot be created. But without DNA there's no blueprint. Just like the relationship between DNA and proteins, neither DNA nor RNA can exist without the other. This being the case, there is only one way the cell could have evolved: the two molecules must have evolved completely independently, fully "anticipating" its interaction with its future partner, and appeared at exactly the same time in exactly the same place, perfectly ready to begin their remarkable interaction. *Reminds me of another story*, Josh mused – *the one about a young girl and a glass slipper.*

By now Josh was really beginning to wonder how a theory with so many unsolved problems and contradictions could possibly have become so universally accepted. *Are people really that blind – or stupid?* he wondered, overlooking his own belief in the theory, which, it was clear, was rapidly deteriorating.

Assuming its formation, the next problem the cell faced was the acquisition of food and the production of energy necessary for maintenance and growth. In the absence of free oxygen – which, supposedly, didn't exist yet – the only method of acquiring food and energy was fermentation. The problem here was that the cells' source of food was the very organic molecules from which they were formed. This process could not continue indefinitely, of course, because eventually there would be no materials from which new cells could be created.

As usual, Josh discovered, evolutionists have a creative solution to this dilemma: in the nick of time, they claim, cells – or was it just one particularly ingenious cell, sort of a "cellular Einstein"? – *invented* the process of photosynthesis! With the energy of sunlight, cells were now able to make their own organic molecules to use for food and energy. It was no longer necessary for them to consume their own building blocks in order to survive. Evolution, apparently, had dodged a bullet, one that could have brought the entire process to a screeching halt. Of course, there was not a word of explanation regarding how this incredibly fortuitous event might have happened, but that was incidental. The important thing is that it allowed the story to continue.

A wonderful byproduct of photosynthesis was – and still is, of course – oxygen. And an isotope of oxygen is ozone. As oxygen and ozone began to fill the earth's atmosphere, so the story goes, the ozone formed a layer high above the earth which shielded the planet from the deadly ultraviolet rays which had been such a hindrance to the evolution of life on dry land. The oxygen, on the other hand, permitted higher life forms to *invent* a new way to acquire energy, which was many times more efficient than fermentation: respiration ... that is, *breathing*.

As Josh read about this incredible series of events, his tolerance was stretched to the breaking point. *It just seems like this whole story of evolution rests upon miracles – one, after another, after another, after another ...* he thought.

The notion that a cell could have "invented" photosynthesis particularly irked Josh. He had a special interest in plants. In fact, he had a small greenhouse behind his house where he grew several kinds of flowers and a few herbs. He knew something about photosynthesis. He was well aware, for example, that it was the principal food production process in nature, the process upon which all life depended. And he knew that photosynthesis rested upon three very complex components, chlorophyll, chloroplast, and cytoplasm, each of which contained thousands of atoms in a very complex and precise arrangement. For photosynthesis to have evolved, all three of these components would have had to arrive at precisely the same point in time and space *completely independently* and *purely by chance! –* just like the protein and DNA molecules, or the DNA and RNA molecules, at an earlier stage in the process.

To Josh, the evolutionists' explanation of photosynthesis was simply unbelievable. *To claim that a cell "invented" photosynthesis is like saying that an earthworm invented our most complex computer. The only difference is that an earthworm is vastly more complex than a single cell – an earthworm is composed of billions of cells all arranged in perfect order – and photosynthesis is actually more complex than our most sophisticated computers. After all, man invented and now builds computers. Given only sunlight and a few basic cells it is inconceivable that man could have ever invented the extraordinarily complex and remarkable process of photosynthesis. But according to the theory of evolution,* **cells** *did!*

It had been another long day. Once again it was close to midnight. Every day for over two weeks, Josh had been totally immersed in this study, and he was very tired. By now it was perfectly obvious to him that the trial that he had subjected the theory of evolution to was not proceeding as he had anticipated at all. He had expected occasional problems, but nothing like this. There was simply no escaping it: the theory that was often referred to as the "bedrock of science" appeared to be built upon a foundation of sand. Most of the evidence in its defense seemed to be weak, at best. Some of it, like the multiverse theory, seemed to be ridiculous. Josh realized, of course, that in a certain sense his exploration of evolution had barely begun. He had only come to the evolution of the cell. The entire evolution of life stretched out before him. At this point, it didn't matter, though. For now, at least, he had seen enough.

On the one hand, what he had discovered saddened Josh. He felt like he was losing a dear old friend. On the other, however, he was quenching his deep thirst for truth, just as Paul had said he would. In a few days, perhaps he would pick up his study where he had left off. Maybe the theory could make a miraculous recovery and regain some credibility.

Right now, however, he wasn't concerned about that possibility. He cared about only one thing: going home and getting into bed. He gathered up his things and headed out into the warm night air. The library doors closed gently behind him. It was midnight.

14

The Light Breaks Through

That night Josh wasn't able to get to sleep. He was restless, and memories of the terrifying dream that he had had shortly before his suicide attempt kept flashing through his mind. The minutes crawled by and turned into hours. Deep into the night, he decided to try reading something, hoping that this might get his mind off the nightmare and allow him the sleep he longed for. As he reached over to turn on the lamp on his nightstand, he knocked a couple of books on the floor. Falling to the floor with the books was a piece of paper. It was the pamphlet that Jennifer had handed to him as he had left the youth group meeting a few weeks ago. Curious, he picked it up. It was the first time he had paid any attention to it.

On the cover was a simple question: "What is truth?" The question immediately sparked his curiosity, for it reminded him of a comment Paul had made: *Ultimately what you are searching for is the truth.* Thinking about it, Josh realized that Paul's insight into his condition was right on the mark. He *was* searching for the truth – about science, about evolution, about God ... and about himself. That's what his recent study marathon was all about: a search for truth. But even though Paul had pointed this out to him, it hadn't really struck him until he had read the cover of this pamphlet. Paul's words had planted the seed; the pamphlet had given the words life.

The pamphlet went on to say exactly what Paul had said, that Jesus is the way and the truth and the life. It added the rest of the verse, also: no one comes to the Father but through Him. It then explained exactly what one must do to become aligned with the Truth, with Jesus. What really caught Josh's attention was that the instructions included the exact passage in Romans that Paul had recently referred to: *If you confess with your mouth Jesus as Lord, and believe in your heart that God raised Him from the dead, you shall be saved; for with the heart man believes, resulting in righteousness, and with the mouth he confesses, resulting in salvation.*

Suddenly, these words came alive for Josh. Like a brilliant shaft of light they pierced the dark wall of depression that had imprisoned him for so long. He sensed that these words had the power to free him from his bondage, and he desperately wanted it. Dropping to his knees at the side of his bed, haltingly he began to pray.

· "Uh, God, I'm not really sure what is going on right now, but for the first time in my life, I think that I might really believe that you're real. I want to be honest with you … I'm not *sure* about this, but I'm a lot more sure than I've ever been before. I know that I've done something really awful, God, and I'm *really, really* sorry. To tell you the truth, I don't know how you could ever forgive someone who had done something so bad.

"But Paul told me that if I confess my sins to you that you would forgive me, and that's what I'm doing right now, and I believe that you will, because I trust Paul and I believe that he was telling me the truth. Like I just said, Lord, I can't even say for sure that I definitely believe in you. But I can say for sure that if you are out there – and I *really* hope that you are – I definitely want you to be my Lord … So I hope you heard me, Lord Jesus, and I hope you'll forgive me. Amen."

The confession had been made. Another name had been written in the Book of Life.

Far above Josh's bedroom, the stars twinkled brightly in the clear night sky, declaring the glory of their Creator, and a gentle breeze rippled the curtain of the window. Josh climbed back into his bed and soon fell into a deep, peaceful sleep. The chains of depression that had held him for so long were finally torn loose. Now he was held in the loving arms of the Maker of the stars.

The next day Paul received an email message that caused his heart to leap with joy. It was from Josh, and it was only two words: *mission accomplished*. Paul quickly replied and suggested that they get together soon. Josh said that he was looking forward to it, but that he wanted a little time to let everything settle in first.

The next morning Josh finally woke up at about eleven o'clock. It was Saturday, and he had no plans. He felt completely rested and at peace. Outside of the large window on the west side of his room was a large old maple tree. Ever since he could remember he loved to lie in his bed and watch the activity in this beautiful old tree: squirrels racing through the branches playing tag, all kinds of birds, the seasonal changes of the leaves. Two of his favorite memories were the brilliant orange-yellow leaves in the fall and ruby red cardinals on the snow-covered branches in the deep of winter. This morning his perspective on this natural beauty was different. For the first time in his life, he had a sense that these things weren't there just by chance, but that they were put there for a purpose, by a Creator. Also for the first time, Josh felt that there was actually someone that he could thank for this glorious natural beauty. And he did.

After awhile he decided to get up and check his email, something that he had neglected over the past several days. He only had a few, but three of them were from David. He immediately gave him a call and told him that he'd go over to his house as soon as he had some breakfast. Among other things, he wanted to tell his friend about the study he had been involved in over the past few days.

About one o'clock Josh arrived at David's house.

"Hey, dude, what have you been up to? I thought maybe you had dropped off the face of the earth or something," David exclaimed as he greeted Josh at his front door.

"No, man, I didn't drop off the face of the earth – but I've sure been learning a lot about it!" Josh replied with a big smile.

In a moment they were settled down in David's den. On the TV was the college kick-off bowl from the Meadowlands in New Jersey. Ohio State was playing Penn State. David was a big Penn State fan. He was thinking of going to college there, in fact.

"So, what have you been doing that kept you too busy to answer your emails?"

"I've been on a trip, Dave – an incredible trip, back to the beginning of time and deep into the universe."

"I thought you said you weren't into drugs. What happened?"

"No, no, I'm not talking about drugs, Dave. I'm talking about truth."

For the next two hours Josh related to David the study of evolution that had absorbed his attention over the past several days.

"You're right, buddy. That was a pretty amazing trip!" David declared. "So what's your conclusion?"

"What do you mean?'

"Like, what do you think about the theory of evolution now?"

"I think I'd have to agree with Paul, that it's a giant lie ... but I'm not absolutely sure at this point. I mean, it's just a little too much to swallow – You know what I mean? – that what we're being taught in school about the origin of the whole world is a huge *lie!*"

"Yeah, and not only us, but every other kid in America, too," David added.

"Yeah, that's right." Josh paused to reflect for a moment. "It's really bizarre, man, when you think about it. It's almost like there's this massive conspiracy going on that includes, like, all the science teachers in the country ..."

"Or the world," David interjected.

"Right. It's crazy, isn't it?"

After another pause, David changed the subject. "Hey, listen. We've taken the last few weeks off, but our youth group is meeting this Sunday at Jennifer's house again. Why don't you come?"

"Whoa, buddy! I don't know about that. You know what a fool I made of myself at the last meeting I attended. Plus, I'm sure everyone knows what I did afterward – right?"

"Yeah, right," David replied, stating the obvious. "But, hey, you've seen the light, now, right? I'm sure everyone would love to hear you describe what you've learned – like you just did with me. It was awesome, man – totally awesome."

Josh nodded his head. "Thanks. Maybe I'll think about it. Speaking of Jennifer, let me ask you a question. If these meetings weren't at Jennifer's house, would you still be going to them?"

"What do you mean?"

"Come on, man ... You know what I mean."

"Yeah, I do. And to answer your question, yes, I would attend these meetings if they weren't at Jennifer's house – as long as Jennifer was still there!"

After they both laughed, Josh asked David another slightly more serious question. "Let me ask you something else about these youth groups. Is your main reason for going to them to learn about God, or to see Jennifer?"

"All right. I'll be honest with you. When I first started going, I have to admit, it was more to see Jennifer than anything else. But as time passed, I've really grown to like the meetings aside from that. I think Paul is very cool, a really good teacher, and I've learned a lot ... Of course, it certainly doesn't hurt that Jennifer's at the meetings, too!" David added with a sheepish grin.

"I'll bet it doesn't!" Josh laughed, slapping David with a high five. "I have to say," he added. "She's definitely hot."

"Yeah, you're right ... hot *looking*, that is. Other than that, though ... Let's just say that she's as good and pure as the driven snow. If I could ever get her to go out with me alone I'm sure she wouldn't let me ..."

"That's what I meant, Dave – hot *looking*. I know what you're saying. She wouldn't let you touch her. Forbidden fruit, man. It's probably the best kind."

"I'm glad you added the word *probably*. Obviously you're not speaking from experience."

"Yeah, like you'd know, Romeo." Josh quickly retorted, a big grin on his face.

Again Josh paused. He wanted to bring something up, but he was hesitant. He didn't know how his friend would react.

"You know," he began haltingly, "after the last youth group I was at, as I was storming out the door, Jennifer gave me a pamphlet. It was, uh, pretty interesting."

"Oh, yeah? What was it about?"

"On the cover was a simple question: What is truth? It really caught my attention because, as I thought about it, that's what my whole study over the past several days was all about: a search for truth."

"So, did you find it? The truth, I mean."

"Yeah, I think I did."

"And what is it?"

Here's the part that Josh was hesitant to bring up.

"Well, I think I discovered the truth about evolution, for one thing. But I think I found a more important truth: Jesus Christ."

"You mean that He is the way, and the Truth, and the life and no man comes to the Father but through Him – and that you must confess Him as your Lord and Savior if you want to be saved from hell?" David replied with a smile.

"Yeah, man, exactly! I didn't think you knew that stuff. How did you find out?"

"Well, the youth group certainly had something to do with it. But Jennifer did, too." David proceeded to relate to Josh the conversation he and Jennifer had had after the meeting with Mr. Potter about their science exams several weeks earlier.

"That's cool," Josh said. "So, let me ask you. Did you confess Jesus as your Lord, like that verse in Romans says you must?"

"Yeah, I did. That very night."

"Awesome. Guess what. I did, too – last night."

The two youths looked at each other and nodded their heads. Suddenly, they embraced. For a long moment, they held each other tightly. They didn't say anything. They didn't need to. It was a powerful moment for them. They had been best friends for many years. Now, they knew their friendship would last forever.

15

Road Trips and Rock Layers

The Sunday before Labor Day the Grace Bible Church youth group had their first meeting of the new school year at Dino's Pizza. Paul thought that it might be a more comfortable place for any new students than the Conley's home, which would be the location of their future meetings. David had encouraged Josh to come, but he didn't show up. About halfway through the meeting, Sue Peterson received an urgent call from home and had to leave immediately. Her little sister had fallen down the stairs and had to be taken to the hospital. She had hit her head and was unconscious. Fortunately, it turned out to be only a mild concussion. When the meeting ended, Jennifer realized that she needed a ride home. She had come with Sue.

"Hey, I can give you a ride home," David offered. "I have my dad's Honda."

"Sure," Jennifer replied. "That would be fine."

As they walked out to the Honda, Jennifer remarked, "I think that was a pretty good meeting, don't you, Dave?"

"Yeah, I do. Those two new kids … uh, what are their names?"

"Cody and Janelle Simpson. They're brother and sister."

"Oh yeah, that's right. Anyway, they seemed pretty nice. What do you know about them?"

"Not much. They moved into town this summer, and I've seen them a couple of times at our church. I thought it would be nice to ask them to our youth group. Hopefully, they'll decide to come to our next meeting."

"Speaking of that – you know, our next meeting – it seems like everyone wants to continue our discussion of creation and evolution, doesn't it, Jen?"

"It sure does. In fact, most of the group seems to be excited about that topic … What about you?"

"What do you mean?"

"Do you think we should continue looking into creation and evolution?"

"Yeah, definitely. I thought the discussion we had last spring was really interesting … and I don't think that we finished it."

For the next few moments the two teens were silent. David glanced over at Jennifer. The full moon cast a pale amber glow on her face. *She sure is pretty*, David thought to himself. As he turned his eyes back to the road, it was suddenly apparent to David that he had never had feelings toward another girl like he had for Jennifer. He wasn't sure exactly what these feelings were, but he knew they felt good – very good, in fact.

Jennifer turned towards David. "What are you thinking about?" she asked.

"Oh, nothing much," David replied with a smile. Actually, that wasn't true. David *was* thinking about something: how he might wrangle a kiss from Jennifer when he dropped her off at her house. He knew that Jennifer was a very good Christian girl, and he suspected that she may never have kissed a boy before, so he knew that he would have to be very careful in order to have any chance of success. According to his way of thinking, this was about the sixth time they had been out together (he knew that he was stretching it to call this evening "going out," but he needed all the ammunition he could muster to make this event happen). To be precise, they had been out once together, to a movie, and three or four other times with friends, to restaurants, if you can call McDonald's and Dino's restaurants.

Jennifer's perspective was slightly different, and more accurate. She figured that they had been out on an official date once, the movie, and she wasn't about to let David kiss her yet. The thought of kissing David *had* crossed her mind, though. She was a good Christian, but she could be attracted to a boy just like any other girl could be. In fact, she was – and he was sitting next to her.

A few minutes later, David dropped Jennifer off at her house. As they said goodnight at the front door, their eyes met, and they stood motionless for a moment. As David leaned toward Jennifer, the door suddenly opened.

"Hi, Jen," her father exclaimed. "Oh, and hi David, too," he quickly added.

David's big moment was foiled – but he had come close!

Later that week Paul was driving down the Interstate one afternoon with David and Josh in a rented truck, picking up some furniture for the church.

They were passing through a long road cut with some eye-catching rock strata. The towering thirty-foot cliffs on both sides of the road made it seem as if they were driving through a canyon. It was late afternoon, and the wall to their left was in deep shadow, obscuring the distinction between the individual layers of rock. On the other side of the road the scene was dramatically different. There, the bright sunlight grazing the face of the cliff caused every layer to stand out in vivid relief.

"Wow!" Josh exclaimed. "Look at those layers of rock. They're incredible. Each layer is so *distinct*. It's hard to believe that they were created naturally. It looks like they were built by a team of stone masons, doesn't it?"

"I totally agree, Josh. They're amazing," Paul assented. "How do you think they were formed?"

"Well, according to our science textbook rock layers build up over many millions of years. The ones in the Grand Canyon supposedly took over a *billion* years to accumulate. They're arranged chronologically … you know, the oldest layers are on the bottom and they get progressively younger as they move toward the top. I guess that's pretty obvious, though, isn't it? Of *course* the older layers would be on the bottom!"

"We'll talk about that in a minute. But back to my original question for now … How do you think they were formed?"

"According to what we learned in school, every now and then, a natural event – like a volcano, or a huge hurricane, or a flood – caused the land to be covered with sediment, like volcanic ash or dirt or mud. The sediment buried all of the plants and animals in the area. As time passed, this layer of sediment would harden into rock, turning the buried plants and animals into fossils. Then, thousands or millions of years later another similar disaster would occur and the same thing would happen again. As time passed, the layers would build up and after a few million years you'd end up with something like the cliff we just passed. ... How's that?"

"How did the layers turn into rock?" Paul asked.

"I don't know. As far as I can remember, our textbooks didn't really get into that too much. I think water might have had something to do with it, though. Like, the stuff had to get soaked with water somehow in order to eventually turn into rock. You know ... Dry sand or dirt doesn't become rock by itself, right?"

"That's right. And you're right about the water, too. Water *definitely* played a role in the formation of those layers. I'll explain how in a minute. First, though, let me clue you in to some interesting news, Josh. It didn't take millions of years for these layers to form. It probably took only a few days – maybe even hours."

"A *few hours* to form a thirty foot wall of rock?! No way, Paul! That's *crazy*, man."

"I didn't say that the layers turned into rock in a few hours. I only said that it took that amount of time for the *layers* to form. It took a little longer for the layers to become hardened into rock."

At that moment they were passing through another road cut. This one included rock strata that were bent into massive folds, called synclines and anticlines. These cliffs were about fifty feet high and at one place the folds looked like a massive "U."

"Look at that folded rock, Josh," Paul said as he quickly pulled over to the side of the highway so they could get a closer look at the spectacular rock formation. "Let me ask you something. How could *solid rock* ever bend into folds like this?"

"I have no idea ... but, wow, that cliff is really amazing, isn't it? I've driven by here quite a few times, but I never really noticed how incredible it is."

Paul smiled. "I'm sure that you're not the only one who didn't notice it, Josh ... But what about my question: How could solid rock ever bend into folds like this?"

"Oh, yeah ... I never thought about it. It does seem pretty impossible, though."

"Not only does it *seem* impossible. It *is* impossible. Solid rock does not bend without cracking."

"All right ... I'll buy that. That makes sense. But, listen, I want to go back to what you said before, that these layers were formed in a few *days*. How in the world could that have happened? It just seems totally unbelievable to me. Like I said earlier, in school we were told that it took millions of years for these layers to form. Are you saying that our teachers are telling us fairy tales?"

"I'm totally with Josh," David chimed in. "What you're saying seems totally unbelievable to me, too. What's the deal here, Paul?"

"I'll tell you ... The material that became these layers of rock was originally sediment that was suspended in massive quantities of moving water. It may seem surprising, but sediment that is suspended in moving water settles out in layers. As the water flows along, the sediment separates according to the size and weight of the particles, and as it settles it forms layers."

"Come on, Paul. That's pretty hard to believe. It just doesn't ...""

"Listen, Josh. I thought it sounded unbelievable when I first heard about it, too. But research within the past several years has absolutely confirmed this process. It has been proven beyond doubt through extensive testing."

"Have you ever seen any of these tests yourself?"

"Actually, it's pretty easy to test the general principal on your own. Take a handful of mixed gravel ... including large-grained sand up to pebbles about the size of marbles, or a little bigger ... and dump it into a tall clear container filled with water – like a tall vase, perhaps, the taller the better. You'll see that, generally speaking, as the gravel falls the larger, heavier particles settle on the bottom and the smaller, lighter ones settle in order above them, depending upon their size and density. The settling of these particles clearly results in layering.

"Now, imagine what would happen in a massive flood with water a mile deep or more. Imagine the water surging about in great waves, both on the surface, in great tidal waves and tsunamis, and below the surface, in deep-sea currents. Suspended in the water would be massive quantities of sediment. As these waves flowed over an area the sediment would settle, in exactly the fashion I just described to you, with the heavier particles settling first and the others settling above them according to their size and density. As time passed, more waves would pass over the land, interspersed with occasional periods of relative calm. Every wave would deposit a new load of sediment, thus creating new layers. When the flood finally ended and the land became dry, in its wake would be many layers of sediment. Over time, these layers would harden into rock – just like the ones in front of us here.

"Listen. I have a wonderful video of some tests of this phenomenon. It's very cool. If you'd like, I'll show it to you when we get back to my house. "

"That would be awesome," David said. "I'd love to see it."

"So would I," Josh added.

"That's not all, though," Paul continued. "There's additional proof that these layers could have been laid down very rapidly. Have you ever heard of Mount St. Helens?"

"Yeah," David replied. "It was a huge volcano that blew up sometime in the 1980's. We heard about it in our geology class."

"What did you hear about it?"

"Oh, not much. Just that it was really huge and that it was a good demonstration of the explosive power that exists in volcanoes. Our teacher told us that its explosive energy was equivalent to about 20,000 Hiroshima bombs. Pretty awesome, isn't it?"

"Yeah, it sure is. But this volcano demonstrates a lot more than just incredible energy. It also proves that rock layers can be formed very rapidly, like I was just saying. For example, there's one thirty foot rock layer in the area that formed in *one afternoon*. The layer consists of thousands of individual strata, or mini-layers, some only one millimeter thick – basically, just about what we're looking at right here."

As he tried to process the extraordinary information he had just heard, Josh paused. Then, pointing to the cliff, he said, "In order to form this many layers of rock in a few hours, there must have been one heck of a lot of water, Paul. Where in the world would the water have come from?"

"The Genesis Flood, of course," Paul smiled. "You know, the one described in the Bible that saved Noah and his family."

"But you just told us that a thirty foot cliff of rock layers was formed by the volcano at Mt. St. Helens," Josh said. "Why do you think that this one was formed by the Genesis Flood. Why couldn't it have been caused by a volcano, too?"

"Well, one reason is pretty obvious. Do you see any mountains around here that look like they might have been a volcano at some point in the past?"

"Uh, no. In fact, there isn't anything around here that really qualifies as a mountain at all."

"Right. But beyond that, there are many places in the world where the layers of rock are a lot higher than this one. You mentioned the Grand Canyon before, Josh. Like you said, it is over a *mile* deep, and rock layers there extend all the way from the bottom to the top. The land around the canyon is flat for miles around. Nobody believes that a volcano had anything to do with the formation of the rock layers there. There's one more thing to keep in mind. At Mt. St. Helens the volcano wasn't the direct cause of the strata. The material that exploded out of the mountain, the steam and volcanic ash, caused massive mud flows. When the steam hit the cool air it turned into water, of course. This was the cause of the layering. The volcano, in other words, was the indirect, not the direct, cause of the layers. Ultimately, the layers were formed by water."

"How long ago did this great flood take place?" David asked.

"Oh, a long time ago," Paul said with a little smile.

"How long ago?"

"About five thousand years ago."

"*Five thousand years ago?!* That's not a long time ago. Compared to the age of the earth, that's, like, yesterday, man," David said.

"So, let me see if I've got this straight," Josh said. "You believe that these rock layers that we're looking at right here, the ones that we've been taught in our science class took millions of years to form, were formed only a few thousand years ago in a giant flood that was never mentioned, not a single word, in our science classes. That's pretty radical, man ... No, make that *very* radical. Let me ask you – and be *honest*, Paul: how *certain* are you that these rock layers were formed by the Genesis Flood? Do you have any doubts at all? I mean, it's pretty wild to think that as we drive down Interstate 80 we're actually looking at something caused by a great flood that covered the entire earth a few thousand years ago. That's a mind-boggling thought ... completely and totally mind-boggling."

"Let me tell you about a fascinating discovery that was made in the early 1970's," Paul said. "You've heard no doubt of the White Cliffs of Dover on the southern coast of England, right? Well, listen to this ...These limestone beds can be traced westward across England, and they appear again in Northern Ireland. In the opposite direction, the same chalk beds can be traced across France, the Netherlands, Germany, Poland, southern Scandinavia, and other parts of Europe to Turkey, then to Israel and Egypt in the Middle East, and even as far as Kazakhstan. Remarkably, the same chalk beds with the same fossils and the same distinctive strata above and below them are also found in the Midwest USA, from Nebraska in the north to Texas in the south. They also appear in the Perth Basin of Western Australia[5]. There is little doubt that these limestone beds scattered around the globe are all different sections of the *same* bed.

"This being the case, it is rather obvious that it must have been created by some natural event at approximately the same time. Furthermore, unless there happened to be a simultaneous series of events all over the earth that resulted in the exact same interconnected layer of limestone, this event must have been the *same* event in every location. Given the evidence, my friends, there's really only one reasonable candidate for the cause of this bed: a worldwide flood.

"So, in answer to your question – How certain am I that these rock layers were caused by the Genesis Flood? – I'm absolutely certain. I've thought and read about it a lot, and I'm absolutely sure about it. Look at those folded layers up there. As you said, Josh, they're amazing. Well, they're one of the things that convince me that the layers were formed in the flood. As far as I'm concerned, a massive flood is really the only reasonable explanation for these great folds. Think about it. In order for these multiple folds to appear, the sediment from which the rock was made must have been in a *plastic* condition at the time of their formation – not completely hardened, in other words. Like I said before, solid rock does *not* fold! Partially hardened sediment, sediment deposited in a great flood, could. Did your geology book offer any explanation for such folds in solid rock?"

"Uh – not that I recall," Josh replied. "I have to admit … What you're saying makes sense, Paul."

"Think about this," Paul continued. "These road cuts are found everywhere, all over the earth. If the rock layers that they expose really were formed in the Genesis Flood, that means that the majority of people in the world have been presented with virtually indisputable evidence of this flood – and not just once, but over and over again. But guess what … Primarily because of what they have been taught in school – or, more accurately, what they *haven't* been taught in school – and learned through the media, *they don't believe in it!* They've seen tons of evidence of this flood with their very own eyes, but they are completely blind to it! You just said yourself, Josh, that this flood was never mentioned in your science class. Think about that. The most extraordinary natural event in the history of the world, by far – an event that completely altered the entire surface of the earth – and not one word about it was ever mentioned in a class that was supposed to be teaching you this very history! It's kind of like teaching American history without ever mentioning the Revolutionary War. If it wasn't so sad, it would be laughable."

"You're right, Paul. It is sad," David agreed. "But let's not forget: before this discussion, Josh and I were blind to these truths, too. We never knew that these rock layers were formed in a great flood, especially the one described in the Bible. It may seem clear to us now – I think – but it wasn't about a half hour ago."

"Let me ask you something, Paul," Josh said. "If you think about it, the explanation that you just offered for the formation of rock layers – the settling of sediment during a massive flood – is completely different than the explanation we learned in school … you know, the explanation I gave you at the beginning of this discussion: lots of local catastrophes over millions and millions of years. Maybe there are two *different* processes that form these layers, so maybe both explanations are correct."

"I don't think so, Josh. First of all, I don't think that the earth has *existed* for millions of years, which would make the explanation you gave invalid right off the bat. But that's hardly the only reason. Let me ask you something: with the process of stratum formation that you described, how thick do you think the individual layers would be?"

"What do you mean?"

"In the process that you described, every time one of these natural catastrophes took place, supposedly it completely wiped out the entire natural environment in that area, all of the plants and all of the animals, right?"

"Yeah, I guess so."

"Well, if they happened, those catastrophes must have been immense, right? So, how thick do you think the resulting rock layer would be?"

"I don't know … pretty thick, I guess. Fifty feet, maybe more."

"So how thick are the individual layers in this road cut here?'

Josh quickly scanned the rock wall in front of him. "It looks like only a few inches, maybe a foot at the most."

"Right. Now, do you think that the explanation that you gave for the formation of rock layers could *possibly* explain how these layers, averaging only a few inches thick, formed?"

"I'd have to say *No* … But, like I was saying before, maybe there are two different processes that form rock layers, and the ones here were formed by the process you described – sediment settling out of a great flood – while other layers, thicker ones, were formed the way we were taught in our science class."

"Let's suppose for a moment that you're right. It raises a question, of course: was the sediment-settling process, the process that formed the layers we're looking at here, ever mentioned to you in school?"

"Hmmm ... Not that I remember. How about you Dave? Do you remember hearing anything about this process in our science class?"

"Nope ... never," Dave quickly replied.

"Just as I expected," Paul said. "Of course it wasn't ... And I'll tell you why. In your science class, you are taught that the floods that cause rock layers are *local*. The idea that a *local* flood was the cause of strata such as this one here, or even much higher ones with much thicker individual layers, would be very difficult to accept. The obvious solution to this dilemma is to consider that the cause of strata like this was not a local flood, but a *worldwide* one. But this would raise the possibility, of course, that the flood must have been the one described in the Book of Genesis. Like, how many other options are there for a worldwide flood? But it's very clear that *this flood is never supposed to be mentioned in your school* – as proven by the fact that it **never is**."

"Like I said in one of our youth groups, it's never mentioned in any of the reference books in our library, either," David observed. "Remember I told you that I had checked this out in our school library and didn't find a single book that ever mentioned any worldwide flood?"

"Yeah, I sure do!" Paul said. "You were checking it out because of what Reverend Strong had said about the Genesis Flood when he was over at your house for dinner."

"That's right," David said. "Nice memory, Paul."

"Thanks," Paul smiled. "So, then, the point I'm trying to make here is that when you think carefully about it, as an explanation for the rock layers commonly found in road cuts, the sediment-settling process of strata formation is far superior to the process you were taught in school ... and, that being the case, like I was saying, every time you pass through rock layers in a road cut you're looking at evidence of Noah's Flood."

"There's something I don't get here, Paul," David said. "If a worldwide flood is a better explanation for these layers of rock than the one in our textbook, why aren't we told about it? It doesn't make sense."

"That's a great question, Dave, and I'd love to discuss the answer, but I think we should do that in one of our youth group meetings. It's really important, and I'd like everyone in the group to be in on the discussion. So let's hold that one until the next meeting, all right?"

"Yeah, sure. No problem."

Staring up at the dramatic cliff in front of him, Josh paused and slowly shook his head. "To think that these rock layers were formed in a great flood that covered the entire earth millions of years ago. Wow! That's incredible ... totally *awesome*."

"Make that *thousands* of years ago," Paul smiled. "But you're right. It sure is, Josh. I totally agree. Like I just said, I always get excited when I see them. No matter how often I see them, I *always* feel this way. It never fails. Sometimes, I'll take an afternoon drive just to look at them. Of course, I always bring my camera. I've got some great shots of them. To get the best shots the light has to be just right – like it is right here, grazing across the surface. I'll have to show them to you. My wife thinks I'm a little nuts, but fortunately she loves me in spite of it!"

"It sounds to me like *she's* the one that's a little nuts – for marrying a guy who gets so turned on by a bunch of rocks!" David said, at which they all enjoyed a good laugh.

16

The Big Decision

"As we were leaving Dino's last Sunday, Sue asked me a very good question: 'If you could pick one thing to prove that evolution wasn't true, what would it be?' I told her that I'd think it over and give her an answer the next time we got together, which is tonight."

Paul Hopkins was speaking at the first official meeting of the Grace Bible Church youth group after summer vacation. At Dino's the previous week, the group had decided that they wanted to continue the discussion of creation and evolution that they had begun the previous spring. There seemed to be a lot of unanswered questions.

"First of all, let me just say that I believe that there is a lot of evidence to demonstrate that evolution isn't true. The one I've chosen to describe tonight, however, is certainly one of the best. It's the origin of life. Now, before I begin my description, I need to make a couple of things clear to you. First, when pressed, most evolutionists will admit that the origin of life is pretty difficult to explain by the theory of evolution. At the same time, however, they will make it very clear that whatever the explanation is, it cannot involve anything supernatural, like a Divine Creator, because the theory absolutely excludes the supernatural. Inadvertently, this exposes the real purpose of the theory: *It is an attempt to explain how the natural world came into being by random natural events, without a Creator.*

"Now, even though it contradicts this fundamental presupposition of their theory, evolutionists will sometimes argue that their theory doesn't even apply to the origin of life, that it only addresses the *development* of life, not its *origin*. Don't be fooled by this claim. It's a cop-out. The only reason it is suggested is that, first, there is not the slightest bit of evidence that life can evolve from non-life through random natural events – which, of course, is the only method that evolution employs – and, second, the more that is discovered about the complexity of the cell, the more difficult it becomes to even *imagine* that such events could have been its cause. If evolution is true, then evolutionists have absolutely no choice in this matter: life *must* have developed through this method, because, according to their theory, it's the only alternative available ... Remember: the theory of evolution is an attempt to explain how the natural world came into being by random natural events, *without a Creator.* Actually, in light of this fundamental presupposition, the inescapable truth is that the theory of evolution applies not only to the origin of life but to the development of the world *from the very beginning.* If a Creator was not involved, then it *must* have evolved naturally. Again, there's no other choice. It's quite easy to prove this. Just look at the literature about evolution. None of it ever attributes *anything* to a Creator. None of it ever states that 'In the beginning God created the heavens and the earth ... After that He created the first living cell, and then He sat back and let evolution take over.' You've all been through courses on evolution in school. I'm sure that you know that what I'm saying is true.

"Now that these things are settled – now that it's clear that from an evolutionary perspective the origin of life must be attributed to random natural events – let me ask you all a question. You've all been taught the theory of evolution in school. By your teachers, and textbooks, how was the origin of life explained?"

Mike Lawton was the first to speak up. "As far as I remember, the first life supposedly developed over a few million years in some warm little pond of goop. First of all, atoms that were drifting around connected to one another to form molecules, and then some of these molecules hooked up to form amino acids. After a few million more years, some of these amino acids got together to form proteins and other stuff, and after a few million more years there was the first life, a cell. How's that?"

"The condensed version of the origin of life. Excellent, Mike," Paul replied. "That's about it. Now, let's take a careful look at it, to see if it really makes any sense. Before analyzing it, though, I want to make sure that you have a very clear understanding of the wondrous complexity of the cell. So, we're going to read together this description of the cell from a book called *Evolution: A Theory in Crisis*, by an Australian microbiologist named Michael Denton. It's rather long, but it's very powerful, and it will serve as an excellent background for our discussion."

Paul passed out sheets with this description and proceeded to read it aloud.

Perhaps in no other area of modern biology is the challenge posed by the extreme complexity and ingenuity of biological adaptations more apparent than in the fascinating new molecular world of the cell. Viewed down a light microscope at a magnification of some several hundred times, such as would have been possible in Darwin's time, a living cell is a relatively disappointing spectacle, appearing only as an ever-changing and apparently disordered pattern of blobs and particles which, under the influence of unseen turbulent forces, are continually tossed haphazardly in all directions. To grasp the reality of life as it has been revealed by molecular biology, we must magnify a cell a billion times until it is twenty kilometers in diameter and resembles a giant airship large enough to cover a great city like London or New York. What we would then see would be an object of unparalleled complexity and adaptive design. On the surface of the cell we would see millions of openings, like the portholes of a vast space ship, opening and closing to allow a continual stream of materials to flow in and out. If we were to enter one of these openings we would find ourselves in a world of supreme technology and bewildering complexity. We would see endless highly organized corridors and conduits branching in every direction away from the perimeter of the cell, some leading to the central memory bank in the nucleus and others to assembly plants and processing units. The nucleus itself would be a vast spherical chamber more than a kilometer in diameter, resembling a geodesic dome, inside of which we would see, all neatly stacked together in ordered arrays, the miles of coiled chains of the DNA molecules. A huge range of products and raw materials would shuttle along all the manifold conduits in a highly ordered fashion to and fro from all the various assembly plants in the outer regions of the cell.

We would wonder at the level of control implicit in the movement of so many objects down so many seemingly endless conduits, all in perfect unison. We would see all around us, in every direction we looked, all sorts of robot-like machines. We would notice that the simplest of the functional components of the cell, the protein molecules, were astonishingly complex pieces of molecular machinery, each one consisting of about three thousand atoms arranged in highly organized 3-D spatial conformation. We would wonder even more as we watched the strangely purposeful activities of these weird molecular machines, particularly when we realized that, despite all our accumulated knowledge of physics and chemistry, the task of designing one such molecular machine – that is, one functional protein molecule – would be completely beyond our capacity at present and will probably not be achieved until at least the beginning of the next century. Yet the life of the cell depends on the integrated activities of thousands, certainly tens, and probably hundreds of thousands of different protein molecules.

We would see that nearly every feature of our own advanced machines had its analogue in the cell: artificial languages and their decoding systems, memory banks for information storage and retrieval, elegant control systems regulating the automated assembly of parts

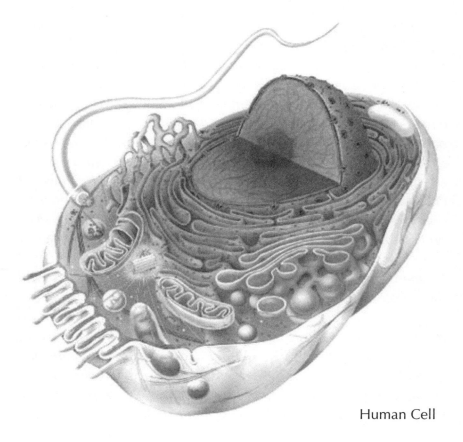

Human Cell

and components, error fail-safe and proof-reading devices utilized for quality control, assembly processes involving the principles of prefabrication and modular construction. In fact, so deep would be the feeling of deja-vu, so persuasive the analogy, that much of the terminology we would use to describe this fascinating molecular reality would be borrowed from the world of late twentieth-century technology.

What we would be witnessing would be an object resembling an immense automated factory, a factory larger than a city and carrying out almost as many unique functions as all the manufacturing activities of man on earth. However, it would be a factory which would have one capacity not equaled in any of our own most advanced machines, for it would be capable of replicating its entire structure within a matter of a few hours. To witness such an act at a magnification of a billion times would be an awe-inspiring spectacle.

To gain a more objective grasp of the level of complexity the cell represents, consider the problem of constructing an atomic model. Altogether a typical cell contains about ten trillion atoms. Suppose we choose to build an exact replica to a scale one trillion times that of the cell so that each atom of the model would be the size of a tennis ball. Constructing such a model at the rate of one atom per minute, it would take fifty million years, and the object we end up with would be the giant factory, described above, some twenty kilometers in diameter, with a volume thousands of times that of the Great Pyramid.[6]

"Before going on," Paul said, "I want to point out that in terms of information storage capacity, the cell far surpasses computer chips. If each of the three billion base pairs in the DNA of a human cell were equivalent to a letter of the alphabet, the information stored in this DNA would be equivalent to the information in about two thousand books of 500 pages each. The storage capacity of DNA is billions of times that of our most sophisticated computer chips. Listen to this. It's a statement I came across from Werner Gitt, an expert in the field of information, regarding this storage capacity:

The knowledge currently stored in the libraries of the world is estimated at 10^{18} bits. If it were possible for this information to be *stored in DNA molecules, 1 percent of the volume of a pinhead would be sufficient for this purpose. If, on the other hand, this information were to be stored with the aid of computer megachips, we would need a pile higher than the distance between the earth and the moon.*[7]

This statement was made in 1996, so the numbers would be somewhat different now. Like, today, instead of this information being stored in DNA that covered only one percent of the head of a pin, the DNA might cover the *entire* head of the pin," Paul grinned, "but I imagine you get the point … So, the cell is a pretty impressive little critter, isn't it?" Paul said, smiling and looking around the room. By the looks on their faces, everyone in the room certainly agreed with him!

"All right, now that we understand what an incredibly complex organism a cell is, let's review the evolutionists' explanation of its origin, to see how much sense it makes. As the song says, let's start at the very beginning … According to evolutionary theory, the earth first formed about 4.6 billion years ago. There are many theories about how the earth formed. I won't waste your time reviewing them, because as far as I'm concerned … well, I think they're all pretty foolish. Anyway, current estimates are that life first appeared about 3.5 billion years ago, about one billion years after the earth originated. As Mike explained earlier, this life supposedly formed in a "little pond" of warm liquid. Supposedly, this process took a very long time, a few hundred million years, perhaps. As Mike suggested, the liquid in this pond was not water, because the basic building blocks of life, like amino acids and proteins, cannot form in water. What this liquid was we are not told. In honor of Mike, we'll call it *goop*. The only things in this pond were the basic building blocks of matter, atoms and molecules.

"Before I go on, I want to make a few comments about one of the key players in this story, atoms. They're incredibly important to the story, but the theory of evolution basically takes their existence for granted. According to the theory, they originated as a result of the Big Bang explosion about fifteen billion years ago. It doesn't explain *how* they were formed. It just claims that they were. There was the Big Bang, and then there were atoms. That's it. But there's something very wrong with this description. Atoms are actually incredibly complex objects that scientists still don't completely understand. They are the *building blocks* of everything in the *entire universe*. To claim that a huge *explosion*, the Big Bang, caused them is a bit like saying that an explosion in a Silicon Valley factory resulted in the formation of billions of brand new computer chips. It doesn't make any sense. Explosions don't *make* things; they *destroy* them.

"Getting back to the story, over the next few hundred million years, very, very slowly, purely by trial and error, some of the atoms and molecules that were aimlessly floating around in this goop began to connect to one another. Exactly *why* they should do this — join together, that is — is not explained. Once again, they just did. After a few trillion of these random connections, all, purely by coincidence, in precisely the right order, lo and behold, as Mike said, something miraculous happened: the first cell was "born." Be careful to notice that not only do these atoms have to come together in exactly the right order, but also that each correct combination must *stay* together over countless millions of years, waiting patiently for the next member of the combination to happen along. A little common sense should tell you that this story is utterly absurd. It's kind of like claiming that a monkey sitting at a typewriter randomly hitting the keys of a computer could produce the Manhattan telephone book if he was able to stick to it for a few million years. Of course, a cell is vastly more complex than the Manhattan telephone book. After all, the numbers and letters in the phone book don't do anything. They just lie on the pages, as lifeless as a stone. The components of the cell, on the other hand, are active and constantly at work, just like the different components of a factory. One more thing: the Manhattan telephone book can't *reproduce itself*, like a cell can.

"Think back to Mr. Denton's description of the protein molecules. Each one is made up of three thousand or more atoms, and there are tens of thousands of them in each cell. In our little pond, therefore, all of these proteins must be forming, one atom at a time, entirely by chance, with absolutely no guidance or direction. Of course, these protein molecules are only one part of the cell's components. After they have formed, they must then somehow produce other components of the cell, such as DNA and RNA. The story must overlook the troubling little fact that in today's world DNA and RNA are required for the manufacture of proteins … which raises the question, of course: How could the proteins have evolved without DNA and RNA? I should add that the same symbiotic relationship also exists between DNA and RNA; neither can exist without the other. RNA is required to produce DNA, and vice-versa.

"Keep in mind that all of this activity is taking place without any master plan. That is, none of the parts that are forming have the foggiest idea that they will one day be part of the first living cell. Furthermore, they are all operating completely independently, totally unaware what their future partners are doing. Its sort of as if workers in ten thousand different factories all over the world created thousands of different parts for some unknown machine, without having any knowledge of what the other workers were making, only to discover that when they were finished and all of the parts were assembled together they had created a Boeing 747! The only difference between this scenario and the origin of the first cell according to the theory of evolution is that the parts for the 747 were being made by intelligent beings, whereas the parts for the cell supposedly were being made by the completely random interaction of lifeless atoms and molecules."

"I have a question, Mr. Hopkins," Kelly Conley said. "I kind of see what you are saying, but, still, I can't help thinking that if there was enough time, couldn't these atoms become just about anything, even a cell? I mean, a billion years is a mighty long time, isn't it?"

"That's a very good question, Kelly, and it's exactly what evolutionists would like us to believe. One of them once said, in fact, that time is the hero of the plot – the evolutionary plot, that is. However, according to the laws of probability, the answer is a very emphatic "No!" I don't want to get into these laws right now, but I'll try to answer your question by asking you another one. Suppose all of the parts to a brand new Corvette were tossed into a big pond and over the years this pond was subjected to earthquakes, hurricanes, floods, etc. … all kinds of natural events that would cause the parts to be periodically mixed up. How long do you think it would be before the parts would assemble themselves into a Corvette?"

After pausing for consideration, Kelly answered, "Like, uh, never."

"Let me make the problem a little simpler, Kelly. How long do you think it would take for a single bolt in the Corvette to screw itself into a threaded hole – the *correct* threaded hole, that is?"

Kelly just smiled and nodded her head. She got the point.

"So, everyone, according to the theory of evolution, that's how the first cell came into being … countless billions of atoms arranged themselves into something that exactly paralleled a giant factory, as described so vividly by Dr. Denton. There were, however, three differences between this cell and the factory. First, in the factory all of the operations were carried out by people, whereas in the cell everything is completely automatic. Second, the factory covered about 400 square miles, whereas ten thousand of these cells would barely cover the head of a pin. And finally, the cell has the ability to entirely reproduce itself in a few hours. Needless to say, the factory could never reproduce itself without a lot of outside help.

"There is, of course, one other difference between this cell and the factory: the cell supposedly came into existence completely by chance, whereas the factory required the combined effort of several thousand highly intelligent beings – people, in other words.

"So, there you have it: some very good reasons why life could not possibly have evolved by random natural events, as the theory of evolution claims. How did I do, Sue? Did I answer your question?" Paul asked Sue Peterson.

"Yeah, you sure did," Sue smiled. "That was *awesome*."

After a brief pause, a question came from the back of the room. "I have a question, Paul. If the theory of evolution is not true – like you claim – does that make our science teachers a bunch of liars?" The questioner was Josh Siegel. This was his first appearance in the group since his traumatic experience several weeks earlier. Most of the kids were very surprised, even shocked, to see him at their group again. A few others, like David, of course, and Jennifer – and Paul – who knew the entire story about what had happened to Josh, were not surprised at all.

"Before answering your question, Josh, I know I speak for everyone here when I say that I'm really glad that you're back – and I certainly hope you'll be a regular in our group."

Josh nodded his head and smiled.

Paul paused for a moment to consider Josh's question. He wanted to make sure that he got the answer right.

"Your question is a little tricky, Josh. Let me begin my answer by asking you another one. Suppose you were driving through an unfamiliar town, and you stopped to ask a man directions. He says to you, 'That's easy. Just drive to the end of this road and turn right. The place you're looking for is about a mile down the road, just past a big red barn on the left.' Before long you discover that the man's directions were wrong. He *thought* they were correct, but they weren't. Rather than turning right at the end of the road, you should have turned left. Now, was the man who gave you the directions lying to you?"

After thinking it over for a moment, Josh replied. "No, I guess not. If he thought the directions were correct, I don't think you could accuse him of lying. He simply provided incorrect information."

"Exactly," Paul quickly replied. "And the situation with evolutionists is the same. If they *believe* that what they are telling you is true, if it isn't, that doesn't make them liars. It simply makes them purveyors of misinformation – just like a man who provides incorrect driving directions."

"So, then," Josh observed, "someone can spread a lie without being a liar."

"That's right," Paul said, smiling and shrugging his shoulders.

David now spoke up. "Personally, I don't really care about what label should be hung on the people who are teaching evolution, whether they should be called liars or not. It seems to me that what really matters is that what they're teaching us are lies."

Scott Martin spoke next. "Here's what I don't understand. From the things I've heard in this group – like what you've just said about the origin of life – it seems really obvious that the theory of evolution is, like, totally ridiculous. So how can so many people that seem to be pretty intelligent – like Mr. Potter, our science teacher, for instance – believe it? It just seems crazy … You know what I mean?"

"That's a very good question, Scott," Paul replied. "Let's throw it open for discussion. How about the rest of you? What do you think about what Scott said? How can so many apparently bright people believe something that appears to be so foolish?"

"I have to tell you, it sure baffles me," Mike Lawton said. "Like Scott, I don't think it makes any sense. As far as I'm concerned, the idea that a bird evolved from a reptile is stupid enough, but the idea that something as complicated as a cell – that description of the cell you read earlier was totally *awesome*, Paul; I loved it! – could have evolved by atoms and molecules randomly bumping into each other is even more unbelievable. It's completely bogus, like totally insane. I just don't get it."

For a moment, there was silence. Scott's question hung in the air.

"Um … I think I might have an answer," Jennifer offered somewhat hesitantly. "I've thought about this before – more than once, in fact – because, like Mike said, it does seem crazy that so many people could believe an idea that seems so bizarre. To me, the problem is that these people are spiritually blind. The Bible says someplace that the minds of unbelievers have been blinded to the light of the gospel, and it certainly seems to me that the creation is part of the gospel. I don't understand exactly how these peoples' minds become blinded, but it sure seems obvious that they are. Like Mike said, anyone who believes that ten trillion atoms could arrange themselves by chance into something that resembles a giant automated factory that can reproduce itself in a few hours certainly should start seeing a psychiatrist before it's too late!"

Paul smiled and slowly nodded his head, once again impressed deeply by Jennifer's keen spiritual insight. "I think you hit the nail squarely on the head, Jennifer. I totally agree with you. People who believe in the theory of evolution certainly are blind to the truth about God's glorious creation. And you're right – The Bible does specify exactly how this happens. The verse is second Corinthians 4:4: *...the god of this world has blinded the minds of the unbelieving, that they might not see the light of the gospel of the glory of Christ, who is the image of God.*"

For the next several minutes the conversation drifted rather aimlessly. The group seemed to be headed some place, but it wasn't clear where – until Josh Siegel spoke.

"Something's wrong here," Josh said. "If what is being said here is true – and I want to make it clear that I totally agree with it – then what we are learning in our science classes about the origin of the world is a complete lie. That is just not right. If we really believe what we're saying here we should *do something* about it. If we don't, it looks like we accept this lie as being true. In my mind people who listen to something that they know is a lie and don't stand up and object to it are almost as guilty as the one telling the lie. In history we're studying World War II right now. Some of you guys are in my class. Isn't this what happened in Germany at that time? Didn't the German people passively accept Hitler's lies without standing up to him? And didn't that lead to countless millions of deaths?"

For a moment the room was silent. Josh had drawn a line in the sand, and no one was sure how to react to it.

"Well, what do you guys think?" Josh asked. "Do you agree with me or not? What about you, Dave. What do you think?"

"Uh, I don't know. Actually, I think what you said makes a lot of sense. But, hey, say we did want to do something about the situation. What the heck could we do? I mean, all of our science teachers seem to believe that the theory is true. What can we do to make them change their minds?"

Josh turned his attention to Jennifer. "What about you, Jen? What do you think? Is there something we can do here?"

Jennifer paused to collect her thoughts. Everyone was very interested in what she would say, because by this time, like Paul, they were all impressed with Jennifer's keen spiritual insight.

"Well, I must say that I definitely agree with you, Josh. I've been thinking along the same lines, but, to tell you the truth, I've been afraid to say anything about it. I'm really glad that you brought these ideas into the open, though. So, yes, I'm behind you one hundred percent. I do think we should do something about these things. I'm just not sure what, however ... What do you think, Paul? Do you agree with Josh?"

Paul took a deep breath before he responded to Jennifer's question.

"Okay, Jennifer. Since you've put me on the spot," he said with a smile, "I have to admit that – well, yes, I, too, agree one hundred percent with Josh that we probably should do something about this situation. I've actually thought about this notion more than once in the past. And I have some ideas, too. However, before I tell them to you I want you guys to talk it over. If anything actually happens, I feel very strongly that it should be driven by you, not me. So, the floor's open, guys. Let's hear what you have to say."

For the next forty-five minutes or so there was a spirited discussion about the issues that Josh had raised. By the time it was over, everyone in the room was in agreement that they should do something to counter the current policy in their school regarding the teaching of the theory of evolution. Furthermore, they were *excited* about the prospect. They recognized that it could be an exciting adventure for them. Paul agreed to investigate the possible avenues they could take and to try to have some information for them by the next meeting.

After the meeting, Josh and David lingered in the Conley's kitchen after the others had left.

"Well, Josh," Jennifer said, "it looks like you've really started something here, doesn't it? We may be about to hit the national headlines. I can see them now: 'The Creation/Evolution War Moves to Madison, New Hampshire.'"

"I don't think so," Josh replied with a big grin. "But hey, Jen ... Don't blame it all on me. You said that you agreed with me one hundred percent. You did, too, Dave!"

"Yeah, you're right, pal. I did … and I do. It's pretty crazy, isn't it? What the heck are we getting ourselves into? But hey, I'm actually kinda psyched. You gotta admit: it could be pretty exciting, right?"

"Yeah, you're right, Dave. It definitely could be," Jennifer replied. "I wonder what our strategy will be. Do you think we should try to have creation taught along with evolution? I know this has been tried before, without much success. One problem that I've read about with this approach is the teachers. Like, if our teachers all believe in evolution, and don't believe in creation, how can we expect them to present our side fairly? It's one thing for them to teach a lie that they believe is true – you know, evolution. It's another thing, however, for them to teach something as possibly being true if they are completely convinced that it isn't."

"Yeah, you're right, Jen," Dave said. "That certainly is a problem, isn't it? … Hey, I have an idea," he continued with a little grin. "Maybe Paul could come in and teach some classes on creation. Then our teachers wouldn't even have to deal with it."

"That's brilliant, genius," Josh observed. "After that, maybe Santa Claus could come in and teach a few classes on the meaning of Christmas."

"Hey, wait a minute," Jennifer quickly interjected. "What's wrong with that? As far as I'm concerned, Santa Claus is more believable than the theory of evolution, and every school in the country allows *it* to be taught. If they allow the theory of evolution to be taught, why couldn't Santa Claus come and teach the meaning of Christmas? And then, just think, in the spring, the Easter bunny could be invited in to teach the meaning of Easter."

"No, no, Jennifer," Josh said, wagging his finger. "Don't you see? Santa Claus is too closely connected to Christianity – remember, he is the symbol of CHRISTmas to most people today – so he could never be allowed in our classrooms. And I'm sure you both know why, right?"

"Of course," David said. "It's perfectly obvious: the separation of church and state."

"Okay, Dave," Jennifer said. "That takes care of Santa Claus. So, what about the Easter bunny? What's the matter with him? What would they have against him? He's just a harmless little bunny."

"Jennifer, how foolish can you be?" Dave quickly responded. "Don't you know that in order to teach in our public schools, teachers must be certified by the state? What were you *thinking*? The Easter bunny isn't certified. Heck, he probably never even went to grammar school!"

"But, hey, he's got one thing going for him that our teachers don't," Josh said. "At least he doesn't believe in the theory of evolution!"

"You're *right*, Josh," Jennifer replied. "Imagine that. A rabbit sitting in front of our classroom munching on a carrot and not saying a word would be a lot more helpful in pointing us toward the truth of creation than a human teaching us the theory of evolution. At least he wouldn't be teaching us *lies!*"

They all had a good laugh.

17

Getting Ready

" I've had a couple of meetings with the School Board about our petition. Here's what's going to happen."

The speaker was Paul Hopkins. It was the second October meeting of the Grace Bible Church youth group. He was referring to the petition that the group had discussed at their last meeting in September, to have creation taught along with evolution in the Madison schools. They had spent a lot of time at this September meeting debating the pros and cons of the idea, and Paul had warned them about the difficulties that they would surely encounter, but by the end of the meeting the decision to move forward was unanimous. Paul was chosen to meet with the School Board members in order to find out exactly how they should proceed.

"First of all, based upon previous similar petitions in other towns in various parts of the country, everyone was well aware that any public forum held to discuss the petition would attract a large audience, and not just people from Madison. Once word got out – and it would have to, because it would have to be announced publicly – the media would be all over it. It certainly had been at other such events. So, it was decided to hold it in the high school gym, which can seat over two thousand people when the entire floor is used for seating.

"The format will be a somewhat informal debate. There will be two panels, with five or six people on each one. One panel will be supporting the petition, the other will be opposed. The seven members of the School Board, who will ultimately make the decision about the petition, will be seated between the two panels. A professional moderator will be hired to regulate the debate. I think this is a great idea, by the way. The debate will be driven by questions from the School Board, but the moderator will be free to allow the speakers plenty of leeway. In other words, the speakers won't be restricted to time limits, as they usually are in more tightly run debates. In a sense, it will be more like a television talk show than a formal debate. Of course, as any of you who have seen these talk shows knows, this format can spin out of control if the moderator is not careful – that's why we decided to hire a professional!

"In addition to questions from the School Board members, questions from the audience may be permitted, also. We weren't able to decide exactly how this would happen. We'll have to discuss it further. So, that's the basic plan. What do you think?"

"When will the debate take place?" Sue Peterson asked.

"Oh yeah. I should have mentioned this … December 3rd, the second Friday after Thanksgiving."

"Who's going to be on the panel supporting the petition?" David asked.

"I don't know. I'll put in my two bits, but, basically, you guys are going to decide who the members will be."

"Really?" Mike Lawton asked. "You want *us* to decide?"

"That's right," Paul replied with a big grin. "Why not? It's your idea."

"That's pretty cool!" Mike said.

For the next twenty minutes or so, there was a spirited discussion about who should be on the creation panel. The selections narrowed down to Paul, Jennifer, and Josh. In addition, it was decided that it would be a good idea to include a lawyer. In regards to the fifth member, they couldn't decide upon any particular individual. They did agree, however, that it should be a professional scientist. Paul agreed to look into the matter.

By the time the meeting ended, one thing was clear to everyone: the event that they had precipitated was very important, and they were all looking forward to it with eager anticipation. Their prayers at the end of the meeting reflected these feelings. They were unusually focused, and passionate. Some people prayed for the first time. Paul closed the prayer time with a Bible verse:

> For our struggle is not against flesh and blood, but against the rulers, against the powers, against the world forces of this darkness, against the spiritual forces of wickedness in the heavenly places.

The last October meeting of the youth group was held on a Saturday night instead of Sunday. The sun was dipping below the western hills as the youth started to arrive at the Conley's home a few minutes before seven, and the air was quite chilly, in the mid 30's, hinting of the cold New England winter that was headed their way. The kids were particularly looking forward to this meeting, because they knew that Laura Conley and Sarah Hopkins had prepared a special treat for them: a big spaghetti dinner, with salad, Italian bread, and hot fudge sundaes for dessert. Laura's homemade pizzas had established her mastery of Italian food, so they fully expected that her spaghetti was not going to be ordinary. They were not disappointed. They had also been informed that they were going to be introduced to two special people: the other members of the creation panel: Martha Parker, a scientist, and Frank Morrison, an attorney. Paul introduced them to the group before they sat down to the meal.

After dinner, everyone moved to the living room.

After everyone was settled, Paul presented a brief description of Mrs. Parker.

"As some of you are aware, I'm sure, Mr. and Mrs. Parker were members of Grace Bible Church for a number of years. A few years ago they moved to Portland, Maine to be closer to their oldest daughter, Elizabeth. They still come down occasionally to visit our church.

"Martha was a geologist for a mining company for about twelve years. Over the years, she has been involved in a number of Christian ministries, including Bridges For Peace, which is an outreach to Jewish people living in Israel. One reason that I thought Martha would be particularly good for our panel is that after graduating from MIT, she worked in a radiometric-dating lab in Boston for almost five years. Radiometric dating is basically the Holy Grail of the evolutionary paradigm, and it will surely be raised in the upcoming debate. I thought it would be most helpful to have an expert on the subject on our panel. I think you would all be interested in hearing about her experience there."

Paul turned to Martha and gave her the floor. In her mid fifties and quite professional-looking, Martha was full of brightness and energy. Her eyes had a constant twinkle and her engaging smile, which appeared often, could melt the frown of the sourest soul, and often had. She was one of those rare individuals who really seemed to take the Lord's commandment in the Sermon on the Mount to heart: *Let your light shine before men in such a way that they may see your good works, and glorify your Father who is in heaven.*

"Thank you, Paul, for that generous introduction. I hope I can prove worthy of your estimate of me!"

For the next twenty minutes, Martha described her experience in the radiometric dating laboratory.

"Whew, that's really amazing," Josh spoke up after she had finished. "It almost seems like you think that radiometric dating is completely bogus, that there's no truth to it at all."

"I wouldn't go quite that far, Josh. It does have some things to tell us, but the notion that the earth is millions – or billions – of years old is definitely not one of them."

"But I thought that the ancient age of the earth is the *main* thing that it reveals," Josh said. "If it's not indicating that the earth is millions of years old, then what is it indicating?"

"I think it may be helpful in determining the *relative* ages of minerals, as opposed to the *absolute* ages."

"What do you mean?" Kelly asked. "I don't get it."

"In comparing two different rocks, Kelly, radiometric testing may be able to indicate which rock was older, but it can't indicate *how* old they are. You know, the ironic thing about radiometric dating is that so many people who completely accept radiometric dating as gospel truth don't even know the first thing about it. Ninety-nine people out of a hundred – or even more – have no idea, for example, that carbon dating is entirely different than the other dating methods, that carbon dating can only be used to date things that are supposedly no older than about 50,000 years.

"Take yourselves. Do you understand carbon dating, and why it can only be used to date relatively 'recent' objects? Have you discussed this issue in your meetings, Paul?"

"Not really," Paul responded. "We've brushed upon the subject a couple of times, but never in any depth."

"I'm not surprised … but, you know, it's a critical issue in this debate." An idea occurred to Martha. " Maybe we could spend a few minutes here and learn a little about it. What do you think, Paul. Is there time?"

"I think that's a great idea," Paul replied enthusiastically. Turning to the group, he asked, "What about you guys. Would you like to hear the inside scoop on radiocarbon dating, from someone who has witnessed it from the inside?"

Everyone enthusiastically agreed, so Martha began her description.

"Great. I'll try to be brief – but I'm not making any promises," she added with a big smile. "At the outset, I need to make something clear. Carbon dating is not used to date rocks; it is only used to date material that was once living, such as bones and plant material. It can date organic material *inside* rocks, but it can't date the rocks. For example, a tree buried by a lava flow can be dated by this method, but the hardened lava around it cannot be. Do you see what I'm saying?"

"How about petrified wood?" Mike asked. "It was once a living plant but is now a rock."

"That's an interesting question … um, What is your name?"

"Mike. Mike Lawton."

"Thank you, Mike. The answer to your question is 'No' – Carbon dating does not work on petrified wood, because petrified wood is entirely stone, primarily silicate, to be exact. The process of carbon dating actually begins high above the clouds, in the earth's upper atmosphere, with subatomic particles, mostly protons from atomic nuclei, called cosmic rays. Some scientists believe that these rays were caused by supernovas – exploding stars – at some point in the distant past, but it's only speculation. With energy far greater than any terrestrial particle accelerator is capable of producing, these rays bombard the earth at the rate of 200 times per second on every square meter of surface area. Like tiny invisible bullets streaking through the atmosphere at almost the speed of light, they silently pass through just about everything in their path, penetrating buildings, mountains – even our bodies. They can even be detected in caves carved into solid rock thousands of feet below the earth's surface. They are …"

"Wait a second," Mike interrupted. "These things pass through our *bodies*?"

"That's right, Mike – thousands *every minute.*"

"Wow!" Mike replied, feeling his chest. "That's unbelievable. Do they do any damage?"

"I agree with you, Mike. It certainly does seem unbelievable. As far as doing any damage, the answer is, 'Yes, they can.' They are similar to x-rays and are known to cause genetic damage to reproductive cells, by means of mutations, which results in birth defects. If there weren't some protection from them, life on our planet would be in grave danger."

"But if thousands of them pass through our bodies every minute, how come we're not in grave danger, anyway?" Sue Peterson asked.

"That certainly is a logical question, and to be honest I don't really know the answer," Martha said. "It's just the way it is. Odd though it seems, our bodies can withstand this onslaught fairly well. Like I just told Mike, though, occasionally these particles do cause mutations and perhaps some other damage, but if it wasn't for two protective barriers, it would be a lot worse. The first of these barriers is the earth's magnetic field, which extends into space and acts as a shield, deflecting cosmic particles toward the poles, where there's very little life to damage. The second line of defense is the earth's atmosphere, which consists, of course, of gaseous atoms, more than 70% of which are nitrogen. As you just learned, despite these protective barriers, a lot of these cosmic rays do enter the earth's atmosphere. And occasionally some of them collide with the nuclei of gaseous atoms. Now, what do you think happens next?"

"The nuclei get smashed to bits?" Ray suggested.

"Exactly! The nuclei get smashed up and their parts go flying into space. One of the things released is neutrons, which are one of the primary components of the nuclei. Now, these neutrons are captured by other atoms, primarily nitrogen, since they are the most common. Now, when these stable nitrogen 14 atoms pick up ..."

"What do you mean by 'stable'?" Peter Bernardo interrupted.

"Oh, yes, I'm sorry. I should have explained this to you. As the electrons in stable atoms fly around the nucleus, they obediently remain in their specified orbits. The electrons in unstable atoms, though, are rebels; they have a mind of their own. For some unknown reason they occasionally fly off into space. These atoms are called radioactive.

"Now, picking up where I left off, when stable nitrogen 14 atoms pick up one of these random neutrons, they become *unstable* carbon 14 atoms – *radioactive* carbon, in other words. Immediately after their formation these carbon 14 atoms are joined by two oxygen atoms ... two oxygen atoms and a carbon atom. What do we have now?"

"CO2 – carbon dioxide," Josh quickly replied.

"Right, Josh. Exactly – carbon dioxide. This carbon dioxide is just like regular carbon dioxide, carbon 12, except for one major difference: the carbon in it is radioactive – unstable, that is. What happens next is that these new unstable carbon dioxide molecules mix together with all of the stable carbon dioxide molecules and become part of the great carbon cycle of life.

"What's the ratio between the two types of carbon?" Josh asked.

"A very important question, Josh, and I'll get to it. Before I do, though, let me ask a question. What do I mean when I say that those molecules become part of the carbon cycle of life?"

"Do you mean the food chain, the process that provides food to living creatures and that starts with plants breathing in carbon dioxide?" Jennifer asked.

"Yes, that's exactly what I mean, Jennifer. Very good. And since some of the carbon in this carbon dioxide that initiates this process is radioactive, the plants are breathing it in along with all of the other carbon dioxide. The carbon dioxide is absorbed by the leaves of the plants – this is their method of breathing – and then, through the process of photosynthesis, converted into sugars. Through the chain of the food cycle, these sugars eventually work their way into the bones and other body parts of animals when they eat these plants."

"So there's some radioactive carbon in our bones?" David asked.

"Yes, David, there is – in your bones and in the bones of every other creature on the face of the earth. Now, as soon as these unstable radioactive carbon atoms form, something starts to happen: they begin to decay by emitting beta particles – electrons, that is. Eventually, they also lose the extra neutron that they had picked up. As a result of these things, they revert back to stable nitrogen 14. This process is called radioactive decay, and it occurs at a constant, steady rate. It's important to understand exactly what is meant by a 'steady rate,' because it's not quite as straightforward as it sounds. Simply put, the term applies to a *group* of carbon 14 atoms, but not to the individual atoms in the group. That is, although the decay rate for the group is known, the decay rate for any individual atom in the group cannot be predicted. It could decay in a minute, a year, 10,000 years, or 100,000 years – nobody knows when it will happen. Furthermore, nobody knows *why* it happens, either. Rather strangely, even though the decay rate of any individual carbon 14 atom is entirely unpredictable, the time it takes for half of the group to decay *is* known. It's called the half-life. And for carbon 14 it's 5,760 years, as best as scientists can determine. If a sample under observation, for example, contains one thousand atoms of carbon 14, in 5,760 years half of them will have decayed into nitrogen 14, leaving only five hundred.

"Now, as long as a creature – an animal or plant – is alive, the ratio of carbon 12 to carbon 14 in his body remains exactly the same as it is in the atmosphere, because his cells are constantly being nourished, and eventually completely recycled, through his food intake and body functions. Since the carbon ratio in the food is the same as that in the atmosphere, and his body is created by this food, the ratio of these carbon atoms will be the same in his body, also.

"When the creature dies, however, this ratio immediately begins to change, because he is no longer ingesting food. This is when the radiocarbon clock begins ticking. The carbon within him is no longer recycled, as it had been when he was alive; it remains within him. As the radioactive carbon decays, the carbon ratio changes. And as more and more of this carbon decays, the ratio of the carbon 12 to the carbon 14 becomes greater and greater.

"Now, based upon the information I have just given you, it is possible to determine how the radiocarbon dating process works. Would anyone like to give it a try?"

"I'll give it a shot," Josh immediately replied.

"Good, Josh. Go right ahead," Martha replied. "I'm interested to see how you do, because I can almost guarantee you that this topic will probably come up in the upcoming debate." Martha had been previously informed that Josh and Jennifer would be members of the creationist panel at the debate.

"Okay," Josh began, "it's pretty simple as far as I can see. Let me use an example. For the sake of argument, suppose that the ratio between the stable carbon 12 and the radioactive carbon 14 in the atmosphere is, say, one hundred to one ... Is that anywhere close, Mrs. Parker?"

"It'll work for now, Josh. Like I said before, we'll talk about this ratio shortly."

"All right," Josh continued. "So, for every radioactive atom of carbon in this example, there are one hundred stable ones. Now, let's say we have a sample from some dead animal, a bone for example, and that in this sample there are ten thousand atoms of carbon 12 and fifty of carbon 14. The bone would be 5,760 years old. Here's why. When it was alive, for every ten thousand atoms of carbon 12 in its body, it would have had one hundred atoms of carbon 14 – a ratio of one hundred to one, just like in the atmosphere. Since in the sample there are only fifty, instead of one hundred, then half of the original ones – the ones in the animal's body when it died – have decayed. So one half-life, 5,760 years, has gone by.

"So, all you have to do to determine something's age is to calculate its ratio of carbon 12 to carbon 14 and compare it to the ratio of these two atoms in the atmosphere. Knowing that it takes 5,760 years for half of the carbon 14 atoms to decay into nitrogen, it's pretty easy to calculate the object's age ... How is that, Mrs. Parker?"

"That's excellent, Josh," Martha replied with a smile, duly impressed. " I couldn't have explained it any better myself."

Mrs. Parker turned her attention toward the others in the room. "How about the rest of you? Did you follow Josh's explanation? Do you have a pretty good idea of how this process works now?" Some nodding heads indicated that at least some of the kids were following the explanation.

"Before moving on, let me ask you a question. Suppose that in Josh's example there were only twenty-five atoms of carbon instead of fifty. How old would the bone be then?"

"Two half-lives – about 11,500 years old," Mike quickly replied.

"Very good, Mike. So, then, the process seems pretty clean and simple, doesn't it? There doesn't appear to be any reason to doubt the results, right?"

As Martha expected, there was general agreement with her statement.

"Well, I hate to disappoint you, but the process is nowhere near as accurate as it appears – not even close. It's actually riddled with assumptions and uncertainties, which cast a very dark cloud over its results."

Martha paused. "You know, we've been going on about this subject for quite some time now. Perhaps you're getting a little tired of listening to me. I know that this subject can be pretty boring. I wonder if it might be a good idea to …"

"No, wait!" Jennifer blurted out. "I don't know about everyone else, but I really want to find out what the problems are. It's starting to get exciting. You can't stop *now*."

As Martha had hoped, it was apparent that the others shared Jennifer's feelings

"Well, I'm very pleased to see your interest. It's great. I'm sure that in time it will become very clear to you that the time we're spending here tonight will prove to be well spent! Now, let's talk about the assumptions underlying radiocarbon dating. Can anyone tell me what one might be?"

After a pause, David spoke up.

"Well, Mrs. Parker, one assumption, I guess, is that the ratio of carbon 12 to carbon 14 in the atmosphere has always remained constant, at least over the time period that the process is supposed to cover – like, I think you said about 50,000 years, or so. If this ratio had been different in the past from what it is now, there would be no way to tell how old a sample was. Like in Josh's explanation, for example, if the ratio of carbon 12 to carbon 14 had been two hundred to one a few thousand years ago, rather than one hundred to one, if scientists assumed that this ratio had always been one hundred to one, the dates that they came up with would just be wrong."

"Exactly, David. You zeroed right in on one of the major assumptions of this process, that the ratio of carbon 12 to carbon 14 has remained consistent. Now, I want you to think about this assumption for a moment. How justified do you think it is to assume that this ratio has been perfectly constant for tens of thousands of years?"

"Why wouldn't it be justified?" Mike asked. "What would ever cause it to change?"

"A few things, Mike. Tell me, what is it that causes carbon atoms to form?"

"Cosmic rays from outer space."

"Right ... and what did I tell you were the two barriers that protected the earth from these particles, that kept most of them away from us?"

"Well, one of them was the earth's magnetic field ... and the other was the earth's atmosphere."

"Right, Mike. First of all, in regards to the mixture of carbon 12 and carbon 14 in the atmosphere, you need to know that all the while that radioactive carbon is being created by cosmic rays in the atmosphere, some of the radioactive carbon that has already been created is in the process of decay. Radiocarbon dating is based upon the assumption that these two processes are in balance, that for every atom of carbon 14 created in the atmosphere, another such atom decays. If this wasn't so, if these processes were not in balance, then the radiocarbon dating method would be invalid, because a fundamental element of the process, the carbon 12 to carbon 14 ratio in the past, would be impossible to determine. Now here's the truth: the decay and formation rate of carbon 14 in the atmosphere is *not in balance at all.* The decay rate is about 30% less than the production rate in the atmosphere. This means that the concentration of carbon 14 is constantly increasing, which means, of course, that the carbon 12 to carbon 14 ratio has been changing over the years and that it undoubtedly was not the same in the past as it is today..."

"Which means that the dates acquired by this dating method aren't reliable," Mike observed with a knowing grin.

"Exactly," Martha replied, smiling at Mike. "Now, what is the other thing that shields the earth from cosmic rays?"

"The magnetic field," Josh quickly replied.

"That's right, Josh. Now here is a very interesting fact. It has been conclusively demonstrated that the strength of the earth's magnetic field is decreasing, and at a surprisingly rapid rate. The field, in other words, was stronger in the past than it is presently. So how do you think that might affect the ratio between carbon 12 and carbon 14, and the entire radiocarbon dating process?"

"Well, if the field was stronger in the past," Josh said, "then it would have blocked out more cosmic particles than it does now, which means that less carbon 14 would have formed – which means that the ratio of carbon 12 to carbon 14 would have been higher in the past than it is now."

"Right," Martha replied. "And if this ratio was greater in the past than it is now, how would the radiocarbon dating process be affected? I mean, suppose, for example, that the ratio between carbon 12 and carbon 14 was two hundred to one at some time in the past rather than the supposed current ratio of one hundred to one, but that the C14 had been decaying ever since at the current rate …"

"Then the estimated date would be older than the real date," Josh quickly interjected.

"Why, Josh?"

"Well, let's say, for example, that 5,760 years ago the carbon 12 to carbon 14 ratio in the atmosphere was 200-1, like you suggested, instead of 100-1, as it supposedly is now, and that a bone from some animal that died at that time was tested by the radiocarbon method. According to the test, the ratio in the bone was 400-1. Now, if the scientists testing the bone assumed that the atmospheric ratio of carbon 12 to carbon 14 has always been what it supposedly is now, 100-1, they would assume that two half lives, about 11,500, years had passed since the animal died. The way they figured it, in one half-life, 5,760 years, the ratio would have only increased to 200-1; it would have taken another half-life to increase to 400-1.

"The problem here is that if the carbon 12 to carbon 14 ratio had actually been 200-1 5,760 years ago – when the animal died – then it would have taken only one half-life for the ratio to become 400-1. The bottom line is that the scientists' estimate of the bone's age was wrong because the assumption it was based upon – that the atmospheric ratio of carbon 12 to carbon 14 has always been the same – was wrong."

"That was good, Josh – very good," Martha said with an appreciative smile. "Thank you."

"Uhh, I'm a little confused, Mrs. Parker," Sue Peterson said. "I'm not sure I get the connection between the earth's magnetic field and radiocarbon dating. Could you go over it one more time."

"Certainly," Martha replied, eager to do whatever she could to help everyone understand this very important matter. "The central feature of radiocarbon dating is the ratio between radioactive carbon, carbon 14, and stable carbon, carbon 12. In order to obtain an accurate estimate of an object's age, this ratio must be known at three specific points: the object being tested, the current atmosphere, and the atmosphere at the time the organism died. As I explained earlier, most radioactive carbon is caused by cosmic rays bombarding atoms in the upper atmosphere. Now, the earth's magnetic field shields the earth from these cosmic rays, and the stronger the field, the greater the shield. It is now known that the strength of the magnetic field has been decreasing over the years, which means, of course, that it was stronger in the past. If it was stronger in the past, less radioactive carbon would have been created in the past – and if less radioactive carbon was created in the past, the ratio between carbon 12 and carbon 14 would have been greater in the past than it is now. Radiocarbon dating is based upon the assumption that this ratio has always been the same, at least over the past 50-100,000 years. But the decreasing magnetic field implies that it wasn't. And if it wasn't, the dates attained by radiocarbon dating can't be accurate.

"Does that help?"

"Yes, it does. I think I get it now," Sue replied. "Thank you."

"You're welcome," Martha responded with a warm smile. "Now, there's only one more item I want to bring to your attention – the *actual* ratio of carbon 12 to carbon 14. In his illustration Josh used a ratio of one hundred to one. In reality, the ratio is a bit greater than this. Would anyone like to venture a guess as to what it is?"

"A thousand to one," David guessed.

"A million to one," Josh offered.

"Not quite," Martha said. "What about you, Jennifer? Do you want to venture a guess?"

"Hmmm … Let's see. Eenie, meenie, minie, mo …" Jennifer said, shifting her finger back and forth from David to Josh. "How about five hundred thousand to one?"

Smiling at Jennifer, Martha said, "I'm afraid you're all just a little bit off. The current atmospheric ratio is about one part carbon 14 to *765 billion* parts carbon 12. For argument's sake, let's just round this off to a trillion to one. And let me give you an illustration of just how huge a number this is. What size container do you think would be required to hold a trillion grains of sand?"

The guesses were a five-gallon can, a trashcan, and a 55-gallon drum . Martha then told them the correct answer.

"No, I'm afraid you're a little bit off once again. To hold a trillion grains of sand a *swimming pool* would be required! The size of the pool would depend upon the size of the grains of sand. Large grains would require a large pool, seventy to seventy five feet long. Medium and smaller sized grains would require a smaller pool.

"No way!" David exclaimed, reflecting upon the image. "A *swimming pool!* That's unbelievable!"

Martha quickly demonstrated the logic behind her analysis. After explaining that there would be about 1,500-5,000 grains of sand per square inch, she showed that this would translate to about 60-250,000 grains per cubic inch, and about 100-400 million per cubic foot – which would mean that a handful would contain about 1-4 million grains, she added. From here, demonstrating the number of grains held within a swimming pool was a couple of quick steps.

"So, then," she said, "the ratio between carbon 12 and carbon 14 is approximately the same as a single grain of sand to an entire swimming pool full of sand. Needless to say, such an extraordinarily large ratio could make accurate testing a bit difficult – which is precisely the reason that this dating method can never be trusted to date anything more than about 50,000 years old – assuming, of course, that anything actually even existed that long ago, which I certainly do *not* believe, of course.

"You see, with the passing of each half-life the carbon 12 to carbon 14 ratio doubles. Thus, in only four half-lives, about 23,000 years, the ratio is about twelve trillion to one, and in seven half-lives, about 40,000 years, it is one hundred trillion to one. Obviously, at such astronomical ratios, it becomes increasingly difficult to accurately calculate it.

"So, my young friends, there you have it: the inside story of radiocarbon dating. The stuff you don't read about in your science textbooks or encyclopedias. Now, perhaps you'd like to hear about some of the other radiometric dating methods. There's only three or four that are really significant. I'm sure we could cover them in about ..."

"Okay, Martha," Paul interrupted with a smile, knowing that Martha was just fooling around. "I'm sure that the kids here would love to stick around for a few more hours to hear the exciting tale of the uranium/lead or potassium/argon dating methods, but I think we've had about enough for tonight. I do want to say, however, that that was a wonderful explanation of radiocarbon dating. I had never heard that analogy of the sand in the swimming pool before. Where did you find it?"

"Actually, Paul, I figured it out myself. It's quite good, isn't it? You know, even though I've checked over the figures very thoroughly, I still find them very hard to comprehend. It sure is a heckuva lot of sand, isn't it?!"

"Before we move on, I just have a quick question, Mrs. Parker," Josh interjected. "Is radiocarbon dating reliable under *any* circumstances?"

"When used carefully, Josh, the dates seem to be reasonably accurate when limited to recorded human history, say back to 2,500 or 3,000 B.C. Even when restricted to these dates, however, there have been many instances in which the dates were proven to be completely mistaken."

The time for the meeting to end was nearing. Before it did, however, Paul wanted to introduce the final member of the panel, Frank Morrison. Morrison was forty-seven years old, of medium stature and common appearance, humble and friendly. He was also an outstanding attorney who had worked on several cases for the most powerful Christian law firm in the country, The American Center for Law and Justice, the ACLJ. He believed deeply in biblical creationism and was thrilled when Paul asked him to consider being on this panel.

"Thank you very much for inviting me to be on your panel, Paul," Morrison said after Paul had introduced him. "It is an honor. I think you all are doing a great thing here. In light of all the problems with the theory of evolution, some of which we've heard here tonight, it's outrageous that it has gained such a stranglehold on our nation's educational system. As you know, your petition is not the first effort of its kind. As I'm sure you also know, most of the previous ones have met with failure. But that doesn't mean there's no hope. There's a wonderful quote that applies very well to this situation. It's usually attributed to the eighteenth century Irish statesman, Edmund Burke. Perhaps some of you have heard it. It states that, *the only thing necessary for the triumph of evil is for good men to do nothing.* I believe very deeply, as I know that you all do, that the theory of evolution is a blasphemous evil that turns people away from their Creator. If people do nothing to oppose it, it will continue to reign supreme in our school's science curriculums. But you, good people, have chosen to do something about it. You have chosen to fight for the truth, and I commend you for it. Furthermore, I guarantee you that, whether it's in this life or the next, your efforts will be rewarded.

"I just want to say one more thing. The proponents of evolutionary theory fight with an unholy vehemence to see that creationism doesn't get its foot in the door of our nation's science curriculum. Considering the fragile foundation of the theory of evolution, this vehemence makes no sense. Science is supposed to be a search for the truth about the natural world. If that was true, educators should welcome the presentation of alternative theories about our origins ... Lord knows, there certainly is a need for them! This vehemence, however, clearly indicates that there is something far more at stake here than a defense of science. What these people are desperately seeking to keep out of your classrooms is not a theory about the world's origins, my friends; it is the One who created it: Our Lord and Savior, Jesus Christ – our Creator. As the apostle Paul said so wisely, *Our struggle here is not against flesh and blood, but against the spiritual forces of wickedness.* I'm sure you all know what *the spiritual forces of wickedness* is referring to, right?"

"Yeah," Scott Martin quickly responded. "Satan and his armies."

"That's right. So, once again, I thank you for the opportunity to help you, and I promise you that I will do everything in my power to see that you emerge victorious. This is going to be an exciting journey, and I'm really glad, and honored, to be included in it," Morrison closed, with a pump of his fist.

About fifteen minutes later the meeting ended.

After the meeting, Jennifer, Josh, David, Mike, and Paul hung around for a little while in the kitchen talking about the upcoming meeting and imagining what it would be like.

"I was at a similar meeting one time in Ohio a few years ago," Paul said, "and I'll tell you, it was pretty crazy. The meeting was held in a high school gym, which is exactly where ours will be held, and the atmosphere in the building was absolutely electric. The purpose of the meeting was exactly what ours is going to be: to try to get creation taught in the school alongside evolution. I had such a strong sense that the room was going to be the scene of a battle, a spiritual battle, that is ... and, man, I'll tell you, it sure was! The room was packed with people, including representatives from many major media companies. I could tell you a lot more, but I don't really need to. I think you'll all see a live reenactment of the meeting in a few weeks – right in your own gym!"

Soon, Paul, Josh, and Mike left, leaving Jennifer and David alone.

"So, what are you going to do the rest of the evening, Jen – homework?" David asked.

"No, I'm all caught up. I think I'll watch a movie."

"Oh yeah? What's on?"

"Oh, I'm not going to watch one on TV. I think I'll watch a DVD we have: *Chariots of Fire*."

"Hmmm … that sounds pretty good. I've heard something about it, but I've never seen it. Is it any good?"

"No, not really. I prefer watching lousy movies," Jennifer said with a little grin.

"Funny," David said, his cheeks a little red. "It's about some Christian athlete, isn't it?"

"Actually, it's about two athletes. One, Eric Liddell, is a Christian, the other Harold … uh, I can't remember his last name … is a Jew. It's an awesome story. And what's better is that it's true. I'm sure you'd really love it."

"It sounds pretty cool. Maybe I'll get to see it some day."

Jennifer paused for a moment. A thought had come to her.

"Hey, why don't you stay and watch it with me tonight. I don't think my parents would mind."

"That's a great idea," David instantly replied. "I'll call home and let them know what's going on."

In a minute David and Jennifer moved into the den, where the TV was. There were a couple of easy chairs and a big, comfortable couch. David let Jennifer sit down first, hoping she would choose the couch. She did. As casually as he could, David joined her on the couch, not too close – but not too far away, either.

As the minutes passed, David tried hard to concentrate on the movie, but he was distracted by a plan he had in mind. Casually, he inched closer to Jennifer, hoping that she wouldn't notice the diminishing distance between them. To his surprise, she didn't appear to. After about twenty minutes, the first goal of his mission was secured: he was right next to Jennifer. His next goal, getting his arm around Jennifer, loomed as a far more formidable challenge. He knew what he had to do: move his arm. And he knew that this move would have to be very subtle. After several false starts, he slowly placed his arm behind Jennifer, resting it on the back of the couch. It was an important move, a major advance, but it was not contact. Finally, he dropped his hand upon Jennifer's shoulder, sure that this would bring his mission to a screeching halt. To his utter amazement and joy, she didn't offer the slightest resistance! Slowly but surely, he inched his hand down Jennifer's arm until she was actually wrapped in his arm. Then, something incredible happened. Jennifer turned towards David and gave him a warm smile! It turned him into putty. He couldn't believe his fortune! Of course, at this point, Jennifer took a firm grip on David's hand – to make sure that it could move no further!

For the remainder of the movie – fifteen minutes – David had trouble focusing on the movie. It's hard to focus on earthly things from cloud nine.

Once the notice of the petition appeared in the local papers, it quickly spawned a steady stream of feature articles and letters. Hardly a day went by in which the issue was ignored. It wasn't long before the story's scent was picked up by, first, the large regional media outlets and, second, the national media.

One of the feature writers of the *Manchester Daily Messenger* found the story particularly enticing. He knew from past experience that the evolution/creation debate was guaranteed to ignite interest and controversy, and he didn't waste any time lighting the first match. His name was Karl Bond. His first article on the subject appeared two days after the petition was announced:

A long time ago, probably when I was in high school, I first learned of the famous "Monkey Trial" that took place in Dayton, Tennessee, in 1925, in which a young high school teacher, John Scopes, was indicted for teaching the theory of evolution to his innocent students. At the time, my young mind placed the event in the dim past, when people lived in log cabins and read books by candlelight and didn't really know too much, and I assumed that the thinking that inspired it had long since disappeared. In fact, if I hadn't discovered that the trial had gained the appellation "The Most Famous Courtroom Trial in American History," I might have thought it was a comedy (to tell you the truth, I'm still not convinced that it wasn't). I mean, think about it, the central purpose of the prosecution was to outlaw the teaching of a scientific theory that has been proven to be about as certain as the law of gravity! Could that really have been a *serious* trial?

From such a perspective, you can imagine how dumbfounded I was to find out about the petition that has
been initiated by a local fundamentalist youth pastor
that proposes to have creation taught alongside the
theory of evolution in our local schools. What I re-
garded as a completely obsolete theory that had been
utterly abandoned by anyone who had made it through
grammar school is actually alive and well – right here
in our own backyard! And guess what … The antiquated
views of our esteemed youth pastor are hardly isolated. According to a recent Gallup poll, when asked
about human origins, 44 percent of Americans checked
the box that said, "God created human beings pretty
much in their present form sometime in the last 10,000
years or so."

When I saw that poll, you could have knocked me over
with a feather. More than eighty years after Clarence
Darrow made William Jennings Bryan look like a buffoon
on the witness stand and a century and a half after
Charles Darwin's brilliant revelation of the master
plan for the evolution of life, almost half of the
American populace apparently know absolutely nothing
about Darwin's magnificent theory – despite the fact
that it's taught in every public high school in the
United States.

Most people who have any familiarity with the
Scopes trial have acquired it from the movie "Inherit
the Wind." This movie portrays Clarence Darrow as the
shrewd leading man of the story and William Jennings
Bryan as his naïve stooge. This is a misrepresentation
of the actual events, for the truth is that Bryan racked
up just as many points in the debate as Darrow. Unlike
Darrow, however, who peppered his remarks with pearls
of wisdom from biology, geology, archaeology and other
branches of science to back his claims, Bryan took a
somewhat different approach. His source of wisdom was
limited to a single book – the Bible. It was as if the

last five centuries of scientific discoveries had never taken place. Some of you may know that the prosecution ended up victorious in the Scopes trial. The biology teacher, John Scopes, was declared guilty. Based upon the Gallup poll cited earlier, what's unbelievable is that if the trial had been held today and the decision was left up to a jury of average citizens, the verdict might end up the same!

As loyal readers of my column, perhaps you are wondering where I stand on this great debate about evolution and creation. I am a great believer in the truth, and I believe that in science as in every other field children ought to be exposed to all views so they can make up their minds for themselves. They should learn that some people believe that the world is round while others believe it is flat; that some believe that mice are generated spontaneously from dirty underwear while others believe that a mouse can only be generated from another mouse, or two; that some believe that we should study the stars in order to expand our knowledge about astronomy, while others believe that they should be studied because they can provide guidance for our lives, like who we should marry and where we should invest our money; that some believe that with the proper hocus-pocus base metals can be magically transformed into gold while others believe that the only place to find gold is in, well, gold mines.

In other words, along with astronomy, biology, and chemistry, I believe that students should learn about astrology, abiogenesis, and alchemy. To round out their education, they should also be exposed to the notion that the moon is made of Swiss cheese, that Bigfoot is alive and well, that the earth is an inverted bowl, and that Mars is inhabited by little green men. In other words, students should be exposed to all theories, regardless of their relationship to reality. Surely, bright young students can separate fact from fiction on their own – even though it apparently presents an insurmountable problem for about half of their parents.

Needless to say, Mr. Bond's article instigated a number of letters of response. Here is one of them:

In his recent article blasting the recent petition to include the teaching of creationism in Madison's schools Mr. Bond maligns the intelligence of William Jennings Bryan: "Unlike Darrow, however, who peppered his remarks with pearls of wisdom from biology, geology, archaeology and other branches of science to back his claims, Bryan took a somewhat different approach. His source of wisdom was limited to a single book – the Bible. It was as if the last five centuries of scientific discoveries had never taken place."

Mr. Bryan attended Illinois College where he studied classics, graduating in 1881 as valedictorian, and earned his law degree from the Union College of Law in Chicago. After practicing law for four years, he went to serve in the US House of Representatives from 1891 to 1895. He was the Democratic candidate for the President of the US three times and was secretary of state under Woodrow Wilson. As a delegate to the Democratic National convention in 1896 Bryan delivered his famous "Cross of Gold" speech, which has been called "the most famous speech ever made before an American political convention."

He is widely known as being one of the most popular and commanding speakers in American history. He obviously left an indelible mark on history.

Does this man sound *unintelligent* to you?

Over eighty years after his death, Google lists over half a million Web sites under Mr. Bryan's name.

How many Web sites mention Mr. Bond? And how many will mention *him* eighty years after his death?

18

In Defense of Evolution

"Basically, Dick, what I'm asking is this: why are you, and so many others around here, so strongly opposed to this petition? It seems to me that the petition has some merit. After all, not everyone agrees with the theory of evolution. But the way science departments operate today, that's the only theory of origins that kids ever hear about. What would be so bad about hearing an alternative view? If the theory of evolution is true, it should be able to withstand a little friendly competition, shouldn't it?"

The questioner was Bob Campbell, a reporter from the *Portland Press Herald*. His questions were directed to Dick Potter, who was sitting across the table from him at Carney's, a pub on the north end of Madison. The old hand-hewn beams that framed the lounge in the pub showed the hands of a skilled carpenter: tight mortise and tenon joints, pegged corner braces, and a rich, hand-rubbed oil finish. The striking beauty of these beams was complemented by the natural wood furniture: dark oak tables and chairs and a spectacular native cherry bar. In the rear of the lounge were two high-quality regulation pool tables and three dartboards. It was a classy pub and over the years had become a favorite gathering place of professors from the University of New Hampshire, particularly those in the science department. It was also Mr. Potter's favorite hangout.

Two others were at the table: Brian Miller, a biology professor at UNH and a friend of Potter's who would be joining him on the opposition panel at the upcoming hearing, and Neil Goldman, a reporter from the *New York Times*. It was a few days before Thanksgiving, less than two weeks before the hearing. Campbell and Goldman had been sent to Madison early to do some background research on the meeting. With their well-honed intuition for sources of information, all it took for the two reporters to locate Carney's was a few questions in the biology department at UNH. They had met Potter and Miller at the pool table earlier in the evening, and they had sat down for sandwiches. It hadn't taken long for the conversation to turn to the hearing.

"Okay, Bob, let me see if I can answer those questions for you," Potter said while sipping his beer. "In our science classes, we're supposed to be teaching truth, or at least concepts that are as close to the truth as possible. Now, I'll admit that there are elements of evolutionary theory – like the origin of matter and the bridge between non-living chemicals and living organisms – that are still to some extent or another mysteries. But apart from these few gray areas, almost all scientists accept the rest of the theory as fact.

"The biblical creation story, on the other hand – and this is without a doubt the creation account being promoted by those who presented this petition – is not literally true. It was written, I'm sure you know, almost 3,500 years ago, millenniums before the invention of even the microscope or telescope. But it wasn't just the microscope and telescope that didn't exist in those days; practically speaking, *science* didn't even exist in those days. The creation account was a poetic attempt to give meaning to the vast, mysterious natural world that the people of those days were so intimately involved with. As poetry, it is very beautiful and powerful. It introduces all the major elements of the natural world: the universe with the stars, the earth and the sun and the moon, and all the classes and groups of creatures, including us. But it's not *factually true*. It's *poetry*. My God, Bob, look at some of the things the story claims ... first of all, that the whole universe and everything within it was created in six literal, twenty-four hour days! Of course, *that* part of the story is not poetry. I have a name for it, but, not knowing your beliefs about religion, I don't want to appear blasphemous in front of you guys. Every literate person today, even kids in grammar school, knows that the world ..."

"Wait a second," Neil Goldman interrupted. "A lot of creationists believe that these days were actually much longer periods of time, thousands of years, perhaps, or maybe even longer."

Potter had heard this idea before, of course – many, many times, in fact – and had little patience for it.

"Yeah, you're right ... theistic evolutionists. And why do you think they believe these days are not literal?"

"I suppose that they think that if these days can be stretched out long enough, then their creation account won't conflict with the evolutionary account."

"Exactly. Now, corresponding to that thought, let me ask you a question: how old is the universe?"

"You mean according to evolutionary theory?"

"According to *science* – you know, *reality*," Potter responded impatiently.

"Well, according to what I read in my paper, about fifteen or sixteen billion years, I guess."

"Right. Now, if the creation account is lengthened to harmonize with evolutionary theory, how long would each day be?"

"Hmmm, let's see … that's not too difficult: fifteen billion divided by six – about two and a half billion years each."

"Right again. Now, in the biblical account, on what day was the sun created?"

"I'm not a Bible scholar," Goldman said, smiling, "but I'll take a stab at it … how about the first?"

"Wrong," Bob Campbell spoke up. "It was created on the fourth day."

"Correct, Bob," Potter said. "And when were plants created?"

"On the third day," Campbell said. "Hmmm … I think I see where you're headed here. If the lengths of the days of the biblical creation account are made to harmonize with evolutionary theory, then the plants would have had to exist for a few hundred million years without any sunlight. A bit unlikely, I'd say."

"You got it!" Potter exclaimed. "Totally absurd, isn't it? And that's just one of the many inconsistencies that cause me not to take these theistic evolutionists seriously. I mean, has this point *ever* occurred to them?! It seems so *obvious*, doesn't it? How can they possibly not recognize it? God, those folks drive me nuts. They think that their theory ties together the biblical account of creation with evolutionary theory, but they obviously don't realize that this is absolutely impossible. It's like trying to reconcile the Ptolemaic theory of the earth being at the center of the universe with the Copernican one, in which the sun is at the center of our solar system. It's simply impossible. They both can't be right – unless, perhaps, the sun and the earth agree to switch places every few years!"

"Here's another problem with the attempt to reconcile the two theories," Brian Miller offered. "In the biblical story, the birds were created before the reptiles, which belonged to the 'creeping things and beasts of the earth' created on the sixth day. The birds were created, along with the fish, on the fifth day. We now know, of course, that birds evolved *from* reptiles – so they couldn't have existed *before* them."

"How do you know that with such certainty?" Neil Goldman asked.

"From the fossil record, and radiometric dating, of course," Miller replied. "There's really very little doubt about it."

Mr. Potter returned to the subject of theistic evolution. "You know, for all practical purposes, the beliefs of theistic evolutionists are almost exactly the same as those of evolutionists. The only difference is that they believe that God played some role in the process. They accept the whole process of evolution, in other words, but insist that God designed it, or started it, or had something to do with it. Hard-core evolutionists, on the other hand – which includes, of course, almost all real scientists – make no claim at all about any role God might have played. Maybe He was involved, maybe He wasn't. There's no way we can tell from examining the evidence, so it really doesn't concern us. If religious folks want to believe that a Creator was involved in the process, that's their prerogative, and they're welcome to it … as long as they don't try to push their beliefs into our classrooms, that is."

"Let me point something out here, Neil," Brian Miller said. "From listening to what Dick has just said, you might think that scientists' attitude toward God's role in evolution is 'take it or leave it.' You know, like he said, maybe God was involved in the process, maybe He wasn't. I know Dick will agree with me that that's not precisely accurate. Evolutionists actually make a conscious effort to exclude God from the process. You see …"

"Which is exactly the issue creationists have with your teaching," Bob Campbell interrupted.

"Okay, that's right, Bob. But just let me finish my point, okay? Scientists believe that the natural world, the world that we can observe and study – the cosmos, as Carl Sagan put it – is all there is and that everything must be explained in terms of the things of this world. God, on the other hand, is supernatural. If He exists, He exists in a spiritual realm that is outside the natural world. This is the realm of not only God, but also, supposedly, of angels, demons, the devil, heaven, hell, etc. Now, we're not making a judgment on the existence of this world, but we are saying – and very emphatically – that the supernatural cannot be factored into scientific observations and conclusions and theories. The reason is very simple: there's no way to scientifically test, or prove, something that's supernatural. Once supernaturalism is accepted as an explanation for things in the world, it can explain anything – without any scientific evidence. As scientists, we simply cannot accept such a parameter. Wouldn't you agree, Dick?"

"I certainly would, Brian. That was very well said."

"What about the laws of nature – you know, gravity, electromagnetism, etcetera?" Neil Goldman asked. "How can you explain their origin? They control the entire world, but it's pretty difficult to imagine how they could have evolved. I mean, what did they evolve *from*?"

"Ahhh, that's a very good question, Neil," Mr. Potter said. "And I'm afraid I don't have the answer for you. Let's just say that it's one of the mysteries of the process that yet remains to be revealed. Oh, and one more thing … If the audience is permitted to ask questions at the hearing December third, please do me a favor – Don't ask that one!

"If you don't mind, I'd like to wrap up my thoughts about theistic evolutionists. I want to make sure that you understand that the people behind this petition – or any similar petition that has ever been presented – are definitely not theistic evolutionists. In fact – and you have probably already discovered this at previous similar hearings – whenever the theory of evolution is challenged, theistic evolutionists are invariably *with* us, not against us. The people behind this petition are fundamentalist Christians who interpret the Bible absolutely literally. Most of them are reluctant to come right out and say it – they're too nice, if you know what I mean – but they think that theistic evolution is just as far off the mark as we do. Practically speaking, these people believe in a six-day creation, a very young earth and a worldwide flood that took place only a few thousand years ago. Plus – and this is huge – except for horizontal variation at the species level, they utterly reject the entire theory of evolution. Theistic evolutionists, like evolutionists, basically reject every one of these notions."

"Speaking of the age of the earth, do those who initiated this petition believe in a young earth?" Bob Campbell asked.

"Like I just said, Bob, this is an integral feature of their package. Of course they do," Mr. Potter answered.

"How young do they say it is?"

"About six to ten thousand years old – with most of them leaning toward the younger age."

"That's really unbelievable, isn't it?" Goldman replied, shaking his head. "I mean, it would be one thing if they said a couple of hundred million years, or even just a million years. But *six thousand* years! That is simply incredible."

"You know, it's strange," Bob Campbell said. "In regards to the age of the earth, it seems that there are basically only two beliefs: one is that the earth is very, very old, about four and a half billion years. The other is that it is very, very young, like six thousand years. Hardly anybody seems to believe in some intermediate age, a few million years or so, like Neil mentioned. You'd think that with all the evidence that has been uncovered and with all the sophisticated technology that is available one or the other of these two extremes would have been absolutely, irrefutably disproven, wouldn't you?"

"One of them *has* been, Bob. These fundamentalists just don't accept it," Mr. Potter declared.

"Perhaps this whole problem could be solved if everyone agreed to compromise and accept an age for the earth that averaged the two extremes – you know, add four billion and a few thousand and divide by two, and you come up with about two billion years," a stranger chimed in with a smile.

"Hey, I recognize you from your picture in the *Daily Messenger*. You're Karl Bond, right?" Potter asked.

"In the flesh, my friend. I was at the bar, and I overheard you discussing the hearing."

After everyone introduced themselves, Bob Campbell said to Bond, "I read your article in the *Daily Messenger* that compared belief in creationism to belief in a flat earth, alchemy and astrology. It was quite amusing … a bit harsh, but amusing nevertheless."

"Hey, I'm not a reporter like you guys. I already did that, for about twenty years, in fact. I write feature articles, and if I'm going to keep my job I need to stir up some controversy, so people will buy the papers I write for. Plus, I try to keep a smile on people's faces."

"So you don't really think these creationists are as foolish as you make them out to be?"

Bond smiled.

"Actually, I do."

"One thing's for sure." Potter offered. "If the response to your articles is any indication of the interest you're creating, I don't think you have to worry much about keeping your job!" Pausing, he added, "I must say, too, that I doubt if your article caused too many creationists to smile."

"One argument that you hear all the time from evolutionists is that the vast majority of scientists today accept evolution as a fact," Neil Goldman observed. "You know the claims… 'Today virtually all scientists recognize evolution as the best explanation for the development of life on earth,' etcetera."

Turning to a page in his notebook, he added, "In its official Position Statement, the National Science Teachers Association calls evolution *a major unifying concept of science which should be included as part of the K –* that's kindergarten – *through College science frameworks and curriculum* and *There is no longer a debate over whether evolution has taken place.* Apparently, the person who wrote those words hadn't heard about the hearing we'll all be attending in a few days! Anyway, claims such as these, which evolutionists make very commonly, seem to be an attempt to win the debate by the shear force of numbers. You know, if enough people believe in something, then it *must* be right.

"Creationists, as you know, dispute these claims and argue that there are actually many reputable scientists who oppose the theory of evolution and believe in creation – even *young earth* creation. I'm hardly an expert on this subject, and I have no idea how many scientists really reject the theory of evolution, but, trying to be as objective as possible, it does seem to me that the evolutionists' position here is pretty persuasive. Like, every science textbook that I've ever seen presents evolution as a fact ... which is true of most media articles, or presentations, on the subject, too. So what's the truth here? Is there really any *serious* disagreement in the scientific community over the theory of evolution? If there are so many scientists who reject the theory, like creationists claim, where are they? How come we hardly ever hear from them?"

"I was participating in a discussion panel on this subject a short while ago," Miller said, "and a creationist in the group – his name was Bill – said that he had a list of five thousand scientists who rejected the theory of evolution. One of the evolutionists responded that she could provide him with a list of twice as many scientists who accepted the theory – all of whom were named Bill!"

"Cute," Bob Campbell responded with a smile. "Nevertheless, no matter how you look at it, five thousand scientists is not an insignificant number. If there really are that many legitimate scientists who reject the theory, it's hardly accurate to claim that virtually all scientists accept it."

"It depends on your definition of the word 'virtually,'" Dick Potter said. "Let me ask you something, Bob. How many scientists do you think there are in the United States?"

"Gee, I don't know ... maybe a few hundred thousand?"

"Well, it depends on what is being used as a definition of a scientist, but whatever definition is used, the number is well over a million, perhaps as high as five or six million. Even at the lower number, five thousand is only one half of one percent of the total. In other words, if a minimum of ninety-nine and one half percent of scientists accept the theory of evolution as a fact, I wouldn't call it a stretch to say that virtually all scientists believe in it."

Campbell shrugged his shoulders, not entirely convinced by Mr. Potter's logic, but not wishing to pursue this particular point any farther.

"So, then," he said, "let me see if I've got this perfectly straight, Dick. The main reason that you object to the petition is because you believe so strongly that the creation story presented in the Bible is absolutely untrue from a scientific perspective and, as such, must be kept out of the science classroom."

"Yes, Bob, that's exactly right. It's not science, and I'm sure it was never meant to be interpreted as such. Like I said earlier, it's poetry, written thousands of years before real science even existed. Why in the world should it be taught alongside of the modern theory of evolution, as if they were equals? I've heard that there are still some people that believe the earth is flat and that they belong to an organization called the Flat Earth Society. Should we allow them to come into our classrooms and present their theory, also?"

"I noticed that you mentioned the flat earth in your article, Karl. What about it? Do you know if there really is a Flat-Earth Society?" Campbell asked Bond.

"Oh, yeah. I checked them out on Google. They exist, all right. In fact, I'm thinking of becoming a member. I suspect that it would be a rather fascinating group of people, don't you think? For example, I've heard that they're arranging an expedition soon to look for the abominable snowman. That would be quite an adventure, wouldn't it?"

"Whatever turns you on," Neil Goldman grinned. "Anyway … When you think about it, it really is incredible that some people still believe that the biblical creation account is literally true, isn't it? I mean, the whole universe created in *six days?!* It's really mind-boggling," he added, shaking his head in disbelief.

"You got it, Neil – *mind-boggling*," Mr. Potter agreed. "Now, is anybody interested in some pool? The table's open."

"Yeah, I am," Goldman said. "But before we kick your butts again, Dick, I want to ask you one more question: do you think the petition has any chance of passing? I mean, any at all?"

"Well, I've never been through one of these things, so I can't say for sure. You guys would probably be able to answer that question better than I can. You've said that you've covered a few of these events before. And you said that they never really got anywhere, right?"

"Yeah, that's right, basically. One of the hearings I covered ended with a decision that evolution could no longer be taught as a fact. Or, to be more precise, *should* no longer be taught as a fact. You probably remember the case. It was in Jefferson, Indiana, a few years ago. In the other cases that I covered the petitions were soundly defeated."

"There's something that needs to be kept in mind here," Mr. Potter said. "Even if the petition did pass by some fluke, who's going to teach creation as a serious alternative to evolution at Madison High – me?" he added with a chuckle.

Everyone laughed at the thought of Mr. Potter teaching creation.

"Hey – maybe it would be challenging, Dick," Miller said. "Just think. You'd have an opportunity to explain how Adam named all the creatures on the face of the earth in a few hours."

"Yeah, Brian, you're right. That certainly would be a challenge!" Mr. Potter said laughing. "Before we drop this subject, let me mention one more thing about this petition. Suppose it passed and teachers were forced somehow to teach creation along with evolution. It would really only add a few minutes to our lesson units. Even a cursory description of evolution requires one or two weeks. Fundamentalist creation, on the other hand, could be explained in one or two minutes, at the most: 'In the very beginning there was nothing except God. Then God created everything in six days. Finally, after all that work, He rested on the seventh day.'"

"That's a little windy," Miller joked, "You don't really need that last sentence."

Everyone laughed.

"Hey, if that's the case, Dick – that it would take only a few minutes to teach creation – why all the fuss?" Neil Goldman said. "Like Nike says, why don't you *just do it*? As you just showed, it certainly wouldn't be very difficult!"

"You're kidding, right?"

"Not entirely. Maybe it's an easy way out for you."

"It's the principle of the thing, Neil. I'm not going to allow myself to be forced to teach something I absolutely don't believe in. Suppose you were writing a story for your paper and were told that you must report something as being true that you knew was not true. Would you do it?"

"Hmmm … a good point."

"Any more questions?" Mr. Potter asked. "Or can we go win our money back now?"

"I think we better be careful, Neil," Bob Campbell said to his partner. "I think I overheard someone saying that Dick Potter's a *hustler*."

A minute later the group was at the pool table.

While they were leaning against the wall waiting their turn to shoot, Brian Miller turned to Mr. Potter. "Hey, I heard a rumor that that brilliant kid you've told me about in your class, Josh … uh, what's his last name?"

"Siegel … Josh Siegel."

"Yeah, that's it. Anyway, I heard that he might be on the panel supporting the petition. How in the world could that be? I thought you and he were really tight. I find it hard to believe that someone like that could be on the panel supporting creation."

"I've heard that rumor, too, Brian. A few days ago. I haven't had a chance to verify it. I guess I should, though."

The truth was that Mr. Potter *couldn't* bring himself to question Josh about this matter. He wouldn't know how to handle it if the rumor proved to be true.

19

The Last Meeting Before the Hearing

The last meeting of the youth group prior to the public hearing was on the Friday before Thanksgiving. Before it started David, Josh and Jennifer had met to go over the various requests for information that had been received from the media. As word of the hearing leaked out, these requests had been increasing every day. They included a number of invitations to appear on television, but Paul and Martha had declined them. They knew that the event could easily disintegrate into a media circus if they were not on their guard. The media, however, had no sympathy for this attitude. This was a good story, and they knew that it would generate an enormous amount of attention and controversy, which would make great copy, of course, and generate increased sales.

Once the meeting got under way, the discussion soon turned to the general approach that the panel members would be taking at the hearing.

"I'm curious, Paul," Mike Lawton inquired. "Are you all planning to attack the theory of evolution, to try to point out its flaws, or ..."

"Well," Paul replied. "that will certainly be included in our strategy. It's unavoidable. I might add, though – It gives us plenty to talk about!"

"Are you going to refer to God, or the Bible?" Kelly asked.

"We've discussed this at some length, Kelly. Our feeling is that other efforts such as ours have gone too far to avoid references to God. We think that this might be one reason that they haven't been more successful. If what we're promoting is *creation*, why should we try to avoid talking about the *Creator*? So, we're going to do everything we can to emphasize the *scientific* legitimacy of the creation account, but we're certainly not going to neglect God. We know that our opponents will object to this on the basis of the separation of church and state. We're going to let Mr. Morrison deal with that matter when it comes up."

"Let me put in my two bits here, Paul," Frank Morrison said. "The truth is that the whole notion of separation of church and state is essentially a bogus idea that was invented by liberals – or, perhaps more accurately, anti-Christians – to suppress the influence of Christianity in our country. I have to tell you, though, that I have some very strong feelings about this subject, and when the opportunity presents itself at the hearing, which we're sure it will, I'm going to show exactly why the idea is illegitimate. To tell you the truth, I'm really looking forward to it."

The meeting ended early, around 9 p.m.. Afterward the group sang a few songs, ending with one of their favorites, *Great is the Lord Almighty*. The singing was followed by customary prayer. This time the prayer lasted considerably longer than usual, about forty-five minutes. For the first time, everyone at the meeting, over thirty people, stayed to participate. The group sensed that the upcoming meeting was going to be a mighty spiritual battle and that they *really* needed God's help.

By 10:15 everyone had left the Conley's except for Jennifer, David, and Josh.

"How do you think the meeting went?" Jennifer asked.

"Okay, I guess," David replied apathetically.

"That doesn't sound very enthusiastic."

"You're right, Jen. It doesn't, does it? I don't know exactly why I feel like this. Maybe it's because of the way the media have reacted. It looks to me like the whole thing might turn into a freak show ... and we'll be the freaks."

"Hey, I don't see anything wrong with the media being so interested. Don't we *want* our position to get publicity? It seems to me that the more people learn about our side, the more they'll support it. After all, it is the *truth*."

"That would be fine and dandy, Jen – if it happened. But you've seen what it's been like the last few weeks, since we presented our petition to the School Board. The media has had a field day. And it's perfectly clear what most of them think about us. Basically, they think we're fools. Like, how many times have you heard us compared to flat-earthers?"

Jennifer nodded her head in agreement.

"I just have kind of a bad feeling," David added. "Like, we're going to lose this battle, just like all the others before us have."

"Hey, buddy, what kind of an attitude is that?" Josh said. "So what if we lose. At least we're making an effort to stand up for the truth. Isn't that what this is all about – the truth?"

"Totally right, Josh" Jennifer said. "That's definitely what it's all about ... and I'm sure God will bless our effort in some way."

Jennifer was a bit tired of the whole subject by now and just wanted to relax.

"Hey, I got an idea," she said enthusiastically. "How about if we watch a movie?"

"That's cool," Josh said. Then, thinking he would be a third wheel, he added, "but I'm a little tired. Maybe I'll get going."

"No, no," David quickly protested. "It's barely 10:30. When was the last time you were tired at 10:30 on a Friday night? Plus, I drove you here."

"It's no problem, man. You know, I don't live far ..."

"You're not going anywhere, Josh," Jennifer said. "There's a great movie on TV: *Casablanca*, with Humphrey Bogart and Ingrid Bergman. I love old movies, and this is one of the greatest. Some people say it's the best movie of all time! So, sit down – *both* of you. I'll get us some popcorn and soda. What do you guys want?"

A few minutes later the three youths were settled down ready to watch the movie. David and Jennifer were next to each other on the couch, and Josh was in the big leather recliner. In the past few months, they had become great friends, and they were looking forward to spending a relaxing evening together.

During a commercial, Jennifer asked Josh, "So, how are you feeling about the hearing, Josh? Do you feel prepared?"

"To tell you the truth, Jen, I'm a little nervous. It looks like there's going to be a mighty big crowd, and I'm afraid that I might get asked some questions that I might not be able to answer. I mean, there's going to be that biology professor from UNH on the evolution panel. What's his name ... oh yeah, Brian Miller. And then I'd end up looking like an idiot in front of everybody in the whole town ... and, in case you've forgotten, you guys know how much I'd hate *that*. What about you, Jen? How are you feeling about it?"

"Well, I know what you mean about being nervous. But I'm thinking if I get asked a question that I can't handle, I'll just pass it on to Paul, or Mrs. Parker, or Mr. Morrison – or maybe even you! I think you're right about the crowd, by the way. Like, there have already been a few articles about the meeting in the *Boston Globe* and the *New York Times*, and then there was that report on *Fox News* a couple of nights ago. Did you guys see it?"

"Yeah, I caught it," David replied. "I thought it was pretty good."

"I saw it, too," Josh replied. "It was all right, I guess. You know, Jen, I'm awfully glad those other three are going to be on our panel. They really know their stuff when it comes to this subject, don't they? I'm really looking forward to watching them in action at the meeting. I think a lot of people are going to be very surprised at how well they do – especially people from the media ... like the *New York Times* and the *Boston Globe*, for example. I've seen their reports on the meeting, too, and it's very obvious what their opinion of creationism is. Basically, they think that people who believe in biblical creation are living in the Dark Ages. Putting it bluntly, they think we're uneducated morons – which, as you know, is exactly what I thought a short while ago," Josh added, shaking his head in shame.

"Do you think you'll be able to handle *any* questions, Josh? Or will you defer all of them to the adults?" David asked.

"I don't know ... But I've been doing my homework, buddy. I guess we'll just have to wait and see," Josh replied, raising his eyebrows with a slight grin. "Let me put it this way: I don't intend to leave anyone with the impression that I don't know what I'm talking about. I already tried that once – and it didn't work out too well."

Jennifer and Dave looked at each other and smiled in response to Josh's remark. They had reflected recently upon how Josh might do at the hearing and had agreed that, in light of his extraordinary intelligence and his newly found passion for creation, he was certainly going to be worth watching. What he just said didn't do anything to change their minds.

The flurry of articles and letters in the *Manchester Daily Messenger* concerning the upcoming hearing was continuing unabated. They clearly indicated the keen interest in the debate that would determine the decision on the petition. Karl Bond had this to say in a recent feature article:

> As regular readers of the *Daily Messenger* are well aware, the upcoming hearing on the petition about creationism has generated an unusual amount of response. One example of this is an article that appeared two days ago entitled, "Is there *REALLY* any doubt about evolution?"
>
> Fortunately, the article was not written by me, because I hardly qualify as an expert in scientific mat-

ters. It was written by a molecular biologist and professor of biomedical sciences at UNH, Brian Miller. In the past few weeks, a number of letter writers in this paper have argued that the theory of evolution is a source of great controversy among scientists throughout the world. Professor Miller begs to differ. His opinion leaves little room for doubt: "In over three decades of professional experience, I have never met a single scientist who rejected evolution."

According to Professor Miller – as well as virtually every other real scientist in the world – species evolved over millions of years as a result of Natural Selection acting upon random mutations. Of course, this is certainly *not* what most of those in these creationists believes. According to them, the entire world, not just the earth mind you, but the *entire universe*, all 100 billion galaxies, was created in six days a few thousand years ago by a being with supernatural powers – an *Intelligent Designer*, as some claim – who lives in the clouds and jump-started Adam's life with a high five ... or, at least, a handshake. Furthermore, based upon the careful research of Bishop James Ussher of Ireland, who lived about 400 years ago, these folks have even pinned down the exact date of this extraordinary event: October 23, 4004 B.C – a Sunday, if you please.

Let's be clear about precisely what the creation crowd would have us believe. Plainly put, they imply that when it comes to the subject of origins, the biologists, geologists, paleontologists, chemists, astronomers, and all the other scientists in the world, at every major university and research institution in the world, have simply missed the truth and got it wrong. Clearly directed by God's Word, the Bible, only the creationists are privy to the truth.

Before leaving you today, I can't help mentioning one more story that many of you have referred to in your letters and that is another of the creation

crowd's favorites. You know the one. Like me, you may
have heard it in Sunday School when you were a small
child: the extraordinary tale of Noah, and his ark. At
the ripe old age of about 500, perhaps while tending
his garden one day, Noah heard a voice. It was his old
friend, God, who instructed him to build a giant boat,
because in about 100 years (since they didn't have
chain saws and power tools back in those days, God figured it would take that long for Noah and his boys to
build such a great vessel) God was going to create a
flood that would cover the entire earth, because He was
sick and tired of all the violence in the world, and He
wanted a do-over with the entire human race. Noah would
only be permitted to include his wife and his three
sons and their wives on this ship. The reason the boat
was so huge, almost 500 feet long, was that in addition
to these eight people it would also include a whole
lot of animals – either two or seven of "every living
thing of all flesh" including, presumably, 330 species
of dinosaurs, including some that might present some
challenges when it came to feeding time, like Tyrannosaurus Rex. As God had warned, the flood came, of course
– right on schedule no less – and lasted about a year.
When it finally ended, all of the passengers exited the
boat, said some fond farewells (some of the animals
could speak in those days – remember the serpent in
the Garden of Eden?), and quickly started reproducing,
each after its own kind. I should add that according
to our old friend Bishop Ussher the ark touched down on
Mt. Ararat on May 5, 2348 – seriously, I'm not kidding,
that is what he actually concluded!

I suspect that some of the things mentioned above
aren't familiar to most of you. Of course, I wouldn't
be surprised, because creationists generally don't
like to discuss them. After all, would you like to try
to defend the idea that the entire world was created
in six literal days on Sunday, October 23, 4004 B.C.

by a Superman with a long white beard who lives in the clouds? I didn't think so. Neither would I.

Of course, to me it's rather obvious why these folks like to keep mum about most of the details of this unbelievable story. It's because it is completely contrary to the views of virtually every real geologist, astronomer, biologist, paleontologist and every other scientist in today's world. With the spectacular advances of modern science, most people understand that the story about the creation and the Genesis Flood in the book of Genesis is a myth, like the ancient Gilgamesh Epic from Babylon, rich in spiritual lessons (although I must admit that I haven't determined exactly what these are yet) but hardly to be taken literally. But the creation crowd believes that they are to be understood exactly that way: literally. I'm dying to find out exactly what those behind the upcoming petition believe about these things. Fortunately, it won't be long now before we'll find out.

One thing I need to warn you about. If you wish to get a seat at this hearing, you better get to the gym early, because I can guarantee you that there will be a very large crowd. If you're searching for me, look in the front row!

One final note: Brian Miller, the biology professor mentioned at the beginning of this article, will be on the panel defending evolution at the upcoming hearing.

As usual, the *Daily Messenger* was swamped with responses to Mr. Bond's article, far more than they were able to print. Many of the supposed problems that Mr. Bond raised were addressed in these letters. One writer addressed the issues Mr. Bond raised about the dinosaurs. He pointed out, first, that there is a significant difference between the biblical term used for the groups of animals included on the ark, "kinds," and the term Mr. Bond used, "species." He used the example of dog "kinds" to demonstrate this difference. The dog "kind" includes a number of different species, including wolves, coyotes, jackals, and all varieties of dogs. Technically, all of these species can be produced from one original kind. Similarly, there were undoubtedly far fewer than 330 kinds of dinosaurs.

Second, he noted, the dinosaur kinds on the ark could very well have been – and undoubtedly were – young animals that would have needed far less space than full-grown representatives. In conjunction with this point, it was noted that the average adult dinosaur was only about the size of a small sheep.

Whatever else can be said about Mr. Bond's articles, one thing is certain: they certainly inflamed people's passions and stirred up interest in the upcoming hearing – and sold a lot of *Daily Messengers*!

20

The Hearing Begins

December third was a cold, raw day in Madison. The temperature never rose out of the twenties. In the late afternoon, as the sun began to fade below the western hills, a light snow began to fall. It looked like winter was going to make an early appearance in New England this year.

The hearing was originally scheduled to last from 8 to 10 p.m. in the high school gymnasium, but in anticipation of an unusually large turnout and extensive media representation the starting time was pushed forward to 7 p.m.. It was still supposed to end at 10 p.m., but everyone knew that it probably wouldn't.

The expectation proved to be accurate. Traffic into town began building around noon, and media crews began showing up in the early afternoon to get their equipment set up. The organizations represented included CBS, CNN, and Fox News, several major newspapers, including the *Boston Globe* and the *New York Times,* and a number of well-known New England media companies, including the *Manchester Union Leader* and several of the larger area television stations. Kevin Pierce, the head of the Madison school district's Building and Grounds Department had been warned that he would have a busy afternoon, but he didn't expect anything like this. People hoping to be seated in the gym began arriving shortly after 4 p.m.. By about 5 p.m. the seats were filled and a long line of people was still waiting to get in. Anticipating such a scenario, the organizers of the meeting had arranged for live video of the meeting in the cafeteria. These seats filled up quickly also. The rest of the crowd, and there were many, would have to return to their homes and find out about the proceedings on the late night news. Interest had been building steadily since the day the petition had been publicly announced, and among the spectators there was eager anticipation. Although many of them were not sure why such an event attracted so much interest,

they were sure about something else: nothing like this had ever taken place in Madison before.

Concerning the format of the meeting, the two opposing sides would each have a panel of five or six members. Seated between them, at the rear of the large stage, would be the seven-member School Board. A well-known talk show host from a Boston television station, Henry Knox, would moderate the proceedings. Questions would be presented mainly by the Board members, and, under the supervision of the moderator and the Board chairperson, Susan Marshall, the discussion would be free flowing, more like it is on a television talk show than in a formal debate. Limited participation by the audience would also be allowed.

The creation panel, of course, consisted of Paul Hopkins, Martha Parker, Frank Morrison, Jennifer Conley and Josh Siegel. Their opponents, the evolution panel, included Richard Potter, the attorney Allan Kennedy, Reverend John Strong, Professor Brian Miller, Barbara Jenkins, associate professor of biology at the University of Vermont, and Peter Salisbury, a high school biology teacher from Manchester. Representing the School Board were Susan Marshall, the chairman, Janice Holmes, Victor Gregory, Thomas Lawton (Mike's father), Virginia Mitchell, James Quinn, and Randall Decker.

Many in the audience were very surprised that two members of the creation panel were high school students. Considering that only one of the panelists, Martha Parker, was actually a scientist, compared with four scientists on the evolution panel, they figured, understandably, that the deck was heavily stacked in favor of the evolution panel.

Shortly after 7 p.m. Susan Marshall opened the meeting. She explained the format, thanked everyone for coming, and, knowing the potential for disorder at such meetings, appealed for civility and respect from everyone in attendance. Before getting started, she asked Donald Patterson, the principal of the high school, who was sitting in the first row, if he would like to say a few words.

Acknowledging Mrs. Marshall's offer with a friendly smile, Mr. Patterson stood up, turned around and quickly surveyed the audience. "Whatever happens here tonight," he began, "one thing's for sure: the issue that will be discussed here is of unusual interest to an awful lot of people. In all my years at Madison High – and most of you know that there have been quite a few of them – I have never seen anything like this. I mean, look who's here – the *Boston Globe*, Fox News, CBS News, the *New York Times*. It's quite amazing. Now, I don't know how things will unfold here this evening, but similar meetings in other locations suggest that things can get pretty intense. Reasonable discussions can quickly turn into bitter arguments. For some reason, peoples' feelings about this subject tend to be unusually passionate. I don't want that to happen here, so, following up on what Mrs. Marshall said, I encourage everyone to display the courtesy and patience that will allow a thoughtful, intelligent discussion that will help the School Board to arrive at a fair decision on the petition. In my opinion the petition is reasonable and worthy of a serious and respectful hearing. I've done a little research into this subject and have discovered that over 50% of the American public believes in some form of biblical creation rather than the theory of evolution, so ..."

Mrs. Marshall's fears were quickly confirmed. A voice called out from the audience, "Yeah, and some Americans still believe in a flat earth, too – but that doesn't mean that their beliefs should be taught in our schools!"

Mrs. Marshall quickly banged her gavel and warned that such outbursts would not be tolerated.

Mr. Patterson glanced quickly at Mrs. Marshall, gently shook his head and continued. "With such a significant number of people believing in creation, it seems only reasonable to me that it should be taught alongside evolution, as an alternative theory of origins. Personally, I don't see what harm this could cause. If the theory of evolution is true, it should be able to withstand a little friendly competition."

"Thank you, Mr. Patterson," Susan Marshall said. "I agree with you ... but I'm only one vote. We'll have to wait to see what my colleagues think! Now, perhaps you could get things going with a question to our panel members."

"Certainly. I'd be happy to. I'll direct it to Mr. Potter. Dick, you have been a teacher in our school system for over twenty years. Surely you have given considerable thought to the topic that will be discussed tonight. Could you tell us what you think about it?"

The long-anticipated debate was under way.

"Certainly. I'd be glad to, Don. You're right. I have thought about this topic quite a bit. Unfortunately, I don't have any choice. Virtually every time I teach evolution, one of my students raises an objection. One issue that enters into this discussion, of course, is the separation of church and state, and I'm sure it will come up before we've gone very far here. However, it's not the most important issue. The central issue here is *truth*. And the first truth that we must face is that the scientific community, including of course myself, is in virtually unanimous agreement that the theory of evolution is no longer a theory but, for all practical purposes, a fact. The evidence from all branches of science is overwhelming. Even Pope John Paul II essentially acknowledged it as a fact back in the late nineties, and as far as I know the Pope is the number one spokesman for the Christian community."

As a science teacher, Mr. Potter was highly esteemed in the community. Many of the people in the gym this night had either been one of his students or had children who had been. His statement regarding the overwhelming support for evolution in the scientific community carried a lot of weight. It was also one of evolutionists' favorite arguments in their battle with creationists and was used to intimidate those who might venture to question their beloved theory, in particular those who hadn't done much research on the topic. It was quite effective. Not everyone was swayed by it, however. One such person was across the stage from Mr. Potter: Martha Parker.

"Mr. Potter," she interjected, "you say that the scientific community is in virtually unanimous agreement that evolution is a fact. This is actually not accurate. There is a very simple reason that evolutionists can make this statement. According to their own definition, a 'reputable scientist' – a *real* scientist, that is – *must believe in evolution.* According to this definition, anyone who does not believe in evolution – a creationist, in other words – doesn't meet this criterion, and thus, by their definition, is not a real scientist. It's a semantic sleight-of-hand. The fact is that there are hundreds – no, thousands – of scientists all over the world who either are highly skeptical of the theory of evolution or are outright creationists. Many of these people have Ph.D.s from prestigious universities.

"Listen, I know that many folks in this area are passionate baseball fans. I have to admit that I am, too – Red Sox, of course – so let me give you a baseball analogy. The claim that creationist scientists aren't reputable, or aren't *real* scientists, is like the claim made for many years that African American baseball players who didn't play in the major leagues before Jackie Robinson broke the color barrier in 1947 weren't *real* baseball players, that they weren't talented enough to play in the major leagues, that is. Of course they were real baseball players! The only reason they didn't play in the major leagues is that those who controlled the major leagues in those days didn't *allow* them to play … just like evolutionists don't allow creationists to be accepted into their self-regulated fraternity of 'reputable scientists.'"

"Can you give us any examples of these reputable creationist scientists, Mrs. Parker?" James Quinn, a member of the School Board, asked.

"If you look on the Internet you can find a number of lists of some of these scientists. One you might try is Answers in Genesis – AIG. They have a list of hundreds of names, all with advanced degrees in various branches of science. There are others, too."

"That's very nice, Mrs. Parker. Of course, a list of scientists who believe in evolution would include *millions* of names, wouldn't it?" Randall Decker said, shaking his head in displeasure. "Before we get going here," he continued, "I'd like to get something off my chest. I can't believe that we're wasting our time on a subject that, like Dick Potter just pointed out, has been settled for many years. As far as I'm concerned – and I know that this opinion is shared by an awful lot of other people – the biblical creation story is a myth, no truer than a fairy tale, and to teach it in our schools as an alternative to the theory of evolution, especially in our *science* classrooms, would be an embarrassment. We would join the lunatic fringe in Kansas as the laughingstock of the country. No, let me correct that ... we already have! Now, don't get me wrong here. I know that the creation story in the Bible is a very beautiful story that has rich spiritual meaning and all that, but the operative word here is *story*. It's a story, not literal history. My god, it's so obvious! The entire world created in six twenty-four hour days. To continue to believe that as literal truth in the modern scientific age is absolutely *mindless!*"

"Right on, Randy! That's tellin' it like it is," a voice shouted from the back of the gym.

Mr. Decker was visibly agitated at this point. His eyes flashed with anger and his face was creased with a foreboding scowl. Seated not ten feet away, Jennifer had a very good view of him, and she was startled by his appearance. She turned to Josh who was seated next to her and whispered, "That dude is *scary*, isn't he?" Nodding his head and raising his thumb, Josh whispered back, "Oh yeah ..."

Suddenly, Mr. Decker turned his attention toward Susan Marshall. "And, I'm sorry, but I think that you, Mrs. Marshall, are abusing your position as chairman of this School Board by allowing this petition to be debated here. Drugs have become a serious problem in our school. They have become common apparently even in the *junior* high school. Our school taxes go up every year, and our facilities are sorely in need of repair. My daughter tells me that her classrooms rarely get above sixty-two degrees during the winter, yet here we are debating whether a fairy tale should be included in our science curriculum. This is *pathetic*," he exclaimed as he slammed his fist on the table, "and I'm ashamed to be a participant. I'm sorry if I offended you, Susan, but I deeply believe that these things needed to be said – and I know I'm not the only one who thinks them."

Mr. Decker's angry diatribe had stirred up the crowd, and Susan Marshall had to bang her gavel once again to restore order. Mr. Patterson's intimation that people's feelings about this topic tend to be unusually passionate was proving to be prophetic.

The meeting was off to a rocky start, and Henry Knox decided it was time to step in. He turned to the creation panel. Gesturing toward the overflow crowd, he said, "The subject that will be debated here tonight, creation and evolution, is obviously very important to many people. As Mr. Patterson pointed out, people seem to have such intense feelings about it. Other subjects, like climate change and poverty and drugs, or the breakdown in morality, or wars, for example, probably get more attention, but none of them seem to stir peoples' passions quite like this one. Why is this? What is it about this subject that makes it so unique in this respect?"

Paul Hopkins spoke up.

"That's a very good question, Mr. Knox," Paul Hopkins said, "and I'm not sure there's an easy answer. I'll give it a try, though ... Perhaps it is because the subject we will discuss here is foundational to all the others. One's opinion about those other subjects you mentioned – drugs, war, climate change, etcetera – are shaped by one's perspective on the world – their world view, in other words. In contrast, one's opinion about origins – the subject of tonight's debate – is *not* shaped by one's world view; it does the shaping! In comparison to those other subjects, in other words, cause and effect are reversed. Mr. Potter said a moment ago that tonight's debate is about *truth*, and I completely agree with him. Truth is the most vital weapon we can pass on to our children as they head out into the big, wide world. Their understanding of truth will shape their world view, and their world view will have a major impact upon the course of their lives ... and, in time, the lives of many others. There is a penetrating statement about this subject that was uttered by the Duke of Argyle many years ago. Here is what he said:

To accept as a truth that which is not a truth, or to fail in distinguishing the sense in which it is not true, is an evil having consequences which are indeed incalculable. There are subjects in which one mistake of this kind will poison all the wells of truth and affect with fatal error the whole circle of our thoughts.[9]

"Ironically, this man was a friend of Charles Darwin. Think about the question that we are ultimately debating here tonight: how did the world, and the life within it, come into being? In regards to truth, it is difficult to imagine a more fundamental or important question. The answers that are being proposed by the two panels here are diametrically opposed. One side is proposing that the world was created by a supernatural Being – God, to be specific. The other side claims that the world came into being entirely through random natural events, that is, *without* any supernatural intervention. It is very important to recognize that these are the *only* possible causes of the world. Therefore, one of them must be true, and the other, by process of elimination, false. That is, the world is the result of either design, by a Designer, or it isn't. There are no other options. As I think you know, those of us who are supporting the petition here tonight believe that the theory of evolution is *not true*. We don't simply have issues with certain parts of it; we utterly reject the entire theory, and, exactly in line with the Duke of Argyle, we believe that accepting the theory of evolution as being true is *an evil having consequences which are indeed incalculable.*

"Furthermore, we believe that this theory is a perfect example of a subject *in which a single error of this kind can poison all the wells of truth and affect with fatal error the whole circle of one's thoughts.* We believe that if children are taught that the world came into being without a Creator – without God, that is – they will pass into adulthood with a world view that is corrupt at its very core, a view that will have incalculable consequences upon the remainder of their lives, not only in this world but in the world to come.

"So, Mr. Knox, in answer to your question – Why does this subject stir up such passion? – it's because people are aware, intuitively or otherwise, of it's vital importance. To accept the theory of evolution as a fact can affect with fatal error the whole circle of one's thoughts, because it eliminates what should be the center of those thoughts: the Creator. The other things that you mentioned – wars, poverty, the breakdown in morality, drugs, etc. – are all caused by man's broken relationship with his Creator. By presenting a world view that denies this Creator, the theory of evolution fosters and re-inforces this broken relationship. That is why, in a very real sense, it is the foundation of all of these other problems."

"Well, Mr. Hopkins," Mr. Knox replied, "you certainly have made your position clear. Having heard them, though, I must ask you something else. Your opposition to the theory of evolution appears to be unequivocal. Like you said, you don't just have issues with certain parts of it; you utterly reject the entire theory. This being the case, how come your petition requests that creation be taught *alongside* of evolution? If you believe that the theory of evolution is *entirely* wrong, why aren't you requesting that creation be taught *instead* of evolution?"

Paul Hopkins smiled. "I have to admit that you've put your finger on a struggle we've been having among ourselves from the moment we started to consider this petition. To tell you the truth, I'm not sure that we made the right decision, either. I guess you could say that in an ideal world, we would have chosen to do what you suggested, to have creation taught in our schools instead of, rather than alongside of, evolution. The problem is that we don't live in an ideal world." Smiling, Hopkins added, "In fact, in an ideal world the theory of evolution wouldn't exist!"

"Thank you, Mr. Hopkins," Mr. Knox responded. Turning to the evolution panel, he added, "Now, I'd like to hear how your opponents respond to this same question. Why do you think this subject is so important to so many people?"

"I'll give it a try," said Brian Miller, the biology professor from the University of New Hampshire. "On some points I am in complete agreement with Mr. Hopkins. First of all, I agree that this debate is very important. Second, I agree that the main thing we are debating is truth. And third, I believe that one's understanding of truth has a major impact upon their world view. Of course, when it comes to my understanding of the truth – at least as it pertains to origins – Mr. Hopkins and I are worlds apart. Whereas Mr. Hopkins believes that the theory of evolution is not true – let me see, how did he put it? ... *an evil having consequences which are indeed incalculable* – I, and my colleagues on this panel, believe that the theory not only *is* true but that it is the major unifying concept of all science, accepted by the vast majority of scientists throughout the world. On the other hand, we believe that the theory proposed by our opponents, supernatural creation, is based not upon science but upon religion, and, as such, has no place in the science classroom."

"Thank you, Mr. Miller," Mr. Knox responded. Smiling, he added, "I'm not sure how things will turn out tonight, but I'm sure about one thing: the battle lines for this debate are clearly drawn!"

.21

Intelligent Design & the Evolution of Whales

M r. Knox turned toward the creation panel.

"Before we continue, there's a question that I think needs to be cleared up. A couple of weeks ago the cover story of *Time* magazine featured the Intelligent Design movement. The article mentioned our meeting here tonight. I'm sure that most of you saw it. The theory that underlies your petition is called *creationism*. In the popular media these days, however, like the article in *Time*, it seems to me that Intelligent Design, not creationism, is mentioned most frequently as the primary challenge to the theory of evolution. My question is this: are these two theories, Intelligent Design and creationism, essentially the same, or are there significant differences? Putting it another way, in the discussion that transpires here tonight, should we assume that you are acting as advocates of Intelligent Design? If the media portrays this debate as another battle in the war between the theory of evolution and Intelligent Design – as opposed to creationism – would their portrayal be accurate? Would you have any problem with that?"

Frank Morrison took the microphone. In recent years there had been a number of court cases involving Intelligent Design, usually prompted by a debate similar to the one taking place here tonight. As both an attorney and a passionate advocate of creation, Morrison had followed these trials with keen interest. He was well aware that Henry Knox's assessment was correct, that in the minds of many people, especially members of the media, Intelligent Design had indeed usurped creationism as the leading opponent of the theory of evolution. He also knew that this change was completely unjustified.

"I'm very glad you brought this up, Mr. Knox, because I'm well aware that there is a lot of confusion surrounding it, and I agree that it should be cleared up before we move on. The short answer to your questions are, first, yes, there are some differences, some very significant ones, between our beliefs and those in the Intelligent Design movement and, second, at least in a qualified sense, we will not be acting as advocates of this Movement, or theory. If you will allow me, I'll explain exactly why this is so. It might take a few minutes."

"I'll keep an eye on my watch," Knox said, smiling. "Go ahead."

"Good. Thank you. I'll try to be brief. First of all, the fact that Intelligent Design has replaced creationism as the leading opponent of evolution in the public mind is simply not right. We agree with them about one thing, of course: that an intelligent designer was the cause of our world. In regards to many other issues, however, there are very significant differences between our world views. For example ..."

Suddenly, Mr. Morrison was interrupted.

"I'm sorry, but I have to step in here," Reverend John Strong spoke out. "What Mr. Morrison is saying perfectly typifies everything that is wrong with this petition. Those who believe in supernatural creation should *embrace* the Intelligent Design movement with open arms. The central tenet of their theory, that the world is the result of the plan of an intelligent designer, not only the natural process of evolution, is also the central tenet of creationism. It almost seems that creationists *ignore* this. As far as I am concerned, the issues that they have with Intelligent Design are a perfect reflection of the inflexibility and narrow-mindedness of those that cling to an absolutely literal interpretation of the Bible – in particular, the book of Genesis. It indicates why so many people ..."

"Excuse me, Reverend Strong," Frank Morrison interrupted. "But I would like to ask you something: do you support the theory of Intelligent Design?"

"Why ... well, if you mean, 'Do I accept the idea that an Intelligent Designer was somehow involved in the creation of the world?' then, yes, of course I believe this."

"Do you believe that this intelligent Designer is, or was, the God of the Bible, Yahweh?"

"As a Christian, of course I do. But what I believe in regards to this point doesn't really matter. Although those in the Intelligent Design movement are adamant about *not* identifying the Designer, their foundational premise is that there *is* one. That's enough for me."

"But you identified the designer as the God of the Bible. As you just pointed out, those in the Intelligent Design community don't take this step. They don't identity the designer. According to them, apparently, it could be Allah, Brahma, or even some unidentifiable spirit or Higher Power from another world. You're okay with that?"

"Yes. I see where they're coming from. They don't want their theory to be branded as a religion. They don't want to limit their audience."

"Perhaps … But let me ask you something else," Morrison continued. "Do you believe in the theory of evolution?"

"If you are asking whether I believe in the process of evolution – that the world evolved over billions of years as a result of gradual small changes to living organisms – then, yes, I do."

Morrison turned toward Henry Knox. "As you have just heard, Mr. Knox, Reverend Strong supports the Intelligent Design movement, even though its followers are reluctant to identify the designer. There is something else that Intelligent Designers might not agree with him about: evolution. He says he believes in the process of evolution. Those in the Intelligent Design movement do not necessarily share this belief. I say 'necessarily,' because what they believe about this process is actually difficult to determine. On the one hand, in general they are very critical of the details of evolution. This would seem to suggest that they reject the theory. On the other hand, however, you don't find many of them outrightly rejecting the theory. As far as I can determine, Intelligent Designers are not exactly sure what to think about the theory of evolution."

"Do they accept the chronology of evolution, like Reverend Strong does, Mr. Morrison?" Mr. Knox asked. "You know, the belief that the world is billions of years old."

"Generally speaking, yes, they do."

"I'm not sure I understand. If they reject the process of evolution but accept its chronology, what is their explanation for the origin and development of life? If the earth has been around for billions of years, but life didn't evolve, how do they think it got here?"

"Remember that Intelligent Designers' beliefs about evolution are a bit difficult to pin down. Some of them even appear to accept it, although in a qualified sense, I guess. Others apparently believe in a theory called Progressive Creation, which also denies the process of evolution but accepts its chronology. According to this theory, God intervened in earth's history periodically and supernaturally created living creatures."

"That's interesting. I've never heard of that theory before. Why don't creationists consider it?" Knox inquired. "After all, it denies evolution and accepts supernatural creation. Isn't that exactly what you all believe?"

"Yes it is. But, just like Intelligent Design, the theory of Progressive Creation accepts the Big Bang theory for the origin of the world, the billions of years chronology of evolution, and the general order of events proposed by evolution. Furthermore – and this is crucial – both of these groups deny a worldwide flood and accept the evolutionists' explanation for the fossil record. We completely disagree with every one of these notions. The way we see it, they have some of the pieces of the puzzle in the right place, but they have a lot of work to do before it's successfully finished.

"I need to point out something else about followers of Intelligent Design. In addition to being critical of evolution, they are also critical of young earth creationists like us. In fact, some of their leaders go so far as to say that they don't even want to *associate* with us."

"Come on, Mr. Morrison," Reverend Strong spoke up. "I think that's a bit of an exaggeration."

"Not really, Reverend," Morrison replied, while pulling out a piece of paper from the file in front to him. It was a copy of a letter.

"Phillip Johnson is one of the founders and leaders of the Intelligent Design movement. This letter in which he expresses his opinion regarding the age of the earth reflects this attitude about young earth creationists. It was written a number of years ago, but nothing on the official Web site of the Intelligent Design movement suggests that their belief regarding the age of the earth, and their attitude toward creationists, expressed here by Mr. Johnson is any different today ...

"I am not one of that party ... In common usage creationism has come to mean Biblical literalism, and in particular to imply the claim that the earth is no more than a few thousand years old. I have not personally studied the evidence regarding the age of the earth, or the metaphysical assumptions that underlie the methods of measurement, but I have no desire to quarrel with the generally accepted estimate of four or five billion years. More importantly, I am not concerned with whether the scientific evidence agrees with any dating derived from the Bible, nor do I assume the literalists are reading the Bible correctly in its own terms, even without regard to any conflict with the scientific evidence. So I am no creationist, as that term is currently used, although I do believe that God can create. Let me call myself a "theist," in a perhaps futile attempt to avoid guilt by association."[10]

"... the *association* he alludes to here is obviously association with creationists.

"According to this letter, then, Mr. Johnson not only does not want to join forces with creationists, he doesn't even want to be *associated* with them! Mr. Johnson is not alone here, for Intelligent Design supporters are often critical of young earth creation– if they mention it at all. Like theistic evolutionists, many of them appear to find the concept of a young earth embarrassing."

"You know, Mr. Morrison, as I listen to you explain your opposition to Intelligent Design – and I know this is going to sound weird – I can't help thinking that you believe that Intelligent Design is more closely aligned to the theory of evolution than creationism. Am I wrong?" The speaker was Victor Gregory.

"That may be stretching it a bit, Mr. Gregory, but it certainly contains an element of truth. The disagreements that we have with Intelligent Designers probably do seem strange to most people. After all, they're promoting the idea that the world was designed, just as we are. Shouldn't that make us partners? Not really, because, as I've just explained, in regards to many other fundamental issues, the Intelligent Design community *does* line up more closely with evolutionists than creationists."

"I understand what you're saying, Mr. Morrison," Victor Gregory responded, "but, nevertheless, I can't help thinking that you're fighting against your friend. And you know the saying: 'A house divided against itself cannot stand.'"

"I appreciate your point, Mr. Gregory, but, unfortunately, what I have just pointed out is the truth. In addition to the differences I pointed out a moment ago, we believe that those in the Intelligent Design movement are operating under an illusion, which is that with enough coaxing, in time evolutionists will acknowledge that an intelligent designer is somehow involved in the evolutionary process. There's a critical flaw in this reasoning, however: *by definition* the theory of evolution precludes such a designer. The fundamental building block of the theory is chance, or naturalism. Its entire purpose is to explain how the world came into existence and evolved through entirely *natural* events – *without* any involvement by a designer. To ask evolutionists to accept an intelligent designer in the process of evolution is like asking young earth creationists to accept that the Bible contains errors. Both requests are utterly hopeless, for it is asking their believers to abandon a fundamental, nonnegotiable tenet of their theories. It would be like asking Billy Graham, or the Pope, to abandon his belief in Jesus Christ."

"You seem to be overlooking something here, Mr. Morrison," Reverend Strong interjected. "You say that the theory of evolution excludes a designer. But there are many people, like me, who believe in both the theory of evolution and a supernatural Creator. It's called theistic evolution. I'm sure you've heard of it," he added with a slight smirk, knowing perfectly well that Frank Morrison was very familiar with theistic evolution.

"Of course I have, Reverend. Let me ask you something. How many textbooks on evolution have adopted your position about this?"

"What do you mean?"

"How many of the biology textbooks commonly used in public schools endorse the idea that evolution was designed and guided by a supernatural Creator?"

"I don't know. What difference does it make? Whether or not the authors of textbooks agree with us doesn't determine what we believe."

A discussion ensued about theistic evolution. Frank Morrison and those on the creation panel argued that once a Creator was introduced into evolutionary theory, it was no longer the same theory that was taught in our nation's public schools and publicized so broadly in the popular media. Proof of this is that the proponents of this version of the theory are virtually unanimous in their rejection of theistic evolution. Reverend Strong and one or two others argued otherwise. The others on the evolution panel remained silent, because they actually agreed with Morrison. Morrison had been involved in similar discussions many times, and he always found them to be very frustrating, because it seemed so obvious to him that the *real* theory of evolution, the one taught in public schools, had no room for a designer. It baffled him that so many people – mainly theistic evolutionists – were unable to recognize this. He thought of a well-known statement from the American biologist Richard Lewontin:

Our willingness to accept scientific claims that are against common sense is the key to an understanding of the real struggle between science and the supernatural. We take the side of science in spite of the absurdity of some of its theories … in spite of the tolerance of the scientific community for unsubstantiated just-so stories, because we have a prior commitment, a commitment to materialism [essentially the same as naturalism]. Moreover, that materialism is absolute, for <u>we cannot allow a Divine Foot in the door</u>.[11]

After a few minutes, Henry Knox intervened. "This discussion of theistic evolution is interesting," he said, "but we need to wrap up the discussion about Intelligent Design and move on. We have a lot to cover here tonight ... Mr. Decker, I see that you'd like to say something?"

"Yes I would. Thank you." Randall Decker turned toward Frank Morrison.

"Mr. Morrison," he said, "your claim that the entire purpose of the theory of evolution is to explain how the world evolved through entirely *natural* events, without any involvement by a designer, is putting the cart before the horse, as far as I'm concerned. The way I see it, scientists have *proven* that the world evolved from natural processes. The idea that there was no designer in the process is simply an inevitable corollary of this discovery. Scientists don't believe there was any designer in the process, because they've proven that there doesn't *have* to be one."

Morrison shrugged his shoulders. He was very familiar with the idea that Decker had offered. Excluding theistic evolutionists, of course, it was shared by virtually everyone who believed in the theory of evolution.

"I'm familiar with that idea, Mr. Decker. Of course, I completely disagree with it. As this meeting progresses, I hope our panel will help you to see why."

"I have a question for you, Mr. Morrison," Susan Marshall said. "Why do you think that Intelligent Design proponents are so reluctant to specify the designer? I mean, if it's not God, who in the world could it be? It seems to me that maybe they're just going overboard in their effort to not offend evolutionists."

Before Morrison had a chance to answer, Martha Parker spoke up.

"Frank, I've given this question a lot of thought. Do you mind if I step in here?"

"No, of course not, Martha. I've had the floor long enough. Go right ahead."

"Thank you," Martha said, turning toward Susan Marshall. "As far as I can tell, Mrs. Marshall, there are two possible answers to your question. The first is that Intelligent Design supporters actually believe that the designer's identity is a mystery. The second – as Reverend Strong mentioned – is that, regardless of what they believe, they think that identifying the designer as God, or a god, would undermine their mission to have their theory included in the discussion about origins, because, as you suggested, it would cause their theory to offend, and ultimately to be dismissed by, evolutionists. Quite frankly, I have no idea which of these options Intelligent Designers actually believe. Perhaps there's an element of both. I can, however, tell you what our opinion is of them.

"In regards to the first – that the identity of the designer is a mystery – we completely disagree with it. As Mr. Morrison just made clear, our conviction that the God of the Bible is the Creator of the world is an essential, nonnegotiable tenet of our theology and world view. Furthermore, from our perspective the idea that the world was designed but that the designer is unknown directly contradicts the plain words of the very first verse of the Bible – *In the beginning God created the heavens and the earth* – and, because of that, is an insult to God as the Creator. As far as we're concerned, admitting that the world is designed without disclosing its designer is about like awarding the Nobel Prize in literature to a book without disclosing its author. It simply doesn't make sense.

"Concerning the idea that identifying the designer would nullify any possibility of support from evolutionists, Mr. Morrison just addressed that a minute ago. As he said, the problem with this idea is that evolutionists are *never* going to allow a designer into their theory, because *by definition* their theory precludes such a being. If Intelligent Designers are concerned that evolutionists will dismiss a theory that requires a Designer, they are wasting their energy. They already have."

Tom Lawton now had a question for Mrs. Parker.

"I have read that evolutionists often claim that Intelligent Design is a Trojan horse for creationism. You know, that it is creationism in disguise and that its real purpose is to advance creation. Do you agree?"

"Yes I do, Mr. Lawton. Intelligent Design adherents dispute this, but they are wrong. The evolutionists are absolutely right. Intelligent Designers may not realize it, but everyone else does. The plain truth is – and I think that evolutionists are intuitively aware of this even if Intelligent Designers may not be – that accepting an intelligent designer is the first step on a slippery slope that inevitably leads to the demise of the theory of evolution. Obviously, evolutionists are not going to take it."

"I have a question, too, Mrs. Parker," Janice Holmes said. "I'm a little confused about something. Mr. Morrison said that Intelligent Designers generally reject the process of evolution but believe that the earth is billions of years old. Mr. Knox asked him, 'If the earth is billions of years old, but life didn't evolve, how do Intelligent Designers think it *did* get here?' I'm not sure that Mr. Morrison answered that question. Can you?"

"I can try. If you allow God into the equation, the answer could be Progressive Creation. After all, as Frank pointed out, this theory accepts the ancient age of the earth and rejects evolution. The problem with this is that Progressive Creationists believe that the Creator is God, something that Intelligent Designers are not so sure about; to them, it might be God, but it might not be. This uncertainty raises two questions. First, 'Without either evolution or God, How could life have originated?' and second, 'If the Intelligent Designer is not God, who, or what, was he – or she, or it?'

"Concerning the first question, one of the answers that has been proposed is something called panspermia, which is the notion that the first cells came to earth from outer space. If you give this idea a little thought, though, you quickly realize that it raises a lot more questions than it answers. Like, exactly how did these cells get here? Did some very advanced alien beings from a distant planet make a pass over the earth a few billion years ago in a space ship and drop a few cells out of a porthole onto the barren lifeless ground? Why would they have done that? Or was there an explosion of some sort on a planet with life that ejected into space some cells that then travelled trillions of miles and landed on the earth? If this happened, though, how in the world would these cells have survived a multitrillion mile journey through frigid empty space? And even if they did survive this miraculous journey, how could they have continued to survive in an utterly lifeless environment?"

Martha cocked her head as something occurred to her. "Of course, that's exactly the type of bleak environment in which life supposedly began in the evolutionists' little tale of the origin of life, isn't it? … Oh, well. No matter how these questions about panspermia are answered, though, the fundamental question remains unanswered: How did the life on the other planet come into being in the first place? Thus, panspermia doesn't offer a solution to the problem of how life originated at all. It just kicks the can down the road.

"As to the question of who, or what, the intelligent designer might be if it isn't God, I'm going to leave it up to you all to ponder that question on your own. As far as I'm concerned, there are no good answers to this question. To put it bluntly, I think that the idea that life, and beyond that the universe, might have been created by some mysterious being, or 'Higher Power,' that isn't God is, well, ridiculous. I'm sorry if this conclusion offends some of you, but I've thought about this question quite a bit, and I simply can't come to any other conclusion."

She turned to Henry Knox.

"I guess that wraps up my thoughts about Intelligent Design, Mr. Knox," she said. "I hope that Frank and I have answered your question about the relationship between this movement and young earth creationism. As you can see, there are some significant differences between our two world views. There is no doubt that Intelligent Designers have made some significant contributions to the fight against evolution, and we certainly appreciate their efforts to prove the existence of an intelligent designer, but we feel that in their single-minded focus on this one goal they are overlooking many other critical pieces of the creation puzzle, like the Genesis Flood, for example. They are headed in the right direction, but like someone once said about scientists in another context, I think that as they journey up the mountain in search of the truth regarding creation, if one day they reach the top they will discover that young earth creationists were there all the time."

"Thank you, Mrs. Parker ... and Mr. Morrison," Henry Knox said. "This discussion of Intelligent Design lasted a little longer – make that a *lot* longer – than I had anticipated, but I think it was important to get this matter cleared up. I, for one, thought it was fascinating."

Knox wasn't quite finished. He had one more question.

"Before we move on, I can't help asking you a question, Pastor Strong. You claim to be a supporter of Intelligent Design. Unlike those in the Intelligent Design movement, however, you leave no doubt that you believe that the designer is the God of the Bible. I was under the impression that the main division between the two groups represented here tonight is their beliefs regarding the cause of our world. The panel that you are on claims that the cause is evolution. Your opponents claim that the cause is God. It seems to me that you might be on the wrong panel. Am I right?"

Pastor Strong smiled. "I certainly understand your confusion, Mr. Knox, but no, you are wrong. I'm on this panel because, like the others on this panel, as well as virtually all reputable scientists in the world, I too believe that the world came about through the process of evolution. Where I differ from some of my colleagues is that I believe that God had a hand in the process. As Mrs. Parker and Mr. Morrison pointed out, this belief causes a little separation between me and those in the Intelligent Design movement, because, although they believe that the natural world was designed, they don't seem to be too sure about who designed it. Furthermore, as these two members of the creationist panel also pointed out, the Intelligent Design crowd doesn't seem to be too convinced that evolution even happened. To tell you the truth, I agree with Mrs. Parker and Mr. Morrison that some of the positions of Intelligent Designers are rather baffling. I mean, they believe in an intelligent designer but don't necessarily believe that it's God. Come on – Who are they kidding?

"In contrast to Intelligent Designers, those on the creation panel have no doubt at all about evolution. They completely reject it. Like the others on this panel, I think this is preposterous and that it completely flies in the face of modern science, and I do not in any way wish to be associated with such foolishness. In fact, I will do whatever I can to *oppose* it. Does that answer your question, Mr. Knox?"

"Yes, it certainly does. Thank you. Now, I think it's time to begin looking at some evidence from both sides – you know, specific examples that support your beliefs. Who would like to go first?" he said.

Josh put up his hand. "I'll give it a shot, Mr. Knox."

Josh's offer caused a buzz of excitement in the audience. Most of them were surprised to see two high school students on the creation panel and were eager to see how they would handle themselves.

As far as Josh himself was concerned, he was a little nervous – he had never spoken before an audience anywhere near the size of this one – but he was completely confident that the position that he would be defending, young earth creation, was the *truth,* and he felt deeply honored to be selected to defend it. Furthermore, he had great faith in the wisdom of his fellow panelists, especially Paul Hopkins, Frank Morrison and Martha Parker, and he knew that they would be ready to pick him up if he should begin to stumble. He had one other motive for being here, also. He knew that all of the kids in the Grace Bible Church youth group were in the audience. He had grown very fond of them all in the past few months, and he wanted to redeem himself in their eyes from what he believed was his shameful argument with Paul Hopkins that led to his slide into depression and an eventual suicide attempt. He knew very well that none of this group in any way looked down upon him for this event – in fact, when he returned to the group they warmly and enthusiastically accepted him – but, nevertheless, he felt that he had something to prove to them. The irony that he would now be defending the theory that he had intended to rip to shreds earlier didn't escape him. It should be added that the youth group kids most definitely did not wonder about Josh and Jennifer's inclusion on the panel. They were well aware of the keen minds and strong faith of their two friends, and they were eagerly looking forward to their display. In direct opposition to most of the rest of the audience, these kids figured that Josh and Jennifer gave their side a distinct *advantage*.

"I think that the evolutionist's explanation for the evolution of the whale is a pretty good place to start," Josh began. "It just so happens that we have a picture of ..."

"Uh – excuse me," Brian Miller interrupted. "I believe that Mr. Knox said that he was looking for 'specific examples that support your beliefs.' I have a sneaking suspicion that what you are about to present is not evidence *for* creation, but evidence that is – in your opinion, at least – *against* evolution. Am I right, Josh?"

"Well, uh, yeah ... I guess you might say that."

"Mr. Knox," Mr. Miller said, "I think we should establish a ground rule right now that we should all limit ourselves to presenting evidence that supports our positions, rather than attacking and criticizing the tenets of our opponents. Sometimes it seems to me that the only ammunition in creationists' arsenal is criticism of evolution. As far as I'm concerned, they're just firing blanks. I want them to show us some *live ammunition* – scientific evidence that supports their theory, rather than just criticism of ours ... if they have any, that is."

Martha Parker was quick to respond.

"I'm afraid that Mr. Miller is overlooking an important point, Mr. Knox. As Paul Hopkins pointed out a few minutes ago, there are only two possible causes for the origin of the world, and of the life within it: chance or design ... or, to put it into the context of tonight's debate, evolution or creation. This being the case, demonstrating the flaws in one side's evidence automatically enhances the credibility of the other. In a murder trial, for example, a suspect is either innocent or guilty. The more success that the suspect's attorney has at proving that the prosecution's evidence is wrong, the more likely the suspect will be determined innocent. The reason, of course, is obvious: if he is not guilty, there's only one alternative: he's innocent. Tonight's debate is similar. Since there are *only two* possible explanations for the origin of life, any evidence presented against one side inevitably strengthens the other."

"What you said may be true, Mrs. Parker, but it doesn't invalidate my original point," Miller responded, "which is that it often seems that the *only* evidence in support of creation is evidence against evolution. Outside of the Bible, where is the evidence for creation? When you get right down to it, it really seems that your whole argument is summed up in the bumper sticker: God did it and that settles it. What's there to debate about that claim?"

Martha Parker was familiar with the criticism Miller had suggested. She had confronted it many times. Before she responded to his question, however, in order to make sure that everyone else understood exactly what the issue was, she wanted him to elaborate a bit.

"What you're really claiming is that creationism is not science. Isn't that true, Mr. Miller?"

"To be perfectly honest, I'd have to say 'Yes.' Investigation into the origin of the things in the natural world – trying to figure out their interrelatedness and how they came into being, in other words – is one of the main purposes of science … and belief in a Creator precludes this inquiry. Throughout history thousands of scientists have devoted their lives to this research; countless articles and books have been written about it. Many questions remain unanswered, of course, but research into it continues unabated today. Yet in one chapter of the book of Genesis, about twenty-five or thirty verses, the Bible supposedly provides the *entire* explanation for these origins. In less than two pages, that is, the Bible supposedly explains what scientists have been unable to completely explain in thousands of complete books. The truth is that belief in a Creator eliminates the need for scientific investigation, Mrs. Parker. It's not that complicated. If you believe that the entire natural world was created supernaturally by God in a few days, what's left to investigate?"

"The problem with what you're saying, Mr. Miller, is that it ignores the distinction between *applied* science and *historical* science," Parker replied. "Generally speaking, the branch of science that occupies the vast majority of scientists' time is *applied* science, which focuses upon investigation of things that actually *exist* in the natural world. The *origin* of these things is the focus of a completely different branch of science: historical science. It is applied science that leads to all of the discoveries in the world, the advancements in technology and medicine and energy, for example, that makes the world a better place to live in.

"Now, the debate between evolutionists and creationists, like the one we're having here tonight, is focused primarily upon historical science, because its main focus is the origin of things. When confined to historical science, to the origin of things in nature, your claim is absolutely correct. We *do* believe that the biblical explanation for the origin of the natural world, and the things in it, is the truth. We do believe that these things were created supernaturally by the Creator. When it comes to applied science, however – the area of science that occupies the great majority of scientists' attention – your claim is baseless. Creationists are just as committed to investigation of things in the natural world as evolutionists are. Whether these things were created supernaturally or evolved by random natural events has absolutely no impact upon their *investigation*."

"Come on, Mrs. Parker," Miller replied. "I think you're playing semantic tricks here. Of *course* ..."

"No, wait, Mr. Miller. I'll prove what I'm saying is right. It's really very simple. If I asked you to investigate a laptop computer and to then explain to me in minute detail its design and operation, would the fact that it was *designed* make the slightest difference in your investigation? Would you look at it and say, 'Oh, there's no need to investigate that machine, because it's *designed*'?"

"Of course not."

"Well, it's exactly the same with every living thing – and an awful lot of non-living things, I might add. In regards to the study of these things, it makes no difference whatsoever whether one is a creationist or an evolutionist. Just as it does with a computer, one's belief regarding their origin has no impact on the *investigation* of them, on the effort to learn about their structure and function, and to determine whether this knowledge has practical application in the world. For example, a creationist's belief regarding the origin of a living cell certainly does not affect his desire to study it. Actually, in a very real sense, the creationist's belief that God created these things may actually enhance his desire to investigate them, because learning about the Creator's works teaches us about the Creator. As I'm sure you know, throughout history many of the world's greatest scientists were devout creationists. Do you see what I'm saying here, Mr. Miller?"

"I can't say that I necessarily agree with you, of course," Miller replied, "but I have to admit that the distinction between applied and historical science in relation to this issue is an interesting perspective. I hadn't given it much thought before."

"I'm glad that it was helpful, Mr. Miller. Now, can Josh proceed with his thoughts regarding the evolution of whales, Mr. Knox?"

"Yes, of course," Knox replied. "Before he does, though, I just want to say something about debates. I've moderated a number of them. In a debate the opposing sides must be allowed to probe and question the positions of their opponents. Such activities are fundamental features of debates. Without them, a debate becomes little more than alternating lectures. I don't think that's what all these people here tonight came to hear ... Now, Josh, why don't you go ahead and tell us what you think about the evolution of whales."

"Okay ... sure," Josh replied. "There's a picture from our high school biology textbook that supposedly shows this evolution. Let me show it to you."[11] The picture quickly appeared on the video screen. Josh said, "As you can see, it supposedly shows a few of the stages involved in the evolution of a whale. At the top of this page is a picture of a *Mesonychid*, which is supposedly an early ancestor of the whale that theoretically lived about sixty million years ago. Mesonychids were supposedly hoofed, hyena-like mammals that looked like,

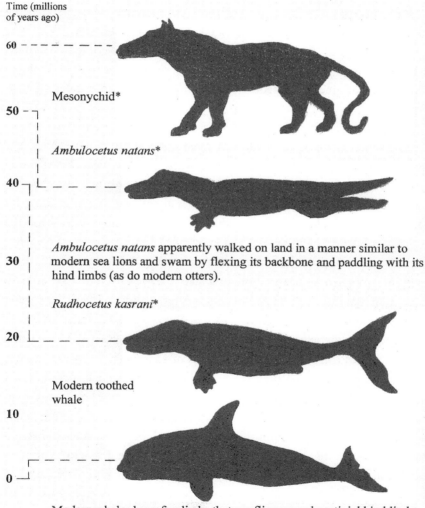

Time (millions of years ago)

60

50   Mesonychid*

    Ambulocetus natans

40

Ambulocetus natans apparently walked on land in a manner similar to modern sea lions and swam by flexing its backbone and paddling with its hind limbs (as do modern otters).

30

    *Rudhocetus kasrani**

20

    Modern toothed whale

10

0

Modern whales have forelimbs that are flippers and vestigial hind limbs, reduced to only a few tiny internal hind-limb bones that have no function.

*based upon incomplete skeleton

and were apparently about the size of, wolves. The animal right below him is called *Ambulocetus natans*. According to the text, as maybe you can see, this guy apparently *walked on land in a manner similar to modern sea lions and swam by flexing its backbone and paddling with its hind limbs, as do modern otters.*

"Now, if you look at these pictures without thinking about it too hard – or, better yet, without thinking at all – the alleged transformation that it describes is perhaps reasonable. If you really start to think about it, though, as I did, it becomes not only *not* very reasonable, but completely *unbelievable*. I'll try to explain why. First of all, let's be clear about exactly what we are being asked to believe … One day a wolf wandered down to the water …"

"Just a second," Peter Salisbury interrupted. "If we're going to be forced to listen to this description, let's make sure that the facts are straight. Nobody said that the original creature, the Mesonychid, was a *wolf*. It is described as wolf-*like*."

"Oh, sorry," Josh replied. "Let me correct myself … One day a Mesonychid, which looked like a wolf, wandered down to the water. About fifty million years later, completely as a result of *accidental* mutations, his offspring had evolved into a creature that looked *absolutely nothing* like him, lived in a completely different environment, and was about two thousand times his size: a whale. Now, let me tell you, although a whale is not a fish, this is the greatest "fish story" of all time, if you know what I mean. Let me show why.

"The story begins a long, long time ago – sixty million years ago, to be exact. Strolling along on the shore of a lake is a Mesonychid … or, at least, something that looked like a Mesonychid. After wading in the shallow water for a few minutes, he decided to go for a swim. Surprisingly, he really enjoyed it. In fact, he *loved* it! Before long, he became the greatest Mesonychid swimmer of all time – the Michael Phelps of Mesonychids. From that day forward he spent as much time as he could in the water. He just couldn't get enough of it. Now, considering that he – or his offspring at least – was eventually going to evolve into a whale, two extremely fortunate things happened at this point. First, a mutation took place in his DNA. The change that this mutation caused was incredibly tiny, of course, because it would be another sixty million years before this transformation would be completed, and an awful lot more changes would be taking place in the intervening years. What was this change? Who knows? Whatever it was, though, it caused him to be a tiny, tiny bit more like a whale than any other Mesonychid. Perhaps one of his legs, or maybe even all of them, became a whisker shorter. After all, by the time the process was finished, he wouldn't have *any* legs, so they had to start getting shorter someplace along the way … unless, of course, some super mutation just eliminated them altogether! … Of course, that wouldn't leave the creature that this happened to very fit for survival now, would it? A Mesonychid with no legs wouldn't last too long, would it? You know the mantra of evolution: the survival of the *fittest*," Josh chuckled.

"The second fortunate thing that took place is that a cute little female found our hero's new interest in the water very attractive and frequently joined him for his swims. The reason that this was so fortunate is that if one of his offspring was ever to become a whale, he must *have* offspring … and in order to have offspring, he needed a mate, of course. It takes two to tango, right?

"Now, in addition to the change caused by the mutation, another thing that Michael – that's our hero – and his mate passed on to their offspring was their love for water. In fact, amazingly, one of these offspring was even more attracted to water than his parents! Furthermore, against all odds, another mutation occurred in the DNA of this creature's cells that caused him to be just a little bit more like a whale than his parents. Perhaps his legs, or maybe his hair – after all, in addition to not having any legs, whales don't have any fur, either … not much, anyway – got a tiny bit shorter.

"Over the next fifty to sixty million years, thousands upon thousands of additional mutations – *positive* mutations, mutations that provided brand *new information* – occurred to some of the offspring of this original pair, until, finally, there was a pair of perfectly formed 75-foot long whales. Now get this … all this happened *even though mutations never provide new information!* A whale supposedly evolved from a something that looked like a wolf through thousands upon thousands of mutations that provided new information, even though in the real world mutations *never* provide new information!

"I have to tell you, the absurdity of this hypothesis is truly mind-boggling, Mr. Knox. Do you *see* what I mean? The more I thought about it, the clearer it became to me: It's certainly not science; it's not even science fiction; it's complete and utter *insanity!*"

"Your colorful description certainly does seem to cast some doubt upon the hypothesis, Josh, but I must ask you a question," Henry Knox said. "Wouldn't the vast amount of time supposedly allowed for this process – sixty million years – make it more plausible? Given enough time, in other words, couldn't random mutations produce just about *anything* – including a whale from a Mesonychid?"

"Not at all. It doesn't matter how many years are allowed, Mr. Knox. The process is still completely impossible, because, like I just said, mutations *never* provide new information. Mutations *damage* cells; they don't improve them! To expect mutations to create a whale from a wolf is like expecting an artist to paint a blue rose from a jar of red paint. It's completely impossible. The ingredients to do it simply aren't there.

"Here's another problem with the story. Even if mutations could produce new information, they would have to occur *in exactly the right order* ... like, the mutations that provided a blow-hole for the whale, for example would have to occur towards the end of the process, not the beginning. What good would a blow-hole on the top of a Mesonychid's head do, eh? ... By the way, how ridiculous is the notion that random mutations created a hole in the top of a Mesonychid's head so that the animal he would eventually become, a whale, could breathe? Anyway, even if they could provide new information, what are the odds that ten thousand, or a million, or more mutations could occur in exactly the right order?

"As I was thinking about this hypothesis before this meeting – I thought I might get a chance to talk about it – I tried to imagine an analogy that would illustrate how impossible this evolution would be, and, believe me, it wasn't easy. Here's one I thought of, though ... Imagine a monkey sitting at a keyboard and banging away at the keys. What are the odds that he would eventually type the entire Bible – that's about four million letters – with all of the correct punctuation? I'll tell you ... It doesn't matter whether this little critter was given a million years or a zillion years, Mr. Knox; the chances that he would eventually type the Bible are absolutely *zero*. In fact, in forty million years the odds that he would type the first verse of the Bible – *In the beginning God created the heavens and the earth* – are exactly the same: absolutely zero. As slim as these odds are, though, the odds of a Mesonychid turning into a whale through random mutations are a lot smaller, because not only does the entire form of the Mesonychid have to completely change, but every single one of the creatures that play a role in the process – the ones that undergo the necessary mutations, in other words – must *survive* ... even though for much of the time they would have been easy prey for creatures like sharks, because they would have been only partially formed and have had no way to defend themselves. Like, what kind of chance would a stubby-legged half-wolf that couldn't swim too well have against a twenty foot great white shark? By the way, in case you were wondering, according to evolutionary theory sharks have supposedly been around for about 400 million years ... and some ancient ones were supposedly a lot longer than twenty feet, too!"

Josh paused for a moment, and Henry Knox assumed he was finished.

"That was very interesting, Josh. I'm sure ..."

"If you don't mind, Mr. Knox, I'm not quite finished. I want to point out one more thing that I think is really important. Can you give me another couple of minutes?"

"Yes, I suppose so. But, please, no more than that. We really must move on."

"Good. Thank you very much. One thing that's obvious from these pictures — not that you needed them to clue you into this fact — is that a whale is a completely different creature than a Mesonychid. One thing that's *not* obvious from the pictures, however, because the picture obscures it — notice that the Mesonychid and the whale are about the same length in these pictures — is that a whale, a blue whale, for example, is about 30 times the length of a wolf and might weigh two or three thousand times as much. In other words, not only did the original Mesonychid undergo a totally miraculous transformation, but he also exploded in size during the process!

"As I've been studying this subject, I've discovered that this practice of turning one creature into another through a few imaginative drawings is very common in evolutionary literature. Here's one I'm sure you've all seen," he said, signaling the student in charge of the video screen. A picture from National Geographic showing the hypothetical steps in human evolution appeared on the screen. "A friend of mine who happens to be a good artist provided me with a few other evolutionary transformations that I thought you might find interesting. His name is Darrin." Pointing to the video screen, Josh said, "The first one shows a small creature similar to a housecat evolving into an elephant." As this amusing picture appeared on the screen, laughter rippled through the audience. "Now, you may think this picture is amusing — I do, too — but keep in mind that the transformation it depicts is actually nowhere near as radical as a Mesonychid turning into a whale, because all of the animals in this picture have one thing in common that the ones in the picture from our textbook didn't have: they all live on the land. An elephant may look a lot different than a housecat, but not nearly as different as a Mesonychid looks from a blue whale!

"Here's another one ... this shows a lizard evolving into an eagle. This is pretty amusing, too, isn't it? The only trouble is that this is actually what evolutionists believe! – that reptiles evolved into birds! Here's one more: a mouse evolving into a killer whale. You might think this is a joke, but, hey, why not? ... If a wolf can evolve into a whale and a lizard into an eagle, why couldn't a mouse evolve into a killer whale? What's the problem? Just like a Mesonychid and a whale, they're both mammals."

Shaking his head, Josh added, "So there you go, Mr. Knox – one reason that I reject the theory of evolution: the idea that whales evolved from wolves.

As far as I'm concerned, the evolutionists' hypothesis for the evolution of whales is enough reason, by itself, to reject the entire theory. The more I thought about it, the clearer it became to me: any theory that includes such a completely absurd hypothesis *must* be wrong."

As Josh sat down, initiated by his buddies in the youth group, a burst of applause broke out.

"That was very clever, Josh, and the audience obviously found it entertaining, but it seems to overlook one little detail: whales had to come from *somewhere*. They didn't just pop out of thin air. Maybe the hypothesis in your textbook does seem a little far-fetched, but at least it's an explanation. Can you offer a better one?" The speaker was Randall Decker, a member of the School Board who was decidedly pro-evolution.

Before Josh could answer, Jennifer spoke up. "I agree that whales didn't pop out of thin air, Mr. Decker. I believe, though, that they popped up in the water, on the fifth or sixth day of creation," she said with a big smile.

"This is a perfect affirmation of the point I was making before," Brian Miller said. "You know, the idea that 'God did it and that settles it.' Jennifer's claim cannot be proven or disproven through the scientific process. Science can only investigate *natural* phenomena. The notion that Jennifer alluded to rests upon a *supernatural* process, one orchestrated by a *supernatural* being, which, by definition, lies outside of science. This is the whole problem with our opponents' petition. We've already seen it alluded to in Mrs. Parker's discussion of Young Earth Creationism versus Intelligent Design. It would bring the supernatural – religion, in other words – into the science classroom. And the Constitution, specifically the First Amendment, along with the Supreme Court, clearly prohibits this."

Miller's statement was a clever sleight-of-hand, an attempt to shift the focus from Josh's impressive dissection of the evolutionists' Mesonychid-to-whale hypothesis to a subject upon which Miller was firmly convinced his side held the higher ground: the separation of church and state. Another reason that Miller wanted to steer away from any further discussion of the Mesonychid-to-whale transition was that he had serious doubts about it himself!

22

Religion vs Science

Before Jennifer or Josh had a chance to respond, Frank Morrison spoke up.

"You're referring to the separation of church and state, right, Mr. Miller?"

"Yes, of course."

"I'm glad you brought that up. As Mr. Potter indicated at the beginning of this meeting, it was bound to come up, and we certainly need to address it. Now, let me see if I understand you correctly ..."

"Perhaps I should take over here," Allan Kennedy, also an attorney, interrupted. "After all, this is a legal issue, and if the discussion on one side is going to be led by an attorney, it's only fair that the other side should be represented by one, too – right? You don't mind, do you, Brian?"

Brian Miller was well aware of Frank Morrison's formidable reputation as a skilled courtroom lawyer and was only too glad to accept Kennedy's offer. After all, his expertise in legal matters, particularly the one about to be addressed, was the primary reason that Kennedy had been selected for the panel.

"No – No. Please, go right ahead," Miller quickly replied.

Allan Kennedy was a successful trial lawyer from the Boston area. He had grown up in Atlanta, Georgia, and had received his undergraduate degree from the University of Tennessee in Knoxville and his law degree from Boston University Law School. Dayton, the site of the famous Scopes "Monkey Trial," was only about fifty miles south of Knoxville, and Kennedy had visited the site a couple of times in conjunction with some law courses. He found the trial fascinating, and when he heard about the hearing in Madison he quickly realized the similarity between these two events and made some inquiries regarding the make-up of the panel to see if his services might be helpful. The other members all agreed that he would be a good addition.

He and Morrison had crossed paths many times in the past and had shared a beer or two together more than once.

After the brief interruption, Morrison continued.

"So, Mr. Kennedy, I assume that you agree with Mr. Miller that the First Amendment prohibits the teaching of creation in our nation's public schools?"

"Yes, of course. It would violate the separation of church and state inferred by this Amendment. More specifically, according to rulings by the Supreme Court, it would violate the first clause of this amendment, the establishment clause, by promoting a religious doctrine."

The separation of church and state was a common issue in this debate, and most of the people in the gym that night were familiar with it. At the same time, they weren't too clear about the connection between this concept and the subject being debated here tonight. To Frank Morrison, however, the connection was very clear – and completely unjustified.

"I'm glad you said that the separation of church and state is *inferred* in this Amendment, Mr. Kennedy, because it certainly is not *stated* there … but I'll get to that shortly. First, though, I'd like to make a request. Since the legal basis of your argument is the First Amendment, perhaps it would be helpful if you told us exactly what this Amendment states."

"Yes, of course," Kennedy replied unhesitatingly. "Congress shall make no law respecting an establishment of religion or prohibiting the free exercise thereof; or abridging the freedom of speech, or of the press; or the right of the people peaceably to assemble, and to petition the Government for a redress of grievances."

"Thank you," Morrison replied. "According to your statement, the teaching of creationism in the public schools is illegal – or, at least, impermissible – for two reasons: first, it violates the notion of the separation of church and state and, second, it would be promoting a religious doctrine, which the First Amendment supposedly prohibits. Is that correct?"

"Yes."

"In regards to the first claim that, based upon the First Amendment, our petition violates the separation of church and state, there are three specific problems. First, as we just heard, the First Amendment prohibits *Congress* from making a *law* respecting an establishment of religion, etc. What we are presenting here tonight isn't a law; it's a petition. Furthermore, Congress has absolutely nothing to do with it. They didn't originate it, they didn't vote on it, they didn't pass it, and most of its members have probably never even heard of it. Finally, as we just heard, the separation of church and state is never mentioned in the First Amendment – or any place else in the Constitution, for that matter."

Oddly, Morrison's point regarding the absence of Congressional involvement in this case, though seemingly obvious, was rarely mentioned in the creation/evolution debate. It may not have been quite an elephant in the room, but in Morrison's opinion, it certainly qualified as a large dog. Kennedy hadn't considered it. He had to think quickly to come up with a response.

"When applying this amendment to this particular issue, Mr. Morrison, the courts apparently have interpreted the word 'Congress' liberally to include any law-making body, including those at the local level. Therefore, this would include the effort that your side is making to force the teaching of creationism into the Madison schools through legal channels, even though these channels are local. In regards to your claim that the words *separation of church and state* are not in the Constitution, of course I'm aware of that. Over time, however, the phrase has become accepted as an accurate description of the underlying intention of the Amendment's authors."

"You're right about one thing, Allan: the court's interpretation certainly is liberal! But that doesn't mean that it is correct. To me, and many others, using the First Amendment as the basis for making a judgment in this case is not only unjustified; it is a glaring example of a justice system run amok, of judges and lawyers manipulating laws and inventing meanings to satisfy their personal opinions. If the writers of the Constitution intended the law-making body in the First Amendment to be something other than Congress, they could have said so. They didn't, so there's no justification to suggest otherwise. Furthermore, the fact that the *separation of church and state* has become accepted as an accurate description of the underlying intention of the Amendment is a perfect illustration of the shenanigans taking place in our legal system. As we just heard, the words *separation*, *church*, and *state* are nowhere to be found in this Amendment.

"In a nutshell, the claim that the words *Congress shall make no law respecting an establishment of religion* establishes a legal basis to prohibit the teaching of creation in our public schools is absurd. It is a vivid example of a justice system that has lost its moorings."

Mr. Kennedy's response was brief. "That may be your opinion, Mr. Morrison, but it's obviously not the opinion of our nation's courts. They have consistently applied the First Amendment to cases like this one."

Mr. Morrison stared at Mr. Kennedy and slowly nodded his head in reluctant agreement. From a factual standpoint, he knew that his opponent was correct. At the same time, he knew that what the courts were doing was dead wrong. Repeating a falsehood over and over doesn't make it true. Mr. Morrison was well aware that in regards to the legal opinions in the country, those of most lawyers and judges, he was on the losing side in this debate. The opinions of most of these people, he realized, just like Mr. Kennedy's, were pretty much set in stone, and it was highly doubtful that anything he said would alter them. At the same time, however, he knew that the evening's proceedings were being carefully followed by countless thousands of the general public, and he realized that it was a golden opportunity to inform them of the truth. It was, in other words, a great "teaching moment," and he intended to take full advantage of it.

"The Supreme Court once decided that slaves of African descent – Negroes, in other words – were private property and could not be taken away from their owners without due process of law. Do you think that decision was correct, Mr. Kennedy?"

"Of course not – and it was duly corrected a few years later, with the thirteenth and fourteenth Amendments."

"Which perhaps sets a precedent for the foolish decisions regarding the prohibition of the teaching of creation in our schools, eh? Like the authors of the thirteenth and fourteenth Amendments, perhaps the people behind these decisions will see the light, too!"

Morrison decided now to head in a new direction.

"Before we go on here," he proceeded, "I think it would be worthwhile to review the historical setting and purpose of the First Amendment. An understanding of these things is very helpful in understanding why it is so unjustified to use this Amendment to ban the teaching of creation in our schools ..."

Before he was able to continue, he was interrupted by Janice Holmes, a member of the School Board.

"Excuse me, Mr. Morrison. I think you're right about the importance of the background of the First Amendment, and I definitely want to hear what you have to say ... but if you don't mind, I'd like to ask you a question first."

"That's okay. What is it?"

"It has to do with the second part of the First Amendment, the section that guarantees freedom of speech. It seems kind of bizarre to me that evolutionists try to prevent the teaching of creation in our schools on the basis of something that is not even mentioned in this Amendment, the separation of church and state, when this same Amendment definitely *does* guarantee the freedom of speech, which, it seems to me, *should* guarantee the right to this teaching. If you ask me, it seems like they're trying to ban this teaching on the basis of something that is plainly *not* in the Amendment, when something that plainly *is* there guarantees this right. And how about this: According to the Supreme Court, because of our freedom of speech it's okay to burn the American flag. If the First Amendment guarantees *this* right, how in God's holy name can the very same Amendment be used to prohibit the teaching of creation in our schools? If you ask me, that is absolutely *crazy*."

"That's a very good question, Mrs. Holmes, and I'm very glad you asked it," Morrison replied with a warm smile. "Needless to say, I sympathize with your perspective one hundred percent – and by the end of this evening, I hope a majority of your colleagues on the School Board will too! Now, if you don't mind, I want to finish my review of the background of this Amendment."

"Yes, of course. Please go ahead. I'm very interested to hear it," Janice Holmes replied.

"The background was the religious system in the homeland of the colonists, England. In England, there was a national religion, Anglicanism, supported by the state. By various means, all other religions were penalized. This lack of freedom of religion was the primary reason for the colonists' exodus from England, and the fact that it was dealt with in the very *first* Amendment of the Constitution was certainly no accident.

"The purpose, then, of this Amendment was to prevent the religious favoritism that existed in the colonists' homeland. The words of this Amendment – *Congress shall make no law respecting an establishment of religion* – precisely reflect this goal. The First Amendment, then, prohibits the *federal* legislative body, Congress, from creating a law that in any way elevates one religion to a position of prominence above all others. In light of this historical background, the idea that this Amendment prohibits the teaching of creation in our schools is *completely ridiculous*, and it's shocking that our legal system supports it. I'm sure that the authors of our Constitution would be in complete agreement with me. In fact, they're probably rolling over in their graves at this very moment!

"Now, Allan, let's move on to your second claim, that our petition is promoting a religious doctrine. Although it is certainly connected to such a doctrine, promoting it is not our primary purpose. The main reason for the petition is our conviction that the explanation currently being taught to our children about origins, the theory of evolution, is *not true* ... which means that these children are receiving false information about very important questions, like, *Where did I come from?* And, *How did the world come into being?* As Paul Hopkins pointed out a short while ago, the answers to these questions are instrumental in the formation of their world view, and if these answers are false it will have a disastrous effect upon these views. Of course, this theory completely undermines the biblical account of creation, as well. Let me call a spade a spade, Allan; In addition to being untrue from a scientific point of view, the theory of evolution is teaching our children that *there is no God,* and to us this is absolutely unacceptable."

Morrison's statement was contentious, and it drew some murmurs of protest from the audience.

"Now *you're* the one who's being ridiculous, Frank! Of *course* your petition is promoting a religious doctrine. According to creation, the natural world and everything in it was created by a supernatural being, God, in six twenty-four hour days, correct?"

"Yes, that's right."

"Where does that theory come from?"

"The Bible."

"My God, man, if that's not a religious doctrine, I'd like to know what it is! How can you possibly say that it isn't?" Kennedy said, shaking his head in disbelief.

"I didn't say that the petition doesn't support a religious doctrine, Allan. I said that that is not its *primary* purpose. Its primary purpose is to ensure that our children are provided with the correct explanation for the origin of the world – the *physical* origin of the world – which is something they are definitely not receiving now. The foundation of our petition, in other words, is a desire that children are taught the *truth*."

"Look, Frank," Kennedy said, "let me be honest with you. You're fighting a losing battle here tonight. No matter how logical your argument appears to be, it's perfectly obvious that the theory you are promoting, creationism, is a *religious* doctrine. No argument, no matter how clever, can change that fact. The bottom line is this: to many people, including myself and the vast majority of scientists, creationists seem incredibly narrow-minded, locked into outmoded and disproved ways of thinking. Until Darwin came along, the notion that the world was created by some superman with a long white beard – an intelligent designer, if you wish – was, for the most part, the only game in town. There really wasn't an alternative. But Darwin's theory changed all that, forever. He unlocked the mystery of life, and scientists ever since have been building upon his theory, until today it is accepted almost universally as the bedrock of modern science. It took awhile, but most thinking people eventually came to realize that Darwin was correct. To most people today, especially scientists, the theory of evolution is as certain as the law of gravity.

"Today the only people who reject his mighty theory are Christian fundamentalists, narrow-minded individuals desperately trying to hold on to a relic from the past. I admire the solidity of your faith, Frank – I really do – but, unfortunately, in regards to what it teaches about origins, in this day and age it's disconnected from reality. Modern science is passing your crowd by. The Dark Ages are over, my friend. It's time to enter the twenty-first century. And, look, giving up the biblical account of creation doesn't mean you have to give up your God. Look at Reverend Strong, for example. He believes in evolution and God. Lots of people do. It's called *theistic evolution*. I'm sure you're familiar with it. Maybe you ..."

Morrison shook his head sadly. It was as if Kennedy had never heard a word he had said.

"All right, all right," he interrupted. "I get your point. I want to ask you something, though. You accuse creationists of being 'narrow-minded' and claim that our beliefs are woefully outdated. What exactly do you mean by narrow-minded?"

"Come on, Frank. What are you talking about? Everyone knows what *narrow-minded* means."

"Bear with me, Allan. Just give me a definition in your own words."

"All right, if you insist," Kennedy replied with a roll of his eyes. "How is this? People who are narrow-minded are stuck in their way of thinking; they are not receptive to new ideas. They look at the world as if they had blinders on. They have limited imagination and tend to always think *inside*, rather than *outside*, the box, if you know what I mean. They don't seem to see the broad picture, in other words."

"There are two possible explanations for the origin of the world, Allan: chance, represented by the theory of evolution, and creation. One group here agrees that both theories should be presented in our schools; the other rejects one of these theories out-of-hand and believes that our children should be prevented from even hearing about it. Which group is thinking outside the box, Allan? And which is being narrow-minded?"

The answer to these questions was obvious. Kennedy was silent.

"The point I'm trying to make here, Allan, is that the ones who are being narrow-minded in this debate are evolutionists, not creationists. Creation requires a supernatural designer, of course. Evolutionists, however, reject any supernatural involvement from the outset. It is a *presupposition* of their theory. You know the mantra: *Everything in the natural world came about entirely as a result of natural processes*, or words to that effect. If there are only two explanations for an event and one group is willing to consider them both and the other isn't, it's perfectly obvious who's being *narrow-minded*, isn't it?"

Morrison was making a very good point, but Kennedy refused to acknowledge it.

"You're creating a straw man, Frank. The reason our side isn't willing to consider creation by a supernatural Creator, or Designer, is that we believe such an event is *impossible*. We're not going to grant credibility to a concept that we believe is utterly precluded by the laws of nature."

"But you already have, Allan: abiogenesis, the theory that life can evolve naturally from non-life. And since you stated that your side cannot give credence to an idea that you believe to be impossible, I must point out that the teaching of origins in our schools forces us to do exactly the same thing. Just like you believe the notion of a supernatural Creator is impossible, we believe that the idea that life arose spontaneously from nonliving matter is impossible. The difference is that your idea is an *opinion*, impossible to prove. Our position, on the other hand, is supported by one of the most basic laws of biology, the law of biogenesis. Are you familiar with this law, Allan?"

"Actually, I'm not. Perhaps you could describe it. I'm sure I'm not the only one who is unfamiliar with it."

"Certainly. I'd be glad to. A fundamental presupposition of the evolutionist world view is that the world has evolved entirely by natural processes. Such a world view has no place for the supernatural – including miracles, of course – because, supposedly, events directed by the supernatural cannot be tested and repeated. Therefore, from an evolutionary point of view there are only two possible explanations for the origin of life: abiogenesis, the idea that life arose spontaneously from non-living matter, and biogenesis, the idea that life is produced only from living beings – that life begets life, in other words.

"Now, the second of these options, biogenesis – the idea that life can only be produced from life – is one of the most fundamental and verified laws of science. Just like the law of gravity, it has been completely and repeatedly certified by experiment and there are no known exceptions to it. In the entire history of the world, in other words, there is not a single example of life evolving from non-life.

"The theory of evolution, however, is based upon *abiogenesis*, the theory that life evolved by random natural events from non-living matter. Because it rejects the supernatural, the theory *demands* it. There is no other option. Now, even though abiogenesis flatly contradicts one of the most fundamental laws of science, it is presented as the truth, as a proven fact, in every public school biology class in our nation. Our children, in other words, are being taught as truth something that according to one of the most fundamental laws of science is *impossible*." After a little pause, Morrison added, "Needless to say, this is hardly our only objection to the theory of evolution. It's a good one, though, isn't it?" he added with a smile.

"Look at the facts, Allan. The standard textbook explanation for the origin of life is that over billions of years the random interaction of atoms and molecules in some warm little pond resulted in the first living cell, and that from that point forward the same such interactions produced every living creature on earth, including you and me. *Even though it utterly contradicts one of the bedrock laws of science*, if one ignored this law this was perhaps a plausible explanation for the origin of life in Charles Darwin's day, when the maximum magnification of the most powerful microscope was several hundred times. The people in those days didn't have the technology to know any better. They at least had an excuse for their ignorance. Today, however, when magnifications of *millions* of times are possible through electron microscopes, a great deal more is understood about the cell. To put it mildly, the cell – which is the most basic form of life, of course – is vastly more complex than Charles Darwin could possibly have imagined. A typical human cell is composed of ten *trillion* or more atoms, all operating in perfect harmony to construct and control our bodies. The information storage unit of these cells, the DNA molecule, has a storage capacity that exceeds that of the most advanced computer chips by a factor of several hundred million, perhaps more.

"In today's world, scientists no longer have an excuse to believe that life could have evolved by random natural events from non-living chemicals. Not only is the notion utterly prohibited by the law of biogenesis, but this law is powerfully reinforced by the astounding complexity of the cell revealed by modern scientific technology. To put it mildly, in today's world, the idea that life could have evolved from non-living chemicals by random natural events, which is exactly what is demanded by the theory of evolution, is indefensible. As Sir Fred Hoyle famously stated, it is as ridiculous as believing that a tornado blowing through a junkyard could assemble a 747 airplane.

"Before we leave this topic, I must point out one more thing, Allan. You say that creationism cannot be introduced into the classrooms because it is a religion and the Constitution, at least as it is interpreted by the Supreme Court, specifically requires the separation of church and state. The problem with this argument is that a religion already *has* been introduced into the science classroom: the theory of evolution!"

"Oh, come on Frank!" Kennedy protested. "I've heard that argument before, and it's silly. The theory of evolution isn't a religion; it's *science!*"

"Actually, that's not right, my friend. It is a religion, and I'll show you exactly why. First of all, it perfectly matches the dictionary definition of religion, which I just happen to have here with me tonight. According to Dictionary.com on the Internet, the first definition of religion is, *A set of beliefs concerning the cause, nature, and purpose of the universe*. Certainly, no one can deny that the theory of evolution is a 'set of beliefs concerning the cause of the universe.' Another definition of religion is *a specific fundamental set of beliefs and practices generally agreed upon by a number of persons or sects*. Again, the theory of evolution fits this definition very well, with its followers being *the number of persons who generally agree about it.*

"In support of this opinion is a ruling by the Supreme Court, from a case in 1961, Torasco versus Watkins, in which the judges specifically classified Secular Humanism as a *religion*. I know that you are familiar with this ruling, but if anyone else is interested, I have a copy of this ruling right here in my folder. The creed, or faith statement if you prefer, of Secular Humanism is the Humanist Manifest, written in 1933, and this Manifesto states that 'Humans are an integral part of nature, the result of *unguided evolutionary change. Humanists recognize nature as self-existing* ... which means, of course, not created by anything *outside* of nature. The foundation of the *religion* of Secular Humanism, my friend, is clearly the theory of evolution.

"There is simply no doubt, Mr. Kennedy, that if teachers in the public schools are only allowed to teach that the natural world is 'the result of unguided evolutionary change' and that it is 'self-existing' – which, of course, they *do* – then they are promoting a religion: the religion of Secular Humanism. The truth is that if religion must be banned from our classrooms, then the ban should include Secular Humanism and its underpinning, the theory of evolution."

Kennedy slowly shook his head and smiled.

"You don't give up easily, do you, Frank? Listen, I want to ask you one more thing. The primary source for the idea of creation, and a Creator, is the Bible. A few minutes ago I said that if creation was introduced into the classroom, questions about the Creator would inevitably follow. This means that the *Bible* would inevitably be discussed in our *science* classrooms. Tell me the truth. Do you *really* think that would be acceptable?"

Morrison smiled. "Of course. What's wrong with it? The Bible was common in our nation's schools for the first couple of hundred years of our existence, and with it there we became the greatest nation on earth. One of the primary purposes of schools is to help children discover the truth. The Bible is the greatest source of absolute truth that has ever been written. It should never have been banned in the first place. In my opinion, reintroducing it would not only be acceptable; it would be *wonderful!*"

Morrison paused for a moment and looked thoughtfully at his opponent, and friend.

"I know you don't believe it, Allan, but the truth is on our side in this debate, not yours. The theory of evolution is headed towards its demise, my friend. In reality, it is useless. It explains absolutely nothing about the natural world. To repeat what I said before, it is an attempt to explain how the world came into being through entirely random natural events, without any involvement from a Creator – from God, that is. You're an old friend, Allan. You are hearing the truth about these things here tonight, some of it probably for the first time. I hope that you will evaluate what is said with an open mind and that one day you will recognize the theory of evolution for what it really is: a blasphemous lie that leads people *away* from their Creator. Look out to the gym. There are reporters and technical assistants from many of the largest media giants in the world: CBS, NBC, Fox, CNN, the *New York Times*, and many others. We are in the midst of a great battle here tonight, a battle that has captured the imagination of the entire nation. Ultimately, though, the battle is not about creation versus evolution. Ultimately, it's a battle for people's souls – including yours."

23

The Debate Continues

"That was quite a sermon, Mr. Morrison." Victor Gregory, another member of the School Board, observed with a smile. "Perhaps you have missed your calling! Now, I'd like to ask Miss Conley a question." Gregory was an acquaintance of Jennifer's father – they had teamed up on the golf course a few times – and had met Jennifer. "First of all, Jennifer, I have to admit that I'm surprised to see you and Josh on this panel. I must admit, however, that I was quite impressed with Josh's critique of whale evolution. It was very convincing. It really made me wonder how anyone could have cooked up such a strange theory – and, more importantly, I guess, how it could have ever found its way into your textbook. Anyway, Jennifer, I really admire you for being here tonight. It shows a lot of courage – and a great deal of faith in your beliefs.

"What I'd like to know is this: we've heard so far from Mr. Potter and Mr. Hopkins regarding their reason for being here tonight. Now I'd like to hear your explanation. Why is this petition so important to you?"

Jennifer took a deep breath. "Thank you for your compliment, Mr. Gregory. I have to tell you, though, that if I had known that there were going to be this many people here tonight, I might have thought twice about being on this panel. The largest crowd I've ever spoken in front of before is probably about twenty-five, in one of my classes at school. This is, like, a little scary, if you know what I mean!" She smiled nervously and took another deep breath. "Okay ... Now, to answer your question. I guess if I had to give one reason for being here, it would be the same one that Paul and Mr. Potter gave. It's pretty simple. It's about truth. I believe that what we are taught in our science classes about origins should be the *truth* – and I don't believe that evolution is true. I know that a lot of people here tonight think that this debate is about science versus religion, but, like Mr. Morrison just explained so well – and I think he did an *awesome* job – it really isn't, not at all. It's about a question: how did the world come into being, by God or by chance? We're being taught that it came about by chance. I believe with all my heart that this is the wrong answer. What's worse, though, is that this is the *only* answer we're told about. If you want to know the truth, Mr. Gregory, I actually don't think we should be taught anything about the theory of evolution at all, but I know that's probably not going to happen – not yet, anyway – so what we're requesting, that creation be taught in addition to evolution, is the best plan we could think of."

"Thank you, Jennifer," Gregory responded. "In my research for this meeting I discovered that *all* of the other biology textbooks used in our country's public schools also teach that evolution is a proven fact. In light of this, has it occurred to you that you might be fighting a losing battle here, Jennifer?"

"Yeah, sure. But if people gave up every time the odds seemed to be stacked against them, the world would be a pretty boring place, wouldn't it? My dad loves hockey, and we own a movie about the 1980 Olympic hockey team and their unbelievable victory over the Soviet Union, which I've seen, like, a million times. It's called "Miracle" and it is an amazing movie. Nobody – except the players on that team and their amazing coach, Herb Brooks – gave them any chance of beating the Soviets. The Soviets were, like, the best team in the *world*. They had just beaten ..."

"That's very interesting, Jennifer," James Quinn interrupted. "I remember the event very well, and it certainly was an incredible and inspiring story. However, what we're here to debate tonight is not a sporting event; it's considerably more important, to say the least. Let's return to it, all right?"

"Sorry," Jennifer replied with a shrug of her shoulders. "I just thought that that game was an awesome example of people winning a victory when nobody gave them a chance – which is what we're trying to do here tonight," she added with a smile.

"I understand, and, like Mr. Gregory just said, I really admire your courage in making this effort," Quinn replied. "I want to point something out to you, though. You say that you don't believe that the theory of evolution is true. We all know that there's an awful lot of scientific evidence that indicates that you're wrong. In regards to its *scientific* accuracy, on the other hand, the biblical creation story definitely isn't true. It *can't* be."

"Why not?" Jennifer asked.

"Oh, my ... Where do I begin? For starters, according to the Bible, the earth was created on the first day – you know, Genesis 1:1: *In the beginning* – *before* the sun, the moon, and the stars, which were created on the *fourth* day. Furthermore, the Bible claims that God also created the light that shined upon the earth and inaugurated day and night – or, as the Bible says, morning and evening – on the first day. But the light that establishes day and night on the earth comes from the *sun*. If the sun wasn't created until the fourth day, where did the light on the first three days come from? The Bible seems to be internally contradictory here. It just doesn't make sense, Jennifer, to take this story literally. Surely you see what I mean, don't you?"

"So, your problem is that you don't believe that the earth could have been created before the sun?" Jennifer asked.

"Yes, of course."

"But how can you be so sure, Mr. Quinn? After all, nobody was there to witness the event!"

"No, I'd have to agree with you on that point, at least," Mr. Quinn smiled, disarmed by what he took to be Jennifer's child-like and naïve perspective.

Before Jennifer could respond, Randall Decker spoke up. "Since you're talking about the book of Genesis, Jennifer, if Mr. Quinn doesn't mind, I'd like to jump in here for a moment and ask you something. How old do you think the earth is?"

Decker's question sent an electric charge through the gym. The age of the earth … This was the issue that everyone had been waiting for, especially the media reps. Opinions about many of the issues that would be discussed in this meeting were open to a wide range of interpretations and were scattered across a broad spectrum. Not this one. In regards to the age of the earth, there wasn't a spectrum at all. There were just two opposite ends of the pole, and they were miles apart. Agreement was virtually unanimous: the earth was either very old: 4.6 billion years – or very young: about 6,000 years. Hardly anyone believed in any other age. No matter what direction the ensuing discussion took, everyone was eagerly looking forward to the debate about this issue. Supporters were afraid that, by itself, this subject could destroy any chance for the petition's approval. Opponents expected to see those on the creation panel make fools of themselves as they tried to defend the idea that the earth was only a few thousand years old.

Based upon research he had done prior to the meeting, Mr. Decker was quite sure what Jennifer's answer would be: 6-10,000 years. Like the majority of those in the audience, he, too, believed that this notion was

the Achilles' heel of the whole creationist argument, and he was convinced that once it was exposed any support for the petition would quickly evaporate. Permitting lip service regarding a Creator, even a supernatural one, was one thing; if that was the only goal of the petitioners, they
would surely get some support. Expecting support for the idea that the
world was created only a few thousand years ago, however, was another
thing altogether. Mr. Decker had been looking forward to this moment
with eager anticipation. He firmly believed that his question had handed
his opponents' the shovel with which they would dig their grave, and he
was certain that as soon as their position had been revealed, they would
be buried in it.

Martha Parker was paying close attention to the exchange between Jennifer and Mr. Decker. Like everyone else, she knew that this subject would
come up this evening – Mr. Miller had already tried to raise it earlier in the
evening – and that it would be a challenging one for her panel. She didn't
appreciate that Decker had selected Jennifer to be the first one on the firing
line, and she stepped in before Jennifer had a chance to answer.

"I'd be delighted to answer that question for you, Mr. Decker."

"Uhh … I believe my question was addressed to Jennifer, Mrs. Parker."

"That's all right, Mr. Decker," Jennifer pronounced enthusiastically. "I'd
be happy to let Mrs. Parker answer that question. I'm sure she could answer
it a lot better than I could!"

Not thinking it would make much difference who answered his question, because he was sure that the answer would be the same, Mr. Decker
agreed to Mrs. Parker's offer.

"Thank you, Jennifer," Parker replied. "It's a tough question. I'll see what
I can do with it," she added with a smile.

She turned toward Mr. Decker. "Now, before I answer your question,
Mr. Decker, I have one condition."

"What is it?"

"That after I tell you how old I believe the earth is, you will tell me how
old you think it is and explain to me your reasons for this belief."

Although he was hardly a scientist, Mr. Decker wasn't concerned about
Martha Parker's condition. He was completely confident that his position
regarding the age of the earth was accurate, and he was also confident that
this position was based upon an irrefutable foundation: radiometric dating.
He quickly agreed to Mrs. Parker's condition.

"Okay," she said, "Now I'll answer your question. I believe that the earth is about 6-10,000 years old, more likely toward the younger age."

Mr. Decker smiled with satisfaction. It was exactly the response he had anticipated.

"Six to ten thousand years old, eh?" Mr. Decker responded. "Let's see ... If a generation is about forty years – make it fifty for the sake of argument – then the entire history of the planet goes back only about one hundred and fifty generations! A mere blink of an eye compared to what scientists are telling us."

At Mr. Decker's comments a little laughter rippled through the audience. Mr. Decker was hardly the only one who thought that this young age for the earth was silly.

"Actually, Mr. Decker, your calculation is just a little off," Martha Parker quickly replied. "You see, prior to the Great Flood of Noah's day, which was probably about five or six thousand years ago, people lived much longer than they do now – as long as one thousand years, in fact. Therefore, there would have been less than one hundred and fifty generations – maybe even less than one hundred!" she said with a big grin.

Mr. Decker couldn't have been happier with Mrs. Parker's correction. His goal had been merely to expose the creationists' belief regarding the age of the earth. Parker had not only done this, but her mention of Noah's Flood and the extreme age of the pre-Flood patriarchs had tossed in *two* bonuses. The way he saw it the grave-digging he had planned for his opponents was way ahead of schedule.

"People living to be a thousand years old! Wow ... that's remarkable," he said, unable to mask his sarcasm. Some more laughter rippled through the audience.

"Actually, considering how different the world – and mankind – was back in those days, it really isn't so remarkable at all," Martha replied. "But that's beside the point. I believe that our agreement was that after I gave you my opinion of the age of the earth, you were going to give me yours – and explain your reasons for believing it. I gave you my opinion. Now it's your turn."

"Yes. Yes, of course. I believe, like most people, that the earth is approximately 4.6 billion years old. And I believe it on the basis of radiometric dating, which, according to everything I have read, has basically proven this age beyond doubt."

Mr. Decker grinned, raised his eyebrows and shrugged his shoulders, as if to say, "You can't argue with that now, can you?" Of course, he was not aware of Martha Parker's extensive background in radiometric dating, the graduate courses she had taken in the subject at MIT over thirty years ago and the five years she had spent working in a radiometric dating laboratory. Unfortunately – for Mr. Decker, that is – Martha Parker knew more about radiometric dating than anyone else in the entire gymnasium that night.

"On the basis of radiometric dating, eh? Perhaps you'd like to tell me a little about this process."

"Well, uh … sure. What would you like to know about it?" Mr. Decker replied, caught off guard by Martha's question. He thought that his mention of radiometric dating would be a satisfactory reply to Mrs. Parker's inquiry. He didn't anticipate that he would have to *explain* it, too.

"Oh, nothing too complicated," Martha replied. "Just a little something about how the process works."

Now Mr. Decker was in trouble. Like most non-scientists, he had never studied radiometric dating in any depth. He didn't think there was any need to. He didn't know that the dates determined by the process were open to debate. He had always assumed that they were facts. After all, in the things that he read that's the way they were *always* presented.

Mr. Decker fumbled for an answer.

"You know what I mean … determining the age of things by using radioactive rocks."

"Yes, I know what you mean," Parker calmly replied. "I'm familiar with the process. I know what it's supposed to do. I was just wondering if you do."

"Of course I do," Mr. Decker lied. "Like I just said, it measures the age of things by using radioactive material."

Brian Miller realized that his partner was in trouble and attempted to come to his rescue.

"Randy, why don't you let me take over from here," he suggested.

"That's very generous of you, Mr. Miller, but I would prefer to continue the conversation with Mr. Decker," Martha said. "He has such confidence in radiometric dating. I just want him to tell me why."

Mr. Miller tried to defend his effort, but Mr. Knox came to Mrs. Parker's defense.

"Mrs. Parker has a valid point, Mr. Miller. If Mr. Decker believes so strongly in radiometric dating as the main proof for the ancient age of the earth, he should at least have a basic understanding of the process. I have to admit that I empathize with his predicament here – for I, too, believe that the earth is very old on the basis of radiometric dating, but I don't really understand how it works."

"You're saying, in other words," Brian Miller said, "that Mr. Decker should continue his discussion with Mrs. Parker – but you're glad that *you're* not in his shoes?"

Mr. Knox smiled. "Well put, Mr. Miller. That's exactly what I'm saying. Now, would you like to proceed with your inquiry, Mrs. Parker?"

"Certainly, Mr. Knox. Thank you. Now, Mr. Decker, you say that radiometric dating measures the ages of things by using radioactive material. As I mentioned just a minute ago, I already know what radiometric dating *does*. I want you to tell me *how* the process works. Let me see if I can help you here. You're aware, I'm sure, that there are a number of different radiometric dating processes, right?"

"Yeah, sure I am," came the uncertain reply.

"All right. Just pick one of these and tell us a little about it. Surely that shouldn't be too difficult."

"Okay … sure. Carbon … How about carbon dating?"

Recalling Martha's wonderful description of carbon dating at the youth group meeting a short while ago, Josh and Jennifer glanced at each other, nodded and smiled. They knew that Mr. Decker was in big trouble.

"I'm afraid that won't do, Mr. Decker," Martha said. "Due to technical features of the process, carbon dating cannot be used to establish dates much older than about fifty to a hundred thousand years. You said that you believe that the earth is 4.6 billion years old. Obviously, this is a bit outside the range of carbon dating. I think you better try something else."

Mr. Decker rubbed his hands together nervously and a few drops of perspiration appeared on his forehead. He knew that his knowledge of radiometric dating had almost been exhausted. With the next words out of his mouth it would be.

"How about uranium?" he offered unconvincingly.

"Uranium, eh?" Martha replied. "And how does that process work?"

After a pause, Mr. Decker admitted, "I don't know. I – I can't answer your question. I just don't know."

Needless to say, this exchange with Mrs. Parker had been embarrassing for Mr. Decker. This had not been Martha's intention, however. Her purpose had been to expose a very important truth about radiometric dating. She knew that most people accepted the dates provided by this process as gospel truth, even though most of them had only the barest understanding of it, at best. She, on the other hand, had been exposed to the process from inside the citadel, so to speak – from inside the laboratories that conducted the tests – and had seen first-hand its' critical flaws and that it was often manipulated to produce the results desired. She knew that radiometric dating was the Holy Grail behind the claims for an ancient age for the earth, and at some point during this hearing she had been determined to take dead aim at the process and expose the public's woeful ignorance of it. Unfortunately for Mr. Decker, he happened to be the one who stumbled inadvertently into her cross hairs. Martha had no intention of becoming involved in a detailed analysis of radiometric dating at this hearing. This was hardly the place for it. She just wanted to illustrate that the public's acceptance of the process was based almost entirely upon blind faith, not understanding. Involuntarily, Mr. Decker had nicely proven her point.

Reflecting a question on the minds of many others, Susan Marshall asked Martha, "What kind of experience do you have with radiometric dating, Mrs. Parker?"

After Martha told of her five years in a radiometric-dating laboratory in Boston, Henry Knox spoke next.

"Very interesting, Mrs. Parker. You know, I don't think I've ever met anyone who has actually *worked* in one of these laboratories. Actually, I *know* I haven't. As you were speaking, something occurred to me. Your panel obviously is of the opinion that the earth is very young, only about six to ten thousand years old. I assume that this belief stems from the creation account in the book of Genesis. Sitting on your opponents' panel is someone whose faith also is based upon this book – Reverend Strong."

Mr. Knox turned toward John Strong.

"I'm a little confused, Reverend Strong. You are sitting on a panel whose members obviously believe in a very ancient age for the earth. Your Christian affiliation, however, suggests that you might perhaps believe in a young earth. I'm very curious. Which is it, Reverend – young or old? How old do you think the earth is?"

"I'm glad you asked, Mr. Knox," Reverend Strong replied. "I'd be happy to answer your question. Let me state unequivocally that, just like the vast majority of scientists throughout the world, I believe in an ancient age for both the earth and the universe – to be specific, about fourteen billion years for the universe and 4.6 billion years for the earth. Furthermore, I think that fundamentalist Christians that promote belief in a world that is only six thousand years old are not only completely mistaken, but they are an embarrassment to Christianity. I mean, I know that they are sincere in their beliefs, but the plain truth is that most scientists consider them to be fools. To them, the idea that the earth is only six thousand years old is a complete joke that is utterly disproven by *all* branches of science: physics, geology, biology, astronomy, etc.

"Mrs. Parker just tried to cast doubt upon the accuracy of radiometric dating, but I've never come across any literature that supports her opinion. Everything I've read indicates that the dates provided by the process are, within certain parameters, very trustworthy. For example …"

"Excuse me, but before going on could you tell me what you know about radiometric dating," Mr. Knox interrupted. "As you just heard, Mrs. Parker actually worked in a testing laboratory for five years, so she obviously was speaking from experience. How much do you know about the process?"

"Look, this isn't a forum to test what *I* know about radiometric dating. That really isn't relevant. Of course Mrs. Parker knows more about the process than I do. But for every Mrs. Parker in the world there are hundreds, perhaps thousands, of scientists with equivalent or greater experience in the field who would completely disagree with her. Everyone who has any familiarity with this topic knows that. Why don't you ask her? She'll tell you that I'm right."

"What about that, Mrs. Parker?" Henry Knox asked. "Do you agree with Reverend Strong? Are there many others with experience in radiometric dating that reject it, like you do?"

Martha Parker hesitated. The question presented her with a bit of a dilemma. On the one hand, she knew that her opinion on this matter was definitely in the minority, a very small minority, in fact. At the same time, she knew that her conclusions were accurate. Truth, she knew, was not determined by majority opinion.

"First of all, in humility I must correct one thing that Reverend Strong said: I guarantee you that there are not thousands of scientists that know more about radiometric dating than I do. Now, to answer your question … No, there are not a lot of scientists who question the results of radiometric dating. Most of the people that I worked with, for example, believed that the dates provided by the process were reasonably accurate. But that doesn't mean that they *are!* Before Copernicus, most people believed that the earth was at the center of the universe – or at least the solar system – and that the sun revolved around the earth. But that didn't make it true. The same thing will one day prove true about radiometric dating; even though most scientists in today's world believe that it can accurately determine the age of rocks, they will one day be proven wrong."

"That's sheer speculation," Reverend Strong responded, "with no evidence to support it. Think, for example, about the dates presented in articles you find in the popular media – television, magazines, newspapers, Internet news sites, etc. – about discoveries of ancient fossils, or new theories in astronomy, for example. These dates are always presented as *facts* – not *suggestions*, in other words – aren't they? If there was any doubt about these dates, don't you think that an occasional article would mention it? Or take another example: textbooks. Virtually all of them present radiometric dating as being an accurate method of determining the age of ancient objects. Are the people who write these books all liars, and is there a giant conspiracy to fool all of our school children about the history of the world? Isn't that notion utterly preposterous?"

To most people in the gym that night Reverend Strong's argument was quite convincing – to most, but not all.

"Uhh ... I think that that idea Reverend Strong just mentioned is exactly right," Jennifer offered. "I think that there *is* a conspiracy to make school children believe a lie about the history of the world. And I think that Mrs. Parker's opinion of radiometric dating is correct, no matter how many people disagree with her."

"A *conspiracy*, Jennifer? And just who is behind this evil plot?"

The question was asked by Mr. Potter.

"Why ... uhh ... Satan, Mr. Potter," Jennifer replied a bit hesitantly, aware that her reply would probably be greeted with skepticism by many, including Mr. Potter. She was right, except that 'derision,' or 'contempt,' would be a more accurate description.

"Very good, Jennifer. Thank you," Mr. Potter responded. "Now, let's take a moment to summarize the position of your side. For starters, you believe that a supernatural Creator who has existed forever created, first, the earth about 6-10,000 years ago out of nothing and shortly thereafter every living thing, including the first man and woman, in six 24-hour days. Furthermore, you believe in a worldwide Flood that took place about 5,000 years ago and destroyed every living creature except those who were on the ark and that prior to this flood people sometimes lived to be almost a thousand years old – about one sixth of the entire lifetime of the world, in other words. Finally, there's a massive conspiracy to prevent school children from discovering these wondrous facts, a conspiracy led by the leader of the underworld, Satan, or the devil ... and our schools here in Madison, New Hampshire are part of this conspiracy. Did I leave anything out, Jennifer?"

"No, you covered it pretty well, Mr. Potter. There is one thing, though, that I need to point out. The Genesis Flood didn't destroy *everything* that wasn't on the ark. It didn't destroy the creatures that lived in the sea – at least not all of them – or the plants, or insects."

Mr. Potter took a deep breath and shook his head in bewilderment. *Is there no limit to these people's stubbornness and naiveté?* he wondered.

"Thank you, Jennifer. I wasn't aware of those fascinating details," he said sarcastically. "In any event, these are the basic details of your side's position, correct?"

Stepping in for Jennifer, Paul Hopkins pronounced, "Yes, that's right. You've summed up our views quite well."

"And these are the beliefs that you think should be taught in our science classrooms as an alternative theory to evolution, right?" Mr. Potter asked.

"No, not exactly," Hopkins replied. "We could probably leave out the part about the people living to be a thousand years old – and we definitely wouldn't include any mention of a conspiracy. That probably wouldn't go over too well with our teachers, would it, Mr. Potter," he smiled.

"No, I don't think it would. That's thoughtful of you, Mr. Hopkins," Mr. Potter replied with a little grin. "In all seriousness, though, do you realize what the outside world would think of our school system if we introduced these ideas into our curriculum? We would become the laughingstock of the entire country – no, make that the *world*. Think about it ... Every science textbook I've ever seen that addresses origins teaches that the world is about fourteen billion years old and *none* of them – not a *single one* – ever mentions a worldwide flood ... or any other earth-shattering flood, for that matter. Do you see how far out of the mainstream we would be? Do you see the damage that could be caused to our students if they were exposed to such radical ideas?"

"To us, Mr. Potter," Hopkins replied, "the idea that is radical is that the incredible world that we live in, and the fantastically complex diversity of living creatures, are the result of random natural events. To us, the source of any damage to our students is the godless theory of evolution that they are being exposed to currently."

Mr. Potter paused, mystified by his opponents' unflappable resolve.

"As far as I'm concerned, the idea that the world was created six thousand years ago is completely *insane*," he continued. "I mean, even if radiometric dates were off by a factor of a thousand – which I don't believe they are, of course – the world would still prove to be a lot older than six thousand years. I've got a hot tip for you: If you folks would forget about your silly notion regarding the age of the earth, I think you'd have a lot better chance of making some progress."

"So, then," Martha Parker stepped in, "if we agreed to leave out the age of the earth, then you'd be all for our petition, Mr. Potter?"

"Uhh … I'd have to give that a little thought," Mr. Potter replied with a smile.

At this point, Virginia Mitchell, another member of the School Board, spoke up for the first time. Her views were similar to those of John Strong.

"I have to agree with Mr. Potter," she declared. "I think that your insistence upon this ridiculously recent date for the beginning of the world is killing any chance for support that your petition might have. I think you'd be better off if you selected a compromise date."

"Like what?" Paul Hopkins asked.

"Oh, I don't know – perhaps, like ten million years ago, or maybe a hundred million."

"What do you think evolutionists would think about that date, Mrs. Mitchell?'

"I don't know … I haven't asked any of them!" she smiled.

"Well, why don't you do that, right now?"

"Sure – Why not? So, Mr. Potter, how about this – would you find an age for the earth of about ten million years more acceptable than six thousand?"

"Well, to be perfectly honest," Mr. Potter replied, "I suppose I could answer that question with a qualified 'yes', but only in the sense that it's a *little* closer to the true date than the alternative. But I have to tell you, Mrs. Mitchell, that ten million years is still far too short of a time for evolution to have worked its magic."

"Well, well, Mr. Potter, I see that you and I finally agree about something tonight," Mrs. Parker quickly spoke up. "We, too, believe that evolution is magic!" she added, bringing big grins to her fellow panel members.

Susan Marshall, the chairman of the School Board, now entered the discussion for the first time. She was in favor of the petition, but she saw one major stumbling block in its path.

"As some of you know, I support the petition – although I have to admit that I agree with its opponents that the idea of the world being only six thousand years old seems pretty unbelievable. However, I don't think that's the main obstacle in the way of the petition's passage. What I'd like to ask the petitioners is, just who do they think would teach the creation message if the petition should pass? As far as I can tell, very few science teachers believe that the biblical creation story is literally true, so how could they be expected to teach it as a serious alternative to evolution?"

Josh was the first to respond to Susan's question.

"Let me ask you something, Mrs. Marshall. Do you believe that the theory of evolution is true?"

"No, I don't."

"So, let me see if I've got this straight … Even though you don't believe that the theory of evolution is true, you're not sure whether any alternative theories should be presented, because our teachers might have trouble presenting information about something they didn't believe to be true. Did you ever study Greek and Roman mythology, Mrs. Marshall? If you did, do you think that your teachers believed that all those gods were real? Did they seem to have great difficulty presenting the information?"

"That's an interesting perspective, Josh. I never thought of it like that before," Susan Marshall responded with a friendly smile.

"Excuse me, Mrs. Marshall," Mr. Potter interrupted. "Let me put a little perspective on this matter. Speaking for myself, nobody could ever force me to teach creation in my classroom, at least not the biblical account of it. Maybe it has something to teach us, but whatever it might be, it sure isn't science! It's a myth or an allegory, or poetry, perhaps, but it's not actual history – *and it sure isn't science!* It's so obvious! My God, why can't you people see this!" he exclaimed, slamming his hands on the table in frustration.

As Mr. Potter finished, the veins on his neck bulged and his eyes blazed with anger. Jennifer had seen him look this way once or twice before, and it sent a cold chill down her spine. After the meeting, Jennifer found out that she was not the only one who had noticed the frightening look on Mr. Potter's face. Furthermore, it quickly became apparent that he wasn't the only teacher who would not agree to teach creation.

"I totally agree with Dick," pronounced Barbara Henrikson as she stood up in the first row of the gym. Henry Knox suggested that she save her comment until the end of the meeting, but she politely refused. "I'm sorry, Mr. Knox, but I go back a long way with Dick Potter. I'll make it brief. I just want to say that it's completely inappropriate for these people to try to force us to teach the biblical creation story in our classrooms. If they're so anxious to have it taught, they should focus their attention upon their churches, not the public schools. Like Dick said, in our classrooms we teach science, not mythology." Looking at Josh, she added, "Speaking of mythology, Josh, I know that this subject is addressed in our ancient history courses. Perhaps the creation story could be included in one of them." With a smug grin, she sat down.

This issue of who would teach creation had touched a raw nerve among not only the panel members and the School Board but the audience, as well. It definitely presented a problem. Following Barbara Henrikson's lead, several people in the audience expressed their opinions. The lively discussion, which included comments from members of both panels and the School Board as well as members of the audience, went on for over twenty minutes. Generally speaking, people agreed with Dick Potter and Barbara Henrikson that teachers should not, and could not, be forced to teach creation against their will. There were, however, a few dissenters – like Janice Holmes, a member of the School Board.

"It seems to me," she began, "that all this discussion about whether it's legal to teach creation or whether teachers can be forced to teach it against their will, is peripheral, not the main thing we should be focused upon here tonight. Shouldn't we be focusing our attention on trying to determine which of these two ideas – creation or evolution – is the truth? I don't think that the main concern of the people presenting the petition is who's going to teach creation. I mean, sure, it's something that needs to be considered, but it's not the *main* thing. If I understand them correctly, they're here tonight because they believe that the theory of evolution isn't true, that the biblical creation story is the *true* explanation of how the world was made. I want to hear more evidence for their beliefs. There's no point in worrying about *how* it should be taught until we decide *whether* it should be taught."

"I think that's a very good point, Mrs. Holmes," Henry Knox said. "You're right. Discussing the potential problems that might arise with the teaching of creation is putting the cart before the horse. I agree with you." Addressing the panel members, he added, "Like Mrs. Holmes has suggested, let's try to focus our attention on the question of whether this theory *deserves* to be included in Madison's curriculum and leave the question of how it should be taught for another time.

"Now, in line with this goal, I have a question for you, Mrs. Parker. You believe that radiometric dating is flawed, that its dates are not necessarily accurate, correct?"

"Yes, that's right."

"Can you give us any clear, specific examples of instances in which dates provided by radiometric dating have proven to be wrong?"

"Why, certainly," Martha quickly replied. "I'd be happy to. In regards to my background in this area, I mentioned a few minutes ago that I worked in one of the world's largest radiometric dating labs for almost five years after getting a graduate degree from MIT. While working in this lab, I remember one report in which volcanic rocks from different parts of the earth known to have been formed during the last two hundred years were provided ages by radiometric dating methods that ranged from 100 million to 10 billion years.[12] And another in which the shells of *living* mollusks were calculated to have been dead for 2,300 years!

"My favorite, though, is one I heard from a friend of mine who was working at the Crinum Coal Mine in Central Queensland, Australia in 1993. The team he was with was digging a ventilation shaft for this mine. At a depth of about seventy feet [21 meters] they discovered pieces of wood entombed in basalt. The wood was organic in nature – not petrified, in other words – and in three states: ash, charred, and intact.

"Basalt is basically hardened lava, so it was perfectly obvious what had occurred here. A lava flow had surrounded this tree, burning its outer surface and killing it. Samples of these items, the wood and the basalt, were sent to a few different radiometric dating labs, without being told exactly where the samples came from. Great care was taken to make sure that the results were as accurate as possible. And guess what the results were? ... The wood was given an age of 44-45,500 years. The basalt, however, was determined to be slightly older – *45 million years!* – a *thousand times* the age of the wood."[13]

"Whew!" Henry Knox exclaimed. "That's pretty incredible. How can you explain such a discrepancy?"

"There really isn't a reasonable explanation, Mr. Knox. It's perfectly obvious that all of the items were part of the same event. It's just a dramatic example of the uncertainty of the process."

A few minutes later Victor Gregory spoke up again. "I want to go back to a couple of things that came up a few minutes ago – people living to be a thousand years old, and a worldwide flood that destroyed every living thing on the earth except those that were on the ark. I'm not sure where I stand on this petition yet, but I'll tell you one thing: notions such as these are sure helping me make my decision. I mean, as far as I'm concerned these ideas are absolutely *nuts!* From everything I've read, people that lived a long time ago lived *shorter* lives than we live today, not longer. And about this ark ... I believe that there are, like, a million species of creatures living today. Plus, I've read that about ninety percent of all the creatures that have ever lived have become extinct, which would mean that there might have been a lot more than a million species five or six thousand years ago. Can somebody please tell me how representatives of two or three million species – and two of each, no less! – could have fit into a boat that was only about two or three hundred feet long? And another thing: where was all the food for these critters stored? And one more thing: what happened to all the waste generated by them? I mean, can you imagine what a nightmare that would have been?! My parents used to have a boarding kennel, and I used to clean up the ... well, you know. Sometimes we'd have a dozen or so dogs, and cleaning up after them was quite a job. When I try to imagine eight people cleaning up after a few million animals – some of them a lot bigger than a dog – every day for a year ... uhh, let's just say that I can't."

For the next several minutes, attention was focused upon the two issues raised by Mr. Gregory. The members of the creationist panel made a valiant effort to defend their position – by pointing out, for example, that the ark was actually closer to five hundred feet long rather than two or three hundred, and that the number of creatures represented on the ark was in all likelihood far less than a million – but the odds were stacked against them. The simple fact was that too many people sympathized with Mr. Gregory's position. Creationists had very reasonable arguments for their positions, but they only made sense to people who were willing to consider them with an open mind. Unfortunately, when it comes to these particular issues, open-mindedness is not very common.

This discussion of the ark was terminated with a question from Virginia Mitchell.

"A short while ago, in his discussion with Mr. Morrison, Mr. Kennedy said that to most people the theory of evolution is as certain as the law of gravity. As far as I know, *nobody* ever questions the law of gravity. I'd like to see what those on the creation panel think about what Mr. Kennedy said."

"I'm very glad that you brought this subject up, Mrs. Mitchell, because gravity is a very fascinating subject," Paul Hopkins replied. "And here's

Isaac Newton Discovers Gravity

why ... Although it holds the entire universe together, *nobody knows what it really is!*"

"Oh, come on," Reverend Strong objected. "Of *course* people know what gravity is. It's a force, and its effect can be precisely calculated. First of all, you're raising doubts about the theory of evolution. Is the law of gravity going to be next on your list of targets?"

"I'm not questioning the *effect* of gravity, Reverend Strong. The question I am raising concerns its *essence*, what it actually *is* ... and the truth is that, like I just said, nobody knows. Its effect can be calculated, but it cannot be found. Science offers no explanation for this profoundly mysterious force. Scripture does, however: Jesus Christ. The book of Colossians declares that Jesus is *before all things, and in Him all things hold together ... in Him all things hold together*. There is the best explanation of gravity you will ever find."

James Quinn now spoke up.

"That was interesting, Mr. Hopkins. I have to admit, I've never thought about what gravity really is before. I've always just taken it for granted, I guess. But now that you brought it up, it seems that maybe you're right. Maybe we really don't know what gravity is. It seems kind of hard to believe, though. I'll have to look into this further.

"But now I want to ask about something else: pesticide and anti-biotic resistance – you know, the ability of bacteria and various insects and other pests to develop resistance to the chemicals that man creates to destroy them. It seems to me that these things are pretty indisputable examples of evolution. If they aren't examples of evolution in action, what are they?"

Martha Parker responded to Quinn's question.

"I'm glad you brought this up, Mr. Quinn, because your opinion about this subject is quite common today ... and completely wrong. The truth is that this resistance is not an example of evolution at all. I'll try to explain why, but first I'd like to ask you a question: why do you think that antibiotic resistance is an example of evolution?"

"Uhh ... well, everything I've read about it says that it is," Quinn answered somewhat hesitatingly. After a brief pause for reflection, he continued. "When you think about it, it seems rather obvious, I think. In order for a living thing to evolve, the first thing it must do is survive. After all, another name for evolution is *Survival of the Fittest*. So, if some chemical is introduced into a population of bacteria, for example, in order to destroy it, and some of the bacteria develop a resistance that allows them to survive, they are fulfilling the first requirement of evolution: survival."

"They may be *surviving*, but they're not *evolving*," Parker quickly retorted. "The question that must be addressed is: What is the cause of this resistance?"

"I don't know," Quinn replied. "I'm not a scientist."

"Well, I am. There's hardly time here to go into the technical details of the process, but a brief summary should be sufficient to illustrate the point. In essence, what happens is very simple. The most important thing to understand is that in any population of bacteria there will usually be some members that have a *pre-existing resistance* to a particular antibiotic. In other words, the resistance does not originate in reaction to the antibiotic; it is *already there*. Therefore, when the antibiotic is introduced, these individuals survive. As they breed and multiply, their offspring replace the individuals that were destroyed by the antibiotic. And one thing is certain about these offspring: they belong to the same species, or kind, that their predecessors belonged to. They have most definitely not changed into anything new. The notion that this is an example of evolution, Mr. Quinn, is completely unfounded. It's simply an example of *survival*."

"But, like I said before, isn't surviving a basic requirement of evolution?" Quinn asked. "After all, if a group of animals doesn't survive, they sure won't be able to evolve, right?"

"Yes, of course ... but just because a creature *survives* doesn't mean that it has *evolved*," Parker replied, slightly frustrated at Mr. Quinn's apparent inability to grasp what she believed was quite a simple point.

Parker paused for a moment.

"Let me give you an analogy to illustrate this point. Imagine a group of fighters holed up in some mountainous caves in a war. A random rocket from their opponents blows up the entrance to one of their caves. Shortly thereafter the enemy swarms into the area, locates the caves and slaughters everyone in them ... everyone, that is, except those in the cave whose entrance had been destroyed by the rocket blast. Because of this damage, the enemy was unable to enter that cave. In fact, they didn't even know it was there! The fighters in this cave survived, but – just like the bacteria that were resistant to the pesticide – it wasn't due to anything new that they had created. It was due to something that had been *destroyed*."

"So are you saying that the pesticide wasn't effective in the bacteria that survived because something in their bodies had been destroyed ... instead of their bodies producing something new?"

"Yes, exactly. Whatever it was that had allowed the antibiotic to become activated in the bodies of the nonresistant members had been destroyed, or altered, in the resistant ones."

Thomas Lawton entered the discussion here.

"It occurs to me that pesticide and antibiotic resistance is sort of like the immunity that some humans have to certain diseases. You know what I mean by immunity ... A community, or some other group of people, is hit with some disease – like measles, for example – but some individuals don't get sick because they're immune. Aren't the germs that are causing this sickness just like an antibiotic, in a sense? Both of them are chemical agents with the potential to harm, or kill, their recipients, but not all of the recipients are affected because some are immune, or resistant to the agents. Humans who are immune to measles, in other words, are just like the bacteria that are resistant to a particular antibiotic. Both of them have a built-in resistance to the poison that is attacking their comrades. I certainly don't think that anyone would ever claim that people who are resistant to certain diseases are an example of evolution in action, so why would this claim be made about creatures that resist pesticides, or antibiotics?"

"That's an excellent connection, Mr. Lawton. It makes my point very well. Thank you," Parker replied.

"What causes this pre-existing resistance in some individuals, Mrs. Parker?" Virginia Mitchell asked.

"There are a number of causes," Parker responded. "But I don't think this is really the place for me to describe them. Like I said before, they're pretty technical. The main point is they are not the result of new information in the resistant creatures, something that evolution demands, of course. Both before and after the introduction of the pesticide, the resistant creatures belong to exactly the same species as the nonresistant ones. In no sense is evolution taking place.

"I'll make just one more point about this matter. When I asked Mr. Quinn why he thinks that antibiotic resistance is an example of evolution, his reply was that everything he's read about it says that it is. I think that this reply is an accurate reflection of the impression that most people today have about this matter. And considering that it is not really an example of evolution at all, it is an accurate reflection of something else: the deceptive power of the theory of evolution, its ability to invent evidence out of thin air and lead people to believe that it's a fact ..."

"Like the idea that birds evolved from reptiles, eh?" Tom Lawton quickly interjected.

"Exactly," Parker smiled.

The meeting continued on for another two hours or so, but it was clear that the Board was not going to be able to arrive at a decision this night. There were too many unanswered questions, especially in the minds of the Board members. The creationist panel had offered some good arguments, but in the end they were unable to successfully remove the strong doubts about the two issues raised by Mr. Gregory: the age of the earth and the Genesis Flood. Therefore, shortly after midnight Susan Marshall huddled briefly with the other Board members and then declared that the decision on the petition would be withheld until another meeting had taken place, in two or three weeks. Their decision was met with instant and loud disapproval by some members of the audience who thought that the petition should have been denied. But they were a minority. Most people agreed that it was too early to make a decision.

It seemed, then, like a stalemate. It wasn't. Almost everyone in the gym had expected that the petition would be defeated and that this battle that had caused such division in their town would finally be over. Thus, from the perspective of those presenting the petition the postponement was a victory. They had survived to fight another day.

As expected, Karl Bond was quick to pounce on the positions expressed at the hearing by the creation panel. His first post-hearing article appeared in the *Daily Messenger* the Sunday after the Friday evening meeting:

As most of you are well aware, the hearing on the "creation petition" took place in the Madison High gym last Friday evening. And what a meeting it was! I suspected that the creationists would provide me with some tasty morsels to offer my guests, but I was mistaken. Overflowing with generosity, they provided me with a great feast, a seven-course dinner! Let me describe it to you.

Let's begin with the make-up of this esteemed panel. Now, you would think – or I would, at least – that if these people were hoping to convince the School Board that the theory of evolution, a theory that is supported by virtually every reputable scientist in the world and which has been called "the foundational theory of all of science," is not all that it is cracked up to be, they would have selected the best "creationist scientists" (how's that for a good oxymoron, eh?) available to argue their position.

But, no, that is not what they did. Not at all. They selected two *high school students*, a youth pastor, and a lawyer … along with one scientist, a woman who apparently worked for a mining company for several years. Do you think that this selection just might indicate that there's not a big crowd of real scientists available for this panel?

One of the members of the evolution panel, a well-respected local science teacher, Richard Potter, pointed out that a few years ago Pope John Paul II threw his support behind the theory of evolution. These creationists are supposedly Christians. What Christian can argue with the Pope? His words are supposed to be infallible, aren't they?

At one point, one of the creationists – I think it was the youth pastor – argued that the theory of evolution is essentially at the root of just about all of the world's problems. We'd better be on our guard. I'm starting to suspect that the real goal of the creation crowd is not just to have creation taught alongside evolution, but to completely eliminate the teaching of evolution altogether. After all, if you believed that this evil theory was behind all the world's problems, isn't this what you would shoot for? Just think: if schools really want to get rid of drugs, for example, all they need to do is have creation taught in their science classes instead of evolution. How simple! Why didn't I think of that?

One thing I found particularly surprising is that these creationists apparently don't consider supporters of Intelligent Design to be their brothers-in-arms. I have to admit that in comparison to the courageous warriors we witnessed at the hearing these IDers do appear rather wimpy. I mean, the main position they champion is that there is an Intelligent Designer behind the natural world – but they don't have the guts to say that the Designer is God. If it's not God, who is it? Zeus?

One of the high school students, Josh Siegel, had the temerity to question – let me be a bit more specific: to *mock* – the explanation for the evolution of the whale in his biology textbook. I did a little research on his textbook and discovered that both of its authors have PhD's from prestigious universities and have been professors in their field – again at prestigious universities – for many years. It would be one thing for Josh to question some of the details of this explanation. But that is hardly what he did. He mocked the entire account as if it was completely absurd. What credibility does this young man have? Better yet, does he have *any*?

In the middle of the hearing the two attorneys on the panels wasted about a half hour debating the legality of teaching a story right out of the Bible in our science classrooms – you know, the religion versus science debate. I say "wasted' because the Supreme Court has already decided this debate in favor of evolutionists, many times, in fact. Sometimes I wonder if any of these creationists are aware of that. Perhaps they have been too busy reading their Bibles to have noticed.

The other high school student, Jennifer Conley, who looks like and probably is a cheerleader, informed us that she believes, as the Bible teaches, that the sun was created *after* the earth, three days after to be exact. Perhaps she isn't aware that the Bible declares that God said, "Let there be light," on the *first* day of creation. Naturally, because He is God, the light appeared as ordered. If light appeared on the first day of creation, but the sun didn't appear until the fourth day, where, Miss Conley, did this light come from? Based upon her comments, Miss Conley's response to this question would undoubtedly be, "I don't know – but nobody does, because nobody was there to witness it!" How utterly convincing.

Now, Martha Parker, the only scientist on the creation panel, made the rather astonishing claim that radiometric dating, which is utilized these days in many branches of science, is completely unreliable. How come there are reports practically every week that describe discoveries of ancient fossils that are millions of years old, and the dates, at least in specific ranges, are always presented as *facts*. Is Mrs. Parker privy to some clandestine information that none of the people who prepared these reports have ever come across? If she is so sure that these dates are all cockeyed, why doesn't she inform the scientific community so that they don't have to continue making fools of themselves by disseminating false information? Surely she must have plenty of evidence to support her astounding conclusion.

Finally, Jennifer revealed what is perhaps the most interesting fact of all. The teaching of the theory of evolution is actually a worldwide conspiracy, she informed us, the intent of which is to prevent children from learning that the world was created in six 24-hour days, that the world is only about 6-10,000 years old, that there was a worldwide flood about 5,000 years ago that destroyed every living thing on the face of the earth – except, she is careful to remind us, some of the creatures that lived in the sea, as well as the insects – and that prior to this great flood people would sometimes live to be almost a thousand years old … and this at a time when there were no life-saving drugs, hospitals, ambulances, or even electricity! Oh, yes, just one more thing. Miss Conley also fingered the evil being who is behind this great conspiracy: Satan, the Devil himself.

Fortunately, the hearing ended without a decision about the petition. Apparently, we will have to sit through another hearing before the School Board arrives at a decision. I say, "fortunately," because if the first hearing was any indication, I can't wait for the delicious treats that I'll have to write about after another one. Long live the creationists!

24

Josh Runs into Mr. Potter

A few days after the hearing Josh ran into Mr. Potter in the hallway as he was leaving school.

"Josh, stop down at my office," Mr. Potter ordered. "We need to talk."

"Uh – yeah, sure," Josh replied hesitantly, knowing that the meeting would be awkward, at best. "I'll be down in ten or fifteen minutes."

The instant Josh entered Mr. Potter's classroom, there was tension in the air. Aside from their encounter a few minutes ago, they had neither seen nor spoken to one another since the hearing. After some brief, uncomfortable small talk, Mr. Potter got right to the point. "You know, Josh, I've known for two or three weeks that you were going to be on the panel supporting the petition. I was going to speak to you about it earlier, but I didn't, because … because, to be perfectly frank, I just *couldn't* believe it. I'm shocked. How could you, of all people, possibly believe the ideas being promoted by that panel? A six thousand year old world that was created in six 24-hour days and an ark that saved eight people and two of every creature from a world-wide flood about 5,000 years ago – not to mention people that lived to be a thousand years old. My God, Josh, that's not history. It's a fairy tale from the Dark Ages – or insanity. How could you have so thoroughly rejected every-thing you learned in school about the history of the universe, and about evo-lution? What could have made you believe such foolishness? Tell me, Josh. Please, tell me. It makes no sense to me, absolutely none." Mr. Potter stared hard at Josh, his glare conveying confusion, disappointment, even anger.

Josh took a deep breath. Ever since the hearing, he had known that this conversation was inevitable. He wasn't looking forward to it.

"I'm not surprised at your questions, Mr. Potter. To tell you the truth, it kind of shocks me, too. If someone had ever told me six months ago that I would believe these things, I would have questioned their sanity – or recommended them to a psychiatrist. Life, however, has taken a strange turn for me in the past few months."

Mr. Potter nodded his head understandingly. He was aware of Josh's brush with death the previous spring and had heard the rumor that it may have been attempted suicide. He had difficulty believing this rumor, however, and had not discussed the matter with Josh. Whatever had happened, Mr. Potter had noticed that Josh had definitely changed recently. From the mercurial, outspoken, arrogant young man that he had become familiar with, Josh now seemed much more calm and peaceful, almost humble. Such a dramatic change was certainly not common. If Josh was about to explain the reason for it, Mr. Potter was going to pay close attention.

Josh began by telling Mr. Potter about the youth group that was meeting at the Conley's, and their investigation into the creation/evolution debate.

"No matter how hard I tried to reject what they were saying at those meetings," he said, "I couldn't help thinking that some of it actually made sense. Believe me, Mr. Potter; I didn't want this to happen when I first decided to attend one of these meetings. To tell you the truth – and I'm really ashamed of this now – I went with the intention of showing everyone there how stupid their ideas were. I figured it would be a slam-dunk. I mean, like you just said, taking the biblical creation story literally – as I knew the people at these meetings did … David had told me something about them before I went – seemed ridiculous to me. And I figured that proving it would be so easy. David had told me that the group leader was the youth pastor at his church. I was sure that he – the youth pastor – would offer me a golden opportunity to tear his little fairy tale to shreds and show all these misguided students, including several of my friends, how silly it was. I fooled myself into believing that I was, like, some sort of ambassador for the truth. Actually, I realize now that I was on a big ego trip, trying to show everyone how brilliant I was. As far as this youth pastor was concerned, David told me that he was about thirty years old and that he had graduated from a pretty good college – Yale, maybe. Of course, that didn't concern me, not in the least. I was completely confident in my intellectual ability and was sure that nobody could get the best of me in any debate about science, especially some youth pastor, no matter where he went to college. It's not a real pretty picture, is it Mr. Potter?"

As he recalled the attitude that had driven him to the youth group, Josh was momentarily overcome with emotion and was unable to speak. The emotion that was choking him, however, was not shame, as his last words had suggested. It was engendered by his awareness of and deep gratitude for the remarkable change that had taken place in his soul in the last few months, a change that had, as if by a miracle, transformed the despair and turmoil that had so long plagued him into peace and joy. He had been aware of this change before, of course, but for some reason this meeting with Mr. Potter brought it into particularly sharp focus.

"Are you okay, Josh?" Mr. Potter asked sympathetically, as Josh struggled to regain his composure.

"Yeah, sure," Josh replied, wiping his cheeks with his shirtsleeve. "Whew, I don't know where that came from!" he added with a big smile.

Gathering himself together, Josh continued with his story.

"So, like I said, some of the things that were being taught at this group actually made sense. I started checking them out on the Internet, and at the library, fully expecting to discover their flaws, but, much to my surprise, I started discovering that the things they were saying were *true!*"

"Like what?"

"Well, it wasn't necessarily the truth about the biblical creation account that first started to turn me around. That came later. It was the lack of basic consistency in the evolution story. Let me tell you what I mean ..."

For the next hour or so Josh proceeded to relate to Mr. Potter some of the problems he had discovered with evolutionary theory, including the flaws with the Stanley Miller experiment, the evolutionary explanation for the origin of life, and more. He also indicated how deeply impressed he had eventually become with the wisdom of the adults he had come to know through the group, especially Paul Hopkins and Martha Parker. Furthermore, he made it clear that the fundamental reason for his transformation was not an intellectual awakening but a spiritual one.

Despite his disagreement with Josh's conclusions about evolution, Mr. Potter didn't choose to debate these matters right now. It was Josh's last comment that caught his attention.

"What do you mean by a spiritual awakening?"

Josh told Mr. Potter about the awful nightmare he had experienced just before his suicide attempt, telling him that the evil figures that were pursuing him in the dream were symbolic of the demons that were pursuing him in real life.

"At this point in my life," Josh said, "I was in really rough shape, but the light of God's truth had already penetrated the darkness of despair that surrounded me, and, despite what lay in my immediate future I was intrigued by this light. The demons could see what was happening, and they hated it. They would much prefer that I would die than follow after this light … and, as you know, I almost did," he added, almost choking up again.

At this point Mr. Potter had had enough.

"My God, Josh! All this talk about demons who are trying to kill you, 'the light of God's truth', your belief that the biblical creation myth is literally true. I hate to say it, but you're talking like one of those religious fundamentalist, like a follower of one of those TV evangelists or something. These are the people who are trying to drive us back into the Stone Age, particularly in the area of science. I am absolutely dumbfounded. How in the world could this have ever happened to *you*, Josh? With your talent in science, the world was your oyster. I have never had a student that was so destined for success. I can't believe what I'm hearing, Josh. I just can't believe it."

Mr. Potter rested his head in his hands and slowly shook it back and forth.

Josh sensed that he might be presenting Mr. Potter more than he could handle spiritually, but he also felt a sense of urgency, an intuition that his teacher desperately needed to hear a little more, right now. So he pressed onward.

"It's about truth, Mr. Potter."

"Truth!" Mr. Potter protested, banging his hand on his desk. "Nobody has an exclusive handle on truth, Josh. Nothing is pure truth. There's always a little error mixed in."

"Respectfully, I have to disagree, Sir. There is pure truth, and He has a name … Jesus Christ."

"Oh, *no!* Don't tell me that on top of everything else, you've become a Jesus person, a born-again Christian, too?"

"Yes, that's right."

Shaking his head in disbelief, Mr. Potter rose from his chair. Josh's suspicion had been correct. Mr. Potter had heard more than he could handle.

"That's it, Josh. I've heard enough for now. Let's call it a day."

Mr. Potter grabbed his briefcase and headed for the door. Josh was right behind him.

As they were departing, Mr. Potter turned to Josh with one final question.

"I suppose you would tell me that the only way to heaven is through Jesus, that one must accept Christ in order to be *saved*, right?"

"Uh, yeah … that's right," Josh replied somewhat hesitantly, aware of Mr. Potter's defiant attitude.

"Saved from what, Josh ... Hell?

Josh didn't reply.

Shaking his head, Mr. Potter turned to head down the hall. "I'll see you tomorrow, Josh," he remarked as he was leaving. "If I don't go to hell first!" he added with a hearty guffaw.

Josh said a quick prayer and departed.

After leaving the high school, Mr. Potter headed straight for Carney's for a bite to eat and a few beers. He was spending more and more time there these days. He was trying not to let his conversation with Josh affect him, but he wasn't having much success. The truth was that the conversation had affected him very deeply. He had tremendous admiration for Josh's brilliant mind, and his shocking intellectual about-face had shaken Mr. Potter to the very depths of his soul. Had it been someone else, he could have rationalized it. But not Josh. He was far too bright to fall for this creation foolishness.

For the next few hours, Mr. Potter tried to enjoy himself by shooting some pool, playing a little Instant Lotto, chatting with friends, and, of course, drinking beer. The night was bitter cold, and with the fire crackling in the big stone fireplace at the far end of the pub, he was in no hurry to leave. Finally, close to midnight, he decided it was time to go. As he stepped out into the frigid night, he was greeted by a blast of snow that swirled about in the wind, stinging his face. While he had been inside almost four inches had fallen. He recalled hearing a prediction of snow earlier in the day, but it hadn't seemed anything to be concerned about. The blustery snow made it difficult to see, and he had a little trouble finding his car. The eight Sam Adams in his system wasn't making his search any easier. When he finally got on the road, the driving conditions were very poor. Visibility was about fifty feet, or less. He wasn't particularly concerned, though. His Explorer had been on this route so many times that he felt it could practically find its way home on its own. Thoughts about his conversation with Josh drifted in and out of his mind. The heavy snow rushing relentlessly into the beams of his headlights and streaking around his Explorer was hypnotic. On and on it streamed, in endless waves.

Suddenly, amidst the swirling snowflakes a great dark shape burst into view. "Oh, my God!" he screamed. He made a desperate attempt to swerve, but it was too late. His Explorer skidded off the road and slammed into a huge old oak tree near Grace Bible Church. The vehicle ripped some gouges in the tree, but the old oak had weathered a few other accidents in the past and it would recover from its wounds once again. The Explorer, however, was not so lucky. It was totaled.

Mr. Potter was alive, but not by much. The police and ambulance workers who pulled him from the twisted wreckage and the doctors who attended him in the emergency room all agreed that it was a miracle that he had survived.

"Five ... six ... sev ... Whoa! That's it for you, Kelly!" David shouted from the sofa, clapping his hands in glee.

Kelly and Jennifer were competing to see who could do the most handstand pirouettes, a common floor exercise element in gymnastics, which they both were involved in. Kelly had never beaten her older sister in these contests, but she was drawing closer.

"Nine ... ten ... eleven ... twelve ... thir – Whoops! There goes Jennifer! She's on the floor. But, sports fans, it's a new record for the Madison High gymnastics team! The crowd is on its feet. Congratulations, Jennifer – congratulations," David exclaimed.

Kelly leaned over and gave Jennifer a high-five. "Way to go, sis. You crushed me tonight ... but I'll get you next time!"

Everyone laughed.

Just then the doorbell rang. It was Paul. Martha and Frank Morrison were right behind him. The youth group was getting together with the panel members to go over material and strategize for the next hearing.

As people moved into the living room, Jennifer pointed at the television set.

"Hey, look at this," she pointed. "It's the weather report. And they're talking about a *big* snowstorm moving across the Midwest that's supposed to hit here next Tuesday or Wednesday. It might even be a blizzard."

"I wonder if the meeting will have to be postponed," Martha asked.

"I heard a report of this storm just a few minutes ago, on my way here from the hospital," Josh said. "They said it could be a real dandy."

"Were you visiting Mr. Potter?" David asked.

"Yeah."

"How's he doing? Jen and I visited him a couple of days ago. He didn't look too good – although I must say he looked a lot better than he did last week."

"He's improving. Although I'll tell you one thing … There's no way he could ever make the meeting Wednesday night. Actually, I don't think he'd be able to make any meeting for a few more weeks. I mean, you guys know what happened to him in the accident: broken leg, broken collarbone, a couple of broken ribs, internal injuries, and some serious cuts and bruises. When I first saw him, two days after the accident, I was really scared that he might not make it."

"Did you talk about the hearing?" Jennifer asked.

"No way," Josh replied emphatically. "The only time I did bring it up – a few days ago – he got really agitated. That's the last thing he wants to talk about right now. Nevertheless, there's always hope. Remember where I was a few months ago?"

"I sure do!" David quickly said. "And I wasn't far from you, buddy … Hey, how about some pies everyone? I picked up a couple on my way over. Two bucks each ought to cover me."

"I'll go get them," Kelly offered.

"Hey, David," she said, poking her head out from the kitchen. "Where did you get the pizza … Dino's?"

"Yeah, sure. Where else?"

"Haven't we told you that you shouldn't get them from there any more? They're *always* a piece or two short!"

David smiled sheepishly.

"That's two less for you, buddy!" Josh pronounced.

25

Jennifer Takes a Stand

After the pizza disappeared, Paul opened the meeting in prayer, and the meeting got under way. Much of the prayer was focused upon Mr. Potter, asking God to heal him, not only physically, but, even more importantly, spiritually. Before long, Martha sensed that Jennifer didn't seem to be herself. She asked her if everything was all right.

"Well," Jennifer began a little hesitantly, "to tell you the truth, something is kind of bothering me. I can't seem to ignore it."

"What is it?" Martha inquired.

"It's about our petition. I think we might be making a mistake."

"What do you mean?" Paul asked. "Do you think we shouldn't have introduced it?"

"On, no. It's not that at all. I don't think we've gone too far. I think maybe we haven't gone far enough ... Let me try to explain. It started a few days ago when I was reading Psalm 94. Here, let me show you," she said, opening her Bible. "Listen to this – verse twenty: *Can a throne of destruction be allied with Thee? One which devises mischief by decree?* As I was reading this verse, it suddenly struck me how it applies to the theory of evolution, and to our petition. I mean, like, think about it. This theory is a *throne of destruction*, because it destroys the truth about who the Creator is, and it destroys the souls of many people who believe it by blinding them to the truth. And if they reject the truth about God, we know where that leads them ...'"

"Yeah ... to destruction. To hell, in other words," Josh offered.

"Right, Josh. So, anyway, I saw the theory of evolution as the throne of destruction in this verse. The verse asks if this throne should be allied with God, which means, of course, that it shouldn't be. So here's what this verse was saying to me about our petition. I don't think we should be trying to have creation taught along with the theory of evolution, because that would be teaming up the story of God's creation with a 'throne of destruction' – exactly what this Psalm warns us against. And, you know, the more I thought about it, the more I thought that what we are trying to do is wrong. I mean, think about it. We all believe that the theory of evolution is a lie, right? A lie meant to explain how the world came into being *without God*, right? Why would God want the beautiful story of His creation taught alongside this horrible lie, as if they were equals? Personally, I really don't think He would."

There was a pause. Everyone had been paying very close attention to Jennifer's words.

"That's very interesting, Jennifer," Paul said. "Compelling – a very keen insight into that passage. It certainly creates a problem for our petition, doesn't it? Have you had any thoughts about what we might do about it?"

"Yes, I have," Jennifer replied. "The answer, I think, is right in the same Psalm – verse sixteen: *Who will stand up for Me against evildoers? Who will take his stand for Me against those who do wickedness?* To me – and I know you guys all feel the same way – the theory of evolution is wicked and evil. And I believe that from God's perspective – which should be ours, right? – those who promote it are 'evildoers.' I'm not saying that these people are necessarily consciously aware of the evil they're promoting, just that ..."

"You're right about that, Jen" Josh interrupted. "In fact, they would vehemently *deny* it in most cases. But they're *deceived* about the truth – just like I was."

"If we follow your line of reasoning to its logical extreme," Martha observed, "we should try to have the teaching of evolution banned from our schools ... Now, there's something that would make the headlines, wouldn't it?" she added with a slightly mischievous little grin.

"Yeah, it sure would!" Jennifer responded.

"I see your point, Jen," David said, "and, I have to admit, it makes pretty good sense. But I don't think the idea would get much support if we ever tried to push it. I mean, a lot of people already think we're pretty crazy. Can you imagine their reaction if we tried to actually ban teaching of the theory of evolution? They'd probably try to lock us up!"

After a few minutes of discussion, Paul said, "You know, the more I think about it, the more I think that Jennifer is really onto something here. Time after time, the attempts in our country to have creation taught alongside evolution have failed. But maybe the reason they have failed is, like Jennifer said, that God doesn't *want* them to be successful, because – as she said — Why would God want the beautiful story of His creation taught alongside the blasphemous lie of evolution, as if they were equals?"

Paul turned to Frank Morrison. "Would there be any legal obstacle to changing the petition, Frank? Could we legally change our goal from having creation taught alongside of evolution to banning all teaching of origins in our schools?"

"Yes, I believe we can," Morrison replied. "I think it would just require formal notification to the School Board and a public notice in the newspaper."

"What do you think about the idea, Frank?" Martha asked.

"Well, from a human perspective, if the petition is changed, I don't think it would have hardly any chance of being approved. On the other hand, however, history has proven that if it isn't changed it probably won't be approved, either. One thing is pretty certain: if it's changed, the media attention will be extraordinary. I mean, think of how much attention these efforts to get creation into the schools generate. Imagine the response if the goal is to have evolution *eliminated!* But wouldn't all this attention be great for our cause, which is to focus attention on this issue, so people can learn the truth about it? So, I say we should go for it. Let's change the petition!"

After a brief discussion, the vote was unanimous: the petition would be changed so that the goal would be the elimination of all teaching of origins from the Madison schools. Everyone was well aware that with this change they would be sailing into uncharted waters.

As usual, the meeting closed in prayer. Paul went first.

"Dear heavenly Father," he began, "we thank you for your blessing upon our meeting tonight, and, God, I thank You for the wonderful way your Spirit works in Jennifer's heart. It is indeed true, Lord, that the theory of evolution is a throne of destruction, and you know that our desire is to do whatever we can to save people from the consequences of bowing before this throne. We offer You our humble thanks for choosing us to participate in this exciting plan.

"As I consider the spectacular beauty of your creation, Lord, the works your hands have made, I think of your Word which tells us that you have given us all these things to reveal yourself to mankind ... *For since the creation of the world, His invisible attributes, His eternal power and divine nature, have been clearly seen, being understood through what has been made* ...and I think also, Lord, that it also says that those who have seen your creation and fail to acknowledge You will be without excuse when they meet You face to face on Judgment Day. We know with all our hearts, God, that the heavens are, indeed, telling of Your glory and that their expanse is declaring the work of Your hands, and we desperately want others to understand this too, so that when they stand before You, Your final words to them won't have to be, 'Depart from Me, you who practice lawlessness; I never knew you.'"

"And Lord Jesus, we pray that you would be with us at the next hearing," Martha continued. "Lord, we are well aware that we are engaged in a mighty spiritual battle here, a battle between good and evil, light and darkness, and You know, God, that we cannot wage this battle on our own, that in our flesh we are too weak. But your strength, we know, is perfected in our weakness. So we pray that You would bless us with your strength and your wisdom and grace at this hearing so that your light, the light of your Truth, would shine into the hearts of everyone in that gymnasium – and the countless other souls who will be watching the event.

"And God, one more thing … Help us do everything in love. We know, God, that Satan will be doing everything in his power to stir us to anger and resentment, but such feelings would not bring glory to You, and we pray that you will guard our hearts from these things."

Jennifer was next.

"Dear God, I thank you so much for what you're doing through our youth group. Lord, when we first came together last spring we could never have imagined where You would lead us. From just a few of us getting together to find out about your creation, and now people from all over are hearing about these things … all over the *country*, I guess. Lord, you are *so awesome*. And God, I too pray that you would be with each of us at the next hearing. You know that I'm pretty nervous about speaking in front of so many people, but I know that you will give me the peace I need to do a good job."

The prayers continued for several more minutes. Everyone contributed.

As Paul, Martha, and Frank were walking to their cars, Frank asked Martha what she thought of the evening.

"I thought it was quite remarkable. It made me think of the verse in the Bible: *and a child will lead them*. As I listened to Jennifer's argument, the question she raised – Why would God want the wondrous story of His creation taught alongside the blasphemous lie of evolution? – seemed so obvious. How could we have missed it? But isn't that something that happens all too often in our lives: missing God's obvious messages? Jennifer is a remarkable young woman, and we are very blessed to have her in our group."

"I totally agree with you," Morrison replied. "Like David said, our new petition will undoubtedly meet a lot of resistance – and probably has very little chance of being approved – but, nevertheless, from God's perspective I think we're doing the right thing. What about you, Paul. What do you think?"

"I'm with you, one hundred percent. And I can't wait 'till the next hearing. People will hear the truth, and, hopefully, it will set them *free*."

Before long, the high school kids decided that it was time for them to leave, too. As Josh got up, he turned to Kelly.

"Hey, Kelly … As I was coming up to your house, I saw through the window that you and Jen were doing handstand pirouettes. How many can you do?"

"Why do you ask?"

With a big smile, Josh replied, "Come on. Let's have a contest."

"You must be kidding, Josh! Get real. I don't want to *embarrass* you – but, hey, if you want to, let's do it!"

Josh went first.

"One … two … three … Uh-oh, our boy is down!" David called out, laughing heartily with his friends.

Now it was Kelly's turn.

"Five … six … seven … eight … nine …"

"Great job, Kelly! Keep it up," Jennifer exclaimed encouragingly.

"Ten … eleven … Oh boy! That's it for Kelly – but it's a new PR for her. Way to go, Kelly!" David said.

Kelly high-fived everybody, grinning proudly.

"That'll teach you not to challenge these girls on their home turf, Josh," Jennifer laughed, jabbing her finger playfully in Josh's ribs.

Just before dawn the following Wednesday, a blizzard howled through western New England. By late morning it had slammed into Madison with blinding fury. It was the worst snowstorm the area had experienced in almost twenty years. Because of the upcoming holidays, the second meeting on the petition was postponed until January 19th. Prior to this date, the youth group met two more times at the Conley's. At the first of these, most of the time was taken up with a discussion of the first hearing ... what was effective, what wasn't, and why.

The second meeting was held a few days before the second hearing. It was a wonderful gathering, with over fifty people, including several parents of the regular attendees. There was a potluck supper with enough food to feed a small army. The mood was very positive. Everyone was aware that it was highly unlikely that its revised goal – to eliminate all teaching of origins in the Madison schools – would be approved. At the same time, however, people were just glad that there was going to be a second hearing, that the petition wasn't defeated at the first one, which is what most people had expected. Everyone agreed that God's hand was upon that meeting, and they were eagerly looking forward to what He had in mind for the second one. Whether or not the petition was approved, the wonderful news about God's creation would be proclaimed once again, this time before an even larger audience than there was for the first hearing.

The meeting ended with prayer, and a song. The song was well-known by almost everyone and had become almost the theme song of the group ...

> You are Lord of creation and Lord of my life,
> Lord of the land and the sea.
> You were Lord of the heavens
> Before there was time,
> And Lord of all Lords you will be!
> We bow down, and we worship you, Lord.
> We bow down, and we worship you, Lord.
> We bow down, and we worship you, Lord.
> Lord of all Lords You will be!

As Josh and Paul headed out the door, Josh commented to Paul, "You know what, Paul? Something kind of odd is happening. In my reading to get ready for the next meeting, it's occurring to me more and more that one of the links in evolutionary theory that evolutionists believe is one of the strongest might actually be one of the weakest."

"Oh, yeah? What's that?"

"Natural Selection."

"That's interesting, because I agree with you one hundred percent. Do some more research into it. Get prepared. Maybe it will come up at the next hearing."

"Yeah, I'll do that," Josh said.

David was the last to leave. Jennifer put on her coat to walk out with him. A light snow was falling. As they stood there holding hands, Jennifer looked up and said,

"You know, I was thinking about snow the other day, and a neat thought occurred to me. You want to hear it?"

"Yeah, sure."

"Well, in God's design of the world, when the temperature drops below freezing, water turns to ice, right? Now, generally speaking, that's a good thing, because we need ice – you know, to put in our drinks to make them cold and to skate on, stuff like that. However, God knew that if water *always* turned to ice under these conditions it would *not* be good. If precipitation always turned to ice when the temperature was below freezing, it would be very *bad*, because then, in the winter all we would have would be sleet or, even worse, freezing rain. And you know what freezing rain causes: *ice storms* – And we all know how awful *they* can be, right? Like, remember that terrible ice storm that occurred in northern Maine and Canada a few years ago? The pictures were just *unbelievable*."

"Yeah, I remember them. They looked like something out of a horror movie or something. It was totally crazy."

"Right. Anyway, God recognized a potential problem, and He did something about it. He tweaked His design so that when the temperature fell below freezing, the moisture that fell from the sky would usually not be ice or freezing rain. It would become something else. It would turn into tiny little crystals – snowflakes. Now, not only would these crystals be incredibly beautiful – we've all seen the amazing design of snowflakes … like, no two are exactly alike – but they would also be very light, so that when they fell to the ground, rather than streaking down like sleet or freezing rain which can actually *hurt* when it hits you, they would flutter harmlessly down like tiny little feathers. Then, to top everything off, even though the crystals are made of ice, which is clear, as they gathered on the ground the blanket that they created would be pure white, and the earth would be transformed into a beautiful winter wonderland – just like this!" she said, sweeping her arm across the snow-covered landscape that lay before her.

Turning toward David with a big smile, she said, "So, what do you think? Because He loved us, God turned something that could have been really bad, something that would *hurt* us, into something really, really beautiful. It's pretty cool, isn't it?"

"Yeah, I like it. It's very cool. God is awesome, Jen ... and so are you!" he said as he gently put his arm around her. "Just one question, though: how come there still are ice storms?"

"It's Adam and Eve's fault – you know, the Fall, in the Garden of Eden. They blew it, Dave. They ate the forbidden fruit, sin and death entered into the world ... So now we have ice storms!" Jennifer smiled up at David.

"What about blizzards? They sure can cause some problems."

"Same thing," Jennifer said, still looking up at him with the same enchanting smile.

Before she knew it, her lips were pressed against David's in a sweet, tender kiss.

The snow was coming down harder now, but David and Jennifer didn't notice ... Their minds weren't on the weather.

26

Reverend Strong and the Flood

One Monday morning in early January Reverend John Strong was in his office at St. Peter's Church when he heard a knock on his door.

"Come in," the Reverend called out.

A stranger entered the room. "Hello," the man said cheerfully. "I'm Mark Snyder. I'm visiting my in-laws in Madison with my wife and three young children, and my wife and I attended your morning service yesterday. My wife's parents recommended your church to us."

"It's nice to meet you, Mark. Here, sit down … Who are your in-laws?"

"Elizabeth and Joseph Murphy. I doubt that you'd know them. I don't think they are, you know, regular attendees," Mark smiled as he headed toward the leather armchair beside the Reverend's large mahogany desk.

In their introductory conversation, Mark disclosed that he was an assistant pastor at a small nondenominational church in Maine. He quickly got to the reason for his visit.

"There's something I want to ask you about, Reverend. In your sermon yesterday, you referred to the Genesis Flood."

"Yes, that's right. I said it was a warning from God to a sinful world. It was just a passing reference."

"You indicated that you believe that this flood occurred some place in the Middle East. I guess you believe that it was local?"

Immediately it was clear to Reverend Strong what this conversation was going to be about: the scope of the Genesis Flood. He wasn't surprised. A little red flag had already gone up when his guest had mentioned that he was 'an assistant pastor at a small nondenominational church.' He knew that the theology of such individuals tended to be very conservative; that is, they generally tended to interpret the Bible literally. And he wasn't surprised that the topic he had come to discuss was the Genesis Flood, for he knew that when it came to debate topics, for such people this was one of their favorites.

"Yes, that's right. Like most experts in the earth's history who are willing to acknowledge such a flood … you know, geologists, archaeologists, etc. … that's exactly what I believe."

"So, you don't believe that this flood was universal, in other words."

"If I believe it was local, I guess I can't believe that it was universal, can I?" Reverend Strong smiled.

"Forgive me. That was kind of a stupid question, wasn't it?" Snyder smiled, his cheeks a little red. He was a little nervous. He was deeply involved in the creation/evolution controversy and knew that the Genesis Flood was a central issue in this raging debate. Creation was his passion, and whenever he encountered what he believed was false teaching about this subject, he felt obligated to challenge it. He didn't relish these confrontations – especially when they involved someone as experienced as Reverend Strong – but he felt it was his duty, or, to be more precise, his mission. Because of all of its media attention, he was familiar with the recent hearing at Madison High regarding the petition, and Reverend Strong's role in it.

He asked another question.

"You believe in the words of the Bible, Reverend, don't you?"

"Of course I do. I'm a Christian!"

Turning quickly to the Book of Genesis in the well-worn Bible that he had brought with him, Snyder said, "But look at what the Bible says about this flood. I'm sure you're familiar with these words:

Behold, I, even I am bringing the flood of water upon the earth, to destroy all flesh in which is the breath of life, from under heaven; everything that is on the earth shall perish, and …

And the water prevailed more and more upon the earth, so that all the high mountains everywhere under the heavens were covered. The water prevailed fifteen cubits higher, and the mountains were covered, and …

And all flesh that moved on the earth perished, birds and cattle and beasts and every swarming thing that swarms upon the earth, and all mankind; of all that was on the dry land, all in whose nostrils was the breath of life, died. Thus He blotted out every living thing that was upon the face of the land, from man to animals to creeping things and to birds of the sky, and they were blotted out from the earth; and only Noah was left, together with those that were with him in the ark.

"How can these verses be describing a *local* flood, Reverend Strong?"

As he listened to his young guest read these Bible passages, Reverend Strong thought back to the time many years earlier when, entering seminary, he too had interpreted these passages from Genesis literally. From his perspective, it had taken many years to recognize that such an interpretation was completely incompatible with modern science, forcing its abandonment and leading to a theology that harmonized the powerful spiritual teaching of the Scriptures with the facts of science: theistic evolution. He hoped that the upcoming conversation might help his young guest recognize the wisdom of this enlightened theology. As far as he was concerned, fundamentalism – interpreting the Bible literally – was a major stumbling block on the road to spiritual enlightenment. In his mind, theistic evolution was the theology for today's world. Fundamentalism was a relic from the past.

"First of all, Mark," Strong said, "of course I'm familiar with those passages. I've read and studied them countless times. Before I address your question, let me ask you something, though. You took science classes in high school, and maybe even college, right?"

"Of course."

"Did any of your textbooks, or teachers, ever mention the Genesis Flood?"

"Well, I don't remember it being discussed in high school or college – I went to Williams College– but it was certainly mentioned in seminary."

"I'm surprised that you went to Williams. Williams is quite liberal. Where did you go to seminary?"

"Wheaton College."

"And what did your Wheaton professors teach about the scope of this flood?"

"Their opinions were mixed, but I guess I'd have to say that the general consensus was that the flood was probably local."

Professor Strong smiled. "So, there you go, Mark ... the flood was never mentioned in all of your high school and undergraduate courses, and in seminary, at what is often referred to as 'the Harvard of Christian colleges,' the consensus is that the flood was local. Do you see a pattern here?" he asked, smiling again.

"Yes, of course I do. I just don't happen to agree with it." Quickly, he shifted the conversation to another subject.

"Are you familiar with fossil graveyards, Reverend?"

"Somewhat … They're locations in which large numbers of fossils are found packed together, like in the Bone Cave in Cumberland, Maryland."

"Exactly – And they're found all over the world. They generally contain huge numbers of fossils, often countless millions, packed tightly together. Furthermore, and most significantly, the fossils often indicate that the creatures were buried in some sort of massive, violent cataclysm, because their bodies are often badly distorted, or even torn apart. Here's something else that is extraordinary about these graveyards. Sometimes the creatures represented in them are natural enemies and sometimes they are from completely different climactic zones. Like, there might be tropical warm-climate animals with Temperate Zone plants. Let me ask you a question: how can a local flood account for these fossil graveyards?"

"Perhaps they were caused by many different local floods, like the ones that take place today."

"But local floods today aren't creating anything that remotely resembles these fossil graveyards."

That's a good point – it hadn't occurred to me before, Reverend Strong thought to himself.

"Okay, Mark, I have to admit, I don't have a good explanation for how local floods could have caused these fossil graveyards, but let's keep something in mind: there are thousands of geologists all over the world who know an awful lot more about these things than you or I do, and these graveyards haven't caused them to believe in a worldwide flood. I'm sure if you asked any of them, they would have a very good explanation for these graveyards."

Hmmm, Mark mused … *Appeal to authority – a common escape when you don't know what you're talking about.*

After a brief pause, Reverend Strong continued. "I assume that you are aware that there are some very good hypotheses regarding the local nature of the Genesis Flood."

"I am. Do you have any in mind?"

"One of the best known was a proposal by two Columbia University geologists, William Ryan and Walter Pitman, in the late 1990's. Their study received considerable publicity, including a major article in *National Geographic*, and was generally praised in the academic world. Even today a Google search reveals thousands of Web sites that reference this study. Are you familiar with it?"

"Yes, I've read about it. In fact, I think I have a copy of the *National Geographic* that you referred to. It's been awhile, though. Why don't you refresh my memory?"

"I'd be glad to. The theory is that as the Ice Age melted, a wall of seawater surged from the Mediterranean into the Black Sea. During the Ice Age, the authors argue, the Black Sea was an isolated freshwater lake surrounded by farmland. About 12,000 years ago, toward the end of the Ice Age, Earth began growing warmer. Vast sheets of ice that sprawled over the Northern Hemisphere began to melt. Oceans and seas grew deeper as a result. Then, about 7,000 years ago the Mediterranean Sea swelled. Seawater pushed northward, slicing through what is now Turkey. Funneled through the narrow Bosporus, the water hit the Black Sea with 200 times the force of Niagara Falls. Each day the Black Sea rose about six inches (15 centimeters), and coastal farms were flooded. Seared into the memories of the terrified survivors the tale was passed down through the generations and eventually became the Noah story."[14]

Snyder slowly shook his head in frustration. "So, you're saying that you agree that this is a reasonable explanation for the biblical flood story?"

"Certainly. It may not be the correct explanation, but for the time being, it's as good as any."

"Let's think about this story, Reverend. How much sense does it make that people involved in a local flood, regardless of its magnitude, would ever believe that the flood was worldwide? Imagine yourself in this event ... An unprecedented surge of water has suddenly inundated the area in which you live and has caused panic among you and all of your neighbors. The water is rising so fast that you are hard-pressed to gather up your most valuable possessions and your family and livestock to move them to higher ground before they are destroyed. All of your crops and equipment will soon be under water. Fortunately, you are able to find safety in the nearby hills. Day after day the water continues to rise, but after many days it finally levels off. The land you are familiar with, your homeland, has dramatically changed, and you and your family are forced to find a new plot of land and begin your life anew. You have never witnessed such a natural disaster in all your life, and you surely never will again. But – and this is a *very big* 'but' – would you have ever thought that the flood you had just experienced was *worldwide,* as Ryan and Pitman suggest you would have?"

Before Reverend Strong had a chance to answer this question, Snyder continued ...

"The answer to this question is perfectly obvious: *of course you wouldn't have!* To imagine otherwise is preposterous. Regardless of the scope of the flood, at all times you would have been able to see vast areas of land – distant hills and mountains and valleys – that the flood had not touched. The flood may have been very bad, but neither you nor anyone else would *ever* have thought that it was *worldwide*."

"Perhaps the survivors portrayed it as being universal for dramatic effect … you know, to emphasize how terrible it was," Reverend Strong suggested.

"And then this lie was transmitted around the world and down through the ages without anyone questioning it, even though everyone knew that it wasn't true – that the worldwide flood immortalized in these stories wasn't really worldwide at all? I'm referring, of course, to the fact that the story of a universal deluge is imbedded in the cultures of literally hundreds of people groups around the world, something that I'm sure you are familiar with. Personally, I don't think that that notion is worthy of attention, and I can't believe that you would either, Reverend. It just doesn't make any sense. A tale about a local flood in the area of the Black Sea is not going to pass into the culture of hundreds of people groups all over the world and then be remembered in their society for *several thousand years* as a *worldwide* flood. Come on, Reverend. That is *ridiculous!*

"So let's be realistic: in regards to the fundamental issue here, the scope of the flood, the Genesis story and the hypothesis developed by Mr. Ryan and Mr. Pitman are completely at odds. Genesis is *obviously* describing a universal flood; the Ryan and Pitman account is *obviously* not. But that's not all. They also differ in many other fundamental details – like, the ark that rescued Noah and his family from the flood. In the Genesis account, Noah was commanded by God to build this boat many decades prior to the flood. The ark was a huge boat; it would be over four thousand years before a larger one was constructed. The foresight and advance planning related to this event is a vital part of the biblical story. Just before the deluge began, a vast number of animals arrived at the ark, which would soon save them from the terrible destruction that lay ahead. The ark and the animals are *essential details* of the Genesis Flood account, Reverend Strong, and *neither* is included in the Black Sea Flood story."

"Perhaps the reason that such details weren't included in this hypothesis is that reasonable people are aware that fitting two of every kind of animal in the world on a ship, regardless of its size, and feeding them for a year is impossible. Therefore, the inclusion of the animals in the biblical description of the ark *cannot* be literal, so any realistic hypothesis of the flood, such as the one offered by Ryan and Pitman, isn't going to include it."

"That's a common argument, and there are very good answers to it. Entire books have been devoted to it. I'd be happy to discuss it in detail, but

I don't think we have time for that this morning. For now, I'll simply say that the ability of the ark to handle its passengers has been thoroughly and convincingly documented by a number of authors, and I'd be happy to give you their names, if you're interested.

"In any event, it completely ignores the point I was trying to make: that the Black Sea Flood story completely omits two absolutely essential elements of the Genesis Flood story, the animals and the ark. But that's not all. In addition to the ark and the animals, this story also omits virtually all of the other key features of the Genesis Flood story, including the reason for the flood – man's transgressions – God's divine judgment, the salvation of a single family favored by God, the landing of the ark on a mountain, the worship offered by the survivors, etc. The fact is, Reverend, that the story proposed by Ryan and Pitman has practically *nothing* in common with the Genesis Flood story, other than the fact that they both involved a lot of water ... although the Genesis account involved a LOT more! And, just think, this story is considered to be one of, if not *the*, best theories in support of the notion that the Genesis Flood was local! Unbelievable. It's about as bad as pointing to the peppered moth as the best example of evolution that has been observed by man. One word describes them both: *pathetic*."

Before Reverend Strong could say anything, his young guest continued. "In light of these things, that people would actually accept this story as a reasonable explanation for the Flood story in the Book of Genesis is mind-boggling. It clearly reveals the extremes that people will go to in order to explain away the worldwide nature of this flood. Of course, don't get me wrong. I'm not saying that this Black Sea flood did not occur. It may very well have. My dispute is with the proposal that this flood was the one described in the Book of Genesis. The claim that these two floods were the same makes about as much sense as arguing that the sun and the moon are exactly the same type of object – because they both are in the sky, are round, and radiate light! Just like the two different accounts of the flood, any similarity between these two luminaries is completely superficial. In *essence*, they are completely different.

"Now, I'd like to ask you a question, Reverend. How in the world could these two apparently very intelligent men, Ryan and Pitman, arrive at the conclusion that these two completely different events were the *same*? Also, why do so many other apparently intelligent people, such as the editors of *National Geographic*, believe such a flimsy theory?"

Reverend Strong thought it was a pretty good question, but he didn't have an answer off the top of his head. He could tell Snyder did, though.

"I don't know. Why don't you tell me?"

"I'd be glad to. All of these people are devoted to the theory of evolution, and they will do anything – absolutely *anything* – to make sure that this theory remains alive. If there really was a worldwide flood it would be the death knell for this theory. So the main reason for the local flood theory – Ryan and Pitman's or anyone else's – is to keep the theory of evolution alive."

Reverend Strong leaned back in his chair and shook his head in reservation. "Come on, Mark. That's pretty wild. I can see why you might think that an historical worldwide flood might present some problems for the theory of evolution, but to say that it would be the theory's death knell is really extreme. How can you say that?"

"There are a few different reasons, but it essentially boils down to the fossil record. Basically, there are only two explanations for the fossil record: a universal flood and the theory of evolution. According to the first, most of the fossils are the result of the massive amounts of sediment created by the vast quantity of water in the universal flood. Except for the creatures that were on the ark, this sediment buried the majority of the living things that existed on the earth at that time, and that was the cause of the fossils – or most of them, at least. The evolutionary explanation for fossils is completely different, of course. According to that theory, fossils were formed over countless millions, even billions, of years by multiple geological events. You know how it goes … Some natural catastrophe – a volcano, or an earthquake or a flood or something – buried the living creatures in some location a few hundred million years ago and the buried creatures became fossils. Then, a million or so years later, after the land had been repopulated by a whole new set of creatures, another catastrophe took place and buried all of them, creating a new layer of rock with a new set of fossils … etcetera, etcetera, etcetera.

"Now, these two explanations for the fossil record are *mutually exclusive*. That is, if one is correct, the other *cannot* be. Therefore, if the fossils were created by a worldwide flood they could not have been created by the evolutionary explanation for the fossil record. But the explanation for the fossil record offered by the theory of evolution is not just one minor feature of evolutionary theory. It is one of its *fundamental cornerstones*. The theory's very existence depends upon it. If the worldwide flood explanation for this record was proven to be correct, thereby proving the evolutionary explanation to be false … remember, the two theories are mutually exclusive … the entire theory of evolution would collapse like a house of cards.

"So, then, it's simple logic: in order for the theory of evolution to remain alive there must not have been a worldwide flood. Aside from completely ignoring it – pretending it never existed, that is – which is the approach taken by a lot of evolutionists, including those who write our students' science textbooks, the only alternative is the local flood theory. So, like I was saying, the main purpose of the local flood theory is to allow for the survival of the theory of evolution. It's just a fact, Reverend, pure and simple: If there really was a worldwide flood, there really wouldn't be a theory of evolution," Snyder said with a smile.

Reverend Strong nodded his head and smiled back. To his surprise, even though he was resistant to it, he found his young guest's logic interesting, even slightly persuasive.

"There may be an element of truth in what you are saying, but I'm sure you realize that the whole idea rests upon a completely unproven assumption," Reverend Strong observed.

"What's that?"

"That a universal flood is a better explanation for the fossil record than the one offered by evolutionary theory."

"Yes, of course. And guess what … it *is*," Snyder replied with a confident smile.

"You might think so, but I'm sure you know, Mark, that the vast majority of scientists in the world would strongly disagree with you. These people reject the whole notion of a worldwide flood. As you told me a short while ago, even most of your professors at Wheaton believe that the Genesis Flood was local."

Mark shrugged his shoulders. "Sad to say, Reverend, you're absolutely right, but that's their problem, not mine. And it doesn't change the fact that the very survival of the theory of evolution depends upon the local flood theory."

"Let me ask you something else, Mark. Do you believe that the people who come up with these local flood theories, people like Ryan and Pitman, realize that their motive is to keep the theory of evolution alive, as you have suggested? I hope you realize that that would be a bit difficult to swallow."

"Oh, no … definitely not, Reverend. They aren't aware of this at all. They would be just as surprised to hear this as you are!"

Mark paused for a moment. "You know, when you come right down to it, people don't want to face the truth about a worldwide flood because they don't want to face the truth about God. A verse in the Bible explains this situation perfectly, Second Corinthians 4:4: *The god of this world has blinded the minds of the unbelieving that they might not see the light of the gospel of the glory of Christ, who is the image of God.*

"But I believe in the local flood theory, because, like just about every scientist in the world, I think the evidence is in its favor. I've been a Reverend in the Christian church for over thirty years. Are you saying that I don't want to face the truth about God?"

"I don't know what your relationship with God is, Reverend. That's between you and Him. I can tell you, however, that the local flood theory is not just wrong. It's far worse than that. If the Flood described in the Bible was local, it makes God – the Author of these descriptions – seem like a fool and a liar, or, even worse, a deceiver. Consider, for example, the size of the ark. As described in Genesis 6:15, the ark was a massive vessel: 75 feet wide, 45 feet high, and about 450 feet long. As I mentioned earlier, it was not until 1884, about 5,000 years after the flood, that a vessel, the Eturia, a Cunard liner, was built with a length exceeding that of the ark.[15] Building such a huge ship, which took Noah and his helpers many decades, to survive a local flood would be absurd. Think about it. Seriously, take a moment and try to imagine it. It would make Noah, and God, appear as fools."

"Did you ever consider that the measurements given for the ark might be symbolic, not to be taken literally, like so many other descriptions in the Bible?"

"But what in the world would they *symbolize*, Reverend? What are the numbers three hundred, fifty, and thirty – the measurements of the ark, in cubits – supposed to be symbolic of? To me, that suggestion makes absolutely no sense. Think about this, too … After the flood, God promised Noah, *I will remember my covenant, which is between Me and you and every living creature of all flesh; and never again shall the water become a flood to destroy all flesh.* If the flood that prompted this was local, then God would seem to be a liar, first because a local flood certainly could not have destroyed *all flesh*, and second because this promise would have been broken countless times throughout history, with every occurrence of a local flood.

"Finally, Jesus Christ Himself acknowledged the global extent of the flood. Speaking of the pre-flood population, in the twenty-fourth chapter of Matthew He said: *The flood came and took them all away.* Needless to say, such utter destruction would not be possible with a *local* flood!"

From Reverend Strong's perspective, what Mark Snyder was saying strained reason to the breaking point. To take issue with a local flood hypothesis, such as that offered by Ryan and Pitman, was one thing, but to say that the primary purpose of the theory was to prop up the theory of evolution was something radically different and, as far as he was concerned, without basis. For now, anyway, he had heard enough.

"Mark, listen ... What you are saying is very interesting, although I don't happen to agree with most of it. I have a lot of work to do here this morning, so, if you don't mind, I'm going to have to end our meeting. Perhaps if you're in town again in the future, you could stop by and we could continue this discussion."

"Oh, sure, Reverend Strong. Please forgive me if I came on a little too strong at times. As you can see, I get very passionate about this subject. And, thank you – the next time I'm in the area, I promise, I'll be sure to stop by and say hi!"

As Snyder headed toward the door, something occurred to Reverend Strong.

"Hey, Mark, I just thought of something!" he called out. "There's a fatal flaw in your idea that the primary purpose of the local flood theory is to allow for the survival of the theory of evolution: the local flood theory was around long before the theory of evolution even existed, so there's no way that could be its purpose!"

"You're forgetting something, Reverend. The Devil is very good at planning ahead," Snyder said with a smile.

Reverend Strong watched his young visitor as he walked down the long hall and disappeared around the corner. Their meeting had not gone exactly as the Reverend had anticipated. It was he, not Mark Snyder, who had been given a lot to think about.

Two days before the Second Hearing, another article by Karl Bond appeared in the *Daily Messenger*.

"Well, all you creation versus evolution junkies, the great day is almost here: the final hearing on the petition to have creation taught alongside evolution in the Madison public schools. My sources inform me that, despite the many reasons for making some changes on their panel – which I have pointed out in my previous articles – the creationists have ignored my wisdom and decided to go with the same representatives they had at the first hearing, which includes, of course, two high school students and a youth pastor. I wonder what Josh Siegel will decide to attack this time … Natural Selection, perhaps? A high school student attempting to falsify one of the cornerstones of what has been called "The Grand Unifying Theory of Science." Now, that would certainly be worth the price of admission, wouldn't it?

Having informed us in the first hearing that the earth was created before the sun, perhaps Jennifer Conley will explain to us another rather remarkable event: how Adam was able to provide a name for all the animals on the face of the earth - in *one day*.

Of course, the big news that came out since the first hearing is that the goal of the petition has been changed. Originally, the petitioners sought to have creation taught alongside evolution in the science classrooms. Now, they seek to have all teaching of origins banned from these classrooms. They're not just adjusting the teaching of evolution to include their religious theory, like they were before. They want it to be eliminated altogether!

The boldness of their effort is truly breathtaking. In the famous Scopes trial in Tennessee in 1925 the defendant, John Scopes, was tried for teaching that man had evolved from a lower animal. The entire theory of evolution was not on trial; it was only this particular aspect of it. In its effort to ban the entire theory of evolution from its classrooms, the current trial in Madison – after all, that's what it really is – propels us backward, not just a few years, but all the way back to the early twentieth century, *before* the Scopes trial. In the national media, this hearing has been dubbed "The

Second Scopes Trial, or "Scopes Retried." That's not really accurate, though; in fact, it's much worse!

Now, I have to admit that I truly admire the gumption of this little group. This is not just David versus Goliath, folks. It's David versus a *whole army* of Goliaths!

One thing about this upcoming hearing is virtually certain: for one night, at least, Madison, New Hampshire will be the center of attention for the entire country, and much of the world beyond. As anyone who has been following this situation knows, the first hearing about seven weeks ago generated significant interest on its own. The long delay since that meeting has provided ample time for the media to whip up interest, and all indications are that this hearing is going to be a media extravaganza. If you are planning to attend the hearing live, if you want a seat in the gym I advise you to arrive early – like around lunchtime, perhaps. I guarantee you that the gym will be completely full at least two hours before the meeting starts, perhaps earlier.

Those of you who are my loyal followers know that I have had a lot of fun writing about this great debate, and I'm sure that this hearing will not end this joy ride. In fact, I expect it will provide much fodder for future articles. However, I want to end this article on a serious note.

What is taking place in Madison is a sign that something is terribly wrong in our educational system. That apparently intelligent people could still believe in this day and age, among other things, that the world is only 6 –10,000 years old and that about 5,000 years ago a great flood covered the entire earth with water and that the only creatures that survived this flood were Noah and his little family along with two of every creature on the face of the earth, all of which just happened to appear at the ark just before the rains descended … Let me tell you, my friends, what, in my humble opinion, this indicates. Far from indicating that the theory of evolution needs to be questioned, or, much worse, ignored, it indicates that the theory needs to be taught *much better*. When over 99% of scientists believe in a theory but less than 50% of the public does, that doesn't suggest that there's something wrong with the theory. It suggests that it is not being taught effectively.

So, then, here's my plan. After the curtain has fallen on this current charade and this little band of creationists shuffle back to their churches where they belong, *I* am going to present another petition to the School Board. This petition will call for an *increase* in the amount of classroom time devoted to the theory of evolution, double the current time, perhaps even triple. My goal will be simple: to have Madison be the first town in the United States to have the beliefs of the general public regarding evolution match the beliefs of scientists. It would offer the people in Madison an opportunity to *redeem* themselves!

Do I hear an "Amen, Brother Karl"?

One more thing … I did a little research on this petition and discovered that it originated in a church youth group led by the youth pastor, Paul Hopkins, on the creation panel. Not surprisingly, the two high school students on the panel are part of this group, too. In light of this discovery, in conjunction with my new petition I thought it might be a good idea to start up an Evolution Club at Madison High – you know, to give this church youth group a little competition. Maybe the group could be called "Darwin's Disciples." Has a nice ring to it, doesn't it?

Hopefully, this club would spawn similar clubs in other towns and villages, until one day there would be such clubs throughout our land. Why not? I'm sure that the youth group led by Mr. Hopkins is not the only such group studying creation.

We're in a battle, folks, and we need to fight for the truth … because, after all, "the truth will set you free."

27

The Second Hearing Begins

By the time the second hearing arrived, Madison was in the grip of a real old-fashioned Northeast winter. The temperature hadn't risen above twenty degrees for several days, and another snowstorm had hit the area a few days earlier, dropping an additional fourteen inches of fresh powder. All the roads were clear, however, and a large crowd was expected for the meeting in the Madison High gym. Anticipation for the meeting had been building steadily since the first one, but the startling announcement regarding the change in the petition had caused this interest to explode. From all parts of the country, and several foreign countries as well, media hounds were converging in the gym. They sensed that blood was going to spill tonight, and they were pretty sure whose it would be: the creationists. In order to create interest they were hyping the event as the second Scopes Trial, often referred to as the most famous courtroom trial in American history. As Karl Bond had noted in a recent article, technically the portrayal was not quite accurate, for in the original trial, in 1925, the plaintiffs were only trying to prevent one aspect of the theory of evolution from being taught in Tennessee schools: the notion that man evolved from ape-like ancestors. They were not, in other words, trying to ban teaching of the entire theory, as the petitioners at this "trial" were attempting to do. No one could recall such an effort ever being attempted before. The media hype, then, was not really necessary; it really was a major story.

The Madison High Buildings and Grounds crew were doing their best to accommodate the technical demands of all of the media representatives, but it was a losing battle. There simply weren't enough outlets, cables, manpower, or time. In the end, it simply boiled down to "first come, first served." Seating was going to be another problem. Latecomers would have no chance of getting into the gym, but additional seating, with live television coverage

315

of the proceedings, was being made available in the high school cafeteria. As it turned out, even that was inadequate. Most of those who were turned away from the cafeteria, however, did observe the meeting that night – on their own television sets.

Once again, the meeting was scheduled to begin at 7 p.m., but people began arriving shortly after four, a few even earlier. By five the gym was just about full. The panel and School Board members had been asked to arrive early for interviews with media reps. They weren't too thrilled about this, because they knew that in all likelihood it was going to be a long and no doubt tiring night. They agreed to these interviews on the condition that they end by 6:30, so they would have a short break before the meeting began at seven. All of the panel and Board members arrived on time except for Mr. Potter, who was still weak from his auto accident. He planned on attending the meeting for as long as he was able but did not feel that he had sufficient strength for the preliminary interviews as well. One of his legs had been badly broken, and he was still using crutches.

By 6 p.m. there were over seven hundred people in the high school cafeteria, well beyond its normal capacity. The tables had been removed, however, so the fire marshal had decided to allow the extra people.

At 7 p.m., with hundreds of people turned away, Susan Marshall banged her gavel and called the meeting to order. She announced that the meeting was scheduled to end at 11 p.m., but added that she would allow it to extend if it appeared to be necessary. She implored people to behave in an orderly and courteous fashion. It was a tall and probably unrealistic order, for people's emotions were on edge tonight. There was an air of electricity and tension in the air, somewhat like that prior to a big sporting event.

A few minutes after seven the hearing began with a question from the moderator, Henry Knox. It was directed toward the creation panel.

"I'm sure that you all are well aware that your decision to change your petition was a stunning surprise, to say the least. A number of attempts to mandate the teaching of creation in public schools as an alternative to evolution have been attempted in recent years, but no one that I talked to could remember any effort to *eliminate* the teaching of evolution – except, of course, in Dayton, Tennessee in 1925. What prompted you to make this decision? … and what chance of success do you think it has?"

Paul and Martha immediately looked at each other. Martha nodded her head and pointed her finger at Paul, giving him the go-ahead to answer the question. Paul knew that Mr. Knox's understanding of the Scopes trial was not exactly accurate, but he let it slide for now.

"To tell you the truth, the decision was a bit of a surprise to most of us, too, Mr. Knox. A short while ago, at one of our meetings, Jennifer raised a question: why would God want the glorious truth about His creation taught side-by-side with the blasphemous lie of evolution, as if they somehow deserved equal attention in the classroom? Her question caused us to think very hard about what we were trying to accomplish in these hearings. As you pointed out, there have been numerous attempts in the past few years to mandate the teaching of creation in public school science classrooms when teaching about origins, but, unfortunately, these efforts have had little success. Time after time, they have been defeated. So, it occurred to us that perhaps the reason they were being defeated is that God didn't *want* them to be successful. This being the case, from our perspective, we were left with two possible goals: either have creation taught exclusively as the explanation for the natural world, or eliminate the teaching of origins altogether. It's pretty obvious that the first option would have no chance of success at all – you know, the "separation of church and state," which, as we have made clear, we don't believe in … although we know the courts do – so, by process of elimination, we were left with the second."

"Apparently, you've missed something. The second option has no chance of success, either. Come on, Paul … *wake up!* If you think you're going to have the teaching of evolution banned from our schools, you're living in a dream world! Seriously, what you all are trying to do here is absolutely crazy." The speaker was James Quinn, from the School Board, and the truth was that his opinion was shared by most of the Board members, as well as most other people observing the evening's proceedings.

"We know that we're facing an uphill fight, to say the least," Paul replied. "But, hey, stranger things have happened … Remember what the Red Sox did against the Yankees in 2004!"

"Yeah, I remember … But I don't see David Ortiz on your panel," Mr. Quinn said with a smile.

"That's okay. We've got someone supporting us who's a lot bigger and stronger than David Ortiz!" Paul quickly replied.

It had been decided in advance that members of the audience would be allowed a limited number of questions, and Mr. Knox now recognized one of these, a man by the name of Edward Douglas. The question was directed toward the creation panel.

"I wasn't at the first meeting, and I just want to make sure that I understand your position. According to what I read, you don't just have reservations about certain elements of the theory of evolution; you completely reject it – every bit of it. Is that correct?"

"Yes, that's correct," Martha replied. "We believe that the theory is a diabolical – uh, *outrageous* – lie intended to explain how the world came into being without a Creator."

"*Diabolical?* Doesn't that mean 'from the devil?' You're claiming that the theory is not just wrong, but that it's from the *devil?*" the man asked incredulously.

Martha just shrugged her shoulders and raised her eyebrows.

"Whew ... incredible. I think I'll leave that opinion for someone else to tackle. What I'd like is some specific evidence for your rejection of the theory? I know you provided some at the first meeting, and I read some of the reports of this meeting, but I need to have my memory refreshed."

"Sure, I'd be happy to," Parker replied. "I think transitional forms are a good example. It's not a difficult subject to understand. Do you know what the term refers to?"

"Yes. It refers to the creatures that supposedly link related species in the evolutionary tree of life – like Lucy, for example, one of the so-called 'missing links' between an ape and a human being."

"That's right. The first thing that must be understood about transitional forms is that classical and neo-Darwinism – the theory of evolution that most people are familiar with – *demands* them. If, as the theory claims, every living creature evolved very slowly, through countless small steps from some previous one, then a great number of these intermediate creatures – or transitional forms – must have lived throughout earth's history. Charles Darwin himself was clearly aware of this fact. Let me read you what he said about it in his *Origin of Species: The number of intermediate varieties which have formerly existed on the earth must be truly enormous.*

"I must tell you that these words were followed by, *Why then is not every geological formation and every stratum full of such intermediate links? Geology assuredly does not reveal any such finely graduated organic chain; and this, perhaps, is the most obvious and gravest objection which can be raised against my theory.*[16]

"This statement makes it clear that the intermediate forms which his theory demanded had not been discovered when those words were written. For Darwin, however, this was not necessarily a prohibitive problem. Paleontology, the study of fossils, was in its infancy, and he could assume – or at least hope – that these missing links would be discovered in the future.

"Other scientists quickly grasped Darwin's point regarding transitional forms and began a massive search to locate them, a search that has continued unabated to this day. Their search, however, has been in vain. The forms are still missing. Today, however, scientists can no longer rest upon the hope that they will turn up in the future, as Darwin could. Billions of fossils have been unearthed since 1859, and there is not a single unquestionable transitional form among them. With each passing year, the conclusion becomes increasingly clear: transitional forms simply don't exist. And since the theory of evolution *requires* them, well ..."

"Just a minute," Randall Decker interrupted. "I object to what you're saying. Creationists always bring up this notion of the lack of transitional forms in the fossil record. It's just not true. The record reveals a great number of transitional forms. The only people who deny it are creationists."

The argument over the existence of transitional forms is a common one in the debate between creationists and evolutionists. It usually ends up in a stalemate because neither side can really prove their case. Creationists, of course, cannot present any tangible evidence to support their position because according to them there isn't any. Theirs is an argument from silence. Evidence presented by evolutionists, on the other hand – presented to the public via photographs of fossils or artist's renderings based upon these fossils, or perhaps bone fragments – cannot resolve the issue because the evidence is invariably subjective. The *claim* that a creature is transitional doesn't necessarily make it one. They don't come with ID tags.

Martha was well aware of these issues, and had personally confronted them a number of times. She was prepared to deal with them.

"You say there are transitional forms, I say there aren't, Mr. Decker. I think we both know that any discussion about this subject is ultimately going to boil down to your word against mine. Neither of us can really prove our position. I can, however, prove that something that you just said isn't true."

"Oh? What might that be?" Mr. Decker replied, surprised.

"You said that creationists are the only ones who don't believe the fossil record reveals transitional forms. The truth is that there are plenty of evolutionists who don't believe it, either."

"Like who?"

"You are familiar with the theory of Punctuated Equilibrium, I'm sure."

"Of course," Mr. Decker responded a little hesitantly. He had heard of it, but really wasn't *that* familiar with it.

"For the sake of others here who are not aware of this theory, perhaps I should briefly explain it. Would that be all right?" Martha asked Henry Knox.

"Yes, certainly. I'm curious myself to know what it is."

"Good. Punctuated Equilibrium, sometimes called Saltationism, is an alternative evolutionary theory developed by two influential evolutionists, Stephen Jay Gould, professor of geology at Harvard University for many years, and Niles Eldredge from the American Museum of Natural history, in the early 1970's. This theory proposes that evolutionary transitions occurred in sudden leaps, as opposed to the gradual changes over long periods of time in classical neo-Darwinism. According to this theory, the fossil record should contain very few, if any, transitional forms, because a sudden transition over a relatively short period of time would be far less likely to be preserved in the fossil record than very gradual transitions over vast periods of time. The window of opportunity for these forms to be captured in the fossil record, in other words, would be greatly reduced. Because of the eminent reputation of its founders – Stephen Jay Gould was widely recognized as evolution's leading spokesman for many years, in fact – the theory has become quite popular. Since a key postulate of this theory is an *absence* of transitional forms, then it's obvious that many evolutionists agree with this postulate – which means, of course, that many evolutionists do *not* believe in transitional forms – at least that there are not very many of them."

"Look, Mrs. Parker, it seems to me that you're making a mountain out of a mole hill," Decker responded. "Perhaps I was mistaken to say that the fossil record contains a *great number* of transitional forms. I should have simply said that it contains *some* of these forms. But even a few of them provide powerful evidence for the theory of evolution."

"Yes, they certainly would … if they existed. The problem is that they don't, Mr. Decker."

"Let me get this straight. You're saying that in all of the billions of fossils in the world there isn't a single one that is indisputably a transitional form?"

"If you mean a transitional form in regards to macroevolution, that's right."

Suddenly, a man in the audience rose to his feet.

"Listen, what difference does it make how many transitional forms there are?! I've never even heard of these things, and, frankly, I don't see why they're important. And this other thing ... Punctuated Equilibrium ... I've never heard of it, either. As far as I'm concerned ..."

As security marshals quickly stood up, Susan Marshall banged on her gavel.

"Sir, I'm going to have to ask you to sit down. You have not been recognized. Furthermore, I will not tolerate ..."

"No, wait a minute," the man said forcefully, holding up an open palm. "I'm not finished yet. Listen, the things these two are arguing about are too technical. I'm not a scientist and I don't imagine many other people in the audience here tonight are, either. I don't think these creationists should be spending their time explaining why some little detail of the theory of evolution might not be perfectly accurate. They don't need to tell us why evolution *isn't* true. They need to tell us why their creation story *is* true. They need to provide us with some evidence that the world is six thousand years old, in other words, even though just about every scientist in the world believes it's, like, a few hundred million years old, or something like that ... whatever. What these people believe in ..."

Another man stood up and interrupted the speaker. "Don't you *understand?!* These people can't *just* talk about creation. They have to point out flaws in the theory of evolution. Otherwise ..."

Susan Marshall banged her gavel hard. "Apparently, Sir, *you* don't understand! People must not speak out until they are recognized. I must ask you to sit down, too."

Apologizing, the man heeded Mrs. Marshall's order.

This interruption, even though brief, had stirred up the audience, and it took a minute or two for everyone to calm down. Susan could see that it was going to be a long night. The tension in the building was palpable, somewhat unsettling.

"I'm sorry for the interruption, Mrs. Parker and Mr. Decker," Mrs. Marshall said. "Were you finished with your discussion? Did either of you have anything else to say?"

"Just one thing," Martha replied. "I'd like to ask the gentleman who asked for some evidence against the theory of evolution. Is this absence of transitional forms helpful?"

"Yes, I think it is," Edward Douglas replied. "That was quite interesting. Thank you."

Janice Holmes, one of the School Board members had another question for Martha Parker. "As you were describing the background of the theory of Punctuated Equilibrium, it occurred to me that the primary reason for the theory, its *raison d'etre* if you will, might be the very thing that it supposedly predicts: the absence of transitional forms. If this is true, don't you think that it's kind of deceptive? … sort of like a weatherman arriving at a *forecast* of snow, because he looks out his window and sees it."

"That's very perceptive, and I believe that you're absolutely right," Parker replied. "I think that this absence of transitional forms had become painfully obvious to the originators of the theory, and they recognized the mortal threat that it posed to the theory of evolution. They recognized that they were confronted with a stark choice: either abandon the current version of the theory of evolution, with its claim of abundant transitional forms, or come up with an alternative version that did not require transitional forms. They opted for the latter, of course, and thus was born the theory of Punctuated Equilibrium – exactly as you suggested."

"You claim, Mrs. Parker, that the lack of transitional forms in the fossil record is a serious challenge to the theory of evolution, serious enough, perhaps, to topple the theory altogether," Victor Gregory observed. "It seems to me, however, that there might be a serious problem with your reasoning. Regardless of whether or not there are transitional forms, isn't the fossil record alone sufficient evidence to verify the truthfulness of the theory? I mean, if the fossil record proves that the theory is true, all this discussion about transitional forms and Punctuated Equilibrium is irrelevant."

"Do you mind if I jump in here, Martha?" Paul Hopkins asked.

"Of course not. Go right ahead. I've said enough for a while!"

"Thanks." Turning to Mr. Gregory, Paul asked, "Why do you think that fossils prove that the theory of evolution is true?"

"Well, as far as I know, there is no argument regarding the ancient age of fossils. Everyone who studies them seems to agree that they are very old – like, millions, even hundreds of millions of years old. If this is so, it proves beyond a doubt that the creation story – at least the one you guys are promoting – is just that: a story, with no basis in reality. If fossils are anywhere near as old as scientists say they are, in other words, we might as well declare this meeting over right now and go home and watch *Survivor*.

"Just one more thing … one more point about fossils. So many fossils are of creatures that no longer exist, creatures that appear to be ancestors of living ones. I read someplace, in fact, that about 95% of all the creatures that have ever lived upon the earth have become extinct. They may not classify as transitional forms – to some people, that is – but whatever they are, they certainly lend support to the theory of evolution."

"I'm very glad you brought up the issue of fossils," Hopkins responded. "They're an extremely important element in this debate. Actually, I'm surprised they haven't come up before. I want to respond to your comments, but before I do I'd like to ask you a question. Do you mind?"

"No, I suppose not," Gregory replied. "I'll do the best I can. But I hope it's not too technical. I'm certainly no expert on these matters. Not by a long shot."

"I understand. I'm sure that very few people here tonight are experts on these things. My question is this: could you describe to me how fossils are formed?"

"I'll give it a try – but what does that have to do with their age?"

"A lot, and you'll see why shortly. Let me be more specific. Perhaps it will make it easier for you to answer the question. Tell me how a fish becomes fossilized. The majority of fossils, over 95%, are of marine life, so this would be a good creature to focus our attention on."

"All right. I'll give it a try. As far as I know, after they die, some fish settle on the ocean floor and get covered by sediment, like silt and sand, stuff like that. Then, over time – many years, I guess … hundreds or thousands, or even more, maybe – this sediment hardens into rock. The fish decomposes so what is left is an impression of the fish inside the hardened sediment – a fossil, in other words. How is that?"

"That was very good. It closely resembles the description of fossilization in most textbooks and encyclopedias. There are a few problems with it, however. You say that after they die, some fish settle on the ocean floor. If this was true, then there should be dead fish on the bottom of oceans and lakes right now, right? After all, fish are still dying today, just like they always have. The problem is that there aren't any – or, if there are, they don't last long. When a fish dies, the first thing that it does is float.

After that – and *always* after that – it is consumed by marine scavengers, other fish, or bacteria and other microscopic scavengers. In today's world, except perhaps in very rare circumstances involving some kind of natural catastrophe, like a flood, it never gets covered by sand and silt and turns into a fossil. The proof of this is obvious. Fish carcasses in this condition – covered by sand and silt, in the process of becoming fossilized – just don't exist. But if the evolutionary explanation for fossil formation – basically, the one you just provided – is correct, they should. They should be abundant, in fact."

"But I don't get it. If this isn't the way fish are fossilized, how are they?"

"I'll tell you, but first let me point out two other features about fossil fish which indicate that the common explanation for their formation is wrong. Now, according to this explanation, fish that become fossilized are dead before the process begins, right?"

"Yes, of course. They're not going to be buried alive."

"Actually, in some cases this is exactly what happened; fish *were* buried alive. Look at these pictures," Paul instructed, pointing to the video screen at the rear of the stage. "They show fossils of marine creatures giving birth, and eating.[17] There are also many fossils of fish with their eyes bulging out, as if they are terrified of something. What do you think these things suggest?"

"Gee, I don't know. I've never heard of these things before."

"Well, you probably wouldn't have seen them in your high school textbooks, that's for sure! But, anyway, they suggest that these fish were buried very suddenly, like before they could even finish swallowing their food."

"How could that have happened?"

"In a massive flood transporting huge volumes of mud and sand very rapidly, like the one described in the book of Genesis – Noah's flood."

"Come *on!*" James Quinn burst out. "We're not going to start talking about Noah's Flood *again*, are we? Didn't we spend enough time on that subject in the first hearing? It's bad enough that you're condemning the theory of evolution, but, like Dick Potter made clear in that earlier meeting, expecting us to believe that the flood story is literally true is just too much ... Two of every animal on earth, including dinosaurs, jammed into one boat for about a year, to save them from a flood that covered the entire earth and killed every living thing that wasn't on the ark?! God, man, that is *ridiculous!* As far as I'm concerned, it's mystifying that supposedly intelligent people in our town – or any place else – can still believe in such ancient fables."

"If you'll give me chance, I think I can explain exactly how it happened," Paul said.

"And just when do you believe that this flood occurred?" Mr. Quinn pressed on.

"Like we said at the first hearing, about 5,000 years ago, maybe a little less."

"So you believe that all these animals that have been fossilized died only about 5,000 years ago – *including the dinosaurs?!*"

"That's right."

"Dinosaurs roaming the earth only a few thousand years ago? You've got to be kidding!"

Suddenly a woman in the audience stood up to say something.

"Wait!" she began. "I'm sorry to interrupt, but I've been trying to get recognized here for several minutes. Could I please say just one thing? It's very pertinent."

Susan Marshall glanced at Henry Knox. He shrugged his shoulders and raised his palms, as if to say, "It's up to you." Susan said she could go ahead as long as she was brief.

"Thank you. Thank you so much. I'll try to be as brief as possible. I just *knew* the subject of Noah's Flood would come up tonight! And I just want to point out that the Bible says that in the Last Days, which I believe we're in, people will deny Noah's Flood, exactly like Mr. Quinn is doing." Holding her Bible open, she proceeded. "It says right here in Second Peter 3, verses three through six:

Know this first of all, that in the last days mockers will come with their mocking, following after their own lusts, and saying, 'Where is the promise of His coming? For ever since the fathers fell asleep, all continues just as it was from the beginning of creation.' For when they maintain this, it escapes their notice that by the Word of God the heavens existed long ago and the earth was formed out of water and by water, **through which the world at that time was destroyed, being flooded with water.**

The woman strongly emphasized the last phrase.

"Do you see what is being said here?" she said excitedly. "This passage not only reminds us of the Great Flood that destroyed the whole earth, but it prophesies that in the End Times people would forget it. And I think we see this everywhere today. Just think about it! So many people ..."

"Thank you. That was very interesting," Susan Marshall interjected. "But I must cut you off now so Mr. Hopkins can tell us how Noah could have fit all those animals onto the ark."

"That's okay," the woman smiled. "I was about finished, anyway. Thank you very much for allowing me to speak, Mrs. Marshall. You're doing a great job here tonight! God bless you."

"And thank *you*," Susan Marshall replied, genuinely appreciative of the woman's kind words. "Now, Mr. Hopkins, would you like to finish your discussion of the Flood?"

"Yes, I certainly would. First of all, however, I want to say to the woman who just spoke that I completely agree with everything she said. The passage she read from Second Peter is a very powerful one. It looks to a time far in the future when people would be ignoring the Genesis Flood, and, as she said, that time is undoubtedly the one we are living in. The science textbooks used in our school are excellent examples of that!" Paul now turned his attention back to Mr. Quinn.

"Now, Mr. Quinn, before I address the issues you have with the story of Noah's Flood, I need to finish my discussion with Mr. Gregory about the formation of fossils, because there's an intimate connection between these two events."

"You mean the formation of fossils and Noah's Flood?"

"Right."

"Go ahead, then."

"Thank you," Paul said. "As I was saying, Mr. Gregory, the standard textbook explanation for fossil formation, the one you offered a few minutes ago, cannot be correct, because when creatures die their carcasses, most definitely including their bones, are completely consumed long before they have a chance to be covered with sediment. Like I said before, the proof of this is that there are no dead marine creatures undergoing this process on the sea floor at the present time. Now, the problem creationists have with this process is not *what* covers the dead creatures; obviously, it's sediment. What we dispute is the manner in which this sediment is laid down. According to evolutionary theory, the process is very slow and gradual. We say that this is impossible – and the fact that carcasses are consumed so quickly is hardly the only reason for this."

"That's interesting," Mr. Gregory said. "What are some other reasons?"

"I mentioned one earlier: the fossils of fish and other marine creatures in the process of eating, and giving birth. Obviously, these creatures were not dead the moment they were buried. The word *moment* is very important in this, and I will return to it shortly. First, however, I want to point out something else that argues very powerfully against the common description of fossilization ... fossil graveyards. These great fossil deposits are found all over the world, and they commonly include a vast quantity of animals, often many millions, packed tightly together. The remains of the creatures in these deposits are often badly broken or torn apart, or in contorted, twisted positions, indicating they died in agony. These features are vivid testimony that the inundation that destroyed these creatures was extraordinarily massive, sudden and violent – most definitely *not*, in other words, the gradual covering process described in your standard geology textbooks. Another extraordinary feature of these graveyards is that some of them contain a wide assortment of different creatures, many of them natural enemies, sometimes from very different climactic zones. The Norfolk forest-beds in England, for example, contain fossils of northern cold-climate animals, tropical warm-climate animals, and Temperate Zone plants.

"Now, Mr. Gregory, put these two features together – the shattered, contorted condition of many of these fossils and the widely divergent climactic zones that they inhabited, as they occasionally are in these graveyards – and look at what you are faced with: massive quantities of disparate creatures, both animals and plants, from a wide range of climactic zones, that have been herded tightly together and then suddenly and violently crushed and buried, and often torn limb from limb. Now, think about this horrifying situation, and imagine what could have possibly caused it."

Victor Gregory slowly nodded his head. "If what you're saying about these fossil graveyards is true – and I can't say for sure, because I've never heard of them before – it certainly does seem inconceivable that they could have been created by a slow, gradual process of sedimentation."

"It certainly does, doesn't it?" Hopkins replied.

"If you're trying to convince me that the best possible explanation for these fossil graveyards is a cataclysmic flood – like, a worldwide one ... like the one described in the Book of Genesis – I have to tell you: you're doing a pretty good job! It just doesn't seem that there's any other reasonable explanation. But I must ask you the same question I just asked about the age of fossils: how come you never see this worldwide flood mentioned as the cause of fossils in science textbooks, or TV shows, or museums? Heck, I've been to a lot of big museums – the American Museum of Natural History in New York, the Smithsonian, the British Museum of Natural History in London, and others, too. And I've never seen this flood mentioned in any of them, not a single word. If the things you've been telling us are true, this silence seems bizarre, like a giant conspiracy to hide the truth. To put it bluntly: what the hell is going on?"

The woman who had read the passage from Second Peter a few minutes earlier bounced to her feet.

"I'll answer that question for you!" she exclaimed. "It's found in Second Corinthians 4:4: *The god of this world has blinded the minds of the unbelieving, that they might not see the light of the gospel of the glory of Christ* ... so they might not see the truth, in other words. Think about the passage I read before from Second Peter, the one that says that in the Last Days people will deny that there ever was a worldwide flood. Don't you see? What you just pointed out about these museums – that none of them ever mention such a flood – is a perfect example of this denial. If you think about it, it's all *so* clear! ... I'm sorry for interrupting, Mrs. Marshall. Please forgive me! I won't say another word," she added as she sat down.

Victor Gregory nodded toward the woman and turned towards Paul. "What do you think? Is she right? I mean, god, there has to be *some* explanation for this unbelievable wall of silence."

"Yes, I believe she is. I believe that she's *exactly* right. *The god of this world has blinded the minds of the unbelieving, that they might not see the light of the gospel of the glory of Christ.*"

Victor Gregory looked hard at Paul and nodded his head several times. "Maybe you're right," he said with conviction. "Maybe you're both right." He sat down.

Henry Knox turned toward the evolution panel.

"According to Mr. Hopkins, the primary cause of fossils is the Genesis Flood. What do you think about this? Do you even believe in this flood?"

The panel members exchanged glances, no one appearing particularly eager to respond. Finally, Peter Salisbury volunteered.

"No, I don't agree with Mr. Hopkins. For one thing, modern scholarship indicates that the flood described in Genesis was a local, not worldwide, event, probably occurring in the Mesopotamian valley, in the vicinity of modern Iraq. This being the case, it cannot possibly account for the vast amount of fossils found through out the entire world."

"And if it was in the vicinity of modern Iraq, I guess it can't account for the fossil graveyard in England, with all of its dismembered creatures, can it?" Josh asked.

Before Salisbury could answer Josh's question, Jennifer spoke up.

"How can you say that Noah's Flood was local?" she asked. "Listen to what the Bible says about it. In Genesis, chapter seven, verses nineteen and twenty, it says that *the water prevailed more and more upon the earth, so that **all the high mountains everywhere under the heavens were covered**. The water prevailed fifteen cubits higher and the mountains were covered.* And look at what it says next: ... *and all flesh that moved on the earth perished, birds and cattle and beasts and every swarming thing that swarms upon the earth, and all mankind; of all that was on the dry land, all in whose nostrils was the breath of the spirit of life, died.*

"Does this sound like the description of a *local* flood, Mr. Salisbury?"

"If the words are taken literally, of course it doesn't. The mistake you are making is to take them this way. This is *not* how they should be understood. These words were written by a man who wasn't even aware that most of the earth existed. To people in his day, the Middle East was all they knew of. As far as they knew, that was the *whole* earth. So he wrote about the flood from his perspective. I'm sure it was a great catastrophe and seemed to him to cover the whole earth. But that was only because his perspective was so limited."

"But how can a local flood cover the highest mountains? A flood that does that must be worldwide," Jennifer replied.

"The speech, like I've been trying to explain, is only figurative. The highest land the observer could see must have been some hills, probably some low ones. But, still, even though it was local, it was surely a very big flood. The man used 'mountains' for dramatic effect."

"But if what you're saying is true," Jennifer responded, "that only explains the fossils in one small part of the world – the place where the flood happened. Like Josh just pointed out, what about all the other fossils? As you know, they're found all over the world."

"Many scientists are coming to believe that the traditional explanation for fossil formation, as Paul Hopkins just has said, is inadequate. More and more of them are coming around to the belief that the majority of fossils were caused by natural catastrophes: mudslides, avalanches, and, of course, floods. These catastrophes, however, were local and occurred at various times and locations throughout the course of history. And in doing so, they have provided us with a record of evolution."

"If what you're saying is true," Paul Hopkins interjected, "if there has been this dramatic shift in the explanation of fossilization, then all of the textbook descriptions of the process will have to be revised and rewritten, won't they?"

"Yes, that's essentially true," Salisbury replied. "In fact, it's already happening. Many of the more recent textbooks already include this revised explanation."

"It seems to me that evolutionists are just stealing the idea that creationists had from the beginning," Josh offered. "The only difference – and it's a mighty big one – is in the size of the catastrophe. Also, fossils are found on the top of high mountains all over the world. How can local catastrophes explain that?"

"That's easy," Salisbury replied. "After the fossils were formed in these local catastrophes, over millions of years the process of plate tectonics – the process that shifted the land masses of the earth and eventually formed the continents – formed mountain ranges, and the fossils that once lay buried in valleys and plains were lifted to the tops of mountains."

"Paul just described these massive fossil graveyards in which many of the animals were twisted up or torn apart. How can your theory explain *those?*" Josh pressed on.

Thomas Lawton from the School Board now entered the conversation.

"Listening to Paul Hopkins's description of the fossil graveyards, something occurred to me. Given the details of these places – the great mass of widely assorted creatures, including mortal enemies and animals from widely divergent geographical locations, whose bones and skeletons are often grossly distorted or torn completely apart – one thing is very obvious: whatever caused them, it certainly couldn't have been the fossilization process described in our children's science textbooks! I mean, just think about it … How in the world could such a catastrophic scene be caused by sediment gradually covering dead animals? The idea is absurd, to put it mildly. Furthermore, a local flood like Mr. Salisbury mentioned, no matter how large, couldn't cause these graveyards, either. For one thing, there wouldn't be enough animals in a local flood. Remember, some of these graveyards contain the remains of *billions* of animals. Beyond that, however, by definition such a flood could never contain animals from different geographical regions, because it didn't take place in different geographical regions.

"A little common sense suggests that by far the best explanation for these fossil graveyards is a great worldwide deluge, exactly as described in the book of Genesis. Now here's what occurred to me. *By themselves* these fossil graveyards utterly destroy the standard textbook explanation of fossilization. Since this explanation cannot possibly account for these graveyards, in other words, it must not be – it *cannot* be – right. It's as if there was a murder investigation that concluded from the evidence that Mr. Smith was the murderer – until footage from a security video revealed that Mr. Smith was in another state at the exact time of the murder. In both of these cases, the new evidence completely invalidates the original theory.

"So, now, let me connect my point here to the debate we are having here tonight. Those on the evolution panel would argue that allowing a worldwide flood to be suggested as a possible explanation for fossils would be a *tremendous* concession to creationists, a concession far too great for them to even consider. But this is flipping logic on its head, because, as we have just seen, a worldwide flood is actually a far superior explanation to the one currently being used. Evolutionists act as if they have circled their wagons to protect the truth from attack, whereas in reality the truth is what is attacking them. They are not fighting *for* the truth here; they are fighting *against* it!"

When he finished, Lawton's remarks were met with a burst of applause from the audience, along with a few shouts of support. Susan Marshall had to bang her gavel to restore order.

A question was now asked by Janice Holmes. Janice was on the fence regarding the petition. Until recently, she wasn't particularly interested in the subject being debated tonight and until the hearings began was unaware of the passion that it could generate. In preparation for the hearings, however, she had been reading up on the subject, and she was becoming more and more intrigued by it. She directed it toward the evolution panel.

"I read about a Tyrannosaurus Rex fossil leg bone that was discovered a few years ago – someplace in the western United States, as I recall – which apparently still contained some soft tissue, even some blood vessels, I think. These dinosaurs were supposed to have died off about sixty or seventy million years ago. How could soft tissue possibly survive for sixty million years?"

"That's a very good question," Brian Miller replied, "and a lot of scientists all over the world are working on it. At first scientists were very surprised, even shocked, by this discovery, but I'm sure an answer will be found before long. This is the way science goes forward. Something new is discovered that doesn't fit into existing paradigms. This spawns new research which in turn reveals new knowledge."

Josh couldn't believe what he was hearing.

"Instead of assuming that this tissue was sixty-five million years old and that scientists would someday be able to explain how it could have survived such a long time, don't you think that there just might be another *much more* reasonable explanation for this amazing discovery … which is that the tissue is actually *nowhere near* sixty-five million years old? I mean, come on, man – the idea that soft tissue and blood cells could survive that long is totally insane. It's so obvious. Can't you *see* that?" Josh said, shaking his head in frustration.

Brian Miller looked carefully at Josh. For a fleeting moment, there was a look of doubt, perhaps even confusion, in his eyes.

"It's easy to see your point, Josh, but I, and just about all of my colleagues in the scientific community, have to disagree with you. The ancient age of these creatures has been far too firmly established for a little soft tissue in one of their bones to create doubt in our minds."

"What if a *living* T-Rex was found? Would that change your mind?"

"I promise you, Josh: the second a live T-Rex is discovered, I'll become a born-again creationist!" Miller replied with a forced smile.

"Fantastic!" Josh said. "I'll be keeping my eyes peeled. If I happen to spot one, you'll be the first to know!"

Henry Knox now reentered the dialogue.

"You folks have expressed great admiration for the creationist organization, *Answers in Genesis* during these hearings," he said, addressing his remarks to the creationist panel, "but, according to information I read on their Web site, they believe that evolution *should* be taught in schools, which is contrary to your position. They believe that since evolution is so pervasive in our society, children must be exposed to it. Your divergence from AIG on this very important point is difficult to understand. How do you explain it?"

Martha Parker stepped up to answer the question.

"We thought long and hard about this issue, Mr. Knox, and it was very hard for us to choose a position that is not supported by *Answers in Genesis*, because, as you pointed out, we do have great respect and admiration for that organization. All I can say is that we arrived at our position after much prayer and careful consideration. Whether or not we made the right decision will be determined by God.

"Now, let me explain the reasons behind our petition. As you know, of course, our original petition sought to have creation taught alongside evolution. As I explained at the beginning of this meeting, however, a few weeks ago Jennifer raised a question: why would the Creator of the universe want the incredible story of His creation taught alongside the blasphemous theory of evolution, as if they are somehow equals? ... which struck at the very heart of our petition and caused us to completely rethink our position, and change it. The problem we have with the idea of teaching creation alongside the theory of evolution is that the theory of evolution is presented as a proven fact in virtually all of the textbooks used in public schools. To us, this is unacceptable. Perhaps you may recall a quotation from the Duke of Argyle that Paul referred to in the first hearing, about six weeks ago. I'll put it up on the video screen for you ...

To accept as a truth that which is not a truth, or to fail in distinguishing the sense in which it is not true, is an evil having consequences which are indeed incalculable. There are subjects in which one mistake of this kind will poison all the wells of truth and affect with fatal error the whole circle of our thoughts.[17]

"As you know by now, those of us on this panel believe very emphatically that the theory of evolution is absolutely not true. In our children's textbooks, however, it is presented as an established fact – over and over and over, in fact. Students are inclined to believe that the information in their textbooks is generally true, as, indeed, they should. Therefore, unless these textbooks are radically reformed – something we don't foresee taking place in the near future – they will encourage our students to believe that the theory of evolution is true. In our opinion, as the Duke of Argyle suggested, this is *an evil having consequences which are indeed incalculable.* Furthermore, we believe that this subject – origins – is a perfect example of a subject in which *a single mistake of this kind will poison all the wells of truth and affect with fatal error the whole circle of one's thoughts.* We believe, in other words, that accepting the theory of evolution as truth has the potential to contaminate a person's entire world view, just like cancer can contaminate a person's entire body.

"So, then, in our opinion, because of the evolutionary bias of existing science textbooks and most science teachers, at the present time we believe it is preferable for students to be taught nothing about origins. At the present time, we feel that any effort to teach creation in the public schools would be perfunctory, at best, and therefore essentially useless. We agree with AIG that it would be preferable for students to be exposed to a fair and unbiased presentation of the topic, but, unlike AIG apparently, we do not believe such a presentation is reasonably possible right now. It is a worthy goal to strive for, but one whose attainment lies in the future. As I said before, we have the utmost respect for AIG and are tremendously thankful for the fantastic job they are doing in spreading the truth about creation, but in this one area we respectfully disagree with them.

"I must add that we are well aware of the inherent problems of our position, such as how can students answer questions about evolution on state achievement exams and SATs if they haven't been exposed to it. In the end, however, we simply came to the conclusion that two wrongs ... learning a lie and then answering questions about it ... don't make a right. The thing that ultimately determined our petition is our conviction that the teaching of evolution as a fact *must* be stopped, and we decided that the goal we have set here is the only way this goal can be achieved right now. If anyone has a better plan, we're open to suggestions," Martha ended with a friendly smile.

"I've got a better idea for you," came a voice from the audience. "Why don't you go back to your own town and let us decide what the students of Madison should be taught in their science classes?"

Before Susan Marshall could bang her gavel, another man responded to this voice.

"Speak for yourself. I'm from Madison, and I think it's about time somebody did what these folks are doing. As far as I'm concerned ..."

"I'd love to hear what you're concerned about, Sir," Susan Marshall said as her gavel pounded on the table in front of her, "but I'm afraid you'll have to save it for later."

"Before we leave this topic, I have a question for you, Mrs. Parker," Tom Lawton said. "Even if the teaching of origins was banned, the students would still be using the same science textbooks that they have now, and these textbooks teach evolution as a fact, from the beginning to the end. Wouldn't this be a major problem?"

"Yes, Mr. Lawton, it certainly would be," Parker replied. "But we decided that we would cross that bridge when, and if, we came to it – after you folks arrived at a decision about our petition."

28

Henry Knox's Eyes are Opened

Another member of the School Board, Virginia Mitchell, now had a question.

"I agree with the fellow who thought that a lot of the discussion going on here tonight is too technical. Like with Punctuated Equilibrium. I never heard of it before tonight, and I'll bet most other people here haven't, either. Like Mrs. Parker suggested, it just seems to boil down to one person's word against another. One says there are lots of transitional forms in the fossil record; another says there are none. How are we supposed to know who is right? It seems to me that there is an avenue that might prove a lot more fruitful than transitional forms. Rather than looking at the fossils of creatures that are long since dead, how about looking at *living* creatures that are in the process of evolving. Surely, if the theory of evolution is true, there *must* be some living examples of it – unless the process is no longer taking place, that is. What about it? Are there any? Has anyone actually ever *seen* evolution taking place?"

Barbara Jenkins, on the evolution panel, quickly spoke up.

"Certainly there are, Mrs. Mitchell. The best-known one is probably *biston betularia,* the peppered moth. Perhaps you remember studying this moth in high school biology."

"Now that you mention it, I think I do. I think there was a picture of it in our textbook. I don't really remember much about it, though. Could you refresh my memory? Why are these moths considered living examples of evolution?"

"The study of these moths took place in Manchester, England," Mrs. Jenkins explained. "Prior to the Industrial Revolution in that country, which began about 1850, the population of the peppered moths living near the major industrial centers such as Manchester was predominantly light, or

337

silver, colored. In fact, in 1849 about 99% of the moths were this color. The remaining 1% were a darker variety. The reason for the dominance of the light moths is very simple. Supposedly, these moths fly at night and rest by day on the trunks and branches of trees. Normally, these tree trunks are covered with light-colored lichen, which camouflage the light-colored moths from the hungry birds that devour them. With the rise of heavy industry about the Manchester area in the 1800's, the toxic gases and soot killed the light-colored lichen on the trees, and the trunks and branches displayed their natural dark color. The light-colored moths, which were previously camouflaged against the light-colored lichen, now stood out in stark contrast and were easily seen and eaten by the birds. The odd dark moth, however, was now protected and began to flourish. In recent years, I should point out, the greater concern for clean air has reduced industrial pollution and the lichen is growing back on the trees, allowing the dark moths to be seen more easily. Now, in a reversal of the original change, the dark moths are diminishing in proportion.[18]

"As you can see, a change in the environment resulted in a dramatic change in the peppered moths. Right before our eyes – or, at least, the eyes of the people who performed the research – evolution was happening."

"I'm a little confused. I don't see why these moths are an example of evolution."

"What are you confused about?" Jenkins replied, her brow furrowed.

"Well, according to your description, before the Industrial Revolution there were both dark and light moths, right?"

"Yes – about 99% light-colored and 1% dark."

"And as a result of this revolution the only thing that changed among these moths was the ratio of their color, right?"

"Yes. But that's what is so significant. In reaction to the change in their environment ..."

"And aside from this change in the ratio of their color, there were no other changes in the moths, right?"

"Essentially, that's correct."

"Before the Industrial Revolution they were called biston bat ... what was their name, again?"

"*Biston betularia.*"

"Oh, yeah – *biston betularia*. So, before the revolution, they were called *biston betularia*, and after the revolution they were called *biston betularia*. They weren't classified as a new species or anything, in other words, right?

That is, there were no characteristics among them that didn't exist prior to the change in their environment."

"Of course they weren't classified as a new species. Evolution takes place very slowly, over hundreds of thousands or many millions of years. These peppered moths revealed one small step in a very long process," Barbara Jenkins replied, a bit frustrated that Mrs. Mitchell didn't seem to be grasping the significance of what she, and most other devotees of evolution, believed was a dramatic example – actually *the most* dramatic example – of evolution in action. "The point of this event is that a real change, a change that was observed and recorded – *evolution*, in other words – took place in a relatively very short time, about fifty years."

"But aside from the ratio of dark moths to light moths, what changed?" Mitchell persisted. "Before the Industrial Revolution, there were dark moths and light moths. After the Revolution, there were dark moths and light moths. Before the Revolution, they were classified as *biston betularia*. After the Revolution, they were classified as *biston betularia*. Where is there any evolution in this story?"

A woman in the audience sprang to her feet.

"I think I can shed some light here," she said. "Can you give me a minute or two, Mrs. Marshall?"

Susan Marshall hesitated. She knew it was going to be a long evening, and she felt a responsibility to keep things moving along at a good pace. Intuitively, however, she sensed that what this woman had to say would be worth hearing.

"Don't worry – I won't take long," the woman persisted.

"All right," Susan Marshall said. "But please make it brief."

"Thank you. I will. I own a kennel. My husband and I raise retrievers. We have Labradors and golden labs, about fifty-fifty. A few years ago, for some reason that we never could figure out the black labs – the Labradors – suddenly became very popular and everyone seemed to want one. For a little while we could hardly keep up with the demand, and during this time we had about ten times as many golden labs as black labs. After a couple of years, the popularity of the black labs leveled off and the ratio between the two breeds returned to normal.

"It seems to me that what happened in our kennel is very similar to what happened with these peppered moths. In both cases something happened that was completely out of the creatures' control that caused the ratios

between the light and dark colored creatures to dramatically change. With
the moths, it was the factories of the Industrial Revolution and, ultimately,
the soot that these factories belched out and covered the trees. With our retrievers, it was the sudden and unexplained rise in the popularity of the black
labs. I doubt that anyone would be stupid enough to argue that the change
in the ratio of my retrievers was an example of evolution! Why is the change
in the ratio of light and dark colored moths any different? Why is this change
supposedly an example of evolution?

"I'll tell you one thing," she said, addressing Barbara Jenkins. "If that's
the best example you can come up with of evolution in action, your team is
in deep trouble!"

The woman sat down, accompanied by some supportive clapping and
nods of approval.

After several minutes of lively discussion of the peppered moth Susan
Marshall acknowledged another member of the audience who had been eagerly trying to be recognized for the last several minutes. The young man
identified himself as Joe Petrocelli. He was fifteen years old. Mrs. Marshall
had decided to be especially sensitive to young people's requests to speak at
this meeting. After all, they were the ones who were going to be most affected by its outcome.

"Thanks a lot, Mrs. Marshall," he began somewhat nervously. "This discussion of the peppered moth makes me think of something I was reading
the other night about the evolution of flight in birds. It was a quote from a
book called *The Origin of Birds*. I don't remember who wrote it. My whole
family is really into this debate about creation and evolution. All of us –
both of my sisters, my brother, my parents and me – have been at both of
the meetings here, and we talk about it a lot. I don't know exactly why, but I
think it's, like, *really* interesting. You know – cool.

"Anyway, this description of how birds got wings seemed pretty bizarre
to me, and I'd like to hear what some of these panel members think about it.
I brought it with me. Do you mind if I read it? It's not very long."

"No. Go right ahead," Susan Marshall replied.

"Oh, good. Wow! I never thought I'd get this chance! It starts out by
saying that 'the original ancestor' – of the bird, that is – 'was a terrestrial
runner,' which means that it lived on the ground ... Okay, here it is:

From being a terrestrial runner the animal now turns into an arboreal
climber ... that means that he climbs trees ... *leaping further and further from*

branch to branch, from tree to tree and from the trees to the ground. Meanwhile the first toe changes to a hind toe so adapted as to grasp the branches. As the hind limbs while running on the ground have abandoned the reptilian position, they are kept closer to the body when leaping takes place. The pressure of the air, acting like a stimulus, produces, chiefly on the forelimbs and the tail, a parachutal plane consisting of longish scales developing along the posterior edge of the forearms and the side edges of the flattened tail.

By the friction of the air, the outer edges of the scales becomes frayed, the frayings gradually changing into still longer horny processes, which in course of time become more and more featherlike, until the perfect feather is produced. From wings, tail and flanks, the feathering spreads to the whole body …[19]

"There's some more, but …well, it was kind of hard to understand."

As the boy talked, Jennifer flashed back to the spring of the previous year when Mr. Potter had been teaching about this very subject: the evolution of birds and their wings. It occurred to her that her questions and doubts about this topic had been the catalyst for the youth groups' meetings about creation and, in an eerie sense, for this very meeting in the gym tonight. A circle was being completed, she felt. She glanced quickly at Josh to see if he might have noticed this connection. Josh was looking right at her, nodding his head with a little smile. Yes, he had noticed the connection. She wasn't surprised.

Joe sat down, apparently forgetting his reason for reading the passage: to ask the panel members what they thought about it. Tom Lawton quickly stepped in. He hadn't forgotten. In the front row of the audience, Mike Lawton smiled. Knowing how his father loved birds, he wasn't surprised that he was the first one to respond to Joe Petrocelli's remarks.

"Joe, that was very interesting, and I'm glad you brought the subject up," Lawton said. "I'll be happy to tell you what I think about it, but before I do, how about letting us in on some of your thoughts. I'd sure like to hear them – and I'm sure everyone else would, too."

Joe was nervous about speaking any further before such a large audience. It didn't stop him from responding, however. He was a bit of a ham, and his love for being the center of attention easily trumped his nervousness.

"Okay," he said as he stood up again. "As my family talked about this description a couple of nights ago, we all agreed that it sounded more like science fiction than science. As we were talking about it, my older sister found a description of a feather in her high school biology book. My dad had been telling us how amazing the design of a feather is, but my younger sister and I wanted to see a description of it in print to make sure he was right. My dad gets a little carried away about these things sometimes. Well, I gotta tell you: my dad sure was right! It *is* amazing! It's just so *perfectly* designed for flight. I mean, I have to admit; I had no idea just how beautifully designed a feather is. We all agreed that for a flat, hard reptile scale to turn into a 'perfect feather' – to quote the guy who wrote it – through *random* changes is absolutely crazy. My dad said that the odds of this happening by chance are about the same as a frog turning into a prince by chance ... although that's exactly what people who believe in evolution believe, isn't it? ... Wow. That's incredible, isn't it? A long, long time ago, there's a little frog sitting on the edge of a pond – and then, a few hundred million years later, just by chance, there's me! Is that nuts, or what?

"Another thing that seemed crazy to me is what happened to all the critters *in between* the reptile and the bird – you know, the *transitional forms*," he said with a mischievous smile directed toward Martha Parker. He had definitely warmed to his task. "According to the theory of evolution, apparently, the process took a really long time – like, maybe a few million years or something. What the heck did all these things *look* like, and how could they have ever survived? I mean, just think about it! All of the transitional forms (Joe liked this phrase!) had 'wings' – or something that eventually became wings – that weren't doing them any good at all. At first, it didn't matter much, because these things were real small, just a little bump or two on their scales, I guess. They had to start *some* place, right?" he grinned. "But as time passed – like, a few hundred thousand years or so, I suppose – these bumps had grown into something a lot bigger ... not wings, of course; they would come about a million years later ... but something a lot bigger than a bump, just a couple of hunks of flesh that didn't have any function at all – yet, at least. And then, finally, millions of years after the process started – Presto! – A perfect bird! My dad pointed out that if birds didn't exist and a team of engineers and designers got together to design one they would *never* be able to come up with a design that was any better – or as good, probably – as the ones that exist. Then he asked us what we thought about the idea that this design evolved in nature *completely by accident* – you know, by chance. We all agreed that it was *completely ridiculous* ... like, just totally *insane*.

"According to the theory of evolution, at least the way I understand it, transitional forms are supposed to possess some kind of survival advantage over the other animals in their group. That's why they survive and the others don't. Well, I have to tell you. I just cannot possibly imagine how the transitional forms between a reptile and a bird could ever have a survival advantage! What kind of an advantage would it be to have partially developed wings? Like, would I have an advantage if I had partially developed legs – or arms? Rather than having a survival advantage it seems to me that these things would be total losers.

"So, as far as we're concerned – you know, my family and me – the whole thing sounds stupid. If you ask me, I think that the people who cook these stories up have partially developed *brains!*"

Joe sat down. The audience, charmed by Joe's youthful courage and enthusiasm, applauded enthusiastically. Joe was surprised and a little embarrassed by this response, but he was grinning from ear to ear. The media loved it, too. Joe had just secured his fifteen minutes of fame. The next day it would be broadcast from coast to coast.

"That was very clever, Joe … but you apparently don't understand the theory that the man is proposing," Barbara Jenkins said. "You seem to think that the incipient wings upon the transitional forms between the reptile and the bird were useless. I believe you referred to them as 'big hunks of flesh that didn't have any function at all.' But this wasn't the case at all. At every step of the transitional process, the appendages would have given their possessors an advantage over the other members of their group, because …"

"Excuse me, Mrs. Jenkins, but I must interrupt you here and ask a question," Henry Knox said. "These transitional forms that you are referring to here … If the process took millions of years and the changes each step of the way were very small, there must have been an awful lot of them, right? So, then, are there examples – you know, *fossils* – of any of them?"

"There certainly is: Archaeopteryx, one of, if not *the*, most important fossils ever found. This primitive bird possessed certain features generally associated with reptiles, such as teeth, a long tail, and claws on its wings, while other features, such as fully developed feathers and wings, are common only to birds. Archaeopteryx, by itself, is sufficient to silence critics who rail about a lack of transitional forms in the fossil record. It's hard to imagine a more perfect example of a transitional form."

"I'm familiar with Archaeopteryx, Mrs. Jenkins, but that's not what I was inquiring about," Mr. Knox replied. "Whatever Archaeopteryx was, its wings were fully developed, as fully developed as a modern bird's according to one report I read recently. One report that I came across even suggested that the entire fossil of this creature might be a hoax. In any event, what I want to know is if there are any fossils of creatures with incipient wings, wings that are only partially developed – the kind that Joe mentioned a minute ago. As I said before, if the transition occurred in a great number of very small steps over a very long period of time, surely there should be evidence of at least some of these steps in the fossil record. So, what about it? Are there any? Is there even a single fossil of a creature with wings in the process of evolving?"

Barbara Jenkins gently shook her head and nervously rubbed her forehead, wishing that Mr. Knox's question would somehow disappear or, even better, that he had never asked it.

"Unfortunately, none have been discovered yet. But we know they're out there someplace – like you said; they *must* be! – and I can assure you that we're going to keep looking until we find them!" she responded with a smile and, to demonstrate her conviction – which she actually didn't have – a wave of her fist.

Mr. Knox was struck by the significance of what he had just heard. Until this point in the proceedings, his reaction to the subject being debated had been fairly neutral. He had entered the gym as a passive believer in the theory of evolution, but, to his surprise, he had been impressed with the arguments being presented by the creation panel. He had been paying close attention to the discussion, of course, but it wasn't because he was searching for the truth. It was mainly because, as moderator, he was obligated to. As far as he was concerned, the discussion was interesting, but he didn't see that it was relevant to him on a personal level. This discussion regarding the evolution of birds had caused a shift in his thinking, however. For some reason, it had struck a chord within him. It seemed completely obvious to him that if birds had truly evolved from reptiles over millions of years there would have to be at least a few fossils of transitional forms of this evolution. The fact that there were absolutely none really surprised him and, more importantly, triggered a radical thought in his mind, one that he had never before considered: perhaps the theory of evolution wasn't all it was cracked up to be. *Perhaps – as those on the creationist panel had been claiming – it wasn't even true.* He wasn't aware of it at the time, but this was a pivotal moment in his life. The truth had broken through.

"Hmmm," Mr. Knox responded, pensively nodding his head. "It is surprising that none have been found, isn't it, Mrs. Jenkins? ... Very surprising."

29

The Second Hearing Continues

Paul Hopkins spoke up next. His comment was addressed to Joe Petrocelli. "Your insight into the theories regarding the evolution of birds was great, Joe. I especially liked your observation that the entire process took place completely by chance."

"But Pastor," Virginia Mitchell interjected, "I don't see why you say that this all happened by chance. I don't see why God couldn't have designed the whole process, after which He – or She – stepped back and allowed everything to unfold according to His plan."

"Ahh, yes ... theistic evolution, Mrs. Mitchell," Paul replied. "The problem is that the two notions that this theory attempts to combine, evolution and creation, are essentially mutually exclusive. The foundation of the theory of evolution is blind chance. As Mrs. Parker just pointed out, the theory is an attempt to explain how the world came into being entirely through such means – random, entirely natural events, in other words. By *definition*, then, the theory of evolution completely excludes any supernatural intervention. Chance, Mrs. Mitchell, is the god of evolution. There is no room for any other one."

Since the earlier discussion about transitional forms Peter Salisbury had been silently observing the proceedings with increasing irritation. He was not at all amused by Joseph Petrocelli's rambling attack upon the evolution of birds or much else that had been said, either. Simply put, the meeting was not proceeding anywhere near as he had anticipated. He didn't think that the petition had the slightest chance of passing, and he considered the proceedings to be, at best, a waste of time, and, at worst, an embarrassment to his profession. The fact that at this point in the meeting his side was on the defensive against a panel that included a couple of fundamentalist Christian high school students and a youth pastor humiliated him, and he decided that it was about time for a change.

"You make that statement with such conviction, Mr. Hopkins, as if it were a fact."

"Which part of the statement are you referring to?"

"Your claim that the foundation of the theory of evolution is blind chance."

"But it is."

"In fact, it really isn't. The director of the process is not chance at all; it is a powerful creative force, a force as fundamental to nature as the law of gravity: Natural Selection. Natural Selection, Mr. Hopkins, does *not* operate by chance. For some strange reason, you creationists just can't seem to grasp this fundamental truth. Natural Selection acts like an omnipotent personnel director of a great corporation, always selecting those individuals who are best suited for a job, who have the best chance to be successful. The corporation in this case is nature, and the job is survival."

Josh jumped into the conversation with a question: "So, like, if something happened to make the environment turn colder, Natural Selection would favor animals that happened to have longer fur?"

"Uh … Yes. Yes, that's exactly right. That's an excellent example, Josh," Peter Salisbury smiled, overlooking the shift in his challenger's identity. "And the difference between Natural Selection and this hypothetical personnel director is that Natural Selection *never* makes a mistake. It uses trial and error, but in the long run it *always* selects for survival those organisms that are best suited to overcome the existing environmental hurdles. In its job, then, Natural Selection is perfect, and, just as it does to the law of gravity or electromagnetism or any other natural law, the natural world responds to it with absolute and unfailing fidelity. Evolution, therefore, is driven by a rigid and uncompromising director, not chance, as Mr. Hopkins has suggested. Do you understand, Josh?"

"Yes, I understand perfectly," Josh said.

"Good," Salisbury smiled smugly. "I'm glad. Perhaps you can take a little time to explain it to your fellow creationists. Most of them could use some elucidation regarding this matter. Now, Mr. Knox, perhaps we …"

"I *understand* your point, Mr. Salisbury. I don't *agree* with it, though," Josh interrupted.

Mr. Salisbury was taken aback by Josh's remark, primarily because in his mind the point he had made regarding Natural Selection was a fact, and therefore not open to debate. In addition, however, Josh was only a high school student. He had proven that he had a sharp mind, but this didn't change the fact that he was only in high school. What in the world made him think that he could challenge the wisdom of someone who had been teaching evolution for over two decades – especially about a concept, Natural Selection, that was a cornerstone of evolutionary theory? Mr. Salisbury thought that Josh was being awfully presumptuous. He was inclined to be gracious and let Josh's remark pass, but it quickly occurred to him that engaging him in a debate about Natural Selection might be just the opportunity he had been hoping for to shift the momentum of the debate. He doubted that Josh would cooperate – he couldn't imagine that he was that brazen – but he figured it was worth a try anyway. There was one other reason for Mr. Salisbury's decision: He still chafed at Josh's cavalier dismissal of the evolution of the whale at the first hearing and figured that Josh could use a little lesson in humility.

He tossed out his hook.

"Oh? And just what is it that you disagree with, Josh?"

To Mr. Salisbury's surprise, Josh took the bait.

"Well, if I have a couple of minutes I'll try to explain," Josh said, glancing at Henry Knox.

"Go ahead, Josh," Knox said. "Maybe it would be a good idea if you started off by briefly describing exactly what Natural Selection is. I'm somewhat familiar with the term, but I'd appreciate a brush-up, and I'm sure others would, too."

"I'll check him for errors," Salisbury said, somewhat annoyed that Knox had not asked *him* for the explanation.

One person that was particularly intrigued by the discussion that was unfolding was Paul Hopkins. He recalled the brief conversation that he and Josh had had after the last youth group meeting in which Josh had expressed special interest in Natural Selection and had indicated that he was going to investigate the subject in case it came up at this hearing. Paul suspected that he probably had. He was right.

"All right," Josh began. "I'll try to make it fairly brief. It's really not that complicated. The basis of the theory is the natural variation of physical characteristics that exists among living creatures – like, you know, size, coloring, body shape, intelligence – things like that. In any given species, no two individuals, in other words, are exactly alike. Take a look around this gym and you'll see what I mean! Most of these traits, of course, are inherited from the creature's parents at birth.

"Now, from the time they are born creatures enter into the great struggle for survival. Since the supply of things that they need to stay alive – basically, food and water – is limited, they must constantly compete for them. Except for the very few at the top of the food chain, like lions and tigers and sharks, for example, most of them must also struggle against predators who look upon them as their next meal. Sharks, you know, don't have to worry much about getting eaten, do they? … except by killer whales sometimes, I guess!" Josh smiled.

"Anyway, because of the natural variations in their physical characteristics, some members of a species have combinations of traits that give them an edge in this struggle for survival. Like, a fast gazelle will have a better chance of escaping the seventy-mile-per-hour charge of a hungry cheetah than a slightly slower one, and a fox with longer fur will be better able to withstand a climate that has turned colder than one with shorter fur, especially if the ground is covered with snow and his fur happens to be white … like the arctic fox. Now, these creatures that have been blessed with these physical advantages are, of course, more likely to survive than their less fortunate compadres. Furthermore, when they reproduce, they will probably pass on these traits to their offspring. So, these favorable traits will survive, while the less favorable ones eventually die out. You know, like good old Mr. Darwin said: the survival of the fittest.

"According to evolutionary theory, over the course of the earth's history there have been countless events that have caused the environment to change, often dramatically. One example of this is the supposed impact of a giant asteroid or comet that occurred about sixty five million years ago and supposedly brought the age of the dinosaurs to an end. In addition, there have supposedly been all kinds of other earth-changing events, like volcanoes, floods, moving continents, ice ages, things like that. When these things happen, the pressure for survival ratchets up. In order for a population of creatures to survive the environmental changes caused by these events, more radical physical changes may be needed. When they occur, if the creatures that possess them are selected for survival, according to the theory of evolution the result might eventually be an entirely new species.

"Suppose there was a major drought on the African plains, for example, that caused a major struggle for the depleted food supply of all the grazing animals, like antelopes … or whatever it was that eventually became an antelope, that is. In order to survive this particular problem, what the, uh

... let's call him a *preantelope* ... needs is not a little more speed to escape the lions – or maybe it was saber-toothed tigers! – although that certainly wouldn't hurt, would it? No, what he really needs is something that would help him to reach food that the others around him can't reach, like a longer neck, so he could reach leaves higher in the trees. Now, if a mutation that extended his neck happened to occur at this time, he would be in luck, right? And if lots of neck-extending mutations occurred afterwards, after a few million years, this creature might just evolve into a completely different one ... like a giraffe!" Josh paused and furrowed his brow. "Of course, after a few million years the drought would probably be over, wouldn't it?

"Anyway, that's the way it works. Mutations and Natural Selection are the twin pillars of evolution. A mutation occurs that gives some creature a survival advantage, and Natural Selection then selects it for ... well, for survival. According to the theory of evolution, every species on the face of the earth was created by this process.

"How's that, Mr. Knox?" he asked.

"I think that was very good, Josh," Knox replied. "How about you, Mr. Salisbury? Are you satisfied with that description?"

"It wasn't entirely accurate, of course, but it was adequate, I suppose. Of course, there's a lot more to it, but I know we don't have time to explore it any further tonight."

"I'll get back to you in a minute, Mr. Salisbury," Knox said, "but first I must ask Josh what problems he sees with the theory. You said you didn't agree with the theory, Josh – so what problems do you see?"

"As far as I can tell, Mr. Knox, there's some big ones, some *real* big ones. To show you exactly what I mean, look at the evolutionists' theory regarding the evolution of the whale – you know, the theory I talked about in the first hearing. If you remember, according to that theory a wolf-like mammal called a Mesonychid wandered down to the water about fifty or sixty million years ago and about fifty million years later became a whale. The numbers here are uncertain, but, believe me, it really doesn't matter.

"Now, in order for this amazing transformation to take place, the first thing that has to happen is a mutation. Imagine, if you can, that the entire process – the evolution of a Mesonychid into a whale – involved, say, ten million mutations, which would be, of course, about one every four years, on average."

"Just a minute here," Salisbury interrupted. "This description already reveals that Josh has no idea what he's talking about, because no one has any idea how many mutations it took for the original creature in this evolution – which may or may not have been a Mesonychid, by the way – to become a whale. Therefore ..."

"All right, Mr. Salisbury," Josh replied, "you're right. Ten million was just a wild guess. Any reasonable number will work. Why don't you pick one for me?"

"That's impossible. Like I said, no one has any idea how many mutations were required."

"I get your point. How about one million? Is that acceptable?"

"I'm not going to play this silly game, Josh. One more time: *nobody knows how many mutations it took for an ancient land-dwelling mammal to evolve into a whale.* The only thing we can be sure of is that it happened."

"What do you mean, 'we?' Speak for yourself, Mr. Salisbury," Thomas Lawton quickly interjected.

"Listen, Josh. We need to move on here," Knox said. "Why don't I pick a number for you. How about ten thousand? Does that seem reasonable, Mr. Salisbury?"

Mr. Salisbury shook his head resignedly. "Ten million, one million, ten thousand ... What difference does it make? No number is really reasonable, because the entire argument that it is connected to is *unreasonable.*"

"I guess I'll have to take that as a 'yes,'" Josh continued. "Okay, so the whole process involved ten thousand mutations, and every one of these mutations supposedly resulted in a completely new feature in the Mesonychid's body, one that also created some kind of a survival advantage for him. Here's the problem with this notion – and, believe me, it's huge. Such a mutation requires new information to be installed in the animal's DNA ... But mutations *never* do this. Research proves this: *mutations never create new information.* They can't. They can only alter or destroy information that already exists in the DNA."

Josh quickly glanced at Jennifer and raised his eyebrows, reminding her of the report on mutations she helped present at one of the youth groups. David had told him about it. Jennifer smiled. She had already been thinking about it.

"If Natural Selection is going to change the Mesonychid into a whale, it needs new features to select from. You know: Natural *Selection.* The only way they can get these new features is through a mutation – but, like I said, mutations aren't able to provide them. Because of this, the process is not only unlikely; it is *impossible*. It can't even get started.

"Problem number two is a variation of the first one. The evolution of a Mesonychid into a whale would require the creation of many completely distinct intermediate creatures. The problem is that research indicates that there is always a strict limit to the potential variation in the physical characteristics of living creatures. Not once in the history of mankind has it ever been demonstrated that these natural barriers could be crossed. Scientists have artificially induced millions of mutations in fruit flies, for example. These mutations have produced all kinds of weird distortions in the fruit flies, like extra wings and legs growing out of their heads, stuff like that. One thing they have never produced, however, is a new insect; every one of the mutant forms is still a fruit fly. The built-in barrier that prevented a fruit fly from becoming anything other than a fruit fly has *never* been crossed. Not once. Once again, Natural Selection is stopped in its tracks. If that old Mesonychid is ever going to become a whale, of course it must break through the barrier that is keeping it a Mesonychid. But science proves that it can't. The only place it ever has is in the imagination of evolutionists.

"Another problem is that if Natural Selection was actually directing the evolution of the whale, it would have to somehow have foresight into the future, to see the end product, in other words, because it is very difficult to imagine many, or any, of the intermediate forms, assuming that there were any, having any survival advantage. I mean, try to imagine a Mesonychid like one tenth on the way to becoming a whale. What in the world would he *look* like — maybe like a cross between a wolf and a seal, with short legs that are starting to look a little like flippers ... remember, in the future he loses his legs altogether — who wanders back and forth between the land and the sea, unable to decide where he belongs? What kind of survival advantage would this strange looking dude have? As far as I can see, the only way Natural Selection could possibly favor him in the struggle for survival is if it could see what he was eventually going to become — because there certainly wouldn't be any reason to favor him like he was!

"Finally, here's the icing on the cake ... Natural Selection's *Terminator*. I've already shown that because mutations cannot provide new information in a cell's DNA, brand new physical features, ones that never before existed, can never appear. But in order for one creature to turn into another, lots of mutations would be required, perhaps thousands or even millions, and – here's the killer – *they would all have to be in a specific order*. In the evolution of the whale, for example, the mutations that resulted in the whale's blowhole couldn't come before he was living in the water, right? Like, what good would a blowhole be on the top of a Mesonychid's head? So then, if mutations can't create one entirely new feature, how in the world could they ever create a few hundred, or thousand, or million, *in exactly the right order?* The answer is obvious: they couldn't. No way – *never*."

Before he was able to say anything else, Martha Parker spoke up.

"If Josh doesn't mind, I'd like to step in here for a moment," she said. "Is that all right, Josh?"

"Yeah, sure. Go right ahead. I was finished, anyway."

"Good. Thank you. Let me first say that I thought your critique of Natural Selection was excellent, Josh, and I agree with everything you said. Now, woven into Josh's critique was the subject of mutations, and this was inevitable, because mutations are such a critical element in Natural Selection. The simple truth is that Natural Selection couldn't exist without them. Of course, as Josh has just pointed out so well, the more important truth is that it can't exist with them, either! Anyway, it occurred to me that a lot of people here tonight probably don't know exactly what a mutation is, and, since they're a critical feature of this debate, I though it might be helpful if I took a couple of minutes to briefly explain them. What do you think, Mr. Knox? Do you think that's a good idea?"

"Yes, I do. Please, though, try to make it brief – like two or three minutes, if possible."

"Two or three minutes, eh? Whew! That will certainly be a challenge. After all, entire books are written about it … graduate level courses at prestigious universities are devoted to it … doctoral dissertations are written about it. To put it mildly, *very* mildly, three minutes is hardly adequate. But I know we need to move forward … Okay, I'll do my best.

"Good," Knox replied with a big smile. "You've got two minutes and thirty seconds left!"

Smiling back, Martha continued.

"You're tough, Henry! All right, let's start with DNA, the famous double helix that James Watson and Francis Crick discovered in 1953 …"

For the next couple of minutes, Martha Parker presented a succinct description of mutations, ending with the vital fact that mutations cannot ever provide a creature with new information.

"The importance of this fact cannot be overemphasized. By itself, this single fact is sufficient to completely invalidate the entire theory of evolution, because if new information cannot be introduced into the DNA – and, as I've just explained, it cannot be – then macroevolution is *completely impossible*.

"Natural Selection can, and does, operate at the species level ... actually, the 'kind' level would be more accurate – this distinction is very important, but, unfortunately, there's no time to discuss it right now ... using genetic material *already present* in creatures' DNA. By means of genetic shuffling – not creating new information, but rearranging information that already exists – a great amount of variation can be created within kinds, such as that we see in dogs and different kinds of rodents and birds, for example. But that is *all* that this process can do. It *cannot* create entirely new features in animals, something that is required, of course, for macroevolution. The abundant experiments performed on fruit flies that Josh just mentioned provide dramatic evidence of this natural limitation. Like Josh said, regardless of how many mutations are induced in these creatures, two facts are clear: they never create entirely new physical features, and when the experiments are over, the creature that remains is still *drosophila melanogaster*, the common fruit fly.

"The bottom line is this: in its effort to win the game of macroevolution, Natural Selection has no chance of winning, because it can't even get in the game.

"Just one more thing," Martha smiled at Henry Knox, knowing that she had already exceeded her time limit, "Josh made a point about the order of the mutations that must occur in the evolution of new kinds, of completely new creatures, that is. He pointed out that these mutations must occur in a specific sequence and that there would have to be a very large number of them. After all, it would take a lot more than ten or fifteen mutations – or ten or fifteen thousand – for a wolf to turn into a whale! Generally speaking, in other words, mutation B must follow mutation A, C must follow B, etcetera. What he was saying was very insightful. If it is in fact impossible for *any* mutation to create an entirely new physical characteristic, how much more impossible it is that a large number of such mutations would occur in a specific order. If it is impossible for a single Chinese letter to ever appear as a misprint in an English book, because Chinese letters don't exist in the program used to print the book, how much more impossible that the entire book could be misprinted in Chinese!

"Okay – that's it. I'm finished," Martha smiled at Henry Knox. "Thank you for allowing me a little extra time!"

"You're welcome. It was worth it. That was very helpful."

Knox now turned toward Peter Salisbury. "So, Mr. Salisbury, what do you think of Josh's description?"

"I'll just briefly address one point that Josh made: the idea that Natural Selection can somehow see into the future. It clearly reveals Josh's lack of understanding, for this is not what believers in evolution claim at all. The idea is quite absurd. Richard Dawkins is a world-renowned scientist and a leading spokesman for the theory of evolution. In his well-known book, *The Blind Watchmaker*, he says that *Natural Selection has no purpose in mind. It has no mind, and no mind's eye. It does not plan for the future. It has no vision, no foresight, and no sight at all. If it can be said to play the role of watchmaker in nature, it is the blind watchmaker.* So then, in complete opposition to what Josh was saying, Natural Selection doesn't select a creature based upon what it will become in the future. It's only basis for choice is the survivability of the creature in the present."

"But what survival advantage would a stubby-legged part wolf, part whale who wanders around in shallow water trying to decide what he should eat have, Mr. Salisbury?" Josh asked.

"Listen, Josh, I think we've heard enough about the evolution of the whale. You've made your point. I admit to you that the current theory regarding this event has some weaknesses, but it's only one very small part of the overall theory of evolution, and I'm sure that further research will eventually clear up its problems.

"Before we leave the subject of Natural Selection, though, for the record I'd like to ask you one simple question, Josh. From everything you said, it sounds like you think that there's nothing at all to the theory of Natural Selection, that it's a complete myth. Is that correct?"

"Not exactly. Like Mrs. Parker pointed out, I think that Natural Selection, or something just like it, definitely operates at the species, or, more accurately, *kind* level, causing variation within the original kinds ... like the variation within canines – you know, dogs, wolves, foxes, etc. – for example. When it comes to macroevolution, however – the process that supposedly causes wolves to evolve into whales, lizards into birds, and monkeys into people – I'd have to say *Yes*, I do believe that Natural Selection is a myth ... because I don't believe that those type of changes ever take place."

"There you have it, Mr. Knox. You just heard it with your own ears. Except at the species level, Josh believes that Natural Selection is completely untrue. Let's put this opinion into perspective. I'll be very blunt. Probably about ninety-nine percent of the scientists in the world believe that the theory of evolution is true and that the organizing force behind it is Natural Selection. Based upon some research he has done in the past few weeks, Josh – a *high school student* – is attempting to convince us that a theory supported by the great majority of the world's scientists is wrong. *Do you see the problem here?* The whole country is watching what we're doing here tonight. Do you see how foolish we're going to end up looking? A high school student who probably has never even read a complete book on Natural Selection ..."

"Is that right, Josh?" Knox interrupted. "Have you ever read a complete book on this subject?"

"No, I haven't. But, hey, this is the twenty-first century, right? ... you know, the *information age.* The Internet has, like, about eighteen *million* entries under Natural Selection. I didn't read them all," Josh smiled, "but I read enough to get a good understanding of what it's all about. Several of the books I read through also contained information about it. Anyway, Mr. Knox, I believe that I understand it pretty well. Like I said before ... When you come right down to it, it's just not that complicated."

Henry Knox nodded his head and smiled at Josh.

"What do you think, Mr. Salisbury?"

"Like I was saying," Salisbury continued, ignoring Josh's defense, "A high school student who has *never read* a complete book on Natural Selection is pitting his opinion on the subject against scientists who have *written* entire books about it! It's ridiculous," Salisbury said, tossing his arms in frustration.

"I'm curious, Mr. Salisbury," Martha Parker spoke up. "Other than his suggestion that Natural Selection must have foresight, exactly what part of Josh's analysis do you disagree with?"

"Uhh ... That's a very good question, Mrs. Parker," Knox responded, "and I'd love to hear Mr. Salisbury's answer, but, listen ... I'm afraid we must move on. It's getting late. We've spent enough time on Natural Selection for now."

"Please, Henry," Salisbury said, "if you don't mind, I'd like to say just one more thing to Josh regarding the evolution of the whale."

"All right. But please, make it quick. We really must move on."

"Thank you. Josh, you obviously have a particular aversion to your textbook's description of the evolution of the whale. The details in your textbook may not be exactly right, but what you seem to be missing is that it *must have happened*. It's not rocket science. Mammals evolved from reptiles on the land, and whales are mammals, so, somehow or other, whales *must* have evolved from creatures that lived on the land. You're obviously a very bright young man. If you don't agree with the current explanation for the evolution of the whale, why don't you apply your considerable intelligence to the issue and come up with a better one?" Salisbury added, dead serious.

"Thanks for the compliment, Mr. Salisbury," Josh replied. "But I think I already know a better explanation: whales never did evolve. They were *created*, by God."

"There we go again … a perfect example of why it's so difficult to argue with these people," Randall Decker blurted out. "God said it; I believe it; that settles it. How can you possibly argue with someone who thinks like that?"

As the exchange between Josh and Peter Salisbury came to an end, Jennifer happened to glance across the stage at Mr. Potter. Their eyes met. Mr. Potter nodded his head, raised his eyebrows and gave Jennifer a little smile and a thumbs up. Jennifer understood the message perfectly. Whatever their differences, they shared a deep appreciation and respect for Josh's extraordinary mind, and they had been waiting for its display this evening. They had just seen it.

Although she enjoyed this little exchange with Mr. Potter, at the same time it caused Jennifer a bit of concern. She didn't think Mr. Potter looked too good. Quickly she passed a note to Josh, who was sitting beside her:

Great job! Hey - Mr. P, doesn't look too good - also he hasn't spoken tonite - have u noticed?

Thanks - I agree - don't know - maybe it's his leg. I know it still hurts him, Josh scribbled back.

The exchange between Josh and Peter Salisbury had created a buzz of excitement in the audience. Jennifer and Mr. Potter were hardly the only ones who appreciated Josh's performance.

Jennifer was about to write something else to Josh, but James Quinn altered her plans.

"You've been pretty quiet tonight, Jennifer," he said. "I'm sure that you agree with everything that the other members of your panel have said during these meetings, but before I reach a decision on this petition myself I'd like to hear a little more from you. So let me ask you a simple question: What

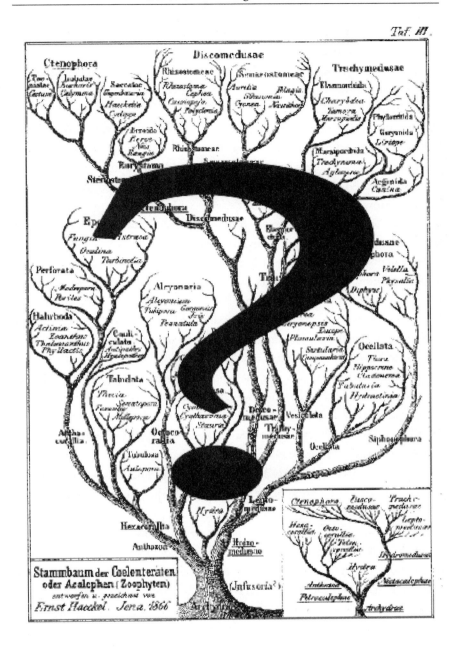

is it that makes you so sure that the world was created by God and not by means of evolution?"

"That's easy, Mr. Quinn. To me the evidence is everywhere," Jennifer replied with disarming candor. "Just open your eyes and look around: the sun and the moon, and the stars in the heavens, the birds in the air, the fish in the seas, the wondrous creatures that inhabit the earth … and *us* – you know: human beings! To me, the idea that these things *evolved* by random natural events, like the theory of evolution requires, is completely ridiculous."

"I appreciate what you've said, Jennifer, and I certainly agree that those things are quite extraordinary, but they're very general, if you know what I mean. I was wondering if you could select something a little more specific … more, I guess you could say, *scientific*," he said with a hint of arrogance.

"All right, I think I see what you mean," Jennifer replied, taking a deep breath. "How about the origin of life? As you know, like I just mentioned, according to the theory of evolution life evolved from nonliving matter through purely random, natural events. You know the story: billions of years ago elements in some 'warm little pond' managed to combine into organic compounds, like amino acids, which in turn combined to form bigger things, like proteins, which eventually formed living cells … all completely by chance. The way I see it, not only does this theory completely reject a Creator – which is one reason I don't believe it, of course – but it is also disproven by *science*. Let me try to explain why."

To those in the youth group it quickly became obvious that the background for Jennifer's explanation was the description of the cell by Michael Denton that they had read in one of their meetings a few months earlier. Jennifer had been particularly enthralled by this powerful portrayal and had read over the description many times.

"In our youth group we read an amazing description of the cell by a scientist named Michael Denton. He pointed out that when Darwin was alive, and for a long time after that, scientists could believe Darwin's explanation of the cell if they wanted to, because they had no reason to doubt it; they just didn't really know much about the cell. Like, their microscopes could only magnify things a few hundred times, and to them the cell was just a mass of blobs and particles that moved about haphazardly, like the little pieces of glass in a kaleidoscope. These days, of course, it's a whole new ball game. Now scientists have electron microscopes that can magnify things *millions* of times their actual size, and they now realize that a typical living cell is like a fantastically sophisticated and complex automated factory, far more complex than any man-made factory that has ever existed, consisting of, like, a trillion atoms, or more. A trillion is a very huge number. I heard a great illustration once of just how big it is. Suppose you lined up some quarters on their edge, like they would be in a quarter roll, on a nice straight road. How far do you think this road would have to extend to hold a trillion quarters, Mr. Quinn?"

"I don't know … A hundred miles?"

"Nope … it would have to extend *completely around the earth* …"

"Wow – that's amazing! I didn't know …"

"*Thirty-seven times!*" Jennifer added delightedly, with a big smile. "So, as you can see, there are an *awful* lot of atoms in every cell. To me the most incredible thing about this description was the idea that the cell could re-produce its entire structure – make a perfect copy of itself, that is – *within a few hours*. To illustrate how incredible this is, Mr. Denton compared the cell to a huge factory the size of a large city, like New York or London, be-cause, in a very real sense, that's how complex a cell really is. As I listened to this description, I imagined myself sitting on a hillside overlooking New York City. I imagined a broad, empty plain nearby. Then I tried to imagine what it would be like to watch the *entire city*, with its tall skyscrapers and bridges and endless roads and highways, duplicated on this plain *in only a few hours*. I mean, think about it, Mr. Quinn. Can you *imagine* what a to-tally awesome sight that would be?! The more I thought about it, the more it blew me away.

"Okay, now, in comparison to a cell, which is the smallest *living* thing, the most complex *non*living thing – say, a crystal, or perhaps a snowflake – is … well, let's just say that there's a giant gap between them, a gap that couldn't possibly be bridged by random natural events. The gap is unimagin-ably huge, like that between a … well, between, say, a tiny dollhouse and a magnificent European castle, but even greater … much, *much* greater, in fact. And the truth is that the more scientists learn about the fantastic design and complexity of the cell, the greater this gap becomes.

"So, there you have it, Mr. Quinn: a good reason – actually, two good reasons – why I believe in creation and do not believe in evolution: the huge, unbridgeable gap between nonliving and living forms, and the fantas-tic complexity of the cell." With passionate conviction, Jennifer then said, "I have to be honest with you, Mr. Quinn: as far as I'm concerned, anybody that considers the awesome complexity of the cell and doesn't see the hand of the Creator must be *blind*."

Jennifer paused for a moment and then said, "There's one more thing I'd like to say before I'm done. It's something that is really incredible, but for some reason hardly anyone ever seems to talk about it. I guess you could call it the *life force*, or something like that. Maybe it's the soul. Anyway, it's the mysterious thing that causes living things to be alive. Like, for example, if I suddenly had a heart attack here tonight and died, my body would be exactly the same as it was when I was alive, except for one thing: it would no longer have the life force that kept me alive. And the thing about this force that's so incredible is that nobody knows what it is and nobody can create it. It's … well, it's just a complete mystery – if you omit God, that is. Because He is the one who creates this force. There's a verse in the Bible – I think it's in one of Paul's letters – Timothy, or maybe Colossians – that says 'In Him' – that would be Jesus – 'all things hold together.' I think that is saying that it is only through God's power that we are alive.

"I was just explaining the amazing complexity of the cell. Well, even if all of the lifeless chemicals that are in a cell ever could come together by accident – like evolutionists suggest – without the spark of God's life force they'd never be alive.

"I probably didn't explain this very well. It's a difficult thing to put into words, I guess. I mean, I know exactly what I want to say, but it's kind of hard to find the right words to say it."

Watching Jennifer intently, it occurred to Paul that the passionate devotion to her Creator, and to His truth, that Jennifer had just displayed was, in a very real sense, the catalyst for the amazing events that had unfolded in the past few months. Suddenly, his heart was overwhelmed with affection for this special young woman, and for the mighty God that they both adored, and for the immense significance of what was taking place here this evening. A line from one of the youth groups' favorite songs came to his mind:

Great is the Lord Almighty; He is Lord, He is God indeed …

Momentarily overwhelmed by his emotions, a few tears trickled shamelessly down his cheeks.

"That was an excellent answer to Mr. Quinn's question, Jennifer," Janice Holmes said. "I'd love to read the book that included the description of the cell that you referred to. Do you remember the name of it?"

"Yes, I do. *Evolution: A theory in Crisis* by Dr. Michael Denton," Jennifer smiled back. "I think Mr. Hopkins probably has a copy of it."

"I'll see if I can get a copy of it from Amazon. Maybe I'll get an extra one for Jim," Holmes added, smiling at James Quinn.

"I, too, thought that your answer was very good," Brian Miller said. "However, it overlooked something very important: just because scientists cannot explain how life could have evolved from nonliving matter through purely natural events at the present time doesn't mean that they won't be able to explain it in the future. With the spectacular revelations regarding the basic building blocks of life in the past few decades, scientists are overwhelmed with new information. It will take time to explore all of this information and produce answers to the mysteries that have been uncovered. Right now the origin of the cell by purely natural events is one of the greatest of these mysteries. I am confident, however, that in the coming years it will be solved. That's what science *does*, Jennifer: it looks into facts that have been discovered about the natural world and attempts to explain them in the light of natural laws and events. It usually doesn't happen overnight, but, so far at least, it almost always happens."

"That's what Mr. Salisbury just said about the evolution of whales, Mr. Miller: even though the process cannot be explained now, it will be in the future. That's a cop-out," Thomas Lawton pronounced. "According to that logic, *nothing* can ever disprove the theory of evolution, because no matter what hurdle is in its path, some future discovery can always remove it. It's the same logic that has been applied to transitional forms: Darwin admitted that their absence was a problem for his theory but was confident that they would be discovered in the future. They haven't been, but according to your logic that doesn't matter, because they still will be – in the future."

"The idea that no transitional forms have been discovered is a favorite argument of creationists, Mr. Lawton, but it's completely ridiculous. The fossil record is replete with transitional forms, and every paleontologist worth his salt is well aware of it," Miller replied.

"Everyone except Stephen J. Gould and Niles Eldredge, eh?" Lawton quickly retorted. "You know, you evolutionists ..."

"I think it's time we moved on," Henry Knox interrupted. "Josh, your analysis of Natural Selection certainly was impressive. You obviously have a deep interest in the subject being debated here tonight and have devoted a lot of thought to it. Now I'd like to ask you a question: what is it about this subject that makes you so interested in it? Something about it fires up your passion. What is it?"

"Hmmm ... That's a great question, Mr. Knox, one that I haven't really considered. Let me see ... I guess one reason would be that this debate – you know, between evolution and creation – is about truth, and truth is something that I'm passionate about. Evolution and creation are two theories, really the *only* two realistic theories – although I guess you know by now that I don't think evolution really is realistic – about how the natural world and everything in it came into existence. As Paul just pointed out, the two theories are *mutually exclusive;* that is, since one of them must be correct – true, in other words – the other cannot be. Getting to the heart of the matter – after all, the whole purpose of this debate is to decide what our teachers should be teaching us about origins – teaching that the theory of evolution is *true* teaches at the same time that creation *isn't.* Teaching that there's *no creation* – and make no mistake, that *is* what we're being taught – teaches that there's no *Creator,* and as far as I'm concerned, that's simply not true.

"It's very interesting to notice that most of the other topics that are the center of controversy today cannot be debated on the basis of whether they are *true* or not. Take abortion, for example. That's certainly a controversial subject, right? Can it be debated in regards to whether it is *true* or not, though? Of course not! People don't argue about whether or not abortion is *true.* They argue about whether it is right or wrong, and when, or if, it should ever be permitted, and things like that. Arguing about whether or not it is *true* wouldn't make any sense, though, would it? Of course it's true!

"Creation and evolution are different. The primary question about them – the only question that really matters, if you think about it – is which one of the theories is *true.* Ever since I first heard of it, starting in about seventh grade, I guess, I believed that the theory of evolution was true. That's what I was taught in school. Why wouldn't I believe it? At first I hadn't heard much at all about the creation theory. In fact, I never heard *anything* about it until Jennifer mentioned it one day in Mr. Potter's science class. And when I first heard it, I thought it was really lame, just like a lot of people here tonight do.

"Not long after that class I got exposed to the idea of creation again," Josh said, glancing at Paul, "this time with a lot more intensity, and it almost killed me ... yeah, that's right ... It almost *killed* me."

Struggling to keep his emotions under control, Josh paused. Jennifer, sitting right next to him, knew exactly what was in Josh's mind and grabbed hold of his hand for support. After a moment, he continued.

"From that moment on, I became intensely interested in the subject. It *consumed* me, man. I *had* to find out whether it was true or not. I spent endless hours reading about it and studying it, and after awhile it became clear to me that the theory of evolution is not only flawed, but that it is a *complete lie.* And when I thought about the fact that this lie was being presented to us in school as the *truth*, it freaked me out … Really, it just *completely* freaked me out …"

"A *complete lie*," Victor Gregory interrupted. "Isn't that a little harsh, Josh. I mean, obviously you don't embrace the theory. But when you label it a *complete lie* I think that …"

"But that's exactly what it *is*, man! – *a complete lie!*" Josh burst out, slamming his hands on the table in front of him. "You've been listening to this debate for several hours here tonight, Mr. Gregory, and you listened to another one a few weeks ago. Have you heard *anything* – anything at all – that suggests to you that the theory is *true*?! If you have, you must have heard something that sailed over my head. Come on! You're hearing the truth about this stupid theory here, something that doesn't happen very often these days. Open your ears, open your heart. God's trying to tell you something here, man. *Receive it.* You may not get this opportunity again. It might just *save your life* – like it did mine," Josh admonished with undisguised passion.

Victor Gregory was not completely convinced that Josh was correct, but he wasn't about to question him about it. Peter Salisbury had already demonstrated the folly of that idea! To be sure, Josh was only a high school student, but he was unlike any high school student Mr. Gregory had ever come across!

"So, Mr. Knox," Josh asked, "does that answer your question about what it is about this debate that fires up my passion?"

"Yes, it certainly does, Josh. Not only did you *explain* the reason for your passion. You did yourself one better: you *demonstrated* it! Thank you. Thank you very much."

At the beginning of this evening some people had questioned the selection of Jennifer and Josh for the creation panel. The last few minutes had laid these doubts to rest. As high school students, they were on the front line of the creation/evolution battle, and this evening they had made it clear that they were well equipped for the fight. They had made many people proud of them – most especially the One who had created them.

A gentleman in the audience now stood up and asked Susan Marshall for permission to say something. Asking that he be brief, she granted it.

"Thank you. Thank you so much. I was listening very carefully to the young lady's description of a cell. I thought her answer was excellent. I believe very strongly in creation, and when I first discovered that the panel supporting this theory would include two high school students, I was worried that that might be a mistake. I have to tell you, though; these two teens certainly have proved me wrong. They have not just held their own; they have been shining stars!"

A burst of applause from the audience affirmed that he was not the only one who felt this way about Jennifer and Josh. Smiling and nodding his head at this show of support, he continued.

"Anyway, when Jennifer mentioned a castle a vision came to my mind. As well as having a keen interest in the subject being debated here tonight, I'm an artist and a musician, and I get these visions sometimes. The image was of a group of people who were lost in a strange place. They assumed that it was a cave. They wanted to escape, but they were unable to, because it was pitch black, and they couldn't see a thing. Having no other option, they waited, assuming that it was nighttime and that the light of dawn might reveal the cave's entrance.

"Sure enough, as time passed light began to dimly glow in the darkness. As the light brightened, the people were astonished, for the reality that the light revealed was radically different from anything they had anticipated. They discovered that they weren't in a cave at all but in a huge palace resplendent with great vaulted ceilings, massive sparkling chandeliers, brilliant tapestries and paintings, and magnificent furniture and accessories, many of them glistening gold and silver. They couldn't believe their eyes!

"I recognized that this was a perfect illustration of scientists searching for the bridge between living and nonliving forms. Just as the light revealed to the people in the cave a reality that was far different from what they had expected, electron microscopes have revealed to scientists a reality completely different than what they had anticipated. As Jennifer explained a few minutes ago, rather than the anticipated bridge that smoothly joins the living and nonliving worlds, what these microscopes have revealed is a yawning chasm, a chasm so great that it has been labeled the greatest discontinuity in the entire natural world.

"It wouldn't be a stretch to say that these scientists have been presented with more empirical evidence of their Creator than any group of people who have ever walked the earth. Incredibly, and tragically, though, many of them ignore it and continue to believe that what they have seen is the result of random natural events – in evolution, in other words. The brilliant truth about their Creator is staring them directly in the face, but they're blinded – blinded by the light." Slowly shaking his head, he added, "How sad ... How very, very sad."

30

A New Beginning

Susan Marshall chose a young girl near the front of the gym to be the next speaker. She identified herself as Katie Benson. She was a friend of Jennifer's sister, Kelly.

"I've been at both of these meetings," she began hesitantly, obviously a little nervous. "Science is my favorite subject, and my parents thought I would find these meetings interesting. They sure were right! They *have* been! I'm fourteen years old, and it's kids my age who are, like, in the middle of this whole thing, if you know what I mean. Joe Petrocelli had a chance to say what he thought about it. Now, if you don't mind, I'd like to tell you what I think about it. I know it's getting late. I won't take long. Do you mind, Mrs. Marshall?"

"You're right, Katie. It is getting late. But I've seen your hand up a few times, and I imagine you have something important to say. So, please, go right ahead." Susan Marshall replied warmly.

"Oh, good. Thank you … Okay, well, I've been listening to everything pretty carefully at these meetings, and something seems weird to me. Right now, evolution is taught in schools and creation isn't. I know that, at first, the people who brought up the petition wanted creation taught alongside evolution, but then they changed their mind and are now trying to see that neither one is taught in school. I don't think that's such a great idea, though, because how can you teach about nature without explaining where nature came from? I'm just sure that a teacher could never make it through a first year biology course, for example, without someone asking where the first cell came from. At least, he could never make it through the course if *I* was in it!" Katie grinned. "So, anyway, I think that our schools have to teach us *something* about where it all began. And if they do, I think they should teach us about creation, not evolution. From everything I've heard at these meetings, creation seems to be a *much* better explanation than the theory of evolution. I don't understand why evolution is taught. From what's been said here, it doesn't even seem that it's true. Why should we be taught something in school that isn't true – especially something as important as how the world began, and where living things come from? To me, it seems really messed up. I don't get it. Thanks, Mrs. Marshall. I'm done."

Katie sat down, and Barbara Jenkins quickly took the microphone. With a condescending smile, she began a response to Katie's question. It quickly became apparent that her remarks were addressed to a larger audience than Katie.

"To conclude from these meetings that evolution isn't true would be a serious mistake, Katie. Certainly, questions have arisen about certain features of the theory, but this hardly invalidates it. It only demonstrates healthy skepticism, something we encourage all of our teachers to stimulate in their classrooms. To conclude that the theory is erroneous because some aspects of it may not yet be completely understood would be missing the forest for the trees. The general theory is the forest, and it is vast and awesome, impossible to ignore and teeming with powerful truths about life on planet earth …"

As Mrs. Jenkins was proceeding with her defense of evolution, the crowd was becoming uneasy. People were whispering to one another and pointing toward the stage. It wasn't because of anything Mrs. Jenkins was saying, however. It was because of Mr. Potter, at the other end of the table from Mrs. Jenkins, who had said nothing all night. Something seemed to be the matter with him. His eyes were shut, and he was biting his lip, as if fighting back tears. As Mrs. Jenkins droned on, he buried his head in his arms on the table. His shoulders were gently shaking.

Suspecting that Mr. Potter was in pain from his injuries and that he might need some help, Mrs. Marshall interrupted Mrs. Jenkins. She quickly walked over to him and expressed her concern.

Mr. Potter slowly raised his head. His eyes were bloodshot. Acknowledging Susan's concern, he nodded that he was okay and asked for the microphone. Hesitantly, Susan returned to her chair.

"I … I want to apologize," he hesitantly began. "I'm so very sorry. I don't know how I can …"

"Dick," Susan Marshall broke in, "you don't need to apologize! We know what you've been through the past few weeks, and we commend your courage for even showing up tonight," she pronounced with heartfelt compassion.

Demonstrating their agreement, a few people in the audience began clapping. Others quickly joined them. But Mr. Potter held up his hand and shook his head to stop them.

"Wait!" he pleaded. "You don't understand. *Please* – Please listen to me!"

The clapping stopped, and the gym became silent.

Mr. Potter directed his attention toward Katie Benson. "I haven't had the privilege of having you in one of my classes yet, Katie, but I hope I will soon. I look forward to it. You seem to be a very bright young lady." He smiled warmly at Katie. Blushing, she smiled back.

Mr. Potter turned away from Katie and looked out upon the crowd. His next words stunned them.

"Folks, Katie is right. The question we should be addressing here tonight is not whether creation should be taught alongside evolution, or whether all teaching about origins should be eliminated from our schools. It is why evolution is being taught in the first place."

Mr. Potter paused for a moment to let the impact of his words have their full effect.

"I realize that some of you may be wondering if I've lost my mind. *How could someone who's supposed to be defending the theory of evolution ever make the statement that I just did?* you're asking yourselves. The truth is, I haven't *lost* my mind – I've *found* it!"

Mr. Potter paused again to gather himself together. He was obviously having difficulty controlling his emotions. Everyone in the gym was hanging on his words. "Let me try to explain to you how I've arrived at this conclusion … Several weeks ago, as many of you know, I was in a very serious automobile accident, an accident that according to all reports should have taken my life. My doctor told me that my survival was truly a miracle, one of the most amazing brushes with death that he had ever experienced in his twenty-five years as a surgeon. Very often, as I'm sure some of you know from personal experience, when someone goes through such an experience, it has a dramatic effect upon their life. They feel as if they've been rescued from the grave and given a second chance at life. This feeling results from another thing that usually happens to them: they start thinking about spiritual things a lot more than they ever had before – which is exactly what I did. I started thinking a lot more about not only God, but heaven, and hell, and my purpose in being here. I'm still trying to figure out a lot of these things. One thing, however, *is* clear to me: I'm very sure that I was saved from death *by God*.

"I also spent a lot of time thinking about this meeting, and I started to become very anxious about it. Something about it was really disturbing me. I sensed it had something to do with the theory of evolution, but I couldn't put my finger on what it was. In any event, I was so confused that I almost didn't come here tonight. You probably noticed that I haven't said anything until now!

"I figured that once I was here, things would get better – but they didn't. They were getting *worse*. But then Pastor Hopkins said something that started to make everything begin to fall into place. He was speaking to Virginia Mitchell, and what he said really convicted me. Perhaps you remember his words: "Chance," he said, "is the god of evolution – there is no room for another one." Immediately, I knew that he was absolutely right, that the theory of evolution *denies God*.

"When Katie spoke, everything suddenly snapped into focus. It may sound trite, but I saw the light. I finally understood exactly why I have been so anxious these past few weeks and why I was so disturbed about this meeting: this theory that I've been teaching with such passion for the last twenty years, the theory of evolution, *denies the very God that saved my life in my accident!*"

Momentarily, Mr. Potter's emotions overwhelmed him again. Several seconds passed before he was able to speak again.

"Isn't that incredible?" he finally continued. "The God that I've been denying my whole life reached out to me the night of my accident and snatched me from the jaws of death!"

He struggled through his next few words. "His mercy ... overwhelms me. It just completely overwhelms me. I've tried so hard to reject Him ... but He saved me ... anyway ..."

By now Mr. Potter wasn't the only one struggling with his emotions.

Collecting himself, Mr. Potter continued. "Whew! I sure wasn't expecting anything like this tonight!" Pausing, he glanced across the stage at Josh and Jennifer. "Compared to this, teaching high school science is a walk in the park," he said with a little smile.

He turned back toward the audience.

"So, what happens now, you may be wondering. Where do I go from here? Quite frankly, I'm not sure ... It's all happening so fast. It's going to take awhile to absorb it all. There is one thing I can tell you for sure, though: I will *never* teach the theory of evolution again, unless to show why it is wrong.

"There's something else I wanted to tell you ... I was just thinking of it. Let's see ... Oh, yes! Now I remember. Why did I say 'I'm sorry' to Susan a few minutes ago? Like Susan, most of you probably thought I was apologizing for the distraction I was causing. That wasn't it at all, however. I had this overwhelming sense of *guilt*. *This* is what I was trying to apologize for. As I listened to Katie Benson, I knew she was right, and it grieved me that I had ever taught something that denies God. In Katie I saw reflected the countless people – hundreds, maybe even thousands, including many of you here tonight – that I had taught as truth this deceptive ... yes, even *evil* ... theory. That's why I was apologizing – because I felt so *guilty*.

"Ultimately, however, it's not you that primarily deserves my apology, is it? No – it's God. It's *His* truth that I've ignored and maligned, and it's *His* forgiveness that I need most of all. I know I don't deserve it, but some friends of mine ..." he said, glancing again at Jennifer and Josh ... "have been telling me about God's incredible capacity for forgiveness recently. He already performed one miracle in my life. Who knows, maybe He'll perform another one. I hope so, because I sure need it!"

Taking a deep breath, Mr. Potter sat down. For now, at least, he was finished. Bowing his head, he folded his hands on the table in front of him. It appeared to some that he might be praying. He was.

There was a long pause. The only sounds were of people blowing their noses in tissues, and the hum of the TV cameras that were transmitting every moment of this dramatic evening, which would soon be seen throughout the country, and the world.

Finally, visibly moved herself, Susan Marshall spoke.

"Dick ... Is there anything else you wish to say?"

Raising his head, Mr. Potter smiled.

"Yes," he said. "As a matter of fact there is. I'd like to ask a question, to Josh."

He turned his attention to his favorite young student.

"Josh, do you think you could find room for another chair next to you?"

For a moment, Josh was at a loss for words.

"Why ... why, of *course!*" he finally exclaimed. "Sure, Mr. Potter! I'd be more than honored to have you sit next to me. Please, come on over ... Wait, I'll give you a hand," he quickly added as he remembered Mr. Potter's injuries.

Mr. Potter held up his hand. "That's all right. I can make it on my own."

He slowly rose to his feet and proceeded to cross the stage on his crutches. Smiling, he shook hands with each member of the creation panel. None of their eyes were dry.

He reached Josh last. Their eyes met, and their minds were flooded with memories – of all the classes they had been in together, of the long discussions they had had, and, more recently, of Josh's numerous visits to the hospital during Mr. Potter's recovery from his auto accident. Josh recalled the times he had seen Mr. Potter's eyes blazing with fury during their discussions about evolution and creation, but all trace of that fire was gone now, and Josh knew that it was gone forever. His eyes now reflected a soul that was weary, but peaceful, like those of a soldier who has returned home from a long war.

Josh rose from his chair, came around the end of the table and embraced his teacher. Through his tears, Mr. Potter whispered, "Thank you, Josh. Thank you so much for leading me to the truth. I never would have found it without you ..."

As the two of them sat down, Jennifer, who was next to him, touched Mr. Potter's hand.

"Mr. Potter," she whispered as their blurry eyes met. "Don't *worry*. God does forgive you!"

A sweet peace filled Mr. Potter's heart.

Some people in the audience began to clap. Others quickly joined in, and soon the entire gym was filled with the sound of heartfelt clapping. For the moment, at least, united by the poignancy of the drama onstage, everyone laid their differences aside. The clapping continued for almost two minutes.

Mr. Potter's startling and completely unexpected turnabout had been highly dramatic, and Susan Marshall couldn't imagine the meeting returning to normal, not on this night anyway. Furthermore it was getting very late, after midnight, and the meeting had already carried on considerably longer than planned. After huddling briefly with her Board members, she announced that the meeting was over and that the Board would convene in a few days to vote on the petition. Nobody raised an objection.

Deeply touched by what they had just witnessed, people filed quietly out of the gym.

Outside of the gym, Jennifer quickly joined up with David and their friends. It had warmed up some, and the night sky was obscured by a light fog.

They especially wanted to talk to Mr. Potter, but he was surrounded by a crowd, including several reporters who were jostling each other in an effort to interview him. David was concerned that all the attention Mr. Potter was receiving would be too exhausting for him in his weakened condition, and he headed toward him, seeking to offer him some protection from the hungry reporters. As he approached, however, he saw Josh standing next to Mr. Potter.

"How is he doing?" David asked his friend.

"He's all right," Josh replied. "Things are winding down here. I don't think we'll be here much longer."

"Good. Come on over when you're done."

"Yeah, sure. I will. Thanks, man."

David smiled, gave Josh a pat on the back and turned away to rejoin Jennifer and their friends.

On his way, he ran into Katie Benson, who was chatting with Kelly and some of their friends. Katie had been one of the stars of the evening and was trying to handle the unexpected attention that her performance had generated.

"Hey, great job tonight, Katie!" David exclaimed, giving her a high-five. "Your comments really hit the nail on the head – especially from Mr. Potter's perspective!"

"Thanks, Dave," Katie smiled. "So what do you think is going to happen now? Do you think they're going to stop teaching evolution in our schools?"

"Gee, I don't know, Katie. We'll just have to wait and see, I guess. The future's hard to predict. Like, nobody would have ever guessed how tonight's meeting would end up, would they? One thing's for sure, though. It doesn't look like we'll be hearing much more about the theory of evolution in Mr. Potter's classroom!"

David stayed to chat with Katie and her friends for a couple of more minutes, and Jennifer joined them. As they were about to leave, Jennifer felt a hand on her shoulder.

"You did a wonderful job tonight, Jennifer," Mr. Potter said to her with a warm smile. "I wanted to tell you something that occurred to me as I was sitting next to you at the end of the meeting. Remember that Bible verse that is hanging behind my desk in my classroom?"

"Yes, I do," Jennifer quickly replied. "I look at it every time I'm in your class. It's burned into my brain! It's Matthew 18:6: ... *whoever causes one of these little ones who believe in Me to stumble, it would be better for him if a heavy millstone was hung around his neck, and he was drowned in the depth of the sea.* What about it?"

"Remember when you stopped by after class several months ago and asked me what I thought it meant?"

"Yeah, sure."

"Well, if you will recall, I told you that I thought it was directed at me, that I was the one who these little ones believed in and that 'these little ones' were my students, and that it placed a great burden of responsibility on me, to make sure that I didn't cause my students to stumble, that I taught them the *truth*. Do you remember?"

"Yes," Jennifer said. "Actually, I remember very well."

"Why am I not surprised?" Mr. Potter smiled. "Anyway, what occurred to me was that my interpretation of that verse was completely wrong. It wasn't *me* who was supposed to be the object of the children's belief; it was Jesus, wasn't it?"

Jennifer nodded her head.

Putting his hand on Katie's head, Mr. Potter continued. "Another thing that struck me was that the verse actually *was* directed at me – but it was saying that I should be drowned in the sea, because by teaching the theory of evolution as the truth I was causing my students to stumble! It's so clear to me now – but it sure wasn't back then! I can't believe how blind I was!" he added, once again choked with emotion.

Then, he looked at Jennifer with a little smile.

"But you already knew all this, didn't you, Jennifer?"

Jennifer smiled sheepishly. "Uh, yeah, I guess I did – but I didn't want to say anything back then. For some reason, I just didn't think it was the right time."

"I guess you were right. It wasn't … You really are something else, Jennifer," Mr. Potter said. And he gave Jennifer a big hug.

"Hey, Mr. Potter, you make me think of a verse I read someplace in the Bible," Josh, who had joined the group with Mr. Potter, spoke up. "The blind will see, and the lame will walk."

Mr. Potter smiled and nodded his head. "The second part of that verse applies especially well to me, I guess – but the first part fits you, too, doesn't it, Josh?"

"Yeah, you're right," Jennifer said. "And it fits the rest of us, too. Because, guess what … Before we knew Jesus, Mr. Potter, we were *all* blind!"

Mr. Potter slowly nodded his head and smiled.

As he headed toward his car, Neil Goldman, the reporter from the *New York Times*, ran into his new friend, Bob Campbell.

"That was quite an ending to the meeting, wasn't it? What did you think about it?" he asked.

Thinking back to their conversation at Carney's with Dick Potter prior to the first hearing, Campbell replied, "Amazing, Neil. I've never seen anything like it. When you think back to how utterly committed Potter was to the theory of evolution, it's just unbelievable, isn't it?"

"Yeah, it really is. In all my years of reporting, I've never seen such a dramatic reversal in a person's thinking in such a short time."

"Me neither. He obviously experienced some kind of religious conversion, don't you think? I'd love to find out exactly what happened. I'll bet it would be a great story."

"You're probably right. Maybe we should try to get together with him sometime and ask him about it."

"Good idea ... Let's plan on it."

Because of his rather frail condition, Mr. Potter had to leave for home. Paul Hopkins, Martha Parker and Frank Morrison stayed around to answer the reporters' questions in the large foyer outside the gym. They were from all over the country, and beyond. The question that they were all most interested in was the outcome of the School Board's vote on the petition. Everyone knew that the vote had the potential to be historic. Paul, Martha, and Frank kept repeating that they had no idea how the vote would go.

Finally, close to 1 a.m., the three of them were able to get away. They headed for the Main Street Diner where they knew that a bunch of people, including a lot of the kids from the youth group and several of their parents had gathered for a bite to eat. Somewhat to their surprise, when they arrived about thirty people were still there. The Diner had to put them in their banquet room.

It turned into one of those special nights when time didn't matter. For a long time – an hour and a half, maybe two – people reminisced about the remarkable evening and all the things that had led up to it. It had deeply touched everyone's heart, and everyone seemed eager to share their thoughts and feelings about it.

Jennifer, David and Josh didn't arrive until after 2 a.m. They went someplace else first ...

After walking Mr. Potter to his car with Jennifer and Josh, David said, "Jennifer and I are going for a ride, Josh. Come with us. We'll go in my car."

"No, you guys go ahead. I'm sure that …"

"Don't bother, pal. You're coming."

"Where are you going?"

"Lookout Ridge. You know what a great view there is from there."

"News flash … It's foggy, dude. Fog's fog. It'll look the same from Lookout Ridge as it does from here."

"We were thinking that the Ridge might be above the fog. Anyway, fogs like this don't usually stick around long this time of the year."

"Hmmm … Maybe you're right. All right. I'm in."

It was normally about a fifteen minute ride to Lookout Ridge from the high school. Because of the fog, however, it would take a little longer tonight.

"That was a pretty amazing night, wasn't it guys?" David said as they headed out of the parking lot.

"It sure was," Josh responded. "Who would have ever thought that Mr. Potter would have reacted like he did? I couldn't believe it. The reporters must have loved it. It'll give them a great story for the evening news."

"You mean *morning* news. But yeah, you're right," David said. "You couldn't invent a script like that one, you know? I mean, think about it. At first – you know, the original petition – our only goal was to get creation taught alongside evolution. When the goal was changed to have evolution eliminated from our classrooms, we were well aware that the petition didn't have much chance of passing. Like, how were you going to stop teachers from teaching evolution, right? But then Mr. Potter – the champion of the theory of evolution, the man who says that the theory is the fundamental theory in all science – stands up and solves the problem by saying that he'll never teach evolution in his classroom again. Who in the world could ever have *dreamed* that story up?!"

"Actually, Dave, I can think of someone else who had that idea before Mr. Potter did," Josh said.

"Oh yeah? Who's that?"

"The person sitting alongside of you: Jennifer!"

"Oops – you're right! How could I have forgotten *that*?" David said, smiling sheepishly at Jennifer.

"It's pretty cool the way it happened, isn't it?" Josh said. "When Jennifer brought that idea up – you know, of eliminating all teaching about origins – we couldn't figure out how the idea could ever be carried out. Remember?

Well, *we* couldn't figure it out – but God could. He knew exactly what to do: change Mr. Potter's heart. Awesome."

"You're right," Jennifer said. "It *is* awesome, isn't it? Hearts, Josh ... hearts ... that's where God works his miracles – you know?"

"Yeah, Jen," Josh responded softly, thinking about the change that took place in his own heart not long ago, "I know."

Just as they reached the parking lot at Lookout Ridge they broke through the fog. It quickly became apparent that they had not just risen above the fog but that they had left it behind, for the broad valley that stretched before them was crystal clear. Pulling up to the guardrail at the edge of the steep precipice that plunged to the valley below, they quickly got out of the car to get a better view. The snow-covered valley and the hills that rose beyond were illumined by the silver light of the crescent moon, and the stars glittered high above like diamonds in silent witness to their Creator against the pitch-black winter sky. Other than the gentle breeze whispering in the nearby pine trees at the edge of the parking lot, all was silent.

"Wow. This is really beautiful, isn't it?" Jennifer said. "Two minutes ago we could barely see a hundred feet. Now it looks like we can see *forever*."

"You're right, Jen. It's totally awesome," Josh said. "I think it might be the most beautiful night I've ever seen. It makes me think of a verse from the Bible – What is it? ... Something about *the heavens are telling about the glory of God, and ... and ...* I can't remember the rest of it."

Jennifer finished it for him.

The heavens are telling of the glory of God,
And their expanse is declaring the work of His hands.
Day to day pours forth speech,
And night to night reveals knowledge.
There is no speech, nor are there words;
Their voice is not heard.

"Psalm nineteen ... Is that what you were thinking of?" she asked Josh matter-of-factly.

"Exactly," Josh replied shaking his head with a smile. "You're something, Jen. You know what's really cool about that verse is that it says that the night sky declares knowledge of God *silently – There is no speech, nor are there words*. When

you think about it, it's kind of an oxymoron. Like, how can something *pour forth speech* without speaking? But, then, look up at the sky. Isn't that exactly what's happening? It shouts to all the world that there is a Creator – but it's absolutely silent. I remember seeing a meteor shower one night a couple of years ago, and it was really spectacular. At one point I counted, like, thirty meteors in a minute. Sometimes there were two, or even three, in the sky at the same time. It was like a giant fireworks display, but with one huge difference. It was completely and utterly silent – just like tonight. It blew me away. It was, like, totally *awesome*."

"Yeah, you're right," David said. "That is cool. You know, I had never thought about that oxymoron angle you mentioned in Psalm nineteen. *Day to day pours forth speech* ... but *there is no speech*. It's very interesting. I guess what people have been saying about you is true, Josh ... you really are a genius, man!"

They all had a good laugh.

For a few more minutes, wrapped in a big woolen blanket, the three friends huddled together in silence, their bodies chilled by the cold night air but their hearts and their souls warmed by the love they were all feeling, for each other, for their Lord, and for His glorious creation. It was a special moment in their lives, not only because of the magical beauty of the night but also because it marked the end of an amazing journey, a journey that had begun innocently enough almost eight months earlier when Jennifer questioned the textbook's explanation for the evolution of birds in Mr. Potter's classroom. Along the way, the lives of many people were changed forever – including, of course, this trio huddled together on Lookout Ridge.

Finally, they got back in David's car, cranked up the heat, and headed back to the diner. Their souls had just been treated to a wonderful feast. Now they decided that it was their stomachs' turn!

As they headed out of the parking lot, Josh said, "I was just thinking Jen ... What we've gone through in the past eight or nine months has been pretty incredible, but if you hadn't stood up for your beliefs in Mr. Potter's class last spring, I don't think any of it would have happened."

Jennifer turned around to Josh and replied, "I was just following my heart." Smiling, she added, "After all, that's where God works His miracles – right, Josh?"

Josh smiled back. "Yeah, Jen ... you're right."

31

Epilogue – The Decision about the Petition

Two days after the Wednesday night meeting in the Madison High gym the School Board gathered in Susan Marshall's home to make a decision regarding the petition. As they entered the living room of the old farmhouse, the heat from the crackling fire in the large stone fireplace provided welcome relief from the bone-chilling air of this sub-zero winter night. Reminders of the recent Christmas holiday were scattered about the house, including the beautiful Christmas tree. It had been almost a month since Christmas, but the Marshall family loved the Christmas season, and they liked to prolong it as long as possible. One year the tree didn't come down until Easter! Before the meeting started, they spent the first few minutes enjoying a delicious coffee cake that Susan had made, fresh out of the oven, along with tea and coffee, and hot cider and fresh fruit. Susan wanted to do whatever she could to start the meeting off on the right foot, because she knew it was going to be a long, and perhaps difficult, evening.

Shortly after seven the meeting began. To review, the petition requested that all teaching about the origin of the physical world and of life be removed from the curriculum of Madison High. It was a unique and radical request. Other groups in the country had proposed that creationism, or Intelligent Design, be taught in conjunction with the theory of evolution, but, as far as the Board members knew this was the first attempt to completely eliminate the teaching of origins. The petitioners' original goal, of course, had been the same as these other groups, to introduce creation into the science curriculum as an alternative to the theory of evolution, but the petitioners believed that there was a fatal flaw with this plan: the teaching of any alternative theories would probably be completely ineffective if those teaching these theories didn't believe in them. And their research had indicated that this was, in fact, the case. That is, for the most part, the current science teachers in the

Madison schools were firmly committed to the theory of evolution and did not consider creation a legitimate alternative. Convincing these teachers to teach creation at all would be a major challenge. Expecting them to do it fairly and effectively was simply unrealistic. The original petition ignored this problem. After the first hearing in early December, however, the petitioners finally decided that this problem *couldn't* be ignored. It would completely undermine the fundamental purpose of the petition. Therefore, the petition was revised.

Another issue that affected the petitioners reasoning was their awareness that any attempt to incorporate creationism into the science curriculum would certainly be challenged on the basis of the separation of church and state. Every previous attempt to achieve a similar goal had faced such a challenge, and every challenge had been successful. Their revised proposal would avoid this hurdle, of course ... because there wouldn't be anything to challenge! This is not to say that the petitioners believed such a challenge had a legitimate basis. Frank Morrison, in particular, had made it clear that they definitely did not. Once again, however, their conviction was trumped by realism. They were *certain* that the ACLU would challenge any attempt to incorporate creationism into the science curriculum, and, based upon history, they were almost as sure that the ACLU would win. What would be the point of having their petition approved if the decision was only going to be overturned in the courts? The petitioners weren't seeking a *moral* victory. They wanted a *real* one. It should be pointed out here that the petitioners were well aware that the goal of their revised petition, the elimination of the teaching of origins altogether, was actually more radical and perhaps less likely to be approved than the original goal. What ultimately caused them to change their petition was not simply the considerations mentioned above, however. It was the penetrating question that Jennifer posed at a meeting after the first hearing. Referring to the theory of evolution, she asked, "Why would God want the beautiful story of His creation taught alongside this horrible lie, as if they were equals?" They had no answer to this question – so they changed their petition.

An air of tension hung in the room. As the hearings in the Madison High gym had made abundantly clear, the subject that would be the background of their discussion this evening, creation and evolution, has a unique capacity to inflame peoples' passions. Since she was primarily responsible for keeping the peace, Susan Marshall was a little nervous about this potential problem. Susan was basically a gentle soul, a lover of peace. The controversy that swirled about this petition had caused her to wonder more than once if she was the right person for this job. Over the last couple of months, she sometimes felt more like a referee in a prize fight than the chairman of a small-town School Board.

Shortly after the meeting began, James Quinn spoke up.

"Before we get going here, I have to be honest with you all ... I can't help thinking that this entire debate is a complete waste of everybody's time. If state education departments and the ACLU have blocked the attempts to introduce creation, or Intelligent Design, into science curriculums, what do you think they'll do if we try to *eliminate* the teaching of origins altogether? They'll go *ballistic!*"

"So what are you saying, Jim?" Janice Holmes said. "Should we just deny the petition right now, have a little more coffee cake, and go home?"

Quinn shrugged his shoulders.

"All I'm saying, Janice, is that even if we approved the petition, our State Board of Education and the ACLU would never allow our decision to stand. It's up to Susan, not me, to decide when we should take a vote tonight ... I like your idea of a little more coffee cake, though," he added with a smile, patting his ample belly, which obviously had consumed more than its share of coffee cake – and many other things – already.

Tom Lawton spoke next.

"Realistically speaking, Jim is right. If we approve the petition as it stands, the State Board of Education and the ACLU will, indeed, immediately challenge our decision ... and I think we know who holds most of the cards in that game.

"But listen – Let me tell you something. We all know that the decision we will be making here tonight is very, very important, and not only for Madison. It will affect science curriculums all over the country. Ultimately, though, there is one thing that must determine our decision, and it's not how our State Board of Education or the ACLU will respond to it. It's a simple question: Is the theory of evolution true, or is it a lie? Make no mistake about it: The decision we make tonight must be determined by how we answer this question. This point cannot be overemphasized. We must not allow our fears about what might happen as a result of our decision to affect the decision itself. Of *course*, approval of the petition would be challenged, but we must forget about that for the time being, and keep our focus on the fundamental question: Is the theory of evolution true, or is it a lie?

"The underlying premise of the petition, the notion that instigated it, is that the theory of evolution is *not* true and that it is unconscionable to teach it as if it is. This premise allows no room for compromise. In order to arrive at a decision about this petition, it is absolutely imperative that we determine what *we* believe about this premise. If we believe that it is true, we *must* support the petitioners. If we believe that they are wrong, then we won't. You probably won't be surprised to hear that I believe that the petitioners are absolutely right, that the theory of evolution is a complete lie and that we must do everything within our power to see that it is no longer presented to our children as the truth.

"The decision we make here tonight, my friends, is probably the most important one this School Board has ever, or will ever, make. The entire nation is waiting to hear it. Let's do everything we can to make sure we get it right."

There was a brief pause as the Board members contemplated Tom Lawton's sobering words.

Randall Decker broke the silence. "That was very dramatic, Tom – and you may be right. But if our decision here is going to hinge upon whether we believe that the theory of evolution is true or not, you can probably guess where I stand. In my opinion, if we approve this petition, we will be the laughing stock of the entire country. You know as well as I do that anyone who doesn't accept the theory of evolution has virtually no chance of getting anywhere in the field of science. You said that the underlying premise of the petition is that the theory of evolution is not true and that it is unconscionable to teach it as if it is. But let's face it … We're talking about a theory that is referred to as "the central unifying concept of biology." Some even refer to it as the most important theory in all of science. You just said that the petitioners believe that it is unconscionable to teach the theory as the truth. I say that it would be unconscionable to allow students to pass through our school system without learning anything about it. The petitioners may not believe that the theory is true, but practically everyone else does … especially scientists!"

Susan Marshall was paying close attention to this conversation between Lawton and Decker, and it was clear to her what needed to be done.

"I don't think there can be any doubt that what you said is absolutely right, Tom – that the decision that we will be making here tonight will be determined by whether or not we believe that the theory of evolution is true.

If the majority believes that it is, then we certainly won't pass the petition. If the consensus is that it isn't, then perhaps we will. So before we do anything else I think we must find out exactly where each of us stands on this fundamental question. We really can't move forward until we do."

It was clear that Susan was right, and for the next hour the Board wrestled with the issue that she had raised. After a very lively, and at times heated, discussion, they arrived at a consensus: they agreed with Tom Lawton. They did not believe that the theory of evolution was true. To be precise, four of them – Susan Marshall, Tom Lawton, Victor Gregory, and Janice Holmes – shared this opinion. Virginia Mitchell still held to her belief in theistic evolution, although not as firmly as she had prior to the debates. Actually, the term "firmly" is a bit of a misnomer here, for prior to these debates she really hadn't thought much about the subject at all. James Quinn maintained his faith in the theory of evolution, although it, too, had been considerably shaken by the debates. Put it this way: before the debates, if the Board members had concluded that the theory of evolution wasn't true, he would have walked out of the meeting in disgust. This evening he stayed, gladly. To say the least, his opinion about these things was definitely undergoing a transformation. Randall Decker still believed in evolution, but he, too, had been affected by the debates and was no longer inclined to defend the theory with quite the same enthusiasm he would have previously. He certainly didn't agree with the majority opinion, but he begrudgingly accepted it. It was clear that he was outnumbered.

The consensus surprised Susan Marshall. As a group they had discussed this issue at only one other Board meeting, the one in November, when the petition first arose – they had not met in December – so she didn't have a clear idea of where the other members stood on it. She did know that Randall Decker would defend evolutionary theory, but she suspected that James Quinn, and probably Victor Gregory, might also. She thought that the result might depend upon the position of Virginia Mitchell. When the consensus became clear, she breathed a sigh of relief. She might not have to be a referee tonight after all!

Having arrived at a consensus regarding this critical question, the group now turned their attention to a major problem that would arise if the petition was granted, a problem referred to a couple of times at the Wednesday night meeting. On the state accreditation exams, which were required of every high school student and were important for their college applications, there were a number of questions about evolution. Under the original petition this would not present a problem, because evolution would still be taught. Under the revised petition, however, the students would be at a great disadvantage. They would be unable to answer the questions on the state exams about evolution because they would never have been taught anything about it. Surprisingly, the revised petition did not address this dilemma. Susan Marshall had this to say about it.

"I've talked about this problem with some of the petitioners, and I'll tell you how they see it. It comes down to a question for them: which would be worse, that our students are taught a theory about the origin of life, and of the world – the theory of evolution – that is not true, or that they miss some questions on their state exams? The way they see it, the origin of the world is an extremely important issue, one of the most important our children will ever face. Perhaps you remember what Martha Parker said about this issue at the hearing. She said that the theory of evolution has the potential to completely contaminate a person's view of the world. In fact, she compared its destructive potential to *cancer*. I have to say, I can't disagree with her. If you think about it, what question is more important than, *where did the world come from?* Like Mrs. Parker suggested, the answer to this question is pivotal in the formation of one's world view, and if the answer is a lie, it results in a world view that is rotten at the very core. For the petitioners, then, the bottom line is this: if creation cannot be presented fairly, leaving a lie as the only theory of origins that our students are taught, it's better that they are taught nothing at all. They are well aware that this is a very imperfect solution in a very imperfect world."

Susan's comments initiated a lively discussion. After a few minutes, Tom Lawton spoke up.

"Listen, this problem of providing the students with the information about evolution that they will need for the state exams is very important. It's very closely related to another one, however, and if you all don't mind I'd like us to turn our attention to it first. Martha Parker mentioned it at the Wednesday meeting. It's the source of this information: the science textbooks. Mrs. Parker pointed out that the theory of evolution is presented as a proven fact in virtually all of the textbooks used in our nation's public schools, and she is absolutely right. She also said that unless the textbooks are completely changed, they will continue to promote the idea that the theory of evolution is a proven fact, no matter what the teachers say. She also said, however, that her panel did not envision science textbooks altering their position on the theory of evolution any time soon, and this is one of the main reasons that the goal of the petition is to eliminate the teaching of the theory altogether.

"Now, as much as I agree with Mrs. Parker's evaluation of this subject, there is one glaring weakness: elimination of the teaching of the theory of evolution does not eliminate its presentation in the textbooks. And the problem with this is that the theory is not confined to just a chapter or two in these textbooks; it permeates the entire book, from beginning to end. The bottom line is that as long as these textbooks are used, the students are going to get the impression that the theory of evolution is a proven fact, no matter what they are told by their teachers. As far as I am concerned, this is a huge problem. In my opinion it is intolerable, and something *must* be done about it.

"Perhaps you may recall that at the hearing I asked Mrs. Parker what she thought should be done about this problem. She acknowledged that her panel was well aware of it, but said that they decided that they would cross that bridge when, and if, they came to it … after we made a decision about the petition, in other words. Well, my friends, we have arrived at that bridge – and we must decide what to do about it. Before we get into a discussion about this, let me just say that I don't think the petitioners really believed the problem would ever arise, because I don't think they really believed that their petition would be approved. They were just being realistic. Of course, you can hardly blame them … Nobody else thought it would be approved, either!"

"Just a minute here, Tom," Decker spoke up. "I'm sure that there's a section in these textbooks that addresses the theory of evolution, perhaps even an entire chapter or two, but to claim that these books teach evolution from the beginning to the end is a pretty bold claim. What makes you think that it's true?"

"Because I have thoroughly reviewed the book with my own eyes, Randy. My son Mike told me about it, and I couldn't believe it, either. But we went through his entire biology textbook together a few months ago, and, sure enough, he was right. There are four entire chapters in the book devoted almost exclusively to evolution. The truth is that there's hardly a chapter that *doesn't* include some reference, either directly or indirectly, to that theory."

"So what do you think should be done about it, Tom? Should the books be *burned*?" Decker challenged with an amused grin.

"No, I don't think we need to go that far, Randy. Just getting rid of them would be sufficient," Lawton quickly replied.

"*Book banning!*" Decker protested in exasperation, pounding his fist on the arm of his chair. "Come on, Tom. You can't be serious! It's bad enough that we're considering banning the teaching of the theory of evolution, but now you want to get rid of the science textbooks, too? What the hell is going on here? What would the books be replaced with – the *Bible*?"

"Really, Tom," Victor Gregory chimed in. "You're not serious about getting rid of these textbooks, are you? If nothing else, think of how much that would *cost*."

"Actually, I am, Victor – dead serious. I don't want my children, and you know that I have five of them, using a textbook that is constantly drumming home the conviction that the theory of evolution is a fact that is completely accepted in the scientific community, especially when I know perfectly well that their teacher is probably not going to be making much of an effort to refute that conviction. Also, in regards to the cost, those textbooks are due to be replaced soon, anyway. They're several years old."

"So what would you do if the textbooks aren't replaced, Tom … homeschool your kids?" Decker asked with an edge of sarcasm, and a touch of anger, in his voice. It was obvious that he was the lone wolf in the evening's debate, and he wasn't happy about it. He was especially annoyed at Quinn. He felt that he had caved in to the opinion of the majority.

"We've thought about it. We've also looked at a couple of Christian schools in the area. But before we make any moves, I want to do whatever I can to see that the current textbooks are replaced. Like I just said, I'm dead serious about this. I'm not going to have my children exposed to these evolution-promoting science textbooks in our schools any longer. I've had it.

"Look, I want to make myself perfectly clear about this. No matter what else we decide here tonight, as far as I'm concerned we must demand that these textbooks are replaced. For our children to be using textbooks that teach as an absolute fact a theory that over half of the people in our country believe is not true and that, furthermore, utterly denies the God that even more of us worship is an utter abomination and should not be tolerated any longer." With deep passion, he added, "No matter what kind of resistance we face – and I'm sure it will be significant – we *must not back down* on this issue."

After a momentary pause, Victor Gregory spoke next.

"All right, Tom ... Now that *that's* settled ... I know that you are a big fan of the creationist organizations *Answers in Genesis, Institute for Creation Research,* and *Creation Ministries International.* I've investigated their position on this matter and have concluded that they would not agree with this petition. They believe that students should learn about evolution in our public schools, but should be exposed to both the positive and negative elements of it. Furthermore, I haven't seen where they would be in favor of banning current textbooks, like you're suggesting. Do you disagree with them in regards to this issue?"

"Like you said, I certainly do have the utmost respect for those organizations. They are unquestionably the leaders in the modern creationist movement. Quite frankly, though, I don't know what their position is on the use of standard science textbooks. I can only repeat what I said a moment ago: I've taken a close look at the ones used at Madison High, and I do not want my children using them. In my opinion, there is far too much evolutionist propaganda in them. Their denial of the Creator is perfectly obvious, and, like I said, this is utterly unacceptable to me. One more thing, Vic ... To the best of my knowledge, the students in our schools aren't learning much, if anything, about the negative elements of the theory of evolution – certainly not from their textbooks, anyway!"

"I agree with Randy and Victor that any effort to get rid of these textbooks would be very controversial, Tom," Susan Marshall observed, "and I'm sure it would encounter considerable resistance. Nevertheless, it's an intriguing idea. Suppose we did decide to try to do it. I'm sure you would agree that the students must have *some* kind of textbook. Where would we get them? Don't *all* current biology textbooks promote the theory of evolution just about as enthusiastically as the one they're using now?"

"Actually, the answer to your question is *No*, Susan. I've done some research into this matter and found that there are a few textbooks available today that present both evolution and creation in their discussion of origins, including the objections to the theory of evolution. They aren't very well known, because they're not published by the major textbook publishing companies. Some other similar textbooks are also in the works."

"But if creation is included that would introduce religion into the discussion, and we all know what the Supreme Court has ruled about that," James Quinn pointed out.

"The authors of some of these books have taken that into account, Jim, and have carefully excluded any reference to God or religion in their works in order to make them acceptable in our public schools. I haven't reviewed ..."

"Come on, Tom!" Randall Decker interrupted. "How in the world can creation be discussed without specifying the Creator?"

"Ask those in the Intelligent Design movement, Randy. They're masters at it. In fact, one of these textbooks was produced by the Discovery Institute, which is the headquarters of the Intelligent Design Movement."

"How do you know that the book doesn't mention God? I thought you just said that you haven't reviewed them?"

"You didn't let me finish, Randy. I was going to say that I haven't reviewed *all* of them. I did review the one available through the Discovery Institute, however, and, sure enough, it doesn't specifically mention God ... aside from saying that God is one of the possible identities of the hypothetical Intelligent Designer."

"I'm a little confused about something here, Tom," Janice Holmes said. "I was under the impression that you are not a big fan of the Intelligent Design movement, that you don't like the fact that they are so insistent about *not* identifying the intelligent designer. Have you changed your mind?"

"Not really, Janice. I just realize that however things play out here tonight the result is going to be far from perfect. Accepting a textbook that teaches about the creation without identifying the Creator is just one of the compromises that we might have to accept. It would be a heckuva lot better than the one currently being used."

"Are these textbooks you have in mind being used at any other public schools, Tom, or would we be the guinea pigs?" Virginia Mitchell asked.

"To be honest, I don't know, Ginny. But it's a very good question, and I think we need to find out the answer to it."

"Let me see if I've got this straight," Decker said. "If the teaching of origins was completely eliminated from our science curriculum, and, just to make sure that our students were not exposed to the idea that evolution is a proven fact we ordered all new textbooks from the Discovery Institute, this would be *far from perfect* in your eyes? Come on, Tom. Aren't you being a little greedy? My god, man, what else could you possibly ask for?"

"Do you really want to know, Randy?"

"No, that's all right. Let's move on."

"No, wait," Janice Holmes protested. "I don't know about anyone else, but I'm curious to know. What would be your ideal scenario for the teaching of origins, Tom?"

The others — except for Decker — agreed with her, so Tom Lawton proceeded.

"Well, the main problem with the changes that Randy specified — the reason that, in my opinion, the program is a *long* way from being ideal — is that there would be a *huge* void: not only would the Creator of the world not be given any credit for His creation; He wouldn't even be *identified!* From my perspective, from the perspective of anyone who believes in the Creator, that would be preposterous. It would be like teaching American history without ever mentioning the Revolutionary War, George Washington or the Constitution! But that's not the only thing that would be wrong with it. According to a verse in the Bible, Romans 1:20, a primary purpose of the creation is to lead people to the Creator. It says, *For since the creation of the world, His invisible attributes, His eternal power and divine nature, have been clearly seen, being understood through what has been made, so they are without excuse. What has been made* in that verse is, of course, a reference to the creation, the natural world. The point is that evidence of God is *everywhere* and that it can be clearly seen by everyone. Every flower, every newborn baby, every star in the sky, every blade of grass — *everything* in the natural world — is unmistakable evidence of the Creator. In an ideal world, then, our science teachers — who would all be creationists, of course, Lawton added with a smile — "would use the creation not only to teach the fantastic truths about the natural world but to point their students toward the Creator of this world, God, so that when they meet Him one day — as they surely will — they will have *no excuse* for not knowing Him. Students in these science classes would not only learn to love and understand the natural world; they would learn to love the One who created it.

"So there you go, Randy: my opinion about how science would be taught in an *ideal* world ... not exactly the scenario we're envisioning here tonight, is it?" Lawton added with a big smile.

While listening to Lawton, Susan Marshall gazed upon the flames flickering brightly in the fireplace. She was captivated by Tom's vision of how origins would be taught in an ideal world, and glancing around the room she could see that she wasn't the only one. As one who believed deeply in the Creator, she was well aware that the teaching of origins in today's schools, so focused upon evolution, was in need of a major overhaul. Even so, she certainly had never envisioned a science curriculum like the one that Tom was describing. *What a beautiful vision,* she thought to herself. *Tom is truly a man of God – what a blessing to have him on our Board!*

"That's very interesting, Tom," Decker said. "You really *are* greedy, aren't you?" he added with a smile. "I'll tell you one thing, though. It's a good thing you realize that that vision is of an *ideal* world, because you're sure never going to see it in this one!"

"Maybe not in our lifetimes, Randy. But I can assure you that someday people certainly will – when the Lord comes back!" Lawton grinned.

"Come on, Tom," Decker said, shaking his head in disbelief. "You're not serious, are you? You don't really believe that Jesus is going to literally return one day to save the world from destruction, like these television preachers do, do you?"

"I sure do, Jim. One day, as the Bible says, *the earth will be full of the knowledge of the Lord, as the waters cover the sea.* One day, in other words, in every school in the world children will be taught the truth about the creation – and the theory of evolution will never be mentioned."

"Do you think we'll live to see that day, Tom?" Janice Holmes asked.

"I don't know, Janice … maybe. It's kind of hard to imagine it, though, isn't it?"

"I agree with Randy, Tom. That was a very interesting perspective," James Quinn said. "I had no idea what you creationists were *really* looking for," he smiled. "But I must ask you something. If you believe that the current petition falls far short of what really should be done, why do you support it?"

"I don't, Vic," Lawton smiled.

Quinn, along with everyone else in the room, was stunned by Lawton's words.

"Wow!" he pronounced. "There's a shocker. I assumed that you would be the strongest supporter of the petition, Tom. I'm speechless."

"I figured what I said would surprise you all, Jim. First, let me say that I completely appreciate the motivation behind the petition. However, as I've thought about it – and I've given it a *lot* of thought – I can't help thinking that it's just too unrealistic to expect that a class about the natural world … you know: biology, geology, etc. … can be taught without ever mentioning where it all came from. You might recall what Katie Benson had to say about this at the Wednesday meeting: *how can you teach about nature without explaining where nature came from.* Katie, I believe, is exactly right. The students wouldn't let it happen. As far as I'm concerned, then, origins *must* be taught – not only creation, but the theory of evolution, as well … although this teaching would point out all the problems with the theory, as well as any of its merits."

"Of course, you don't believe it has any," Janice Holmes quickly added.

"Of course," Lawton smiled. "Anyway, here's what I think we should do. First of all, as I've been trying to make clear, I think that we must get rid of any textbooks that tout the theory of evolution as a fact and replace them with others that not only present creation – or at least Intelligent Design – as a reasonable alternative, but also present the problems with the theory of evolution. Like I've been saying, I know that such textbooks are available. These textbooks are the most tangible evidence of the unrighteousness in the current teaching of origins, and replacing them would be an unmistakable signal that we are not going to accept the status quo.

"Now, let's get back to the problem that came up at the beginning of our meeting: that the teachers currently employed in our schools are not likely to do an adequate job of presenting the creation message, because, for the most part, they don't believe in it …"

"Except for Mr. Potter – I guess he does now!" Janice Holmes interjected.

"Yes, you're right about that, Janice!" Lawton smiled. Thinking back to the dramatic ending to Wednesday night's meeting, he added, "What a moment that was, eh?! The media certainly lapped it up, didn't they? Anyway, aside from Mr. Potter, it's fairly obvious that our science teachers are not enthusiastic supporters of creation. Just like the petitioners concluded, we can't expect these teachers to present a very good case for creation if they don't believe it's true, can we? So, I have an idea to solve this problem …"

"Wait a second, Tom," James Quinn interrupted. "Before you tell us your idea, I think it's time for a reality check here. Are you familiar with the incident a few years ago in Cobb County, Georgia, in which the ACLU had filed suit to force the removal of small stickers in the front of the school's biology textbooks? All these stickers said was that the theory of evolution is a theory and not a fact and that material about it should be approached with an open mind … and the ACLU won!"

"Yes, Jim, I certainly am. It was a deplorable decision – and it shows just what creationists are up against, doesn't it?"

"You'll probably be surprised to learn that I agree with you. I think the decision was ridiculous, too. But the point I want to make isn't about whether the decision was right or not. The point is, if the School Board in

Cobb County was prohibited from placing an innocuous little sticker in front of their school's science textbooks, how in the world do you think that we'll ever be able to get away with replacing all of our science textbooks with ones that not only present the problems with evolutionary theory but also present creation – or at least intelligent design – as an alternative? If the ACLU got up in arms about a harmless little sticker in the front of those science textbooks, how do you think they'll react to *your* plan to entirely *replace* the textbooks?"

"Think about it this way, Jim. About eighty years ago, creation was still the dominant theory of origins taught in our nation's schools. In many states it was actually *illegal* to teach the theory of evolution. Things began to change, however, when the ACLU challenged that law in the famous Scopes trial in Dayton, Tennessee in 1925. Over time things turned completely upside down, until today it's essentially illegal to teach *creation*. In 1925 *nobody* would have ever believed that the teaching of origins in our schools could have evolved to the point that it's at now. A lot of people have a similar opinion about what the petitioners here are trying to do. But the evolutionists eventually won their battle, and the theory of evolution completely replaced creation as the theory of origins taught in our public schools. So, Jim … If the evolutionists won that battle, why can't the petitioners win theirs?"

"Here's something else to think about, Tom," Victor Gregory said. "Even if we could win a legal challenge from the ACLU, I'm sure that our school's science teachers would fight against using the type of textbooks you're suggesting, and in the end don't they have the final say on what textbooks are used?"

"Listen, Vic, what you're forgetting here is *who is in charge of our schools.* It's not the ACLU and it's not our teachers. Ultimately, it's the citizens – the taxpayers – of Madison, and *we* are their elected representatives. Sure, our superintendent is in charge of hiring the teachers, but *we,* the School Board, hire *him.* In the end, everyone who works at our schools is an employee of the citizens of Madison; our taxes pay their salaries. So the bottom line is this: if we decide upon certain guidelines for a textbook, and a teacher doesn't like it, he or she has a very clear alternative: he can seek employment elsewhere. And that brings me to the solution I was about to offer for …"

"Just a minute, Tom," Janice Holmes said. "I want to support what you were just saying about who has the final authority in selecting our school's textbooks. It just so happens that last night, in preparation for this meeting,

I was reviewing the official guidelines of the School Board, and guess what – You are absolutely correct. The teachers are supposed to be consulted, of course, but the final decision on the selection of textbooks is indeed up to us. After all, we're the ones buying the books! Most of the time, this little detail is overlooked, because it just seems to make sense to let the teachers select their own textbooks. Usually, their decisions are rubber-stamped by the School Board. Well, this just might be a situation in which that rubber stamp is set aside, eh?"

Lawton proceeded to explain his plan for dealing with the probable protests from the teachers at Madison High, and about a half hour later, about 2 a.m., the Board finally arrived at a decision. They would not ban the teaching of origins altogether, as the petitioners had requested, for it would unfairly penalize the students in their state exams. They arrived at a three-phase plan. The first two phases were primarily the brain-child of Lawton. First, in the short term, beginning that spring, in coordination with the teaching of evolution in the science classes, a representative from the creationist camp would be invited to the high school as a guest speaker. The details of his presentation, the location and format, would be decided later. There would be no restrictions on his subject matter. Furthermore, he would have to be either directly associated with one of the leading creationist organizations, *Answers in Genesis*, *The Institute for Creation Research*, or *Creation Ministries International*, or be approved by these organizations. The Supreme Court decisions that have been made about such issues would not effect this phase of the plan for these decisions apply only to teaching *in* the classroom, and the speakers that would be invited would be speaking *outside* the classrooms. Of course, this was a technical detail that they were sure would be challenged by the ACLU, or some other legal organization, but they would cross that bridge when they came to it. One thing that made them optimistic was that their school had hosted speakers from Planned Parenthood, and even a LGBT (Lesbian, Gay, Bisexual, and Transgender) group in the past. If representatives from these organizations were permitted to speak, they figured, how could representatives from one of these creationist organizations be denied permission?

Second, the Board would see to it that at least one, and perhaps more, high school science teachers were hired who believed firmly in creation. Having someone like this available to answer questions and offer guidance on a permanent, rather than a temporary, basis would clearly benefit the students. Having more than one person like this would benefit them even more.

Finally, the Board would see to it that any textbooks that taught the theory of evolution as a fact were replaced by ones that pointed out the flaws in the theory and presented the facts about creation, including, if possible, the evidence for a worldwide flood. They knew that this last requirement would eliminate the book from the Discovery Institute – the Intelligent Design community definitely did not support the idea of a worldwide flood in the relatively recent past – and that this might force them to make a compromise. No matter what eventually transpired, the Board was adamant regarding their proscription concerning the theory of evolution being taught as a fact. On this demand, at the very least, there would be no compromise. The current textbooks would *have* to be replaced. Period.

They were well aware that some, perhaps even most, of the science teachers would undoubtedly object to this plan, perhaps vehemently, but that would be okay. Lawton had already proposed the solution to this problem: those who opposed the plan would be welcome to seek employment elsewhere. Of course, if they chose to do this, it would smooth the path for the second phase of the plan ... the hiring of some new teachers!

In regards to the fact that their plan did not exactly meet the goals of the petition, they felt confident that the petitioners would enthusiastically support it anyway, for it was quite obvious that it went considerably beyond these goals. They were quite sure that the difference between the details of their proposal and those specified in the petition would present no legal difficulties, as long as the petitioners approved of the changes. Another petition about a different matter in the recent past had been approved with some changes without any problem, so why couldn't this one be, also?

The plan would be formally introduced into the science curriculum guide and would remain there until a future petition to remove it was introduced, debated, and passed by a new School Board. They didn't expect this process to proceed smoothly, because they knew that in Madison, as in most other towns in the United States, there were many firm believers in the theory of evolution who would not be at all happy with this proposed plan and would undoubtedly fight it. They expected additional resistance from the State Department of Education. On the other hand, they had received enough feedback to know that their plan would receive considerable support from the citizens of Madison. In the midst of this uncertainty, at least one thing was perfectly clear to the Board members: this was not going to be their last meeting about this petition!

Of course, they knew that once their decision was made public, like a spooked cat the ACLU would leap to prohibit its implementation on the basis of "the separation of church and state." Somewhat surprisingly, James Quinn indicated that if this happened, the Board could fully count on his support. Although his opinions were generally liberal, he just didn't like the ACLU. The situation involving the textbook stickers in Cobb County, Georgia, had particularly irked him. He thought that the ACLU had gone way overboard there and had acted like a bully. Also, when it came to legal issues, Frank Morrison's exchange with Allan Kennedy on religion versus science in the first hearing had clearly demonstrated his expertise, and they knew that they could count on his support in regard to any legal issues.

Tom Lawton didn't like the ACLU either. This is what he had to say: "In regards to the theory of evolution, we've compromised far too long. Well, in my opinion, the same thing can be said about the ACLU. Thousands of scientists and almost half the country's population don't believe in the theory, yet, largely because of the ACLU, it is illegal in our schools to present creation as an alternative. This is not only wrong, my friends. It is an *abomination* – an *absolute abomination*. Some day, somewhere, some group is going to stand up to this ungodly organization and finally see that this absurd and unrighteous policy is laid to rest where it belongs – on the scrap heap of history." With passionate conviction, he added, "And let me tell you something, my friends ... that day is about to arrive, that place is going to be right here, and that group is *us!*"

The extraordinary decision made by the Madison School Board was greeted by howls of protest and derision in the nation's liberal media. Some pundits were practically apoplectic.

The *New York Times,* for example, had this to say: As most people are well aware, in recent weeks a petition spearheaded by fundamentalist Christians has been undergoing an intense and closely watched debate in the small town of Madison, New Hampshire. The goal of the petition was shocking: to eliminate the teaching of origins – which essentially means the theory of evolution – from *the school's science curriculum. If passed, the petition would have created a monumental stumbling block to Madison students interested in pursuing a career in science, for the theory of evolution is the central unifying concept of biology and accepted by virtually all scientists as a proven fact. To put it gently, the scientific community does not look kindly upon those who don't accept this simple truth. Approval of the petition rested in the hands of the Madison School Board. With the whole country and much of the rest of the world watching breathlessly, the School Board buckled. They didn't approve the petition, but the alternative they proposed was no improvement. Exactly like the petitioners, they leveled their guns at the theory of evolution. Unlike the petition, however, the Board's plan would not prohibit teaching of evolution; it would emasculate it, though, by forcing teachers to point out all of its problems and presenting creation as an equally valid explanation for the origin of the world. Of course, where there's creation, there's a Creator. Apparently, these people chose to ignore the First Amendment of the Constitution.*

That's not all, though. In addition to the above, the Board is demanding that their school's current biology textbook, which is one of the most popular in the country, be replaced because "it promotes the theory of evolution as a fact from its first page to its last." What a surprise! That which is a fact is promoted … as a fact.

After citing the fact that about half the country's population does not believe in the theory of evolution, the editorial proceeded to point the finger of blame indirectly at the School Board, and directly at their science teachers: *The decision was stunning proof of what can happen when the theory of evolution is inadequately taught and is dramatic evidence of the desperate need to increase the attention given to this vital theory in our nation's public schools. Our nation's position as a worldwide leader in science has already slipped badly, and some have attributed this decline to the endless diversions caused by creationists. If this decision is any indication of the future direction of science education in our nation – and we certainly hope that it is not – things do not look promising.*

Within days the ACLU filed a lawsuit protesting the School Board's decision. Something had happened in Madison, however, that neither the ACLU nor anything else could change. For many years, the students who passed through the Madison school system had been taught that life had evolved as the result of random natural events. This teaching had concealed from them the truth about how the world had *really* come into being, and about the One who had created it. They were the victims of a great conspiracy to hide this truth. The hearings in the Madison gym had unmasked this conspiracy and laid bare the duplicity of its foundation, the theory of evolution.

Driven by the Spirit of God, a mighty wind of change had swept through Madison. No matter how successful they are in courtrooms, against this force the ACLU attorneys are powerless.

They can't turn back the Wind.

Notes

1. Hitching, Francis, *The Neck of The Giraffe*, New Haven and New York, Ticknor & Fields, 1982.

2. ibid., p. 57.

3. The foregoing references are from *Biology: Principles & Explorations*, by George B. Johnson and Peter H. Raven, Holt, Rinehart and Winston, 1998.

4. Denton, Michael, *Evolution: A Theory in Crisis*, Bethesda, MD, Adler &Adler, 1986, p. 328.

5. D.V. Ager, *The Nature of the Stratigraphic Record*, London, Macmillan, 1973, pp. 1-2 ... quoted in *Transcontinental Rock Layers*, by Andrew Snelling in *Answers* magazine, May 7, 2008.

6. Denton, op. cit. pp. 328-330.

7. Gitt, Werner, *Technical Journal* published by Answers in Genesis, volume 10, 1996, pgs 181-187.

8. Jaki, Stanley, *The Road of Science and the Ways to God*, Chicago, The University of Chicago Press, 1978, p. 288 – Original quotation from the Duke of Argyle in *The Reign of Law*.

9. Quoted by: Woodward, Thomas, in *Doubts About Darwin*, Grand Rapids MI, Baker Books, 2003, p. 81.

10. Richard Lewontin, "Billions and Billions of Demons" (review of *The Demon-Haunted World: Science as a Candle in the Dark*, by Carl Sagan, 1997), *The New York Review*, p. 31, 9 January 1997.

11. *Biology: Principles & Explorations*, Holt, Rinehart and Winston, 1998, p. 253.

12. Baker, Sylvia, *Evolution: Bone of Contention*, p. 25, cited in *Evolution: Fact, Fraud, or Faith* by Don Boys, Largo, FL, Freedom Publications, 1994, p. 281.

13. Snelling, Andrew, "Fossil Wood in 'ancient' lava Flow Yields Radiocarbon," December 1, 1997, *Creation* magazine ... *Creation* is a publication of *Answers in Genesis*, located in Hebron, KY ... the article cited includes 15 endnotes that source all of the technical information that formed the basis of the article.

14. For an account of this theory, see *Noah's Flood: the New Scientific Discoveries About the Event that Changed History*, by William Ryan & Walter Pitman, Simon & Schuster, 1998.

15. Henry Morris & John Whitcomb, *The Genesis Flood*, Phillipsburg, NJ, P & R Publishing Co., 1961, p. 11.

16. Darwin, C., *The Origin of Species*, Chapter X (on the imperfection of the geological record), London, J.M. Dent & Sons Ltd., pp. 292-293.

17. See note 9, above.

18. Taylor, Ian, *In the Minds of Men*, Toronto, Canada, TFE Publishing, 1984, p. 171.

19. Heilmann, Gerhard, *Origin of Birds*, Witherby, London, H. F. and G., 1926.

Note: The words Intelligent Design were usually capitalized in order to distinguish the semi-official Intelligent Design Movement from the far larger and more generic group of individuals who simply believe that the natural world was designed and that the one who designed it is intelligent – *really* intelligent, in fact! The latter group includes creationists of all stripes. Many creationists, however, would not consider themselves to be members of the Intelligent Design Movement. That is, they believe in intelligent design, but not necessarily in Intelligent Design.

Acknowledgments

Without the assistance of a few special people, this book may never have been completed. I want to take this opportunity to acknowledge them.

First on the list is my dear sister, Carol, who edited the first draft of the book, which I started in 1996. That draft was entirely handwritten, because at that time my typing skills were in the developmental stage. Carol's suggestions were invaluable. The most helpful, however, was her last: "You've got a good idea here, Bro'... but I don't think it's ready for publication yet." Having worked on the book for over four years, I found her observation quite disheartening. In retrospect, however, I realize that she was exactly right.

Next is Debbi Barnum, who graciously typed the first draft. Not only did she do an outstanding job, but she offered to do it for free. What a saint! My friend Scott Neville was also very helpful with corrections at this stage.

Four years passed before I began the second draft, in February, 2005. For the next three years my only editor was my devoted wife, Sandy. As valuable as her editorial assistance has been, her unwavering support and encouragement throughout this project has been even more important.

A number of my friends have kept this book in their prayers, and I offer them my deepest gratitude. Among these, I want to single out Darrin Anton and Tim Rickert and his family for special thanks. Darrin also contributed a couple of excellent illustrations.

When Sandy and I moved to Lynchburg, Virginia in 2010, a small group of men decided to support me. One of these is Steve Rudolph, who did a fantastic job helping to create the cover and prepare the illustrations for printing. He was truly a joy to work with. Two others are George Caylor and Ken Chalfant. Their support and encouragement is an endless blessing.

A few readers made suggestions that upset me, at first. Upon reflection, however, I realized that their criticisms were valid, and in the end I am very thankful for their candid honesty. The result is a better book. One of these men is John Flora, another supporter from Lynchburg, who was the inspiration for some important changes to the section on inorganic evolution in chapter 13. Another is John Pickett, whose perceptive insight led me to completely revamp the cover and the illustrations.

My search for a publisher, or printer, led me to Believers Press, and Andrew Mackay. I thought the book was finished, but Andrew proved me wrong. He had a few extremely insightful suggestions that were right on the mark. Not only has Andrew provided excellent suggestions, but he has been a complete pleasure to work with. I cannot imagine a better publishing assistant.

For initial feedback, I sent copies of the first printing of this book to a small group of friends. In addition to their general response, I also requested that they notify me of any typos or other corrections that caught their eye. Their feedback was extremely helpful and incredibly encouraging, and I extend my deepest gratitude to every one of these dear friends. Jim LaBate and Gil VanOrder deserve special recognition.

I have saved the most important person on this list for last. In early 2008, with the end in sight, I knew that one thing still needed to be done: the book needed to be reviewed for scientific accuracy. I had no idea who to ask for help. Fortunately, God did: He directed me to Ian Taylor. I was familiar with Ian because I had read his wonderful book, *In the Minds of Men*, but he most definitely had never heard of me. Apprehensively, I sent Ian the first few chapters and asked for his help. To my great delight, not only did he review the technical accuracy of the book, but he so enjoyed it that he wrote a glowing Foreword. Ian found very little wrong with the scientific information. He did, however, make some astute suggestions regarding the overall structure of the book which resulted in some very important changes.

As helpful as Ian's suggestions were, the most important thing that he provided me was encouragement. His belief in this book, and in me, was exactly the inspiration that I needed to see this project through to completion. Ian is a humble man, and despite my efforts to thank him, I'm not sure that he knows how truly grateful I am. I hope and pray that the words in this Acknowledgment will be helpful in this regard.

About the Author

Over the years Stephen Bartholomew Jr. has been a cabinet maker, a furniture store owner, and a mortgage broker – as well as a husband and a father. He is also a talented artist. He first became interested in the creation/evolution debate over thirty years ago. Before long this interest developed into a passion. This passion gave birth to *Scopes Retried*.

Mr. Bartholomew graduated from Williams College in Williamstown, Massachusetts in 1967. His post graduate education includes studies at the Rhode Island School of Design and the Alliance Theological Seminary in Nyack, New York. He served as an interim pastor at a small Methodist church in East Chatham, New York in the 1980's and over the ensuing years has taught many Bible studies, Sunday school classes and youth groups.

Mr. Bartholomew has this to say about his book: "The explanation of origins offered in *Scopes Retried* is obviously at odds with the one that now dominates in the world today, the theory of evolution. I do not expect what I have written to change the minds of many evolutionists. My goal is to reach those whose views on this subject are uncertain and to show them that the ideas promoted here are not only very reasonable but actually far more harmonious with the scientific evidence than those offered in the theory of evolution."

For since the creation of the world His invisible attributes, His eternal power and divine nature, have been clearly seen through what has been made, so that they are without excuse.

Romans 1:20

A Study Guide is available at the *Scopes Retried* Web site:
www.scopesretried.com

Scopes Retried
2233 Rivermont Avenue
Lynchburg, VA 24503

Illustration Credits

* Josh on Floor (p. 108), Easter Bunny (p. 174), Meeting in Gym (p. 214), Genesis Flood (p. 305), Night Scene (p. 376): by author
* Fruit Fly (p. 61), Mouse to Killer Whale (p. 242): by Darrin Anton
* Rock Layers (p. 151): from istockphoto.com
* Human Cell (p. 164): used by permission under the *Creative Commons Attribution-Share Alike License* of the *Encyclopedia of Earth* at the NCSE (National Council for Science & the Environment) Source: Patrick J. Lynch
* Isaac Newton and the Apple (273): used with permission from Photo Researchers – Credit: Science Source
* Fossil Fish (324): used by permission from Answers in Genesis and the Creation Museum – www.answersingenesis.org